The Two Kingdoms

S. J. Garrett

Other Titles by S.J. Garrett

CHRONICLE Series
Chronicle of Destiny
Chronicle of Summer

ETERNITY Series
Ghost Eyes

DESCENDANTS Series
Shadow on the Sea

3rd DISTRICT Series
The Shaughnessy File
The Carmichael File
The Dease File
The Lucino File
The Taber File

THREADS Series
Unraveling Stories

Stand-Alones
Until the Dawn Breaks

There was only one absolute force for the universe. That force was Destiny.

She came to be from nothing, appearing from within the depths of a universe barren of life and existence. As she herself existed, Time came to be. The two joined hands as friends and looked upon the universe around them. They began to prep it, to prepare for more, and their efforts called forth more allies: Life and Love. The four higher powers knew their work would be vast, their duties unending, yet they did not falter. Destiny became their leader as much as their companion and her all-seeing eyes told them what needed to be done.

One day, Time felt a loneliness in her heart, sparked perhaps by Love's meddling, and she turned around to find someone had been by her side all along. Eternity, the perfect complement to her powers. They would bear two children together, twins, who came to be known as Moira and Horatio. They had gifts relating to their mother's powers and soon took up roles in all of existence. Horatio would defend time; Moira would fight for it.

Horatio and Destiny flirted a bit outrageously, teased one another across space, and eventually they had a rather interesting affair. A child would come from that union as well, a young god named Orion who would become Guardian of Destiny and protect his mother and her power.

Into the empty universe around the gods and demi-gods came to be worlds and stars. Other demi-gods began to appear as well. Destiny, still fond of her former lover, set Horatio onto a path that meant he encountered a demi-goddess named Mortality. The two loved, mated, and soon had two children of their own. The eldest, Claret, became quite beloved to her grandmother, and Time herself gifted the girl with the ability to effect time. The youngest child, Pallas, had gifts all his own that would soon be useful as well.

A celestial baby boom seemed to be springing up! Life and Love had always been soul mates, and they also bore a child. A boy they named Lycander who, by appropriate nature of his birth, became the Guardian of Desire. With all the new life, all the new powers and gifts, the physical plane began to slough off into another, more metaphysical, plane. The Ephemeral Plane, as they called it, began to house that which physicality could not.

Within its endless fields appeared a place only Time and Claret could access: the Hall of Records where all memories of all that ever lived would be kept. It would be the central hub for those of Time power, would keep time moving as needed, and even allow someone to move through time—in extreme circumstances. Claret became Librarian of the Hall, and into her possession came an hourglass made from stardust that would mark her position.

The Immortal Fields that made up the rest of the Plane needed their own caretaker as well; they held a vital and critical role to all that existed. Pallas became their Archon to manage the day-to-day maintenance, and Orion stepped forward to serve as their Knight to police anything bad that may come. Unfortunately, the Fields rejected Orion as Knight. When eyes turned to Destiny, she only smiled, and all knew that that meant someday someone else would rise up.

The existence of the Plane bolstered the power of Life in the universe, and worlds began to cluster into galaxies. One galaxy, at the very heart of the universe, began to evolve faster than the others. Two large worlds formed some distance from the star that would be their sun, and behind those worlds came eight more smaller—four behind each. The two largest worlds developed Cores first—that which would give the world its power—and each took in the most potent of elemental magic in the universe. That of Light and Dark themselves, as well as the lesser two, Illusion and Nature. The remaining eight elements dispersed to the Cores of the other worlds, and all was primed for life to begin, but . . . nothing happened.

Life tried. He tried so very hard. His power just could not

penetrate the frozen lands. It *should* have. It *could* have. Yet something . . . the worlds needed *something*. Claret, just a girl of fifteen then, looked out upon the worlds and felt her heart ache with love for the one at the end of the four following the Dark planet. A powerful love, almost as if the same as for her mother. She went to visit the small planet, walked upon its surface . . . and flowers began to bloom.

In a rapidly spreading wave from where she stood came acres upon acres of delicate flowers whose petals had the same pink and lavender hues as Claret's own hair and eyes. The statice blossoms consumed the surface of the world, and the Core took its first breath as life at last arrived. That first breath breathed into Claret's lungs to become her own, and beautiful marks appeared on her bronze skin. A statice blossom, in two places. One directly over her heart and the other over her upper left arm. The world, Statice, had claimed her as its Daughter.

A shockwave released in the process. Other Cores took their first breath and flowers exploded across the surface of all lands. The largest worlds took on protea and delphinium, the former to Dark and the latter to Light. Behind Protea came hyacinth, orchid, and daffodil to join Statice. Behind Delphinium came aster, gladiolus, carnation, and iris. On Protea and Delphinium, at a point where the two worlds could see each other, particularly large blossoms began to grow ever bigger and bigger until they unfurled to reveal the new life sheltered within. A young girl, one to each world, bearing coloring that bespoke of her mother planet's flower. Black and pink to Protea, white and gold to Delphinium.

Blossom marks also appeared on them, but only over their hearts. Destiny carried them to the Plane to meet one another, and to also meet Claret, and a curious thing happened when they did. Claret looked upon the two younger girls and loved them. Loved them so deeply, so powerfully, that she wanted nothing more than to protect them. The mark on her arm glowed brightly, and into her hands came a shimmering mask. When she put it on, her power evolved into something more tangible. Armor reminiscent of her patron flower formed on her body.

The other gods clamored at Destiny to explain. So, finally, she came before the three girls and said, "You are made of magic born of the flower magic of your worlds. Flower Elements, as they should properly be called."

Claret looked at the other two, and they at her, and then the young Protea stepped forward to demand, "We have no names. We should have names to know who we are before you tell us what we are."

Destiny smiled. "You are Shanta." She looked at the one of Delphinium. "You are Enaya. You two are like Claret, but yet different. You are all Cultivators, but where she is both Ruler and Defender, you are only Rulers."

"Ruler?" Claret protested. "You want me to *rule* Statice?"

"Of course, sweetheart. Only a Child of Statice could rule it. Just as only Children of the other worlds can rule them. The Ruler Cultivator magic inside you comes right from the Core of your world. It cannot be taken. Cannot be diminished. It can only grow, can only be inherited by your children. As long as there is a Ruler, the worlds cannot stagnate. But, you, Claret." She turned to the Librarian with a warm smile. She could not help but be most fond of this child of Horatio, the one most like him. "You are also a Defender Cultivator. It will be your duty, your honor, to protect not just your world, but also Shanta and Enaya. To protect all descendants of their lineage. The Cores of Protea and Delphinium are critical for they maintain the elements that infuse all of life: Dark and Light."

Claret took a long breath and then removed her Mask. Her armor disappeared and became instead a gown that in its own way reflected her flower. Both Shanta and Enaya also wore flower gowns of their own. "I will accept that duty, with honor."

She would not be alone for long. The other worlds began to blossom large blooms of their own, two to each world, and from each came another Ruler or Defender. Defenders bore their Flower Marks on their arms for they would take up arms to defend, and Rulers bore their Flower Marks on their hearts for they embodied the heart of their world. Only Claret stood as both for Statice, but when eyes turned to

Destiny for answers, she again only smiled and said nothing.

Each Defender protected their world, their Ruler, and then also the two queens of Protea and Delphinium. For two Defenders, the need to protect went literally into their souls. The Daffodil Defender bonded to Shanta, and the Gladiolus Defender to Enaya, in the way of soul mates, but in a purely platonic sense. They were twin souls, each possessing half a soul that looked identical and therefore overlapped to fuse them together. All the intense love and joy of a romantic soul bond, but without the tricky entanglement of desire. No, *that* problem lay somewhere else for the two queens: Orion and Lycander.

One day, as Shanta and Enaya neared the end of their second decades of life, they unexpectedly happened upon Orion and Lycander. The four had never met before, for the two demi-gods tried not to interfere with events on the worlds unless needed, yet they were not strangers. Even before their births, half their souls had been made to interlock. Shanta soon made Orion her king, and Enaya took Lycander for her own. In not long a time, each bore a daughter of their own who came into life with a Ruler blossom over her heart.

Life, finally, could use his power on the worlds. He populated them with animals, plants, and people, and the Ruler Cultivators became the queens of their planet's kingdom. Shanta and Enaya also took into their command the four worlds behind their own, making them the High Queens and overseers of the Blossom Field galaxy as a whole. Neither could use the Dark or Light power of their planet's Core, however. Instead, each embodied the other element of their world, that of Nature to Protea and Illusion to Delphinium. Peace and harmony spread across the galaxy as a whole.

The other queens bore daughters to become Rulers someday in their stead, and in the same year, new Defenders were born—except for Statice. Claret had yet to meet her soul mate, and though many offered, the queen remained unmoved. She would rule and defend alone until, perhaps, someday her perfect match be born.

As things settled, the highest gods began to leave the physical plane for one where only they could go. Losing Destiny and Time meant that Mortality had to gift humans with shorter lifespans, and

Orion had to remove from all people the ability to know the future. Only Cultivators maintained immortality for they possessed undying magic, and only Aster Defender Cultivators, Claret, and Orion's own Protean daughter maintained their Sight. All Protean children would receive Sight by nature of their shared blood with the Guardian.

Aster Defenders kept their Sight for it allowed them to see if danger approached those they lived to defend. Claret maintained hers for she needed it in order to fulfill her role as Librarian. Having the gift of Sight allowed her to keep the flow of the timeline from getting out of order. She had to be able to see aspects of the future to ensure the past did not change in detrimental ways. If anyone else ever were born with the gift of Sight, it would only be because they fulfilled a role of critical importance to all existence.

Peace could have remained forever . . . if there had not been an unknown consequence for Shanta's birth. The Ephemeral Plane relied not only on Dark and Light power, but also on the power of Nature infusing Protea. Thus, Shanta became the Ruler of the Plane as well, keeping the balance of the space moving easily. The Immortal Fields soon began to house the dreams of all that lived, and Pallas ensured that both good and bad dreams remained in harmony for both held important roles.

Unfortunately, a conflict waged inside Shanta's soul. The powers of Nature and of Dark worked against each other in many ways for Nature depended on sunlight and the Dark absorbed all light. Shanta could not control the Dark of her world's Core, and there could be no harmony without it. They fought for dominance within her soul until they sloughed over into the Immortal Fields. Bad dreams became nightmares that Pallas could not control, and without a Knight, could not destroy. Nightmares rooted, seeded, and moved beyond the reach of the elements. They began to take on a will of their own, began to twist and corrupt, until nothing good remained. Until they had become something never before seen in the universe: they became Evil itself and gained consciousness.

He spilled over into the physical plane before he could be stopped, and he went right after Shanta. He stood as such an adversary to her that all began to call him only Nemesis. He could not reach the High Queen immediately; first, he had to contend with the Defenders who immediately put on their Masks and rushed to protect their liege. They could not touch him, however. Could not wound him. He bowled over them and claimed their lives on his mad quest to reach Shanta. He wanted only her. How he wanted her! His obsession with her was violent and dangerous, and nothing would stand between him and consuming her.

Nothing except Shanta herself. Her people lived in fear, the galaxy trembled around her, and the price of such a thing lay on her shoulders and her weakness. As she watched Nemesis bearing down on her palace, she covered her Flower Mark and felt inside her soul the Seed that made her a Cultivator. Without fear or guilt, she tore out her own Seed and unleashed the rawest magic inside her soul.

The cataract of magic could not destroy Nemesis—not without any harmony—but it could banish him. She hurled him violently away into the sun where the bright light of Nature would keep him weakened and entrapped for millennia. In the process, she thoroughly burned out her Seed and, with it, her own life. When she fell, it was into the arms of her beloved almost-sister Enaya.

"Shanta!" Enaya clutched her closer and felt tears clogging her throat. They two were almost like twins themselves, deeply connected by the opposing force of their worlds' Cores. Enaya had already been devastated through her soul by losing her twin, but this only poured salt in the wounds. "How could you?!"

Shanta did not open her eyes, but she managed to smile. "Aya, how could I not?" She felt a hand take hers and forced her eyes open to see her husband's face above her as well. "Orion."

Orion's handsome face seemed strangely calm, though lines of strain edged his eyes. "It had to happen," he admitted roughly. He brought her hand to his cheek. "I knew this had to happen." He closed his eyes. "Shanta, Enaya . . . someday in the very far future there will be born two Apexes. They will wholly embody the elements of Dark and Light in a way no other could. They will possess infinite power known as arcanery that rivals Destiny herself, and they will stabilize the universe. But . . . they will pay a price. A terrible price, for arcanery cannot come without it."

Enaya took a long breath. "What price?"

"I do not know. I only know it will exist. Mother does not tell me everything either, unfortunately." He closed his eyes. "The Apex of Dark will be the only one who can bring harmony to Dark and Nature. She will destroy Nemesis. Something will face the Apex of Light as well, make her the only one who can destroy it. I know not what."

"Then," Shanta whispered, "I will hold to the hope of a future where my sin is cleansed." Her lashes fluttered closed and the Mark on her chest faded away entirely. Her body had nothing to hold without its Seed, and it began to dissolve into shimmers of color. It took only moments before she no longer existed in the physical realm.

Enaya barely bit back a cry as she reached out. She dropped her hands as her body shook with the force of her pain. "You can't leave me," she whispered. "I have no one left but Lycander and Claret." Her lips twisted into a sad smile. "No wonder Tarveel forced Claret to retreat. She has no successors." She looked at Orion. "But we do. Our daughters are grown. They will become queen in our stead. I will follow Shanta and my Defenders to the afterlife."

Orion felt no surprise; this, too, he had known would happen. "Lycander and I are demi-gods. We can ascend to the Realm of the Gods where Shanta has gone without any trouble. Enaya, are you sure in your decision to abandon your life?"

"What life is left for me here, Orion?" She felt her husband kneel behind her and covered his hands when he placed them on her shoulders. "Our time is done. It is time for the next generation to rise."

"Then so be it."

It was time in more ways than they had guessed. Curious events happened across the galaxy within a year that led the remaining Ruler Cultivators and their mates to leaving behind one life for another. The next generation of Rulers and Defenders rose at the same time to take their positions to maintain balance. Claret mourned those she had lost, but found comfort in the new companions she had gained. She loved Shanta and Enaya's daughters no less than she had loved their mothers, and so she gave them her dedication instead.

Hundreds of thousands of years passed. Every generation, a new crop of Cultivators would be born. They would rise to fight evil in all its forms, for though Nemesis had been sealed, he had planted disgusting seeds that would spawn weed after weed of evil that only the Defenders could destroy. The prophecy that Orion had once spoken passed between generation to generation, but details slowly began to be lost. It took only a few millennia before it lingered only as a memory within the Hall of Records.

Only a legend yet to come to pass.

The Royal War

All that lived, with few exceptions, had to eventually die. How you lived determined how you died, though there was always some *flexibility* to the rules. The average person went on to reincarnation after death, and they eventually re-entered life as someone else. Some people went on to rebirth instead, and they came back to a new life almost exactly as they had left it. Reincarnation reconstructed a soul. Rebirth brought it back intact.

But if you possessed power, if you had gifts, then there could be a third option. People with power ascended to the Realm of the Gods where they continued their life as an afterlife, as a new plane of living. They did not truly die, though they seemed as such to the people left behind in the physical living realm. Rules bound the Realm: except under very specific circumstances, those in the Realm could neither return nor reach out. Even Goddesses and Guardians obeyed those rules.

Some people who entered the Realm were immediately turned around and sent back out to rebirth; if you left something undone when you arrived, you went back to complete it. Only those who had finished their destined tasks could remain. Such was the order of the High Goddesses Shanta and Enaya. Orion had a list of names that he wore on his belt, and every arrival was checked against it. If your name was not lined through, back you went.

Shanta and Enaya had ruled the Realm from the moment they arrived. None of their subsequent descendants had held enough power on arrival to take their place. They watched over the land of the living and interfered wherever and whenever they felt it necessary; only they had that authority. They were quite shameless about it, and Claret often had to remind her fellow Cultivators that the two goddesses wouldn't hesitate to use their power if someone needed a push.

Frankly, someone *really* needed a push. Shanta's foot tapped on the ground as she scowled at her planet through a crystalline sphere. Her husband's arms lightly looped around her waist, and he told her mildly, "Tarveel told me to keep you from causing trouble."

She snorted rudely. Tarveel had been the first Defender Cultivator of Daffodil and was Shanta's twin soul mate. "She knows that will never happen." She leaned back against his chest and sighed heavily. It had been three million, five hundred twenty-seven thousand, six hundred and forty-nine years since she had fought Nemesis. Every year had branded itself into her heart. Every year only deepened her fear that her prophesied descendant would be born. "They grow stronger every generation," she murmured to herself.

He followed her gaze and saw the younger of the two generations of living Cultivators. No more than three generations of Defender Cultivators could exist at once, but it somehow invariably fell that no more than two of either sort would be alive at the same time. Something always happened.

And, as Shanta had said, the magic kept *growing*. The younger generation of Defender Cultivators as well as the younger generation of Ruler Cultivators were exponentially more powerful than their predecessors, who also held more magic than their forbearers. It was not an uncommon happening: magic would climb, peak, and then drop off before the cycle repeated. It had not dropped off in generations, however, and therefore it had reached some . . . unusual levels. "Mother said it would," he reminded her gently.

"And when it finally coalesces physically," she continued softly, "the Apexes will be born."

"They who will be your heirs," her husband concluded in his deep voice. He buried his face in her fine black hair for a moment. He ached watching her suffer under what could not be changed. They both knew intimately that the Apex of Dark would be a Defender Cultivator as well. She could be nothing else. Being a Defender as well as an Apex would give her the gifts she needed to utilize her power and bring harmony to Nature and Dark in order to destroy Nemesis. Yet, because she could not exist alone, her perfect counterpart would have to be born in the Apex of Light. They would balance each other perfectly. Balance. Such a blasé word for a force so critical.

"It terrifies me," she admitted on a half-laugh. "Enaya, too. The kingdoms have drifted apart after all these years to where they are barely allies any longer. One little misstep and the two High Kingdoms might be provoked to war by evil. They can*not* be at war when the Apexes are born!" A shudder went through her body at the very idea. "The Chaos that would be created by the two Apexes at war could not be controlled by anything except a third Apex, and existence itself would collapse under that power! The universe is just too young to support that!"

"Could it ever?" he asked her.

She frowned. "Well, maybe. It would have to be millennia from now." A soft premonition shivered through her that she ignored. Lovers tended to trade bits of power with one another, and she had absorbed the gift of Sight from her soul mate after millennia together. She usually ignored it unless it decided to be specific. Would there be three Apexes? It wasn't worth thinking about. There was too much else riding on the two already known for *fact* to be coming. "We have to reunite the kingdoms." Her voice sounded flat. "No questions asked."

He sighed with a combination of humor and exasperation as he turned her in his arms. He *never* ignored his premonitions or visions of the future. He had a personal core of pure Light that conflicted often with his lover's Dark core. Light could always see clearly where Dark tended to be a bit blind. "Shanta." He caught her face in his hands. "Why aren't you and Enaya interfering? The younger Ruler Cultivators of Protea and Delphinium have never actually met, and the Defenders already look for a way to arrange such a thing. At just thirteen, they are the perfect age to become friends and pull the two kingdoms back together."

"Oh. Oh!" Her eyes widened. "Of course!" She gave him a smacking kiss and then got free of his grip. "I'll be back."

She rushed through the castle calling for her sister, and her husband grinned as he heard the First Cultivators groan. There was always trouble when the sisters were in cahoots. At least this time the trouble would be of the good sort! He ambled off to find Lycander and warn his brother-in-law of the events. The Guardian of Desire would have some work of his own to do in the near future. Uniting the kingdoms would be fine, but the bloodlines of the Rulers needed to continue as well. Lycander would need to figure out just who Destiny had created to perfectly match the young princesses' souls.

* * * * *

The Defender Cultivators of the Dark worlds consisted of twin sisters Sandra and Krystaline Mirages, Tessa Chandler, and—as always—Claret Statice. The Defender Cultivators of the Light worlds consisted of Sara Sukio, Melissa Johnson, Jessica Kalri, and Amanda Rai. Sara stood as twin soul to the young High Princess Hannah Delphinium, and Tessa stood for High Princess Genevieve Protea. Tessa also served another role, that of Lead Defender for her generation, meaning that she possessed the strongest gifts and magic and acted as the leader for her team when they would enter battle. Her Metal element served her well in the role; her friends and partners knew better than to provoke her stubborn and unbendable will.

Her generation of Cultivators—both Defender and Ruler—had been biding their time until all hit their teenage years and could begin to act under their own authority. They would not hit full adulthood and control of their lives until twenty-five, but thirteen marked the start of when they could begin gaining personal responsibility. In particular, it meant that the younger Defenders did not need to bring along an older Defender if they wanted to travel, and they could serve as a sole protector to their princesses if one wished to travel—Rulers could not travel alone, period.

All Cultivators had been born within the same year—not uncommon—and Tessa was eldest while Genevieve was the youngest; also not uncommon. Leads were always eldest, and Nature elements tagged along behind everyone else. The moment Genevieve's thirteenth birthday passed in December of Harmonic Era Year 4675, the Cultivators began to plan how to get her and Hannah to meet in person.

Answer came in the form of Melissa receiving a vision through her Aster Cultivator gift of Sight. It knocked her out in the middle of the throne room, but it was entirely worth it to wake and know how to arrange things. It seemed rather simple, when it got boiled down the most basic concept. She just needed to nag Claret into making a distraction. While she did, Tessa and Sara had the task of convincing their High Princess that meeting each other was worth it.

No pressure.

Sara had to comb the Delphinium palace grounds until she finally located Hannah hiding in the gardens. The princess had escaped there to avoid her mother's wrathful eye, and helpful servants more than willingly tattled on the refugee's hiding spot. Sara rounded the heavily-laden flower bushes and winced in wry understanding.

Hannah had a terrible tendency to get clumsy, and it increased exponentially as she got nervous. Delphinium gifts of Illusion lay wholly within magical confines thanks to their Light core, and therefore Ruler Cultivators of the planet tended to be both a bit plump and also not very strong unless they actively worked against it. Hannah had tried, but she had given up before even age ten. Nothing could therefore counter her innate clumsiness.

Sara looked at the rather impressive juice stain on Hannah's Ruler Cultivator gown and winced anew. Nerves had gotten the better of her again. The problem looked only worse since Delphinium's main color happened to be white; her dress often made a tempting target to bad luck. "Oh, Hannah. What happened this time?"

Tears shimmered across Hannah's pale gold eyes. Her naturally fluffy and curly white hair had begun to escape its pins as well and locks hung around her shoulders. Her creamy skin carried a distinct pallor despite its fair hue. "I accidentally tripped over my skirt, bumped a waiter, and sent a tray of fermented juice glasses flying. The juice hit me and the delegate from Ranunculus alike."

Ranunculus was another Flower Planet located in the next

galaxy over. They had never been a formal ally though they seemed fond enough of Blossom Field to visit now and then. Sara moved closer and tugged Hannah into her arms to comfort and soothe. She stood barely an inch over Hannah's five-four height, but having trained from childhood to fight in battle as a Defender meant she had developed a stronger frame. Hannah loved nothing more than to be cuddled by her twin.

"I take it your mother unleashed the sharp edge of her tongue," Sara sighed. Not for the first time, her Glass element-based temperament made her anger boil under the surface. Glass elements, like Fire ones, ran hot.

"I'm a disgrace to the Delphinium Kingdom apparently."

"Actually, your mother is just a bitch."

Hannah winced. "You said it, not me."

"And keep it that way! I'm already in hot water from Melody repeating something I said!" Melody Carnation was the princess of the Carnation Kingdom and therefore also under Sara's protection as Carnation Defender. "Hannah, how would you like a distraction?"

Hannah frowned at her twin. "Such as?"

"Meeting Princess Genevieve from Protea."

Hannah winced. "Mother won't like that. She thinks Protea people are savages for leaning toward physical gifts more than magical."

Sara snorted. "Protea's queen thinks Delphinium people are snobs for leaning toward magical gifts more than physical."

"We are not!" Hannah blurted. "That's unfair to judge before knowing us!" She fell silent as Sara lifted a brow at her. "Oh," she said only. She thought for a few moments and then nodded. "Alright, I would like to meet Genevieve. I want to prove that her mother is wrong and we are not snobs, and perhaps I can prove to *my* mother that they are not savages."

Sara could only smile. It was that very attitude of Hannah's that made her entire kingdom long for the day when she would ascend to the throne as queen. Hannah's mother had a terribly nasty streak inside her, unfortunately. It cropped up only every few generations of

Ruler Cultivators but thankfully only lasted for one when it did. "Alright then! Let's get you changed into a fresh gown and head for Protea."

Things, perhaps ironically, were not nearly so harmonious on Protea.

"No."

"Yes."

"No."

"Yes, damn it!"

"*No*, damn it!"

Tessa scowled at her princess and was met by a matching scowl as they sat across from each other at the table on Genevieve's bedroom balcony. They had been playing cards until Tessa had dropped her bombshell: she wanted Genevieve to meet Princess Hannah Delphinium. Genevieve, showing trademark Protean stubbornness, had outright refused. Tessa had more than once given thanks for her own Metal element that allowed her to keep up with her twin.

Genevieve and Hannah could so perfectly complement each other if they met, though. Both in personality and even visually. Hannah had the coloring of her maternal bloodline as it had existed for millions of years, and so did Genevieve have her own as well. Her short hair hung fine and straight in the pitch black color of her Dark core, and her vibrant pink eyes reflected the same color as the Flower Mark on her chest. Her Nature magic, being related to the sun in many ways, gave her a lovely golden brown skin color with a soft red hue beneath. She was also tall to contrast Hannah's shorter frame, and she had a both lean and strong build from her years of training. Even Ruler Cultivators of Protea tended to be warriors thanks to Dark cores leaning to physical skills.

One an extrovert, the other an introvert. One the cheerful eternal optimist, and the other the sarcastic pessimist. Really, Protea and Delphinium just seemed meant to balance one another for they each had the strengths and weaknesses the other did not. And while Tessa loved her princess more than anything else, she did sometimes envy

Sara's easier task. "Gen." It was sighed. "Please. Just meet her. Do you really want to just pretend Delphinium does not exist? The palaces can see each other every night between twenty-one and twenty-two hours! It's hard to ignore *that*."

Genevieve scowled. "I have no intents of ignoring Delphinium or its royalty, but I also know my mother would pitch a fit if she thinks I wanted to fraternize with those magical 'snobs'. Tch!" She shook her head. "As if their lack of physicality makes them worth less. I wouldn't mind standing back now and then and shooting things with magic rather than jumping in."

Tessa grinned. "I would pay to watch that. You'd lose your temper partway, grab someone else's weapon, and rush in."

Genevieve snorted at her. "If you didn't tackle me to the ground to stop me."

"Well, *someone* has to do it. At least I'm bigger than you." By only an inch in height, yet enough muscle and strength to physically remove her princess from danger as needed. It happened that way; twin souls always received whatever strength they needed in order to protect the one they loved most. It usually translated into a taller height along the way, for which they were grateful. Tessa never saw anything funnier than the petite Iris Defender—who stood barely over five-foot even—tackling down Genevieve's five-nine figure in the inevitable dangerous moments that always surrounded high-ranking royals. Rulers did not enter battles against evil, but plenty of other issues always came around. "Gen."

Genevieve sighed deeply. "Are you serious?"

"Dead serious. Claret herself has taken it upon herself to distract both your mother and Hannah's—at the same time. We're not asking how because she already scares us. The Elder Cultivators are pretending they don't know what we're doing. Everyone knows this needs to happen. Evil could too easily take advantage of your mothers and bring us to war."

"Tessa." Genevieve's soft voice instantly commanded her twin's attention. "I had a premonition the other day."

Tessa's body tensed. Every Protea Ruler Cultivator had the gift of Sight thanks to being descended of the Guardian of Destiny. Some were stronger than others, and Genevieve had a particularly potent gift. She did not have the common Present Sight that showed current events; instead, she saw future events, known appropriately as Future Sight. No Cultivator of her generation had *ever* doubted the things she saw. "What did you See?"

She took a long breath. "The entire prophecy. It scares me a *lot*. And . . . well, Hannah has a right to know as well. I don't know why it was shown to me," although she feared what it implied, "but she needs to know as well. I was going to make Claret tell her, but . . ."

"What did you See?" Tessa demanded. She caught Genevieve's shoulders, and her copper colored eyes narrowed. They perfectly suited her long peach hair and brown skin, both visual reminders of the Daffodil magic inside her body. "Tell me what I need to know to protect you."

"I can't." Genevieve let her head rest on Tessa's shoulders and took comfort from hearing the heartbeat of the one she loved most. She knew her mother loved her, but it was not the same selfless, unending, love that her twin gave her. When she had her own daughter—if she did—she would love her child with everything she owned. "Alright. Let's go meet Princess Hannah." She smiled wryly as she lifted her head. "Is she as clumsy as I've heard?"

Tessa grinned a bit. "Worse, I'm afraid."

One of the more critical aspects to having a Ruler Cultivator on a world was the ability to use magic in ways both wonderful and yet mundane. Only Cultivators received magical gifts, and nearly all the rest of humankind possessed none. All had an affinity for the elements, but most did not possess actual gifts. Most, but not all. There were a few exceptions—namely, among Caretakers—but they still did not use magic wholly in the way Cultivators did.

The most beloved to all in the galaxy had to be the use of Portalpads, or just Pads for short. These flat discs had been installed in key locations throughout all cities and kingdoms to allow for instant transportation between worlds. You had to pay a fee to use one, of course, but the money went right into the local community to provide improvements to the lives of those living there.

The Pads drew on the power of a Core by directly harmonizing through a Ruler, and that meant that Rulers themselves could use transporting magic without a Pad. Defenders could also use the same magic, but only if they were traveling either to Protea, Delphinium, or their own home world. That very gift therefore allowed Sara to escort Hannah to Protea without anyone noticing they had gone, and it allowed Tessa and Genevieve to meet them at a location well away from the palace.

All four landed at the same time, and Tessa and Sara found themselves staring at one another as their princesses hid a bit behind them. Pink and gold eyes peeked around the arms of the ones they loved most as both Genevieve and Hannah evaluated each other.

Genevieve found Hannah to be lovely and soft and thought she looked like she needed someone to protect her. Hannah found Genevieve to be strikingly beautiful and strong and thought she looked like someone who could handle anything.

Neither said anything for long moments, and yet neither Defender felt any surprise when it was finally Genevieve who spoke first. Curiously, the introverted Protean princess had not a shy bone in her body, and the extroverted Delphinian princess could be *painfully* shy. Genevieve stepped around Tessa and calmly walked forward to lean down to eye level with Hannah. "I don't bite," she whispered.

All of Hannah's nerves simply melted away. In a matching whisper, she said, "I do, but only if someone tickles me."

Genevieve straightened on a grin and then gave a graceful curtsy that made the pinkish petals of her Ruler gown flare over their black underskirt. "Genevieve Protea, High Princess and heir to the throne of the Protea Kingdom."

Hannah matched her curtsy, though she did wobble a bit on the uneven terrain. "Hannah Delphinium, High Princess and heir to the throne of Delphinium Kingdom." Her gold eyes lit with warmth. "Do the Defenders act as overprotective to you as to me?"

"Worse, probably," Genevieve groused.

"That's because you get in worse trouble!" Tessa and Sara retorted in the same voice.

Genevieve winced but did not deny the charge. Instead, she reached out and took Hannah's hand. "Let's walk! Tell me about Delphinium, and I'll tell you about Protea."

With the two Defenders ambling along behind them, the two princesses walked and talked and laughed for nearly two hours. It took less than a few minutes for them to be friends, and only a few more beyond for them to be dear friends. By the time they realized they really should get home, they may as well have been sisters. The only thing they regretted was that they weren't. "I wish we could have children to marry one another someday," Hannah lamented. "So we could be real family!"

"I do as well," Genevieve sighed.

Only daughters had been born to the Ruler Cultivators for millions of years. No one yet knew why, though many investigated the reasons. Moreover, only one child had ever been born to the bloodlines as well. Ruler Cultivators in other worlds often had more than one child, with the younger ones being considered "Deactivated" because their Seed lay dormant inside and would not be useable unless their elder sibling either died without an heir or deliberately chose to activate the dormant Seed. Neither Hannah nor Genevieve could ever expect to have anything except a single daughter in their lives, not even Genevieve with her deeply fertile Nature magic.

Thinking it, Hannah looked around the lush landscape stretching in all distances. Protea both did and did not look anything like the rest of the worlds. Its abundance of Nature power just somehow made it more beautiful. More fertile as well; agriculture tended to be its biggest export. "Protea is different."

Genevieve knew what she meant. "The one in harmony with all of life." She closed her eyes and tilted her face to the sun. "Just the right amounts of this and that. The heart of the galaxy, I've often thought." She grinned. "Delphinium is the conscience! Keeps us from doing anything we may regret later."

Hannah had to smile as well as she thought of some things she had heard the Defenders saying about Genevieve. Perhaps it could be said that the princess of Protea was also the heart of her world as well as the royal houses as a whole. "I can be your conscience." She took Genevieve's hands. "I think I really love you, Gen. I don't want our kingdoms to barely acknowledge one another! We need to be allies. To be friends."

"I don't know why we aren't," Genevieve complained. She blew out a hard breath. "Yes I do. Our mothers." She pursed her lips. "I may have a plan."

"Uh-oh." Tessa winced as she and Sara drew close. "Is this going to get one of us almost killed? Because last time . . ."

"I apologized to Amanda about that!" Genevieve shook her head. "No, I'm thinking of the laws. A princess cannot become queen until she is a minimum of twenty-five years . . . but she can push to ascend at age twenty-three providing she can prove her mother is unfit to rule." She nodded firmly when the other three stared at her. "Hannah's and my mothers . . . they treat each other as a vile beast and care not about the other world. That is unacceptable. The balance of the *universe* depends on Protea and Delphinium maintaining the Light and Dark Cores as well as our powers of Nature and Illusion. Protea ensures all worlds can sustain growth, and Delphinium keeps them safely protected within magical shields. To deny one or the other exists would be like someone denying their left or right lung exists!"

Slowly, Hannah said, "So, by denying one another and putting the entire universe in a state where people suspect a war could brew, they are threatening the very balance of our existence. Protea and Delphinium going to war would place the Defenders in the terrible position of choosing one queen and princess over the other, and it would make the perfect target for the forces of evil that our Defenders are already dealing with often enough."

"That sounds fairly damn *unfit* to me," Sara agreed. Her gold eyes narrowed a bit. "And is more than a little unnerving, really. Is that the plan, then? To take the throne from your mothers as soon as you're twenty-three?" At the nods, she lifted her chin. "So be it. We Defenders will stand by you through that choice."

"What of the Elder Defenders?" Genevieve asked.

"They no more like this than we do!" Tessa shook her head. "They just knew there was nothing they could do about it. They will aid us by not doing anything. They love your mothers and must support them first, but that does not mean they will actively stand against you."

"Then that is the plan," Hannah decided. "And we will all hope we can maintain peace and patience until the day the galactic baby is old enough!"

Genevieve scowled. "Don't you start on me. I get that enough from the others!"

* * * * *

Eleven years passed. Claret frequently provided a distraction to the queens to allow the princesses to steal time to visit together. Their other Defenders aided them as well, arranging times to meet and enjoy each other's company on the other worlds. All Ruler Cultivators of the Lower eight planets simply pretended they knew nothing about it.

The very day after Genevieve turned twenty-three, the coup prepared to launch, but the moment never arrived. As if Destiny herself had interceded, there came a vicious attack on the galaxy by forces of evil. The younger Defenders spirited all of the younger Rulers away within a secret location and stood guard over them. The Elder Defenders rushed into battle to defend all that lived. As fighting grew only uglier, the Elder Rulers began to link their worlds' Cores together. Even the High Queens willingly joined for neither wanted to see their galaxy crumble.

Deep within the secret bunker, the younger generation knew as Elders began to fall. The first signal came in Claret's arrival. She landed a bit unceremoniously in a heap in the middle of the room from a hasty transport. Her armor had been damaged horribly, and her Mask had cracks. Blood stained most surfaces.

"Claret!" Sandra scrambled to reach her side and dropped to her knees. Water magic from her Orchid-based Flower Element glowed over her hands as she called up her healing gifts. At least one Defender per generation had the gift to heal, and while it did vary elements, it usually ended up in the hands of either Orchid, Daffodil, or Iris, for their Water, Metal, and Ice elements adapted best to the skill.

The princess of Orchid, Karalyn, hurried over to give her aid. She had a similar gift on a lower scale—not uncommon among Cultivator generations. Also not uncommon, she and Sandra looked more like sisters than Sandra and her own twin did. All Cultivators shared identical coloring that derived directly from their Flower Element. Both Karalyn and Sandra had vibrant ultramarine hair and haunting purple eyes offset by light brown skin. Krysta and Princess Skyla, being of Hyacinth, had bright blue hair paired with white eyes and offset by fair skin dotted with freckles. Only in facial features did Krysta and Sandra reveal their twin relationship.

The joint magic helped start easing Claret's pain. She reached up to remove her Mask, and her armor disappeared to be replaced by the nearly casual clothing she had been wearing prior to battle, though it looked damaged as well. Her pink hair hung heavy, matted by sweat, and her bronze skin had lost luster. "It's bad," she managed to say. She sat up as Genevieve and Princess Harriet of Gladiolus aided her. "Guilie forced my retreat." It had happened a million times before, yet it never stopped hurting when her partners forced her to retreat for the sake of her life and the future generations she needed to Defend.

Amanda's hands clenched together, and her olive skin took a little flush of combined hurt and grief. Guilie was not just Lead Defender for the Elder Defenders but also of Gladiolus. The two Defenders and Harriet shared their olive skin tone as well as silky yellow hair and bright green eyes. "Then they expect . . ."

Melissa took a sudden sharp breath and lost all color in her light brown skin. She barely noticed her princess, Rebecca, grabbing her in support. The two Aster Daughters had identical orange hair and fiery yellow eyes. "My Seed." She did not need to say more; all could see the Flower Mark on her left arm, and the two blossoms had taken on a sparkling edge that meant she stood as the only Defender. The Elder had fallen.

All younger Defenders had two blossoms to their Mark; the number of blossoms denoted the evolutions their Seed had gone through, something often inevitable in battles against evil. Defenders forced their Seed to evolve in order to gain stronger magic to fight back. Claret only had one despite her long life; she had a particularly potent magic to begin with, perhaps because she was the only one of Statice.

One by one by one the Defenders' Marks gained a sparkling edge as their Seed registered they were the only ones alive. Amanda's went last—nature of her Elder being Lead—but no sooner had her Mark taken on the sparkling than did every princess feel a wrenching in their own Seed. Something rattled the bunker like a shockwave and all felt a sweeping rush of combined Flower Element magic. Into the eerie silence following, every princess found the Flower Mark on their chest taking on its own edging.

Princess Melody of Carnation slowly covered her Mark as tears rolled down her ivory cheeks. She lowered her head and her red hair fell forward to hide her face. "Why?" she whispered. "Cultivators are *immortal*. Why is it they never live even to a natural human lifespan? History is stained with our blood."

"The simple fact," Claret admitted, "is that no more than three generations of Defenders can be alive at one time. A Core simply cannot support more than three. Rulers are different; they are the lifeblood of a world, so there can be as many as needed. A world must always have a Ruler to last through eternity, but it does not always need a Defender. Some worlds do not have them; we are called on the basis of need in the fight against evil. Therefore Defenders will always be born as long as there is evil. And as long as Defenders are born, they will die young if it will prevent the overlapping of more than three."

Gentle Tokala of Iris shouted, "There were only *two*! Many of us have not even yet found our soul mates! Until we bear children, more Defenders are not needed! They could have had more time!" Tears fell from her golden yellow eyes, and even her purple ombre hair seemed to have lost its shine. A flush brought only a bit of color to her fair skin, and she barely noticed her Defender holding her. Not even Jessie could comfort her now.

"I don't like it either!" Claret said raggedly. "Do you think I want to be forced to abandon my partners? Be forced to watch my queens die?" She broke off as everyone near her who could reach threw their arms around her. Tension fled her shoulders. "Damn you, Destiny," she said softly. "What is it you want someday?"

The sacrifice by the Rulers and Defenders of the Elder generation had, at least, succeeded. All evil in the encroaching wave had been destroyed. A somber cast hung over the galaxy as the princesses ascended to their thrones and became queens. Genevieve and Hannah became the new High Queens and immediately launched a peace treaty to reunify their two worlds. The galaxy heaved a sigh of relief, and so did all others beyond.

The shift in power, as well as the ascension of new queens not yet fully adults, caused a shift in the very fabric of Time. Eras governed the universe and changed when power levels reached absolute peak. It usually happened within the first few years of the birth of a new generation of Cultivators, with the birth of those Cultivators often being seen as a sign of an Era *truly* beginning.

Claret saw this shift in the fabric the month following the Ruler changeover and notified Hannah and Genevieve. The Harmonic Era would end in December of Year 4699, and January would start Year 1 of a new Era. The queens, after conferring over the whys of the change, determined the new Era would, appropriately, be called the Royal Era, and the universe accepted it.

Only a week after Genevieve turned twenty-four, the new year and new Era began, and all eyes shifted to the kingdoms in curious wonder over just what sort of future Ruler Cultivators would be born. Some queens had already found soul mates, and had been waiting to be an adult to marry. Others had suitor lists not yet perused, and others had already begun their search. The queens could rightfully choose to wait to twenty-five if they so desired, or they could take advantage of their early adulthood. Most had no desire to rule alone and so began the search early, or got married if their search had ended.

Soon it remained only for the two High Queens to find their soul mates and future kings, and neither of them had any clue of the events about to be set into motion by Lycander himself. Not even Shanta or Orion quite knew just what Destiny had up her sleeve for the royal houses of Protea and Delphinium. It was time for blood outside the galaxy to be added, and events would be set into motion to change all of existence.

The future rode on such a thing.

The next closest galaxy to Blossom Field held several planets though only three sustained life of any sort. One, known as Aria, held the black poppy as its Core flower, and the other, Celia, held the forget-me-not. Neither world had Defenders—there had never been need—but both had Rulers. Aria tended to keep to itself for the most part, but Celia *loved* to have alliances and had been happily making friends with planets all across the universe. Perhaps fittingly for a world that loved to make friends and gave generously of its assets, the Flower Element of Celia was Nature. They had prodded at Aria as well, and succeeded; testament to the stubbornness of the Ruler Cultivator lineage of Celia.

Now that even the slightest hint of war had evaporated from between Delphinium and Protea, Celia wanted to contact both worlds to more formally ally with the galaxy as a whole. They had tentatively reached out to both Statice and Iris who sat closest to the edge of the galaxy, but both queens had directed them to look to the High Queens.

The kingdom of Celia had three children. The eldest and heir was a fully Activated Ruler Cultivator within his own right thanks to being firstborn. He had a younger sister and brother alike, and both had Deactivated Seeds. At twenty-six, Matthew could have inherited the throne if he had been inclined, but he felt no hurry. He also felt no hurry to give serious attention to his suitor list, much to the mutual frustration of his parents and suitors alike.

His companion-at-arms and pseudo-bodyguard also happened to be his best friend. Quint Haven came from a noble family of his own, and he had volunteered to keep an eye on Matthew simply because it meant they could spend more time together. They acted almost as brothers, really, and sometimes even Matthew's parents would forget that they weren't! Some jokingly called Quint "Prince

Quint" and he took it with good humor. He had an upbeat and cheerful manner from a clearly Light personal core that contrasted his serious friend's Dark one.

All that lived had a Light or Dark core inside their soul. It was the deepest foundation of their personality and mannerisms, and while some people could sometimes show aspects of both, no one ever actually *had* both. The presence of Light or Dark deep inside all living beings was what made Protea and Delphinium's roles so very important—and made another valid reason for Matthew's parents to tell him to get in a ship and make his way out there. He went willingly enough, but he dragged Quint along.

The Blossom Field galaxy, for obvious reasons, had border patrols along their galactic edges. Matthew's small ship had to stop at Statice to not only refuel but also get papers giving him safe passage. When he returned to the ship after obtaining them, Quint lifted a blond brow over pale pink eyes. "You look somewhere between confused and wary."

"An accurate summation." Both emotions mingled in Matthew's violet eyes. His eyes and hair alike reflected the violet hues of the Core flower that had birthed his Seed, but his eyes held a red tint while his hair had a blue. "I met with Queen Claret Statice. I would swear she had been internally laughing at my telling her our intent to make alliance."

"She doesn't think we'll get it?" Quint held the door to the ship open for Matthew and then followed him inside and sealed the door behind them.

"She says she's very confident in a powerful alliance forming. *That* is why I'm befuddled. She seems to know something I don't." He sat down in the pilot's seat and fastened in before starting up the systems.

"Isn't Statice the *only* world in existence to hold Memory as its element? That may have something to do with it. Rumor says they tend to be pretty sensitive to events as a whole, almost borderline the gift of Sight."

Matthew didn't think there was anything *borderline* about Claret

Statice's potential Sight. He had heard rumor that the Statice Defender Cultivator was Librarian to the Hall of Records, and that meant the Defender had to have Sight to do her job properly. It seemed unlikely that the Ruler Cultivator would not have it herself. "Well, here's hoping that whatever she did or did not see will not make our job more difficult. I'll hold hopes on her being right about the alliance being easy."

Quint snorted softly as he took control of the ship to navigate out of the spaceport. "You mean unlike Aria?"

"The fact that it took until my grandmother's generation to get that sealed says it all." He leaned back and linked his hands behind his head. He usually let Quint pilot; the other male had far more talent at such a thing. "Can't say as I'm sorry to be getting off the planet for a bit, though."

His companion laughed outright at him. "Is someone feeling a wee bit of pressure to find his soul mate?"

"I should marry you just to make them shut up!"

"I'd be willing to help in that way, if it weren't for the fact that no one would believe us to be anything more than friends, *and* the expectation of you having to have an heir means your mate ought to have the right equipment to bear you a child."

"I have siblings that could have an Activated heir if I should mate to someone not birth-capable," Matthew reminded him dryly. "And I was mostly joking. I pity anyone you finally marry. They'll have their hands full keeping you in line!"

Quint grinned. "Which is why I do a good job of protecting your rear if there's trouble. Still say they shouldn't be paying me for that. I have so little to do. You're pretty damned skilled within your own right, Matt."

"Eh, makes the kingdom feel more secure where I'm concerned. I endure because I know they love me. Makes the fuss over a suitor more tolerable, too. They want me to be happy."

Though the specifics of laws could vary among galaxies, some things remained constant where Cultivators were concerned, just to keep things tidy. A Ruler Cultivator would receive a suitor list at age twenty that any eligible folks could vie to be on. Then, at twenty-five, the Ruler would have to actually look at the list and start the search for a soul mate. Some didn't even get to looking at their list by being lucky enough to find their soul mate early. *Very* few made it past age twenty-six without being successful. Defenders also tended to find their soul mates around the time they became adults, though exceptions existed there as well. Destiny provided for her Cultivators.

Matthew and Quint alike had recently turned twenty-six. Quint, not being royal, did not have to bother with a suitor list though he had had plenty of offers. Matthew had gone over his list already, and no one on it had stood out in any fashion to him. Most soul mates sparked desire right from the first meeting. Others simply sparked an intense friendship that developed into more. Either way, *something* happened instantly, especially after age twenty-five.

Twenty-five was not merely the age where someone became an adult; it was also the age where someone could truly, deeply, recognize a lover soul mate and feel the full force and fury of their emotions. You could recognize a lover soul mate sooner, and feel desire for them as early as age twenty-one, but you never knew the true depths of a feeling into your soul until full maturity. Matthew had felt nothing so far, of any fashion for any person.

"Thinking about Rulers and laws and marriages and the like," Quint said, "didn't I hear that the High Queens we're going to meet are the only Ruler Cultivators in their galaxy not yet to find their soul mates?"

"You did indeed. The information I collected says that all Rulers took their thrones at twenty-three or twenty-four after a horrific battle against evil that took their parents and the Elder Defender Cultivators alike, and over the last year plus, all queens have married their soul mates except for the High Queens. In fact, the next generation boom has already begun. I understand Carnation Kingdom just celebrated the birth of a daughter. Veronica, I believe."

"Royal Era Year 2, bringing to you the Blossom Field baby boom of the latest generation." The words were slightly dry since most everyone knew that it inevitably fell where all members of a generation were born in the same year.

"Considering I believe that Aster, Hyacinth, Orchid, Gladiolus, and Iris are all expecting as well, indeed." Matthew had to grin. "At least that makes it easy to plan the celebrations of the birth of new heirs. They just have to pass the decorations from kingdom to kingdom!" He stretched and watched out the viewscreen as they passed beyond the orbit of Hyacinth and Aster and approached Protea and Delphinium. The two larger worlds seemed to nearly glow within space as if to radiate the power of their Cores. He didn't think he was imagining it; any Core that could hold two elements would surely *have* to glow from its importance.

He actually looked forward to this mission. He had heard some amazing things about High Queen Genevieve Protea and wanted to meet her to see if they were true. He felt a bit as if he might meet a kindred spirit; rumor said her suitor list might rival his own. Poor thing.

His reverie broke as the ship lurched a bit violently and only his seat's fastenings kept him from taking a nosedive into the console. "Quint! What are you doing? Don't brake so hard!"

"That was not braking." The muscles of Quint's arms had bunched as he fought for control of the ship. "That was a meteor hitting us. We're losing propulsion rapidly."

Matthew hastily began typing commands on the console and the litany of abuse that came back from the system made him wince. "Communication systems completely down. Propulsion is definitely lost, and we're about ten minutes from being completely dead in space."

"Or just dead!" Quint said something vicious under his breath. "Apparently we have meteor magnets on the ship! Others are coming right at us. Screw it!" He gave up on control and unfastened his belt. He freed Matthew as well and hauled his friend along out of the cockpit. Though Matthew was not small at six-foot in height with a lean frame, Quint stood fractionally taller and had a broader build. "We're heading to the escape pods. Crash-landing isn't exactly the most polite of hellos, but I doubt they'd prefer calling home to say

Cindy is going to be the next Ruler instead of you!"

Matthew did not argue. The escape pods were personal devices, so each male got into one and strapped in. The pods ejected out into the relative safety of space and their smaller stature allowed them to quickly navigate past the strange onslaught of meteors. The ship did not fare so well; another few blows cracked it open entirely. Matthew tried to navigate his pod toward Quint's, but he had gotten too close to Protea without realizing. The planet's exceptional pull on space—one of the ways it helped keep the planets behind in line—meant that small objects floating around would get sucked in, and Matthew lost control of the pod as the planet towed him into the atmosphere.

He hit the communication system. "Quint! I'm going to be making an unscheduled landing on Protea."

"I'll let you know how mine on Delphinium goes," came the dry answer.

If Matthew had ever envied anything about his almost-brother, it was Quint's ability to always have a cheerful spirit even in the middle of danger. "You ever get the feeling Destiny herself might be setting you up?"

"Every day of my life, friend. Every last day."

* * * * *

"Hey," a woman said softly, and gently. "Can you hear me?"

"Umph," was the best Matthew could manage. It felt as though his entire body had been slammed face first into a wall. He did not remember crashing, though, so perhaps he had gotten lucky and passed out on impact. Some traumas he just did not need to remember.

"That would be a 'yes,'" another woman's voice put in dryly. "I told you, Gen. He's just fine. He's just going to be feeling that crash for a few weeks. Or years," she added with an audible wince. "I've had my share of crashes."

Matthew gingerly opened his eyes and briefly squinted at the bright sunlight. His eyes finally adjusted, and he found himself staring at one of the most beautiful women he had ever seen. Concern had turned her rich pink eyes to the color of a protea blossom in full bloom, and he knew he would *never* forget her face. Dazzled by her, the best he could manage was, "Hi."

"Hi to you too!" She grinned, and dimples flashed in her cheeks. "Welcome to Protea. And watch out for that first step, it's a doozy."

"You really need a sign." He very carefully tried to sit up but couldn't quite manage alone. He would have fallen back again if hands hadn't braced him to help keep him upright. He glanced back to see who had aided him and found a blue-haired woman in a mask and armor. The colors of her armor as well as her eyes and hair bespoke of Hyacinth origin, and the mask belied her position. Her sleeves hid her Flower Mark, but he did not need to see it to know her identity. "You're a Defender?"

"Hyacinth Defender, indeed," Krysta confirmed. "You made quite a ruckus in your landing, friend. I wasn't about to bring Genevieve here unless I came in armor to protect her." Her eyes swept over him and his distinctly flower-inspired suit. "You look like a Ruler Cultivator, so," she removed her Mask and her armor disappeared to leave her in a more casual uniform, "I'll trust you."

He squinted one eye closed on a sigh as the name and situation clicked belatedly. "If you're a Defender, then . . ."

She grinned. "Turn and introduce yourself to High Queen Genevieve Protea."

He turned again and found Genevieve grinning as well. Looking at her again, he could not mistake her identity. Not just her hair and eye color spoke to her Cultivator magic, but also the gown she wore. It looked very much like the protea blossom that effused her world's Core and had given it its name. "I promise that I intended a *far* better first introduction."

"Oh, I've seen worse, trust me." Genevieve looked her unexpected guest over more closely and found his Ruler suit reminded her of a forget-me-not; he could only be from Celia. No surprise; she and Hannah alike had expected the friendly planet to come knocking eventually. She just had not expected the Crown Prince to be quite so devastating to her senses.

He definitely went to the top of the list as one of the most attractive men she had met, and she put her hands behind her back before she gave in to the urge to brush his hair out of his eyes. Unexpected yet recognizable feelings began to surge inside her body and soul with violent force. Desire. Love. Breathless, she could only stare at him. The premonition that had led her to needing to find the pod had not warned her that her destiny might lay inside.

The silence stretched. Krysta slowly lifted a brow as she realized the silent sparks looked *very* familiar. She had seen before, and personally felt, what could happen when soul mates of the romantic quality met for the first time. At the point where Destiny, Love, and Life came together, a cataclysmic force could be unleashed as souls began to interlock in something far more intimate than making love alone. She cleared her throat and watched both jump as if they had forgotten her presence. "Introduction?" she asked Matthew again, this time with heavy dryness.

"Crown Prince Matthew Celia, of the planet Celia from within the Tarmol Galaxy. And, yes, as that implies, I am a Ruler Cultivator. My Flower Element is of Nature, and my Core's flower is the forget-me-not." He picked at the grass in his hair and clothes with a rueful smile. "I was sent as a delegate to Blossom Field with my best friend, but our ship was hit by meteors and we had to escape in the pods. I saw him getting towed toward Delphinium. He hopefully landed there somewhere."

Krysta winced and pulled a small version of her Mask off the bracelet she wore. It glowed and she said, "Gladiolus." After a pause, the Mask turned green. "Mandy, keep an eye out for an undignified entrance from a dignitary. A ship got smashed, and one of the two inside landed here. The other supposedly headed Delphinium way."

"I was wondering what that sound was," Amanda muttered in response. "I'll grab Hannah and check."

Genevieve smiled at Matthew as Krysta put away the communications mask. "There we go! They should find him very quickly." She got gracefully to her feet and brushed out the petals of her long skirt. "Really, this does work out. We would have sent one or both of you there anyway to see how both kingdoms operate. Is he authorized?"

"Well, after a fashion. He's *technically* my companion-at-arms, but he's such a part of my family that even my parents forget he's not part of the bloodline. He's of noble blood within his own right, though." Matthew shook his head in bemusement. "So, yes, he's authorized to act as a delegate as well, as far as I'm concerned."

She hesitated and then said, "We can trade the two of you, if you like." The words nearly got stuck on their way out, and that confused her deeply. He couldn't be her soul mate! No Ruler Cultivator of Blossom Field had ever found a soul mate outside the galaxy, not even all the way back to the daughters of the original generation!

Matthew gingerly gained his feet as he said, "I think I'll stay here a while." He turned in a slow circle to look at where he had landed, and he found a beautiful grassy plain for as far as his eyes could see. In the distance to the east, he could see the line of a majestic castle and knew that had to be the capitol. He studied every line of the land and sky and felt entranced. Celia had a different sun than Protea did, so their worlds looked vastly different for that reason alone, but it seemed as though something more about Protea made it different. Made it seem to feel more lush and overwhelming with life. Perhaps the Core of Dark had something to do with it; Dark types were known for being protectors. "It's beautiful," he said in a soft voice. "Amazing. Rumors don't do it justice."

"I know." Genevieve followed his gaze and then tilted her head back to look up at the sky. She smiled softly. "It might be just because I'm a Daughter of Protea, but I think I love this world more than anyone else does. I hope you'll love it too," she added as she turned to smile at him. "I want everyone to feel the love I do."

He looked down at her. Her taller height meant she came up past his shoulder, which he much enjoyed. She felt both young and yet mature, evidence of an early adulthood forced on her by terrible events. He wanted nothing more than to ease her burdens. The powerful emotions churning inside him were the ones he had been waiting all of his life to find. He couldn't stop himself from tucking a stray strand of hair behind her ear and then tracing the line of her cheek. "I think I will," he said softly, huskily.

She had a feeling he was no longer talking about the planet, and she couldn't find a single word to say. "Uhm."

His fingers slid down to cover her hand. "Are you accepting more suitors?"

Breathless, she stared up at him. "I can't get rid of any of them, so what's one more?" The smile that flashed across his face only made it harder to catch her thoughts. She was in *so* much trouble.

"I would like to be added to the list." He brought her fingers to his lips. "Please."

Suitors *very* rarely asked permission of the one they wanted to court; it was normally asked of her mother. Yet, Genevieve was an adult whose mother had passed. Most had assumed that meant they didn't need to ask at all, and they just had to show up and state their intentions. Matthew's respect for her only made him dig his way into her heart in the way he had already dug into her soul and body. Truly, if it hadn't been for what marriage meant to her kingdom, she would have accepted him then and there and happily booked a honeymoon trip. Fear for the future made her hesitate though she knew her chance at eternal happiness stood before her. "I'll think about it," she said softly.

"That's all I ask," he said simply.

Krysta barely refrained from whistling merrily. She gave them two days before thinking was forgotten about entirely. The explosion would be spectacular.

* * * * *

"Well," a woman's dry voice said somewhere above Quint's head, "if we're going to have strangers crash land on Delphinium, at least they have the decency to be really gorgeous."

"Gladiolus, really!" It was a scolding from another woman, but there was a trace of amusement in her gentle voice. The gentleness seemed ingrained, almost as if it came from the very center of who she was, and yet there also existed a youthful edge to the tone that made her sound very impish as well.

Quint was instantly intrigued, and he cautiously opened one eye. He promptly closed it again on a curse as a light shined merrily right in his eyes and seared his battered head. "Blast and damn, let me die in the dark, will you?"

"Okay, I *really* like him," the woman called Gladiolus said on a snort. "Hannah, you need to keep him. If you don't, he goes home with me. Harriet will love him!"

"*Amanda!*" The rebuke sounded both exasperated and embarrassed. "Will you stop embarrassing me in front of our guest? And move that light while you're at it."

The light moved, and Quint carefully opened his eyes again. This time his eyes focused, and he found himself staring into the lovely face of a woman who literally took his breath away. She looked soft and wonderful and magical. Her coloring echoed the flowers of the world where he had landed, and he very badly wanted to get his hands into her fluffy white hair and see if it felt like the flowers it emulated.

Crash landing had *not* been the first impression he wanted to make on the High Queen of Delphinium, but he felt no desire to knock the circumstances. His head rested comfortably on her lap and her perfume gently teased his nose. Too many emotions to name raced through his heart and soul, and his body ached to feel her soft curves pressed against him. Happily falling in love with his longed for soul mate—and recognizing that he was doing so—he smiled up at her. "Marry me."

Pink touched her cheeks as she tried to ignore her madly racing pulse and the ache inside her heart and soul telling her to grab him now and not let go. From the moment she had pulled him from the wreckage, she had just somehow *known* he was her destiny. Her soul mate. But, he couldn't be! A little desperate, she looked at Amanda. "Can brain damage affect someone like that?"

"He looks lucid enough to me." Amanda set down the lamp she carried and then pulled her Mask up to sit on her head. Her armor disappeared back to her casual uniform, and she shook her head a bit. "His eyes responded to the lamplight—and sorry about that, but we had to be sure. We'll grab Sandra later and have her examine him to make certain there are no internal damages we can't see. Sandra is our resident healer," she told Quint.

"My brain is just fine," Quint assured them both. "And I'm also serious." He tried to sit up, but even though his brain worked fine, the rest of his muscles were another story. He felt as though he had been beaten, wrung out, and then pulled backwards through a keyhole. He tried again to lever upright, and this time Hannah helped. He managed to stay seated and some of the aches went away as he got control over his muscles again. "Very serious," he told her pointedly.

"Mm-hmm." She ignored both proposals. She also ignored the rising urge to fidget and brush out her hair and dress. No clumsy attacks around delegates, damn it! That was her rule, and she would stick to it, no matter how often her own genetics tried to literally trip her up. "Welcome to Delphinium. I am High Queen Hannah Delphinium, and the other person is Amanda Rai, the Gladiolus Defender Cultivator as well as one of my personal bodyguards. It's an honor to meet you."

He nodded his head at Amanda without taking his eyes off Hannah. "Quint Haven. A nobleman from the planet Celia in Tarmol, and the companion-at-arms and sort of bodyguard but mostly best friend to Crown Prince Matthew Celia." He slowly smiled as he took Hannah's hand and brought it to his lips. Her blush only deepened and charmed him more. "Believe me, the pleasure is all mine. I don't suppose Matt's shown up anywhere, has he?"

"He's on Protea," Amanda confirmed, and she did her level best to keep a smug smile hidden. She herself was a veteran of that first moment meeting a soul mate, and she was intimately familiar with the signs. It was about damn time Hannah found a good man to love. She had been ruling alone for long enough.

Hannah tugged at her hand unobtrusively, but Quint held tight without any effort. Recognizing she was up against a particularly stubborn type, she abandoned subtlety and looked him directly in the eye. "I'd like my hand back, please."

"Does it belong to anyone else?" he teased. "Say, perhaps, a suitor?"

"My suitors don't suit me."

"And it's such a pretty hand, too. Won't you give it to me instead?"

"I'm a bit attached to it. You'd have to take all of me with it." As she heard her words, she realized what she had said. Her eyes widened. "Wait!"

Too late. "Deal!" he said cheerfully, and he scooped her up into his arms as he stood. He grinned merrily at Amanda and asked, "Do you mind if I sneak to the front of the line and run away with her?"

"Put me down!" Hannah looked around quickly, but to her relief the only person near them was Amanda—who would be of no help because she had almost doubled from laughter. Hannah could only be glad none of her subjects were around. How would she explain this? "Put me down this minute!"

"Your wish is my command." He dropped her lightly onto her feet only to have to quickly catch her when she tripped on the edge of her Ruler gown's skirt. "Oops!" He grinned when she covered her face with her hands. "Dear goddess, you are *adorable*." There was no response, and his smile slowly faded. He gently pulled her hands away from her face and lifted her chin until she met his eyes. "Hey," he said softly. "I was teasing, Hannah. Everyone's clumsy once in a while."

"I'm clumsy *most* of the time." She struggled to keep the tears back. Stupid Light core often made her emotional, leading her to cry at the silliest things. "Byproduct of being an Illusion element. We're squishy and not strong, and we usually trip over everything, including allies!"

"Tessa forgave you for that," Amanda murmured dryly.

Quint ignored her and reached out to tenderly wipe away the tears escaping Hannah's control. She looked up at him in surprise— she barely reached his shoulder—and she found herself caught by the shimmering promises in his beautiful eyes. His breath caught in turn, and he slowly leaned down to touch her lips with his. Nerves drowned in a searing wave of something heated, hungry, and achingly lonely for what only his heart and soul could give her. He truly was her destiny. Her lips trembled as she stared at him in dawning understanding. "Where have you been?" she whispered.

"It doesn't matter," he whispered back. His thumb caressed her cheek. "I'm here now."

Amanda smiled in satisfaction. "I get to make the bouquet for the wedding."

* * * * *

"You're *what*?!"

The words echoed down the hall, and Hannah winced wryly. "I said," she repeated patiently, "that I'm getting married."

"To *whom*?" Genevieve could only gape at her best friend. She had walked in and, with her normal cheer, dropped an unexpected fireball. "I thought you disliked your suitors!" Her brain finally clicked. "Wait, hang on. You're getting married, and you showed up with our missing delegate. Let me guess, you're marrying him?" She jerked a thumb toward where Quint patiently stood.

"You make me sound like a disease," he said drolly.

She aimed a finger at him. "I like you for that alone. Go talk to Matthew and get out of my drawing room. I want to talk to your fiancée."

"Yes'm." He winked at Hannah and amiably headed out into the gardens.

"Alright," Genevieve said once he had left, "he's gorgeous, smart, personable, and he'll make a damned good king. He also obviously thinks you walk on water, which is just better. But, really, Hanny? I thought *I* was the impulsive one!"

"You're Dark," Hannah countered simply. "You don't see as clearly as I do. And, well, you always let your mind win over your heart, Gen." She took her friend's hands tightly. "He's my soul mate. It scared me. It still scares me. But I knew him." A surprisingly shrewd light entered her eyes. "Not unlike how you knew that handsome prince wandering your gardens?"

Color rose on Genevieve's face. "I don't know what you're talking about."

"Oh, yes you do!" She pushed Genevieve into a chair and sat down beside her. "I'm not that naïve. The moment you introduced Matthew, I could *see* the sparks between you. The *way* he looks at you says volumes." She lifted her brows. "And of course, the way you look at him. Has he said anything?"

"He asked to become a suitor," Genevieve reluctantly admitted.

"And you said?"

"I'd think about it."

She sighed gustily. "I have every confidence that Quint is giving Matthew the same lecture I'm about to give you."

"Lecture. Goddess save me, my conscience is giving me a lecture." Genevieve braced her shoulders. "Let's hear it."

"Why are you sitting here brooding when there's a gorgeous and sweet man who is head over heels in love with you, thinking that you don't know he's even a man, pacing in the gardens with my fiancé?"

It took a few moments to untangle the mess of the statement, and Genevieve eyed Hannah warily. Normally her tirades went on much longer. "That's it?"

"It sums things up, doesn't it?"

"Fair enough." She sighed. "It's complicated."

"So *tell* me." Hannah reached out to cover Genevieve's hands. "Gen, I know there's something important you've tried to tell me. For over a decade, you have tried. Each time you dare approach the subject, *something* happens to stop you! Short of the ceiling collapsing on our heads, I'm not moving until I know what scares you!"

"The prophecy." Genevieve waited, but no cosmic force interrupted this time. She could finally tell her best friend what she had seen. "I saw the whole prophecy, Hanny. Everything lost to time." In a very soft voice she said, "Nemesis will be destroyed by the descendant of Shanta *only when the kingdoms fall*." When Hannah's hands fell from hers, she didn't move to take them again. "I had another premonition recently. The Apexes . . . they will be born within our lifetime. My daughter or granddaughter. One of them will be the one foretold."

"Let me see if I'm clear on this. You're thinking that it's better to not marry and therefore not have a daughter, hopefully stopping the process entirely." Hannah scowled. "Genevieve, you just said it yourself! If you saw a premonition, then it's going to happen! You know you can't stop your Sight! *No one can.* Why are you even trying? Why make yourself suffer more when you could be happy for what time is left? Besides, what would happen to Protea if you don't have a child anyway?"

Genevieve's head lifted quickly. "I didn't . . . that never crossed my mind."

"*You think too much.*"

She winced. "Yes, I heard you the first time."

"Gen." Hannah took her hands again. "Cherish every minute. We can steal every selfish moment we need. Our happiness will give our daughters happiness. We know that. We saw what the opposite did to us. We can't regret anything." She squeezed her fingers for a moment. "Go find Matthew, accept his suit, and demand he marry you before the other suitors can protest."

After a thoughtful moment, Genevieve asked wistfully, "How much fun was it to tell them you were off the market?"

She grinned. "Far, *far* too much fun."

Matthew was partway through the massive gardens when Quint caught up with him. He felt absolutely no surprise with any of the events. Things happened symmetrically a lot of the time where they were concerned. The moment he had realized he was Genevieve's soul mate, he had predicted Quint would be Hannah's. "Fast work," he noted mildly.

"I know what I want." Quint grinned. "I knew she was my destiny, and I moved quickly to claim her. Give Hanny half a chance and she'll talk herself out of things that really are in her best interests." He arched a brow. "On what I suspect is a similar note, any particular reason that you and the beautiful Protea queen are barely speaking?"

Matthew gave a little salute. "We would seem to be soul mates as well, but something frightens her. She said she would think about accepting me as a suitor." His gaze lowered. "After talking to some people and learning more about the prophecy clinging to the universe, I think I understand her fear. The whole ordeal with ancient evils, nightmares, and the destruction of all that lives? It's centered right here. Her very bloodline."

Quint grimaced. "That'd be enough to convince any woman to reconsider marriage and children." He slowly lifted a brow as he saw Genevieve approaching them quickly. "Or reconsider something. Hello, Genevieve."

She didn't even spare him a look. She grabbed Matthew's sleeve and spun him around. "I have two things to say," she told him briskly.

He watched her very warily. "Yes?"

"One, I'm willing to accept you as a suitor."

Relief tangled with wariness. He couldn't quite read the look on her face, and her eyes were full of determination for . . . something. "I'm grateful. What's two?"

She went on her toes, buried her fingers in his hair, and dragged him in for a kiss that damn near put the heat of the sun to shame. It took only a second for him to drag her off her feet and return the embrace with the same fiery enthusiasm. He had been craving her taste from the moment they met. Sunshine and nature and everything wonderful about summer. She was all of it and more.

Quint turned a laugh into a cough and edged away from the scene as quickly as he could. He didn't know what Hannah had said, but it sure as hell had worked! He managed to keep the laughter in only until he was back inside the castle. The *look* on Matt's face when Genevieve had grabbed him!

The kiss continued until the sudden giggle of a maid going past reminded them where they were and what they were doing. Genevieve slowly released Matthew and looked up into his melting violet eyes. They darkened with his moods, and they had become a beautiful rich purple right then. Aching, longing, and hungry. Desire and love and a promise of happiness waited for her in his eyes. "Two," she said huskily, "is that I've decided I want to accept your suit as well."

"After that kiss, I would hope so!" He tightened his arms around her waist and held her closer. She had gone far too long without someone to hold her. "What changed your mind?"

"I can't change my heart." Her gaze dropped to his collar because continuing to hold his gaze felt nerve-wracking. "I want to marry you. I want you to be my husband, and I want my world to have you for her king." She took a breath. "I want you to be the father of my daughter."

"So then it is true that no Rulers of this galaxy can have sons?" he asked softly.

"It's true. It's been that way forever. We do not yet know why. I know I ask a lot, that you forsake your world as Cultivator in order to be my Caretaker, but—" She broke off as his fingers tenderly touched her lips.

"I have a brother and sister. When my sister turns twenty-five in a few years, I will return home and Activate her Seed so that she may be the Crown Princess and pass along our Flower Element bloodline." He smiled. "I want nothing more than to be your husband, the king to your world, the father of your daughter, and your Caretaker who tends to the deepest needs of your soul as a Cultivator. Why shouldn't a Cultivator be a Caretaker as well, if it is what Destiny decrees? We can be Caretakers to one another."

The term Caretaker applied to all soul mates of Cultivators, and nearly all Caretakers had mild magical gifts of their own. Whatever made them up had been very carefully selected to perfectly complement the Cultivator they would love, and allowed them the strength to tend to a Cultivator's sometimes fragile soul. Very rarely, though not impossibly rare, two Cultivators could end up being Caretakers to one another when the two involved needed not just support, but *understanding* from someone who, literally, knew how they felt within their given role. Curiously, it only happened between male-female Ruler pairs, and any subsequent children would be especially hardy and resilient.

Genevieve's lips trembled into a smile as she looked up at her Caretaker. Though their child would be wholly of Protea and not inherit her father's magic, she would still be regarded as an almost-daughter of Celia and deeply beloved to that world as well. How better to make an alliance than by blending the royal lines? And how was it possible that a single person, this single person, could finally make her world complete? She had both of her soul mates now. Her soul was at last whole. "You know," she told him as she wound her arms around his waist, "it's January." When he lifted a brow, she helpfully explained, "The Blossom Field baby boom. We have until December to keep up tradition. I need to get pregnant by March, though maybe April, since Nature elements are usually born premature."

He scooped her up into his arms and began to walk toward the castle. "If my queen insists, I can only oblige. But we really do need to plan the wedding too."

"Tomorrow work for you?"

"Only if I can watch you tell off your suitors."

She could only sigh happily. "I'll make it a party and invite all of the Cultivators." She rested her head on his shoulder and closed her eyes as she sent up a prayer of thanks to Destiny and Love. They had worked perfectly with Life to give her the perfect mate.

* * * * *

Lycander went looking for his wife and found her bathing in one of the large waterfalls near their castle. He perched on one of the rocks and openly admired her naked full figure. She was the one who fueled his power over Desire, and he would have it no other way. "Happy?" he asked her. "Everything ended as you wanted. Now why don't you tell me what else you two are planning? You're obviously not entirely happy yet."

Enaya winced wryly. "Busted." She slung wet white hair out of her eyes and looked over her shoulder. A smile instantly touched her lips as she saw her lover. His chest was gloriously bare since he had tossed his shirt aside. Guardian of Desire, indeed. A mere look at him was all it took to have her entire body aching for his touch. It had always been that way and always would be. She considered herself quite a lucky goddess. "I won't be truly happy until the threat is gone."

"That won't be for a while yet," he reminded her.

"It'll be sooner than we think." She waded toward where he sat and rested her head on his lap. He gently ran a hand through her hair, and she let out a sigh. "Orion, Shanta, *and* Genevieve all felt it. Nemesis is growing strong, and the time is coming soon. Soon the kingdoms will fall. In the meantime . . ."

"In the meantime," he interrupted, "there's nothing you can do. These cards were dealt a long, long time ago. No matter how you meddle, you don't have absolute control, remember? Destiny has her own will and plans."

"I know, I know." With a sigh, she pushed thoughts of the future aside. "Let's think about something else." She smiled slowly. "Want to scrub my back?"

"A newcomer to the kingdom?" Genevieve looked up from reading over a farming complaint and frowned at the Defender standing in front of her. The news was unexpected but a welcome distraction. At seven months pregnant, her loved ones had gone into a tailspin as they tried to coddle her. Hannah had it even worse; she was ready to deliver at literally any moment, and neither Sara nor Quint would leave her side. Luckily, her patience was up to the task of dealing with them.

November had arrived, marking the eleventh month since the marriages that had formally put a seal on the alliances between Protea, Delphinium, and Celia. The Crown Princesses of all the other worlds in Blossom Field had been born. Hannah's daughter would arrive any time, and while Genevieve was technically due in January of Royal Era Year 3, she fully expected to deliver in December. Nature always came early, and Illusion always came late; Hannah had already reached two weeks overdue.

The Ruler baby onslaught had an unspoken side effect that the average person did not know: all Cultivators tended to be the same age. That meant that even as all ten Ruler Cultivators were born, already born were most of the next generation of Defender Cultivators. They could not be uncovered until their fifth birthdays when their Mark developed as they Activated, but they would share their age with their princesses. Whoever would be Lead Defender would be the eldest, as usual.

It would be interesting to see which element claimed that role this time. It tended to fluctuate among the Metal, Fire, Thunder, and Glass elements. Only rarely had some of the others taken Lead, and never once had it been Iris' Ice magic. Ice too strongly reflected defensive skills, so it would take a particularly special Defender of Ice to be a lead.

While Genevieve looked forward to the new generation, particularly her own daughter, terror lurked under the surface of her heart. Would it be her who became the Apex of Dark? Or would it be her own daughter? Genevieve almost hoped for the latter; based on history, she may not survive to see the events, and that honestly relieved her a little.

She fiercely shook it off and looked at her patiently smiling friend. "What kind of newcomer, Sandra?"

"Barely younger, powerful, and fascinating. She only turned twenty-five earlier this year, but you'd assume she was thrice that from the power and talent she possesses. She's from the Faith of the Goddess." Sandra propped a hip on the edge of the table and smiled. "A priestess, no less."

"Really?" Genevieve heard Matthew clear his throat and realized he hadn't a clue what they discussed. "Oh, Matt, I'm sorry. I never did get a chance to tell you about the Faith." She smiled. "The Faith of the Goddess is a religion of sorts based on elemental majik and a belief in a Mother Goddess and Father God. They're incredibly powerful and do so many wonderful things that we could only hope to emulate. They're known as witches, though there are a very, *very* few who are powerful enough to become wizards. This woman must be a wizard herself."

"She claims she's only a witch, but I'm not sure I believe her," Sandra agreed.

"Interesting." Matthew slid an arm around Genevieve's waist to draw her closer, and his hand rested warmly over her belly. He looked at Sandra. "Does she want to meet us?"

"She does." She coughed. "I'm warning you now that she's quite sweet and quite gentle, but she's also a bit of a smartass. She and Krysta almost went to war."

"Your twin is a typical Hyacinth Cultivator," Genevieve countered dryly. "She can't beat me at word games, so she looks for an easier target."

"She didn't find it."

"Ha! I think I'm going to like this priestess. Show her in." She watched Sandra head out and then looked down at her husband. He had yet to turn loose of her. She covered his hand with one of hers. "Are you pleased, my king?"

"Very." He turned his head and pressed his lips to her rounded belly. The punch of love for both his lover and his child nearly felled him. He wanted a little girl with Genevieve's sass and stubbornness and his fearlessness. It would be a scary combination, but he wanted it.

A woman delicately cleared her throat, and both king and queen turned to see a slender figure in the doorway. Pale brown hair hung braided down to her knees, and her eyes looked an interesting pale brown as well. The utter loveliness of her face felt somehow surprising. Her beauty seemed to be more than merely physical; it came from somewhere inside her soul as well.

She wore a dark green dress with a white bodice laced on the top, and a blue cloak fastened around her shoulders. She seemed younger than her age implied until Genevieve looked into her eyes. This woman had seen and done a lot in her short life, and there was a core of steel inside her not dissimilar from the Defender Cultivators themselves.

Something moved against the blue cloak, and Genevieve's eyes widened as she realized there was a small blue and white dragon sitting on the woman's shoulder. The dragon had eyes in a matching shade of color to its owner, and it looked an eerie replica in shape to the silver pendant that the woman wore around her neck, including having very unusual horns. Dragons did not normally possess horns. "It's not often lately that we have dragons on Earth," Genevieve said softly. "They left us not long before the end of Harmonic Era. Twenty-five years ago now, or around that, since the Majik War."

"Indeed. But they do still sometimes come to the physical realm if they find a witch to bond with." The faintest hint of an accent flavored her words though it was not recognizable. She smiled. "This is my guardian, Haeth. I am Priestess Liena Aria." She dipped into a graceful curtsy. "It's a pleasure to meet you, Your Majesties."

Matthew kept an arm around Genevieve's waist as he stood. His eyes studied Liena curiously. He recognized her last name, and he thought he recognized her face as well. Since she had not remarked on it personally, he kept his mouth shut. It would be her business alone. "The pleasure is ours, priestess. What brings you here?"

She linked her hands before herself. "A vision of the future."

That startled Genevieve and Matthew alike. No mortals were capable of having premonitions, let alone visions, of the future. It was a gift left only to those of the Protea Kingdom, Aster Defenders, and Claret. If Liena had the gift of Sight, then the Guardian of Destiny had decreed she was of critical importance somehow. "Really?"

"Really. It is of Blossom Field in general, and the two High kingdoms in particular. I wish to share it, but on a condition."

"And that is?"

"If my vision is correct, I would like to become part of the kingdom." She smiled a bit ruefully. "I'm a bit solitary, and I am . . . gifted. None of the covens here suit me. I would like to find a place within the Protea Kingdom. Witchcraft majik, as you know, blends well with the magic of Cultivators. I wish to be the High Priestess of Protea, if you will have me."

"Does it?" Matthew asked Genevieve.

She nodded slowly, thoughtful. "We've never really had a chance to see how much, though. The kingdom has never found a witch with a gift powerful enough to truly affect Cultivators. Witches are the only beings other than Cultivators to have elemental powers. We call what they use 'majik' since it is like our magic yet different. Karalyn can use Water Flower Element magic in ways to bolster and benefit her world. Sandra can use Water Flower Element magic in ways applicable to battle such as directed blasts and the like. A witch with Water majik could actually control and manipulate bodies of water. Healing skills are not dependent on an element, so Karalyn and Sandra's ability in that regard is irrelevant in comparing the differences between Ruler, Defender, and witch. Witches can heal, too, if they have that particular skill. Certainly, some elements are more suited to it than others, but in Cultivator history, there's been at least a handful of healers of all elements."

Liena smiled. "We witches received our majik as a gift for claiming Destiny as our Goddess. Witches are not too terribly different in some ways from Cultivators, but we do have some distinct qualities. We can evolve into wizards, for example. A witch must choose one or two elements to specialize in and once chosen cannot deviate. She will learn one or two specialized categories of majikal skills, and never really go beyond that since she cannot flex her gift that far. Contrarily, if she were to evolve into a wizard, she could pick up to three more elements and up to two more skills. Wizards are quite rare, though. One in a few hundred thousand or so."

"I understand there's a third level." Genevieve cocked her head.

"Indeed but it has never been seen or obtained yet. It would require a witch to be born with infinite majik, and as we all know, infinite power of any sort is not exactly *common*." She smiled. "We are otherwise much alike to Cultivators. We have either a Light or Dark personal core, and we call ourselves White or Black witches depending on that."

"What do you possess?" Matthew asked curiously.

"I am a White Witch who chose Ice and Illusion as her elements and Sensing and Spiritual Healing as her skills. Sensing means I can sense when energies are out of balance, events are moving or holding still, or even read the energy inside other people to determine their own personal stability. It enhances my Sight to make me a good prophet."

"And certainly a fit for the kingdom!" Genevieve held out a hand with a smile. "May I?"

Liena smiled and took her hand. Genevieve's eyes immediately began to widen as she felt the majik shooting up through her arm. Cultivators could recognize the elemental core of majik inside any witch, but she had never felt anything that strong before. Sandra was right: no matter what Liena claimed, she was *not* merely a witch. If she did not stand on cusp of being a wizard, Genevieve would eat her crown.

Silvery majik glowed across Liena's eyes. "Ice, melt into the warmth of Nature."

Genevieve could feel a sudden flood of elemental magic moving into her body from where their hands clasped, and it not only made her suddenly feel refreshed, it also soothed her somewhat restless unborn child. "How did you . . .?" Her wide eyes stared at Liena. "What did you do?"

"I changed my element into yours in order to bolster you. *That* is what a witch can do for a Cultivator, should we manage to resonate properly."

Genevieve shook her head. "Well, I'm not about to turn you away! You have a deal, Liena. I do not doubt that there are many things you will be able to do for us that no one else could." She smiled. "Including ease my cranky daughter where no one else could!" Her eyes narrowed a bit as Liena winced. "Priestess, why does that make you pull a face?" She crossed her arms. "Just what vision did you have?"

"Uhm." Liena coughed. "Here, Your Majesty, please sit down." She nudged Genevieve's chair closer. "Please trust me, you want to be sitting." Once the queen had complied, Liena sighed. "The status quo of millions of years is about to shatter. Queen Hannah shall deliver a son any minute now, and your own will be born within the next month, Queen Genevieve."

"Just Genevieve," the queen corrected only to break off as the rest of the statement sank in. "What?!" She looked down reflexively at her rounded belly and then up again. "A *son*?!" She looked down again, this time in consternation. "Is *that* why I could not think of a name for you?" she demanded.

Matthew shook his head. "I'm having mental whiplash. To be told only daughters ever come to the Blossom Field kingdoms and then to discover, actually, no, not this time." He frowned. "Why? What caused this sudden change after so long?"

Liena smiled. "You and King Quint. You are from outside the galaxy."

"But why would it matter if my husband is from inside or outside the galaxy?" Genevieve protested. "I know it was unprecedented for me and Hannah to have soul mates from outside, but, is it truly that big a deal?"

She shook her head. "Gender is determined by a father, Genevieve, but magic always plays havoc with genetics. Only potential fathers who have not been subjected to the interplanetary inbreeding of the galaxy would have genes strong enough to potentially override the incredibly potent Ruler Cultivator magic of the queens. Didn't you wonder why *every* Cultivator of a planet has the *exact* same hair, eye, and skin color of her lineage, no matter what her father brings to the mix? Even the Defender Cultivators have magic that has become inbred, proof that it is not wholly blood alone that plays a part."

"It feels a bit scary to hear you say it that way," Matthew murmured.

"With good reason! Unless the lineages are someday rebooted, they might become too inbred to reproduce at all, and no world can exist forever without a Ruler. But," she carried on despite their horrified looks, "*that* is not likely to happen. Destiny would not allow it! She is now starting the reboot process by bringing in intergalactic blood, and it has already had an impact to produce male Ruler Cultivators for Protea and Delphinium."

"Is that the only change in our way?" Genevieve asked dryly.

"Hmm, no, but I'm not sure quite yet just what they will be." Something powerful moved through her eyes. "Time changes," she murmured. "Destiny waits." She shook it off. "There is one other thing to warn you about, though I know not how it will play out. I only know it will. Neither High Prince will be able to pass along their Ruler Cultivator magic to a child as more than a flavor of Dark Nature and Light Illusion. So the reboot probably has more in store that we may not expect."

Genevieve rubbed a hand over her belly and then linked her fingers with Matthew's when his hand covered hers. "I'm not sure what to say." A sudden flutter of panic filled her heart. "Is this . . . is this a sign of . . . of the Apex coming soon?" Silence answered her, and it spoke volumes. She took a deep breath and then let it out. Her granddaughter or great-granddaughter. She would not have to see the kingdoms fall; honestly, she did not think she would be strong enough.

The door to the drawing room burst open and a maid scrambled inside with barely a bow. "Queen Hannah just gave birth to a *son!*" she blurted.

Liena grinned, and Genevieve scowled at her large belly. Matthew just sighed. "What are they naming him?"

* * * * *

Not quite a month later, Genevieve went into labor early as had been expected. Liena tended to her as right of her position as High Priestess, and both Tessa and Matthew stayed by Genevieve's side. After many exhausting hours, finally, the next Protea Ruler Cultivator was born. And, as had been predicted, it was a little boy.

Though the intergalactic blood of the princes' fathers had been enough to bring a new gender, it had not been enough to completely override the lineages. High Prince Robert Delphinium had his mother's unruly curly white hair and light gold eyes, and High Prince Evan Protea had his mother's glossy black hair and vibrant pink eyes. The familiar Flower Mark of their world had etched itself on their small chests over their hearts. Fully Activated Ruler Cultivators, yet male. The whole universe could only shake its head. Leave it to Blossom Field to take something common elsewhere and make it unusual.

It took only a few months before people realized that the princes had, in fact, inherited something more from their fathers: their personalities. Robert hauled himself to his feet at four months of age, took off running, and no one could catch him again unless it involved bribery with sweet things. Evan opted to crawl before running, but as soon as he did gain his feet, he rarely stopped to catch a breath.

The poor Defender Cultivators found themselves with a whole new respect for their predecessors. They had not just the precocious two princes but also the Crown Princesses of their worlds to watch over. Finding the next generation of Defenders could not happen soon enough!

As the Protea Prince's first birthday was celebrated with a party, Shanta observed from within the Realm of the Gods. She watched for a bit before turning away, and she then turned into her husband's chest and bumped her nose on his powerful muscle. "Ow." She rubbed her nose as she stepped back again. "Orion, don't sneak up on me!"

"I wasn't sneaking." He lifted a brow. "You weren't paying attention." He tugged her into his arms and rocked gently. "It's nearly time, isn't it?"

She took a shaky breath. "Yes. I knew that the signs would start becoming more blatant, but this was not in my list of possibilities!" She rested her head on his shoulder. "I wish I could warn them."

He frowned and pulled her away enough that he could see her face, but what he saw didn't reassure him. "You mean you didn't give the priestess that premonition?"

"No." Her protea-pink eyes slowly widened. "I thought *you* had." She slowly turned back to the globe and watched Liena create majikal creatures to entertain the ten young Ruler Cultivators. "She saw it on her own," she murmured.

"She has a direct connection to Destiny." Orion didn't make it a question because it wasn't one. "She is not Protean, and she is not an Aster Defender. She is certainly not related to Claret or Pallas, so, if I did not give her the vision, then she has Sight directly from Mother. I had wondered why I felt such a kinship to her," he admitted. "I now wonder just how we are connected." A thought occurred, and his eyes narrowed briefly. He would have to check to see if he was correct. It could be important.

As if she could read his mind, and there were times it truly seemed she could, Shanta murmured, "Everything that happens now is important. Destiny has something planned for Liena's bloodline. There is a reason for everything."

* * * * *

Time, as Liena had noted, always changed, and it always passed along. Little over four years went by before the next significant change began to rear its head. Evan had just had his fifth birthday, meaning that all young Ruler Cultivators were of the right age where their magic would expand outward, connect to the magic of their Defender Cultivators, and draw out the awakening of the next generation. Robert and Evan would connect to their twin, and the now Elder Defenders would use those invisible beacons to find the next generation.

At least, that was how it *usually* worked. Robert, as was his way, started off the oddities anew by not sending out any pulse of magic. His parents and the Defenders urged him to do it—stifled magic could be dangerous—but, despite the concern, he felt no desire to try. In a way, it did not surprise anyone who knew him. Fearless was not the word for him; 'foolhardy' was more often heard uttered by more than one Defender.

Worse still, he had proven to be a quick learner and early bloomer where Delphinium gifts were concerned. Amongst those gifts was the ability to utilize Illusion magic to literally phase in and out of spaces without being found. The boy could not be kept still! When Hannah went to fetch him for lunch, she could only sigh at seeing his room empty. "Quint!" she complained, her tone aggrieved as she went into her husband's study where he was reading a letter from his family, "your son has done it again."

He didn't look up, but he did grin. "That's my boy." Her hand lightly rapped him in the back of the head, and he laughed. "Hanny, we knew from before his birth that he had magic. Before we even knew he was a *he*. We knew what we were going to be in for with a child of Illusion and Light—we just had to look at *you*." He sat back on a sigh. "He is a fully Activated Ruler Cultivator of Delphinium whether he can pass along that magic or not. That means we have to deal with the quirks that go along with it. Honestly, my only concern is for your lineage and how it will someday carry on."

Hannah had some suspicions on *that* score but said nothing. Sometimes her planet's Light core gave her borderline Sight of her own, but never in a way she could express in words. "I have every confidence it will work itself out somehow," she said only, though dryly. "Even if I do feel as if Delphinium is in for an adventure with our child as a king!"

He grinned and tugged her down onto his lap to link his arms around her lightly. "He's a boy just like his father, love."

"Why couldn't I have gotten a nice girl who would behave herself?" she sighed.

"You would be bored *senseless*," he countered cheerfully. Because she had to grin at that, he had to kiss her, and they very quickly forgot what the subject had been to begin with.

They heard Robert making a gagging noise and broke apart with laughter to find him watching them from underneath Quint's desk. Quint released Hannah so he could reach under the desk and pull the small boy out. Or rather, young boy. At five, Robert already showed signs of getting his father's height as well. He stood closer to the height of an eight-year-old.

"C'mon, you," Quint said. He waited for Hannah to stand and then stood with Robert in his arms. "Lunchtime." He put Robert down and smiled as his son scampered out of the room. "His mother's appetite. I don't think it's entirely being a magically-oriented sort that makes you plump, my love."

"Is that a complaint?" she asked dryly. Her breath stopped as his hands curved around her waist and deliberately flexed to test the softness of her flesh. He leaned down to nip at her ear, and a flush came to her skin. "Quint."

"I love every inch of you exactly as you are," he murmured huskily. He teased her nape for a moment before releasing her. "I'll prove it again tonight. Best go catch our son before he eats the furniture."

She beat a hasty retreat before she insisted on a long lunch of their own, and he grinned as he followed her out into the hall. He had gotten halfway toward the large banquet hall when he felt a familiar power. "Liena?" He glanced to the side just as she rounded a corner, and he smiled. "What brings you here?"

"Courier service!" she countered dryly. "I volunteered to deliver some books back to Hannah, and I caught wind of the erstwhile Light prince, so I thought I'd offer to hunt him down. I saw him go tearing past, so I guess that's not needed anymore."

"Ha! Not this time, though it was close." He ruffled her hair affectionately. "But I am sure he'd like to see you."

"I'll stop to say hi," she started to say as she removed his hand from her head, but the moment their skin touched, she went utterly still. Her eyes unfocused as she seemed to stare at nothing at all.

Quint's entire body tensed. He knew that look far too well. It was the familiar gaze of someone with Sight who had just had a vision enter behind her eyes. Better than entering directly into her mind; it knocked her out when that happened, and usually gave everyone a panic attack until they got reassured it was 'just' a vision. "Liena?" His alarm only mounted as tears began to well in her brown eyes and then spilled down her ashen cheeks. "Liena!"

Her eyes focused on him and her lips trembled open. "Oh no. Oh gods no." She buried her face in her hands. "Why did you make me See that?" she demanded raggedly. "Damn you, Destiny!"

"*Liena!*" Quint grabbed her shoulders to give her a quick shake. "You're scaring me!"

"Don't make me tell you!" she pleaded. "I don't want it to be true!"

"Then you had *really* better warn me what is so terrible!"

"You won't see your daughter's birth!" she nearly shouted.

He froze and his hands dropped from her shoulders. "I and Hannah will have a daughter as well?" He let out a long breath. "That explains the problem of the lineage, then. How won't I see it, Liena? How much time do I have?"

"I don't know." Her shoulders slumped. "I don't. I . . . just don't. I'm so sorry, Quint. I'm so very sorry!"

He caught her in a tight hug. "I don't blame you! If anything, I am sorry you had to see it if it has to happen!" He let go and added, "And I think you'll forgive me if I rush to hold my wife and son."

"Go, please." She watched him run off and then curled her hands into fists. "Damn it!" she whispered again, more viciously. "Why me? Why am I the one you chose to see that?" She swung around on her heel. She would head back to Protea and immerse herself in the kingdom and try desperately to forget what she had seen. It would come to pass far, far too soon.

She found an unexpected reprieve in the form of landing on the Portalpad of the garden only to discover that not only was it unusually raining, but there was a familiar Nature magic lurking in the gardens. She could only sigh. Protea had a very temperate climate that nearly never rained, and what rain *did* come tended to come without warning when Nature power overflowed. "Because, of course. Evan!" she called as she headed into the bushes. "You had better come out before I play dirty!"

Inside the drawing room on the second floor, a conversation not unlike Quint's and Hannah's happened between Genevieve and Matthew. It centered on a prince with more sass than sense, and the unfortunate effects of a child being given two doses of the same Flower Element magic. "He left a tree in his playpen! Which he climbed to get out," Genevieve complained at her husband. "Trees are *your* specialty!"

Matthew could only wince wryly. "Guilty as charged. But it is *your* ability to meld into the land that makes him impossible to track! At least Krysta's Air magic makes her a good tracker, even of people who can disappear into the ground."

"She practiced on me," Genevieve admitted ruefully. "And we have Liena as well. She should be back from Delphinium any time. The Elder Defenders have their hands full. Though neither Evan nor Robert have sent out magic, the princesses have, and the younger Defenders have begun to respond. Tessa said that she hopes to have found the new Defender Cultivators within the next week."

"I suppose we'll then see why our son didn't . . ." He trailed off as a figure filled the open doorway. "Uh-oh."

Genevieve turned and discovered their priestess had returned as expected, but she was soaking wet, muddy, and distinctly unhappy. Her arms held an equally muddy and soggy Evan. A grumpy Water dragon draped over her shoulder. Genevieve tried her best, but she finally had to laugh. "Afternoon walk, Liena? What *happened*?"

"A botched land meld in the middle of a storm!" She shifted her hold on Evan when he tried to squirm out of her arms. "I'll get him cleaned up. Let's go, boyo." She caught him higher when he tried to get his feet on the ground. He, too, stood taller than average. "No, you don't, you little scamp!"

Matthew began to frown as he realized she would not look at him directly. "I'll give you a hand," he offered. He followed her out into the hall and then asked softly, "Liena, are you upset with me for some reason?"

"No!" Her lashes flinched. "Damn it all." She heard the small device he wore to allow communication with the other worlds began to buzz and could only be grateful for the distraction. "Go ahead and answer." She hurried into Evan's room and divested him of his dirty clothes before taking him into the bath and running water in the tub.

"That was Quint," Matthew said a bit grimly from the doorway behind her. "And I think I now know what's wrong. He told me what you saw, Liena. May I assume you saw the same for me?" She said nothing, but her silence was an answer all its own, as was the sight of Haeth beginning to pace over the counter in an echo of her mistress' upset. "Why, Liena? Why are these things happening? Second children born to the kingdoms after sons were born? Quint and I apparently dying before our daughters are born? *Why?*"

"I don't know!" The words were torn out of her, and she fought back her pain when Evan frowned at her. "It's okay, honey." She put him into the tub of hot water and distracted him with a toy penguin. "I've had some bad visions." It appeased him, and she moved out of the bathroom. He was too smart to risk hearing the conversation. "I didn't ask to see what I did," she told Matthew in a low voice. "I asked even less to break down in front of Quint and have him force me to tell him what I saw. I don't *know* anything. I just feel things."

"Do you feel that my daughter will be the one of the prophecy?" Silence again met him, and his stomach clenched painfully. "What is Destiny planning with all this?"

"I don't know that either." She sank down onto a chair. "I just don't."

"Is there anything else strange happening?"

Her lips twisted into a wry smile. "So to speak."

(Iris Palace)

The planet of Iris sat at the end of Delphinium's line, and it could see the preceding Carnation in varying phases across the day. The mostly snowy landscapes of the lovely world had as much to do with its Flower Element being of Ice as it did being one of the furthest from the sun. Protea and Delphinium's Cores protected all worlds and allowed life to not only live, but thrive. Snowy or not, the world's namesake flower bloomed across the surface year-round. It particularly covered the stone castle, but those blooms were ever only the purple iris that could be seen as the Flower Mark on Cultivators of the world.

Jessie considered it an honor to be Defender Cultivator for her world and protect not only Hannah and Genevieve, but also Tokala and her husband, Taben. She considered it even more of an honor to keep an eye on Tokala and Taben's daughter: Crown Princess Yvette Iris. The girl looked as much like her mother as she did her guardian, possessing the same purple ombre hair and yellow eyes. Her Flower Mark, of course, sat right over her heart.

On that particular day where things began to change, Jessie had taken Yvette out into the city to visit a favored park. Jessie sat down on a bench to watch the small princess build snowpeople and a snow-city. She had her senses so attuned for potential danger that it took her quite a few minutes before she discovered that fog had rolled in around her.

"Yvette!" she ordered as she shot to her feet.

The girl ran over to her and clung onto her leg, as she had been taught from birth to do in the case of trouble. "What's wrong?" she whispered.

Jessie put a hand on top of her head, and her other hand held her Mask in case she needed to don it. "I don't know. Someone just used an Ice fog." She shook her head. "I would swear only Defender Cultivators could do that." Her breath stopped for a moment. "Wait." She knelt down to look at Yvette intently. "Send out the pulse again. I think we're close to your Defender!"

Yvette closed her eyes and obligingly set out an invisible pulse of magic. With her eyes closed, she did not at all see it expand outward, gather the fog, and draw it back in toward her. She *did* feel her hands suddenly tingle and hastily opened her eyes to look down at them. Into her hands formed a small Mask identical to Jessie's. Yvette stared at it and then looked at her guardian. "Jess?"

Jessie slowly reached out to push back the cape covering Yvette's shoulders, and there, on her left arm, now glowed a familiar Flower Mark. The same as the one over her heart. "Just like Claret," she whispered, "though it never happened to our other worlds until now. A Daughter of a world being both Ruler and Defender. And it won't be just you. It'll have to be everyone."

"I'm a Defender, too?" Yvette whispered.

"Yes, you are. And I promise I'll help you learn what you need to know to protect yourself as well as the High Princes." She covered the Flower Mark on Yvette's arm wholly with her hand and felt an incredibly powerful wellspring of magic that eclipsed Jessie's by far—who had eclipsed her own predecessor. The magic may have finally reached a turning point and would be capable of being no stronger unless something new added.

She looked into the distance toward the north beyond which, many ages away, lay Delphinium. She had seen absolutely no signs of a twin bond between the two princes and any of the younger princesses. Evan and Robert alike seemed closer to Asheria and Arista than the others, but not in any way that bespoke of a twin bond. Therefore, the princes must have had twins somewhere else. But, then, did that mean no Defenders would be twins?

Things were still in fluctuation somehow.

(Aster Kingdom)

While it was true that the gift of Sight relating to future or present events had a *very* limited scope, a lesser form of Sight known as Ghost Sight happened to be in the possession of all Aster Ruler Cultivators. Perhaps the very nature of the orange aster flower that hallmarked the world's Core had caused it, or perhaps the element of Fire and its rebirth properties had, but Aster held an exceptionally high concentration of spirits of those who had passed. Spirits of people who chose to either not go to the Realm or beyond to a new life. Somehow they all ended up on Aster. In order to communicate with these invisible subjects, Ruler Cultivators had Ghost Sight.

Melissa, therefore, was quite used to the way Crown Princess Asheria Aster would be seemingly talking to herself, but would instead be simply talking to those Melissa herself could not see. The Defender took it well enough in stride; Rebecca had done that to her since childhood, and Rebecca's husband, Goliath, had picked it up as well. She kept half an ear on the conversation side she could hear and made sure nothing was out of line.

On that particular day, as she and Asheria sat within the gardens in Aster Kingdom's grounds, she could hear again as her princess chatted casually with someone invisible to the common eye. Melissa merely kept reading her book; her husband, Jared, had gotten it for her when he had visited his brother recently. He was younger brother to Cedric, king of Daffodil, so for obvious reasons, Aster and Daffodil considered each other stronger allies than most.

The hot air and dry desert weather always made her feel peaceful. Aster's Flower Element of Fire had turned the world into mostly desert landscape, with only pockets of greenery here and there. The sands did not stop anything from growing; in fact, they sometimes helped too much!

Her quiet stopped when a shadow fell over her book. She looked up with a smile to find Asheria peering down at her where she sat on a blanket. "What is it, Ashe?"

"I saw something."

"In the garden?"

"In my mind."

Melissa went very still and then slowly closed the book. "Your imagination?" she asked carefully.

Asheria shook her head and made her orange hair swing. She bore the familiar coloring of her planet's lineage, and could almost pass for Melissa's daughter instead—a useful trick for the Defender to utilize to protect her. "No, I saw something that hasn't happened." She tilted her head. "I saw another princess. She looked like Robert. She needed me."

Heart racing madly, Melissa said, "Ashe, send out the pulse again."

Asheria obligingly released her magic as a wave, and where it had normally disappeared into the distance with no response, it this time seemed to bounce off nothing and come right back to her. Fire rippled over her hands and formed into a small Mask. Melissa reached out to touch her left arm, and though silk covered the Flower Mark, it could easily be felt burning brightly. Asheria looked at the Mask she held and then her hands tightened on it. "I wanted to be one," she whispered. "I wanted to protect Robert and Evan."

Melissa had to smile suddenly as she thought of all the times the princesses had, more than once, tried to be bodyguards to the princes. Well, that made sense of a lot, didn't it? And so did Asheria's vision of a princess looking like Robert. That could also explain a great deal as well.

(Gladiolus Kingdom)

Amanda served as bodyguard to Queen Harriet Gladiolus and her husband, Raphael, and the two royals' young daughter, Crown Princess Julianna Gladiolus. Raphael took it with good nature that he was the only one who did not have yellow hair and green eyes, but he insisted that it was his own olive skin tone given to his beloved daughter. No one corrected him; they liked to think it, too, especially since Julianna acted a bit like him right down to her need to nurture those she loved.

That included even her own guardian, much to Amanda's

bemusement. Still, the Defender did not argue. She had lost out on a great deal of love in her childhood thanks to her parents being unaccepting of the honor bestowed on her to be a Gladiolus Defender. Some of the pain had eased from Harriet, more still from her own soul mate, and now Julianna.

"Mandy," came her husband's dry voice as he walked into the kitchen where she had been assembling pies, "I found something wild. Should we risk feeding it?"

She looked up and grinned at finding Tristan in the doorway with Julianna clinging onto his back. "Maybe. At least it's cute."

"Mandy!" Julianna hopped down and scampered across the room to happily hug her guardian. She then released her and climbed onto a chair. "Teach me!" she demanded.

Tristan mock shook his head as he grabbed a cookie from a jar near his taller wife's elbow. Being shorter had never stopped Tristan from serving properly as her Caretaker and holding her together when the weight of evil pressed her down. "I think Gladiolus types are born not with genes but recipes inside their blood!"

"Stop complaining," Amanda scolded him. "At least we feed you, too!" She grinned at Julianna. "How did you get over here? Did someone drop you?" Amanda and Tristan's home sat on the palace grounds, but a storm had begun outside that meant Julianna should not have been out alone. Storms were exceptionally common on Gladiolus thanks to the Flower Element of Thunder, and the ones that fired off lightning usually made everyone stay indoors.

"I walked," Julianna told her. She grabbed the cookbook and dragged it closer. "Everyone was busy."

"That's damn dangerous," Tristan reminded her. "You could have been struck by lightning!"

"I was, but it didn't hurt. I almost didn't feel it!"

Tristan paused with a cookie halfway to his mouth, Amanda's hands halted over her pie dough. Both knew that only Gladiolus Defenders could actually absorb lightning strikes; Rulers had to actively try to catch them, and Julianna was still too young to learn that. If she had been hit, she should have at least been knocked down.

"Juli," Amanda said softly, "hold out your hands and send out your magic."

Julianna did as asked, and lightning seemed to come in through the windows to spark over her hands safely. A small Mask formed in her grip. She stared at it in a combination of surprise and relief, and then frowned at Amanda. "Does this mean I can protect the princes without them complaining?"

Amanda grinned as she tugged up the sleeve of Julianna's Ruler gown to reveal the glowing Flower Mark on her left arm. She almost didn't need to check, really. Defender Cultivators across time had been vexed by Protea and Delphinium Rulers' natural stubbornness. "I wonder what will happen next," she murmured. "When will the fluctuation end?"

(Hyacinth Kingdom)

Krysta had always known that she would be in for trouble once the heir to Hyacinth's throne was born. She could be in for nothing else when she knew intimately not only just how much trouble Skyla had given her, but also how much trouble she herself had given her predecessor. She just had not expected Destiny's terrible sense of humor to give her the most strong-willed princess *ever* to watch over! Skyla had been bad enough without adding her husband, Phillip's, extra hardheadedness.

On more than one occasion, Krysta had gone hunting for Crown Princess Arista Hyacinth only to discover she had skipped merrily off castle grounds without a care for her age or the danger. She also left parties in the middle of them, already said whatever she wanted when she wanted, and effectively did nothing at all expected of a five-year-old royal. Krysta figured that if she did not have gray hair by the time Arista reached puberty—and goddess help her when *that* occurred—it would be a minor miracle.

It was business as usual in the Hyacinth Kingdom. Krysta had been in the middle of a bath when her wife and Caretaker, Irminia, had poked her head in to tell her a bit politely that Arista had disappeared again. Krysta hastily dried and scrambled into her clothes but still had soap in her hair as she rushed out of the castle. Thank the gods that Arista did not yet know how to hide her trail; Krysta got cold sweats at the very idea.

She picked up the wayward princess just beyond the gardens and trailed her around to a shadowy patch behind some trees that the average person might not normally find. Arista sat on the grass with her chin on her hands as she stared at something intently. Hyacinth's Flower Element of Air lent itself to a very temperate climate that never got too hot or too cold, though winds blew nearly all the time. Most of the world consisted of flat grasslands, though trees grew in some select places. Wherever trees grew, something unexpected happened.

Krysta came to a stop and just sighed. "Arista. Damn it. You gave everyone a heart attack again."

"It's blooming, Krissy."

"What is?" Krysta moved around the tree to kneel behind Arista and discovered, to her surprise, a single black protea blossom. "What the? How . . . how did that get here? Black proteas only grow in the Protea Kingdom! Hell, all of the specific colored flowers for our Marks only grow in the kingdoms. Blue hyacinths are only here, for example. Well," she amended, "with a few exceptions. I've seen black protea and white delphinium on other worlds."

"Why?" Arista asked as she looked up curiously.

"Well, it usually means that the planet where the flower appears is the one belonging to the twin soul of the appropriate High Princess—or prince as may be the case this time." She broke off as she heard her own words. "Wait. That means that the Hyacinth Defender of your generation will be twin soul to Evan!" Her frown deepened. "Which makes no damn sense when Evan hasn't sent out magic."

Arista visibly hesitated and then admitted, "Evan told me something. He Saw it."

Krysta felt the inescapable presence of Destiny and sat down on a sigh. Evan had Sight, of course, from his lineage, so the fact that he had already started having visions did not come as a surprise. Though he be limited to the Present, he might still get occasional glimpses of the future should Orion or Destiny determine he need it. "What did he

See, and why won't I like it?"

"He said he saw a girl who looked like him. Said she had the Flower Mark of Protea, too. And . . . he saw me."

"You?"

Arista paused again and then pulled down the left sleeve of her small Ruler gown. And, there, on her left arm, glowed the familiar Flower Mark of Hyacinth. Identical to the one over her heart, but on her arm. She bore both Ruler *and* Defender magic. "I'm his sister's twin soul," she said softly. "I think that's why the protea is here." She reached out to touch the flower and then pulled her hands back as Air magic began to blow around her fingers. A glow centered in her hands and then formed into a small Mask.

Krysta looked at it in resignation, but did feel a small measure of relief. At least she would not have to chase *two* Hyacinth Cultivators around!

(Orchid Kingdom)

The Orchid Kingdom, possessing the Flower Element of Water, consisted of nearly all water. Land existed as copious islands, many of which remained unpopulated except for animals, and only a few strips of continental land. Even then, the land tended to be rather saturated as well with rivers and lakes and marshes. Cities had been built right on top of the water, and sometimes floated from place to place. The palace itself set upon a strip of land, but it butted up against the ocean.

Sandra considered herself extremely lucky compared to her partners. Water elements, almost as a rule rather than an exception, tended to be patient and calming sorts whose tempers might be terrible but usually took so long to arrive that the owner gave up on even keeping a grudge. That meant that Sandra had been blessed with Karalyn's levelheaded nature, and had likewise been blessed with Karalyn and her husband, Yang's, daughter. Crown Princess Delilah Orchid was usually the most levelheaded of the Cultivator heirs and could usually be counted upon to do what she was told and when she was told it.

Usually.

Sandra had just settled down in the drawing room of the castle to wait for Delilah to finish an art lesson when her own Caretaker walked in. He had a familiar look on his handsome face, and Sandra winced. "What now, Wyatt?"

Cerulean eyes lit with humor as he leaned against the doorframe. "Did you know that it's time for a swim?"

"I had *not* known. Do tell who informed you." She was already getting to her feet as she spoke.

"A certain little princess who, I think, is as much a fish as a human, since she spends so much time in the ocean." He ambled along behind his wife as she strode down the hall. "Should I get a net or a fishing pole?"

"Very funny. Did she even bother going to the lesson?"

"She had paint on her hands, so, presumably, yes."

"We're improving!" She made her way through the castle and then out into the back gardens. An exit in the massive stone walls led directly to a private strip of beach. And, sure enough, happily frolicking in the waves, was the small Cultivator. At least she had opted to put on a bathing suit this time instead of just running into the ocean while still wearing her Ruler gown. The gown came as something conjured directly from her Mark, but it was considered somewhat rude to just treat it as any other clothing piece.

Wyatt hung back a few paces to keep an eye on things as Sandra headed down to the shore. "Delilah," she sighed. "Honestly! Ashe is a terrible influence on you."

"But I'm a good one on her," Delilah reminded her a bit impishly.

"Well, fair enough! Fairly common among us Water types when we're friends with Fire types. What brought this on?" She knelt down to be on eye level. "I know you don't like art, but, you had promised to do better. This isn't like you, to break a promise."

"The water called me," Delilah admitted. "I couldn't ignore it. I think it wants to tell me something."

Sandra suddenly remembered how, at age five, she had felt the water calling to her. She had gone to the shore only to encounter Karalyn and awaken as an Orchid Defender Cultivator. Hoping, fingers crossed, she said, "Send out your magic."

Delilah did as told and sent out her magic. It touched the waves and then repelled back right to her. It swirled down around her hands with whorls of water and formed into a small Mask as the familiar Flower Mark of Orchid appeared on her left arm.

"So that's it," Sandra sighed. "I admit, I had begun to suspect. Your generation hasn't felt like us or even your mothers." She touched the Mark on Delilah's arm and felt it burning with immensely strong magic. Stronger than anything preceding it, to be sure. "Destiny has decided to create more Dual Cultivators at last."

"Are there others?"

"Very, *very* rarely on other worlds," Sandra confirmed. "But like male Defenders, Blossom Field just never had any except for Claret." In a murmur she added, "We never needed it before. Somehow we do now. I wonder why."

(Daffodil Kingdom)

Tessa's full name was actually Theresa, but only two people ever called her that. Brianna, when she was pretending that being queen made her pompous; and Laura, Tessa's Caretaker and wife who used it when she wanted to make a point. Genevieve tended to go the other direction entirely, and called her beloved twin 'Tess' half the time. Brianna and Cedric's daughter, Crown Princess Kacey Daffodil, also swung mostly to the informal side but sometimes was very much her mother's daughter.

Tessa found it a bit curious in many ways. She felt far closer to Kacey than to Brianna, almost with the sense of being kindred spirits somehow. It did not bother her, though she had been a Lead Defender for over two decades by then and knew that when something different happened, then something *very* different would follow. She already had her suspicions, to be sure.

The definitive answer came one day as she and Laura took Kacey out for a walk amid the fields around the palace. Daffodil, being of the Flower Element of Metal, had a curious landscape that held mostly rocky crags and mountains full of volcanoes that spewed fragments of natural metals into the air. The craggy fields surrounding the palace looked as if a giant had been rolling rocks in play and then just left them where they had fallen. The token pink daffodil of the world dotted the landscape like merry spots of color.

Kacey skipped merrily around the boulders and climbed over a few of them. As she did one time, Laura spotted something and bit back a smile. "Tessa, is she wearing shorts under her skirt?"

"She is," her lover confirmed dryly. "I can't keep her from climbing things, so at least I make it more comfortable for her." She gave a deep sigh, which prompted Laura to lace their fingers together. "I'm concerned."

"About?"

"Veronica."

Laura's brows shot up. "A curious thing to hear from a Daffodil Defender. Why would you be worried about Carnation's princess?"

"Because I feel that I'm looking at myself as a child."

It took only a few moments for that to sink in. Laura's pink eyes slowly widened. "You mean she is showing the traits of being a Lead Defender? But Ruler Cultivators don't *have* a lead!" Her wife looked at her evenly, and her heart skipped a beat. "But if she is . . . then . . ." Her eyes shot toward Kacey. "It would have to be all of them."

"Which is why I haven't yet pushed Kacey to again search for her Defender," Tessa admitted.

Kacey had barely been paying attention to them; only enough to know they stayed close, but not enough to listen. She had been listening to the air. Or maybe not the air. It didn't feel like when messages carried on the wind of Hyacinth. It felt . . . different. A voice whispering in her ear. Or maybe three voices. She liked the voices. They made her feel happy.

Seemingly from nowhere, two of the voices got more insistent. She stopped skipping and held very still to listen. The intense look on her face immediately made Tessa and Laura move to her side. Tessa knelt down and caught her face in her hands, and Kacey focused her eyes on her. "I heard it," she whispered.

"Heard what?" Tessa whispered back.

"Hope. I heard the Whisper of Hope. It's coming soon."

Laura frowned. "The whisper of hope?"

Tessa was nearly not breathing. "The Whisper of Hope," she managed to say, "is the legendary force to exist inside the Apexes. It is what lets them create miracles by gathering the rawest power of all the hope in the universe." She looked up at Laura. "Kacey is saying that the Apexes will be born *very* soon, and her ability to hear the Whisper is evidence that it will be in her generation." She shook her head. "No one has ever heard the Whisper before. It's a sign of something great in Kacey's future."

Kacey patted Tessa's cheek soothingly. "I will be okay." She nodded firmly. "I will be strong and help the Apexes."

"She really does sound like one of you," Laura murmured, trying to hide a smile.

Tessa could not dispute that and released Kacey from her hands. "Kacey, send out your magic."

Kacey's nose wrinkled slightly as she sent out her magic into the galaxy, and it spread outward in a wave that grabbed the floating particles of metal that always carried on the wind like unliving bugs. The metal melted together into streams that flowed down to Kacey's hands as she lifted them, and a Mask formed on her palms. Under the petal of her gown, her left arm could be seen, and so could the Flower Mark that appeared.

"You were right," Laura told Tessa. She winced wryly. "And I have an inescapable urge to contact Sara and warn her."

Tessa had to grin. "I'm sure she'll figure it out soon enough."

(Carnation Kingdom)

Sara, despite being one of the more lovely Cultivators in a long while, had a curiously terrible luck where love was concerned. Somehow, she and Jessie had managed to make it into their thirties without finding their soul mates. They had looked, and Sara had been on far too many dates to count, but nothing had ever come from it. It bugged her more than a little; didn't she deserve a Caretaker as well?

The hole, thankfully, had filled a little once Crown Princess

Veronica Carnation had been born. Melody and her husband, Harmon, had produced a child that was, in Sara's opinion, just shy of perfect. The familiar Carnation coloring, her father's incredible beauty, a heart of gold, and a sassy and stubborn nature that made her a force to be reckoned with even at such a young age.

The eldest of all Cultivators of her generation, she had just turned six years old and had already become the unofficial ringleader. If she told one of her fellow princesses to do something, they did it, strangely enough. The princes didn't as much, but she could rather successfully nag them into doing it anyway, as if they somehow knew she did it for their own sake. It bemused Sara to no end, and reminded her a bit of someone else she knew, though she couldn't quite peg who.

"You're upset."

The sound of her princess' voice had Sara looking up quickly from the paper she had been halfheartedly sketching on. She had thought she was alone in the art room of the castle, but somehow Veronica had managed to sneak up on her. The young Cultivator's astuteness did not surprise her; Glass Cultivators often possessed the gift of Empathy that allowed them to feel and identify emotions around them. Sara only had a mild dose of it herself.

Smudges of dirt and sand on Veronica's face implied she had been recently playing in the sandy lands of the world. Carnation's Flower Element, being born of sands, had resulted in a desert world not unlike Aster in many ways, yet one where rain came with relative frequency to turn sand into sludge that would harden into natural glass. Sara had to smile. "Were we outside, Nica?"

Veronica nodded, but a stubborn line set to her chin as she walked closer. She swiped at the sand on her face, and her play clothes disappeared to be replaced by the voluminous petals of her Ruler gown. "You're upset."

Sara sighed. "Loneliness. That's all. I promise." She smiled as Veronica climbed up onto the chair beside her. "What were you up to outside?"

"Magic. I made flexible glass!"

Sara's brows shot up. Only the strongest of Glass elements

actually managed to make flexible glass. It had dozens of applications, and could be extremely dangerous when wielded as a weapon. Nearly no Rulers had ever used it; normally only Defenders found how to make the both hot and yet fragile element work in such a way.

Little pieces began to click together rapidly as Sara stared at her young princess. *Tessa.* That was who Veronica reminded her of! All the details started to fall into place. "Of course," she murmured. "That's what it is. That's why we can't find them. Veronica, send out your magic again."

"Why?" Veronica asked. "It won't find anyone. It never has."

"Yes, it will. I promise it will."

Veronica sighed deeply but obligingly sent out her magic. It ricocheted back into the art room with a wild swirl of sand that formed into ribbons of glass as it arrowed down around her. It pooled into her hands and then formed into a small Mask. The Flower Mark of Carnation appeared and began to glow against her left arm under her sleeve. She stared at the Mask for a moment and then looked at Sara. "It found me."

Sara sighed. "Seems so." She smiled. "You are the Lead Defender for your generation, Nica. You will have to be the one to take charge when needed."

Reasonably, Veronica told her, "I already did. Now they have to listen to me!"

Sara could barely bite back laughter. And here she had thought things could not get more unusual. At least they would now get entertaining, too! A temperamental Lead Defender always kept her teammates on her toes.

Word spread rapidly that the next generation of Defender Cultivators had been found. The entire galaxy seemed to get tipped on its ear over the fact that the Defenders were in fact the Crown Princesses, but with Claret's presence and Duals having existed before in other galaxies, eventually everyone just threw their hands in the air and gave up trying to second guess events. The kingdoms had considered keeping their identities secret, but that would be impossible to do in the long run; who wouldn't guess why the princesses were *never* seen with their Defenders?

Training started immediately with the Elder Defenders working with their charge to teach them everything they needed to know in order to use their magic in battle as well the physical skills they may need. Some, as was common, took to the physical combat better than others. Veronica, Asheria, Arista, and then Julianna ranked at the top of the list for their generation; again, not uncommon. The Lead Defender would always be strongest. Suspicion over the possibility of future princesses meant that neither Melissa nor Krysta felt any surprise to see Asheria and Arista following right behind Veronica in skill; twins usually followed Leads, unless one happened to *be* Lead, such as in Tessa's case.

However, only a bare select few people even knew about the potential future princesses. And with how busy things rapidly got, there became no time for a big meeting to get everyone on the same page. Matthew and Quint left in June of that year, Year 8, in order to return to Celia so that Matthew could finally Activate the dormant Seed inside his younger sister. She had finally turned twenty-five and could rule. She could have been Activated at any age, but the process could so greatly weaken the person Activating her that they had put it off as long as possible. Quint went along to ensure that Matthew had someone to protect him during that weakness, and they left behind their accepting and yet surprisingly cranky wives.

A month ticked by, and confusion mounted among the Elder Cultivators of both Defender and Ruler status as both Hannah and Genevieve became unusually hormonal. Hannah had never been the even-tempered type—Light elements ran hot—but she hit a new level entirely. Genevieve, known for her patience and self-control, seemed even more out of sorts.

During a playdate for the young Cultivators at Protea Kingdom, Sara watched Hannah snipe at nearly everyone and finally demanded in sheer exasperation, "What is *wrong* with you, Hanny?"

Kacey looked up from where she had been shooting marbles with Robert and said in mutual exasperation, "She's going to have a baby!" As the room came to a screeching halt and all eyes turned to her, she pointed at Genevieve. "Her, too!"

Sandra cleared the room in nearly a single bound to grab Hannah's shoulders and search her with magic. The answer came a bit blindingly, though she had not doubted Kacey's ability to sense the new life even at range. "Oh my goddess," she managed to say a bit weakly. "Hannah's pregnant." She grabbed Genevieve's arm and felt the same wild pulse. "Gen definitely is too." She evaluated both and the development of life inside them. "Assuming the normal route of Delphinium always late and Protea always early, Hannah should deliver in November and Genevieve in December. Evan and Robert will share their birthday months."

Both princes brightened and looked utterly delighted by the news. Evan, however, was the only one who did not feel surprised. Neither did Arista, Asheria, or even Melissa and Krysta. The latter admitted, "I had suspected this might be what was going on. A black protea blossomed on Hyacinth's palace grounds."

"At least that explains the hormones," Amanda groused.

"She didn't ground *you*," Robert groused back.

Genevieve and Hannah stared at each other and then mutually sighed. Genevieve spotted Liena in the doorway and demanded of her, "Did you know?"

Liena cocked a brow. "Of course." She leaned against the frame of the door and smiled. "I am the High Priestess," she reminded her queen gently. "I sensed the new life almost as soon as it formed. And I had seen it would happen, so it did not surprise me. You both carry daughters. The lineage shall be safely passed along through their bloodline."

A bolt of sheer terror swiftly went through Genevieve and her hands clutched at her still flat belly as if to protect the sleeping child inside. She immediately had Tessa's arms going around her, and she clung onto her twin with all her strength. Perhaps it would not be her granddaughter after all. Perhaps her coming daughter would be the one. She could not dismiss the possibility, not with all the other unusual events.

Messages were immediately dispatched to Celia to alert the kings as to their coming daughters. A message from Celia's king came back in return, to cheer the addition of new granddaughters to his family, but he warned that Matthew may not be fit to travel for another few months. The process had taken more out of him than anticipated.

Months ticked by without word from Celia, and the queens' pregnancies advanced. A few days before Robert's sixth birthday, almost two weeks late, Hannah went into labor. Liena tended to her personally with Sandra as an aide, and Sara remained steadfastly by her twin soul's side. The baby born that day looked as much like her mother as she did her brother, possessing familiar white hair and light gold eyes, and a creamy skin complexion. Within a few minutes of her birth, the Flower Mark of Delphinium appeared over her heart, which surprised none.

What *did* surprise everyone was that Robert's Flower Mark did not fade into the familiar outline of a Deactivated Ruler. Both brother and sister stood as Activated Ruler Cultivators, meaning both possessed the full potency of their lineage. It was highly unusual for any world; no generation ever had two Activated heirs at the same time. A Ruler who Activated another would effectively Deactivate their own Seed, hence the utter weakness they could suffer. Yet both

Delphinium children had fully Activated Seeds of their own.

Moreover, the new princess had something else entirely to her Flower Mark. Wrapped around the center of the blossom was a pure white crown. It radiated such heat and light that it nearly seared the air. Her entire body brimmed over with untapped magical potential. Liena handed the newborn to Hannah and said, "You have birthed an ultimate being, Hannah."

"The Apex of Light." Hannah looked down at her daughter and felt nothing except overwhelming love and a bit of grief. She would never have asked this fate to have befallen her child, or Genevieve's child. Her suspicions of before had gelled into certainty as soon as she had learned she was pregnant. Knowing what would come, however, had not prepared her for the reality. "Her name is Sayena."

"Lovely." Sara pressed a kiss to Hannah's sweaty forehead. "Well done, you. Should I get the little ones? Robert has been anxious to meet his baby sister, and Asheria has certainly been affixed to your side the whole time."

Hannah smiled up at her. "Please do, though I don't think it will be a *new* meeting. Robert and Ashe alike would talk to Sayena, and I would swear she could hear them. If she was restless, they calmed her."

Sara left the room for a few minutes and then returned shortly with the four Dual Cultivators of the Light planets as well as Robert. The prince immediately climbed up onto the bed beside his mother, and sheer wonder filled his eyes at seeing his baby sister. He knew her. Somehow he knew her. He had missed her, too. He didn't question the strange oddity of missing someone he had not met; they had surely met somewhere before that he did not remember. He gently reached out to touch Sayena's hair, and she peered at him sleepily before smiling. "May I hold her?" he asked Hannah eagerly.

"Scoot in, love." Hannah showed him how to hold the newborn and then wrapped her arms around him to help give extra support. He almost did not need it; the utter reverence with how he handled his sister spoke volumes. "Come here, girls," she added to the Cultivators peering over the top of the bed. "Climb up. There's room."

All four clambered up and then scooted in as close as they could without crowding Hannah so that Liena could continue to tend to her. Asheria hovered right at Robert's elbow and fought the urge to demand he share. "She's so cute!" she said to Hannah. "She looks like Quint!"

Indeed, though both Delphinium children had the coloring of their maternal lineage, they had features that more closely resembled their father. Hannah felt well-pleased with how the genetics had fallen; nothing made her happier than to see tiny replicas of the man she loved. He had kept her on her toes for years, and she looked forward to many more.

Robert saw Asheria eyeing him and smiled. "Your turn." He handed over Sayena without fuss and then looked at Julianna solemnly. "Now you have to stop bothering me because Sayena needs you more."

Julianna eyed him. "We'll still bug you. You get into trouble!"

Asheria barely heard them. She had been transfixed by the tiny baby in her arms. Love ached inside her heart and soul until it welled up and overflowed in a never-ending wave. This princess *needed* her, and Asheria needed her in turn. They shared half a soul, would forever be complete near each other rather than apart. Unlike lover soul mates, twin soul mates could feel their full force and fury of emotion from any age. Perhaps because lover souls also felt desire, and that could only truly come with adulthood. "Just like I saw," she whispered. "I was blessed to be one of the twin souls."

Veronica frowned at Hannah. "Robert deserves a twin too!"

Hannah nodded. "He does, and I believe that one exists. For Evan as well. We are not yet sure how to search for such a person, though. For now, you Dual Cultivators will protect both High Prince and High Princess with the assistance of the Elder Defenders until we can determine our best course of action."

Another month ticked by and Evan prepared for his sixth birthday. Genevieve, near ready to burst at only eight months pregnant, grew more agitated by the day. Knowing she could go into labor too early, even for a Nature element, the Elder Defenders closed in tighter around her. Hannah spent most of her time on Protea to help as well, and Sayena and Robert's presence did, to some extent, help soothe Genevieve. At the least, they soothed her unborn daughter. The baby had a force and will that could be felt in the air around her mother.

No word had come from Celia as to Matthew and Quint's status. They had left only a few weeks before to return to Blossom Field, and not a single bit of communication had been received. Tokala and Claret had their worlds' border patrols on constant lookout for the familiar ship, but nothing had yet been seen. With evil beginning the familiar encroaching once more, tensions ran high as the Defenders waited to be called to battle, potentially to protect their kings' lives.

Liena had spoken to no one of her visions of the kings' future. She had known it would be futile. She simply stayed near to Genevieve as a silent support, ready to deal with whatever fallout may come.

A week following Evan's birthday, the Elder Defenders including Claret, the Dual Cultivators, and the Delphinium Royal Family all visited Protea. Liena had just carried in a tea tray when she stopped dead in her tracks. The tray slipped from her fingers, but Krysta had already been leaping forward. She managed to grab the tray before it hit the ground. She gingerly put it down on the table and then turned back to Liena as others gathered close. No one said a word.

Liena abruptly came back to herself. Her brown eyes looked briefly shocked and then shifted to fierce and determined. "Tessa." She turned toward the Lead Defender. "The kings are in danger! You *have* to go to them!"

Tessa frowned. "Are you sure? What did you See?"

"Just go," Liena ordered. "As High Priestess, I am ordering you to go. While a Caretaker always knows if their Cultivator is in trouble, a Caretaker cannot be sensed in return *unless their mate is a Defender*! Rulers don't feel their Caretakers in danger! Genevieve and Hannah won't feel anything until their mates are near death, and it will be too late! You have to go *now*!"

Tessa nodded sharply. "I'm sure as hell not going to distrust your Sight!" She turned to her partners. "Claret, Krysta, Jessie, Amanda—you're coming with me. Jess, call the Caretakers to meet us to go along; we may need their extra gifts or skills. We will save our kings from anything." She ran for the door, and the four she had commanded stayed right on her heels. Determination burned inside all of them.

"Liena?" Hannah whispered. "What did you See?"

Liena shook her head sharply. "A chance to change something else I had Seen." Her fingers clenched together. "I have to try. I have to try to change destiny."

The others exchanged a quick look. No one, ever, had changed anyone's destiny. Not even their own. Could Liena? Certainly, she had a gift unlike any other.

Genevieve felt a sudden blinding pain radiating from her womb. A familiar pain, if alarmingly more powerful. Terror turned her skin glassy as she grabbed at her belly. "Liena?" she whispered. "Tell me you saw this too."

"To an effect." Liena stepped forward and calmly took command for she knew it was needed. "Hannah, Sandra, I will need you to aid me with Genevieve. Sara and Melissa, take the Dual Cultivators with you to Evan's room for now. Asheria, care of Sayena falls to you." She looked at the remaining Cultivators in the room. "I will call for someone if they are needed."

No one hesitated to do as ordered. The High Priestess of Protea automatically become the one in charge of the kingdom should queen or king be unavailable. On Protea, even Hannah acquiesced to Liena in place of Genevieve or Matthew unless given permission otherwise. Everyone began to move swiftly.

Hannah hurried to Genevieve's side and told Liena, "She's too heavy for any of us to carry. With the additional baby weight, not even Tessa could move her now."

"I am aware." Liena hurried to the door of the drawing room and looked down the hall. Sure enough, a familiar figure stood at the end. "Captain Lieu!" she called. "I need you to help me move Genevieve to her room!"

The Captain of the Royal Knights immediately moved to join her. It was never a hardship for him to be by the lovely priestess' side. "I'm yours to command," he told her simply.

She ignored the double entendre as she pointed at Genevieve. "Carry her and come with me."

Lieu Vanguard calmly lifted Genevieve into his arms and followed Liena through the castle to the queen's grand suite of rooms. He placed Genevieve on her bed and then returned to the hall. After the two other Cultivators had entered the room along with Liena, he shut the door and took up guard. His green eyes narrowed only a bit. Premature birth so soon was not safe for mother or child, even Nature ones, but he knew the odds lay in their favor. All of the galaxy, even the universe, knew what the birth of this child meant.

Genevieve bore the stronger risk of her and her daughter for she would willingly sacrifice her life for her child as needed. Liena would not let her, and neither would Hannah or Sandra. They worked as a team to support Genevieve through the pain-filled hours, unwilling to lose either one of them.

It had been pouring rain outside since early morning in one of Protea's very rare storms, but as the newborn princess took her first breath and let out a terribly annoyed cry, the rain began to cease. A hush fell across the face of Protea as the baby's power spread across the world in an encompassing wave. Liena, unfazed as always, merely took care of the baby while Sandra tended to Genevieve.

Genevieve had slumped against Hannah, but when her daughter was offered, she found the strength to straighten a bit and hold out her arms. The baby she found herself holding had the familiar black hair and pink eyes of her maternal lineage, but, like her brother, had features reminiscent of her father.

She was a surprisingly big baby for being born early! She would never have been born safely if she had gone to term. Unlike most babies, even Sayena, the newborn princess seemed to scorn the fragility that clung to all newly born children. Perhaps an aspect of her Dark core, her Protea lineage, or perhaps even an echo to the warrior nature of both her parents; there was no knowing. And, most significantly of all, the Flower Mark over her heart bore a black crown wrapping about the protea blossom. The Apex of Dark had at last been born as prophesized.

"What's her name?" Hannah asked softly.

"Shanae." Genevieve skimmed a finger down her daughter's cheek and drew sleepy, and cranky, pink eyes her direction. "You little hellion," she murmured. "If I didn't know better, I'd say you chose this moment to be born on purpose." She took a sudden sharp breath and her head jerked toward the bedroom door.

It banged open to reveal Matthew. He was visibly weak, more than a little bloody, and only stayed on his feet because of Tessa and Laura's support . . . but he lived. His lips trembled as he smiled at his wife. "Sorry I'm late, Gen."

"You're here," she managed to say. "You're alive. That's all I could ask." She fought back the tears burning her eyes as he moved closer. "We make beautiful babies, Matt." As he eased onto the bed beside her, she leaned against his arm. Through the ragged tears in his tunic, she could see the now Deactivated symbol on his chest. An outline where there had once been full color.

Liena could not tell if she wanted to cry or to laugh. Had she thwarted Destiny after all, or had she played into a larger master plan? She could not tell. Had no desire to figure it out. She would only be grateful that she *had* done whatever it was she had done. If she had kept her mouth shut, had taken the first vision as set in stone—as all were—the kings would have died. Yet . . . perhaps she had not been wrong then, either. Neither Matthew nor Quint had seen their daughters be born, though they would at least see them grow. "You're a mess," she told Matthew finally.

"The entire scene was a mess," Tessa admitted tiredly. "We arrived to find Matt incapable of protecting himself thanks to Seed weakness, and Quint . . . well, I want to give him a damn *medal*. He was protecting Matt without thought or consequence to himself. He's pretty bloody, too. If we Defenders had been even a minute later . . ."

"You weren't," Hannah told her fiercely. "And that is what

matters." She gave Genevieve and Matthew both a kiss and then rushed to her feet. "I need to see my husband!" She dashed out of the room, tears already running down her face. Too many emotional rollercoasters for her liking over the last day. She would probably cry off and on for the next few hours.

Sandra looked at Liena and got a nod. She nodded in turn. "I will leave Matthew to Liena and go patch Quint back together. It won't be the first time," she added in a grumble as she hurried out.

Tessa leaned against Laura as her wife slid an arm around her waist. "We will go get Evan and the other girls, and bring Claret as well. We will put that entire incident behind us, pretend it did not happen. Liena saved the day this time, not us." She smiled at Liena. "You would make a good Defender."

Liena smiled back as she finished healing Matthew. "Only a good one. I would not be great. I'm better suited where I am."

"Hmm, fair enough." Tessa dropped a kiss on Genevieve's head and then left the room with Laura to go find the children as well as their eldest partner. It was time for tradition to carry on, and for Arista to finally meet the twin she had so longed to know.

Matthew took a long breath as he accepted his daughter from Genevieve. The baby looked up at him for long moments and then contentedly snuggled into his arms. Love ached and overflowed inside his heart. "I want her to be like you," he told Genevieve thickly. "I'm asking for such trouble by saying so, but I do. Evan is more like me. I want our daughter to be more like you."

"Shanae," Genevieve told him on a smile. "Her name is Shanae." Her lips trembled as she wavered between laughter and horror. "And you would inflict my personality on her future Caretaker?"

He leaned down to kiss her tenderly as their daughter rested peacefully in his care. "It hasn't done *me* any harm."

Liena watched the family for a moment and then smiled. "I will spread word of the birth." She left the room to give them privacy and found Lieu still standing loyally in the hall. She told him only, "'tis done. Everything is fine." She started to walk away down the hall, yet was not surprised when he fell into step beside her. "Captain." She turned around and linked her hands together without looking at him. "I am flattered by your attention, but I am not interested."

"Liena." He caught her arm and waited until she reluctantly looked up. "Don't put me off in that way. You must surely know I am in love with you. Please tell me why I don't suit you. Is it the age difference?"

He was ten years her elder, forty-one to her thirty-one. "No." She took a long breath and met his eyes directly. He deserved to know the truth. "Lieu, you are not my soul mate. I have met my soul mate, but I can never be with him. I am not your soul mate."

"No, you're not," he admitted equally, and readily. "I don't *have* a soul mate, Liena. My soul is . . . not properly developed, I suppose. Most humans without power are that way. We don't get the gift of a soul-deep love. But we *can* love with all of our heart." He let his fingers tangle in her messy brown braid. "I could make you happy, my priestess. Maybe not to your soul, but at least through your heart. If you cannot have one, let me give you the other. No one will ever love you the way I do."

"Maybe I'm not attracted to you," she countered calmly. "Did you think of that?"

A smile kicked at his lips as his free hand lifted and he lightly flicked a finger over the rapid race of the pulse in her neck. "No." He slid his hand up to cup her cheek. "Let me court you, Liena. You spurn all suitors, but let me be one. I know that we can be happy. If you can't give me your soul, at least give me your heart and body. I will treasure you for all of our days."

She drew a long and ragged breath. Did she have the bravery to try to reach for happiness? Could she settle for less than everything? Was it even fair to Lieu? The years of loneliness caught her as she murmured, "I don't know if I even know how to be happy with someone that way."

He tenderly brushed her lips with his. "I will teach you. I will court you for a century if needed, Liena."

"Alright," she finally conceded. "You may court me. We will see what happens. Now, let me be. I suspect Quint needs my Spiritual

Healing gifts. His soul surely took a battering in his effort to be Matt's bodyguard while knowing he risked himself as Hannah's Caretaker. I will not let him bear guilt or lingering nightmares for his decision."

"I will come with you." His tone booked no argument. "I know what happens to spiritual healers, Liena. You will need someone to tend to you when it is done. I wish it to be me."

Healers healed by taking in the ailments of their patient and either mending them, as a physical healer did, or expelling them, as a spiritual healer did. Physical healers such as Sandra or Kacey endured painful bruising proportionate to the severity of the wounds they sought to heal, and the bruising would fade within a few seconds.

A spiritual healer such as Liena would endure violent sickness as her body processed the emotional wounds into something physical that could be removed. It could last many minutes, unfortunately, depending on how terribly their patient suffered. Trying to ease the damage done to Quint's soul by him being forced to decide between two people he held a deep emotional loyalty to would take a *terrible* toll on Liena.

Liena could only sigh. "Very well, but it will not be pleasant. Come along, and behave yourself."

He hid a smile as he followed her. Sometimes he felt as if she bordered on being both Light *and* Dark; she certainly showed characteristics of both.

Genevieve had just finished nursing Shanae when she and Matthew heard a knock on the door. They looked up and smiled as Tessa opened the door to let in the four children and Claret. The young Dual Cultivators clustered around the edge of the bed as Evan climbed up to sit beside his mother and father. Claret stayed with her fellow Dual Cultivators, and her lavender eyes looked warm as she smiled at Genevieve. "It's never easy to lose a queen," the Statice Cultivator said, "but it is always easy to love a princess."

"We're loveable sorts," Genevieve agreed on a bit of a grin.

Evan leaned over her arm to look at his baby sister, and wonder filled his pink eyes. She seemed to be watching everything avidly, almost as if she understood the things she looked at. Her eyes would fix on something, study it intently, and then move on. When her eyes fell on her brother, her face wrinkled into a distinct expression of joy.

"This is your baby sister, Evan," Matthew told his son softly. "Her name is Shanae. You must be her tree branches, Evan. She will need you to support her."

"Like Robert and Sayena." Enchanted, he reached out to touch Shanae's hand, and she grabbed onto his finger with a gurgle of happiness. The punch of love he felt for his little sister was staggering but comfortable. He had missed her. How was that possible? How did you miss someone you had never met? She *needed* him. "Can I hold her, Mother?"

Genevieve handed over Shanae with a smile. Evan had held Sayena frequently enough to know how to handle a newborn. He proved it anew by adjusting his grip perfectly to handle his sister, even though she was quite a bit bigger than her slightly elder counterpart of the Light. Genevieve had wondered if the age difference might make things difficult, but it seemed to have utterly no effect. The love and devotion in Evan's eyes could have been no stronger if they had been twins. She gave it fifteen years—max—before they forgot the difference entirely.

"Us too!" Kacey demanded.

Claret bit back a smile as she helped the three smaller princesses climb up onto the bed. She herself sat at the foot and let the warmth of love for new life banish the eternal echoes of sadness for the queens she had lost. Life ended, and life continued. Such was the way things went in her existence; after millions of years, she had seen much of both. It was one of the reasons she stayed in the Hall of Records more often than not. By staying apart from time, she could protect herself to some extent.

Still, as she looked at Shanae, she felt a surprisingly powerful well of love. More than she had ever felt before in her life. She just knew, somehow, that she had never loved a High Princess the way she would love this one, and she would never love another the same way again. Was that, too, a sign of events to change? She did not know for she did not know her own future. She could only wait and see what would happen.

The other three princesses had scooted close to Evan and Shanae. "She's so cute!" Delilah happily sighed. She looked at Kacey. "We will protect her, right?"

"Right!"

Shanae's face suddenly clouded up and she began crying loudly, startling her brother and everyone else alike. Genevieve hastily took her back and tried to rock her, but she just did not want to be calmed. Matthew tried to rock her as well, but she wanted him no more than she did her mother. Her cries grew in volume, and she waved her fists in the air. She clearly wanted *something*.

The pained look on Arista's face at the sight of Shanae's suffering was what finally clued Genevieve in. She had almost forgotten about the little black protea blossom blooming safely beneath the spruce tree in the Hyacinth garden. "Arista, scoot closer."

Arista did as told and found herself unexpectedly handed the crying baby. Shock filled her face, and she hastily shifted her grip to have a better hold. She stared at Shanae wide-eyed, her heart breaking. This most important person in her life was upset, and she couldn't do anything to help. "Don't cry. Genevieve!" She shot a pleading look at her queen and king. "She doesn't like me!"

As if to dispute that very idea, Shanae's tears stopped as suddenly as they had begun, and she stared up at Arista with wide-eyed wonder. She gave a happy gurgle and reached up to pat at Arista's cheek, and the rough and tumble princess stared down at her contented face in surprise. Something, some odd little click inside her soul, seemed to fill her heart with emotion that nearly overwhelmed her. This most important person *needed* her, and Arista needed her in turn.

Genevieve and Tessa exchanged a smile. They remembered that moment themselves. At the least, it finally made sense why the High Princes had not found a twin soul among the Dual Cultivators. They were not truly the heirs to their worlds for they could not pass along their magic to their future children as more than a flavor of elements.

Their sisters, however, would bear the next heirs to the Cores of Light and Dark. That ability to pass along magic made them *highly* valuable and in more need of protection, the likes of which only Defender Cultivators could provide.

Still, that did not mean the boys didn't need guardians of their own. The Defenders would always protect them, but they needed guardians dedicated *only* to their defense. This incident with Matthew and Quint had proven that more than a bit painfully. It had genuinely never occurred to anyone that the kings may need separate guards, for it so rarely happened they went somewhere their queens—and therefore the Defenders—did not. The two High Princes would be at even more risk, for their sisters needed the Defender Cultivators more. If the princesses went one place, and the princes another, then either the boys would be unprotected or the defenses across all four would be minimized by a double split team of Defenders.

Too, the princes deserved the same powerful love that their sisters would receive from the Defenders. They were still children of Protea and Delphinium, and Cultivators of that lineage always needed to be loved with a force not usually found in others. Perhaps because the lineages descended from Destiny and Love themselves—there was no knowing for sure. Once things finally settled down, the search would have to begin.

In the meantime, Genevieve leaned against Matthew and savored the feel of his arms around her. It had been far too close a call. Quint was not the only who deserved a medal. Liena, truly, did as well. She had somehow done the impossible, and she had ensured the younger High Rulers would never suffer only having one parent. That, too, came as highly unusual among Cultivators. And as odd as the times had already become, that was one change that neither Genevieve nor Matthew *ever* wanted to see.

* * * * *

Orion went looking for Shanta as he felt her pain churning inside his soul. It had been too close for anyone's taste. He had seen it too late for anyone in the Realm to even consider stopping the events. No one in their plane had predicted how things would fall; only Liena's vision had given anyone warning, and only Liena's subsequent one had prevented a tragedy. He half wanted to give her a medal himself.

Instead, he sought his wife to give her comfort. Far, far too many millennia had passed for Shanta to easily handle the arrival of her long-awaited heir. Of course, she wouldn't say a single word about it. Her Dark core meant she preferred to take in the pain of others rather than share her own.

He found her sitting on a bench in their garden and staring sightlessly up at the sky. Tears poured down her cheeks. He sat next to her without a word and pulled her into his arms. She turned to cling onto him, and her tears soaked his shirt as the sobs began to tear out of her against her will. He said nothing while he held her. He knew the value of purging emotions held inside for far too long. It was grief for what would happen, fury for what had happened, and a strong dose of fear for what would happen *after* it all ended.

He could only hope that Shanae didn't also inherit Shanta's single-minded determination to keep all her pain to herself. Goddess help her soul mate if she did. From first-hand experience, he knew it wasn't an easy role to have. Yet as Shanta lifted her head to give him a look of indignation that he wouldn't let her cry alone, he knew that he would want no other task than to be the one who gave her a shoulder to rest upon.

6

"Liena!" Genevieve stalked into the rooms belonging to her friend and advisor, Hannah hurrying at her side. "Help!"

Liena looked up with a lifted a brow from where she had been reading a book. "What'd they do now?" was her warm question.

"We've lost them, *again*." Genevieve's tone was aggrieved as she ran her hands through her short black hair. "Merrily disappeared from out of Shanae's room while everyone had their backs turned!"

Hannah sighed, but with a hint of fondness. "Ashe and Arista are training on their worlds; we can't drag them away just to find the missing High Princesses! They haven't left grounds; Genevieve would have felt it if they had. Please find them? They turned five only a month ago, and they could start developing real power anytime!"

Five years of age tended to be the average where a Cultivator developed magic. It was when Defenders could be found, and when Rulers started to really embody their element. It could happen the day of a birthday, or up to months later. Rarely ever more than a year, though. Sayena and Shanae, both only months past their fifth, and both Apexes, could have anything happen.

Liena got to her feet carefully, yet still with a nearly musical grace despite the sixth-month curve of her pregnant stomach. "Ooph!" she said on a laugh. "Such a lazy little girl I'm carrying. She got her father's love of naps."

Genevieve grinned cheerfully. She had been the happiest one of all when she had realized Liena was letting Lieu court her. The courtship had continued for four years as Lieu waited for Liena to learn if she could love him. The patient captain had finally been at the edges of his vaunted self-control when Liena had finally accepted his suit. Much to the humor of all, their first child would be born only a few months after the wedding. Happiness clung to Liena, and Lieu, in a way that it never had before. "I hope she has your personality," Genevieve told her friend wistfully.

Liena smiled. "The women of my bloodline will be not so different from the ones of the planets, Gen. My sons will carry majik, and their children will as well, but it will be my daughters who carry the full weight of my heritage. Once every era, there will be a firstborn daughter of my bloodline who reaches the peak of her majik for that era. She will be the next High Priestess." She thought about what she had seen when she had realized she was pregnant. "Three. There will be three total, including me. I am of the Royal Era."

It was a strangely comforting thought for both queens. "There won't be a need beyond three?" Hannah asked.

She tilted her head. "You know, I don't know. I just feel there will be three total." She headed for the door with a shake of her head. "I'll find the princesses." She laughed. "First the boys, now the girls. Speaking of traits we hope don't carry on in future children!"

She had a fairly good idea of where she needed to go, and her steps were calm. They were calm enough, in fact, that she could hear a soft shuffling of other feet behind her. She stopped, and so did they. She hid a smile and felt the air, and she caught the trace of magic that was white and Illusory. A flick of her fingers sent a spell winging at the owner, and she was rewarded by a shriek of laughter.

She laughed as she turned and went around the corner to discover Robert wiggling helplessly in the spell. He was only eleven years in age, but his height could quite easily throw people off. His handsome looks had only begun to refine more, and he had bucked the Delphinium tendency toward plumpness by picking up a scimitar as soon as he turned five and working on becoming as strong physically as he was with magic. A softness still clung to him in many places, though, which only added to his growing appeal.

Liena would expect him to be a heartbreaker eventually if it weren't for his inability to *dent* hearts let alone break them! The boy wore his heart on his sleeve, gave openly and generously of his emotions, and he was the first to jump forward if anyone needed anything. He really was a Delphinium child in every way. "What are you up to, boyo?" she asked as she banished the spell and helped him stand.

He smiled at her and rubbed the laughter tears from his eyes. She was one of his favorite people; she was actually a favorite among all Cultivators. Both young and Elder found her presence utterly comforting and soothing, and she always listened when someone needed to talk. Something about her wonderful majik soothed them all. "I know where Shanae and Sayena are. They're hiding in the protea bushes of the garden."

"Little wonder," she agreed. "Shanae has hid it, but she is struggling with her gifts."

He frowned at her curiously. He stood only an inch or two shorter than her height, and would be taller before the year was done. "None of the rest of us have struggled, not even Sayena, and she's as powerful as Shanae."

"Shanae has a different sort of power." She ran a hand over his thick white hair. "You know the legends, Robert. You know what her being the Apex of Dark means, don't you? What it means as well for Sayena to be the Apex of Light? We have not yet uncovered the price to Sayena's birth, but that may more fully reveal itself when she actually starts developing her power, as she should any day."

His face darkened. "I don't like it. Either of it. But why would it make Shanae struggle and not Sayena?"

"Inside her, the power of Nature and the power of Dark are fighting for supremacy. They have fought inside the Protea Ruler Cultivators for millions of years. Every last Ruler has eventually swayed to Nature—for they cannot embody Dark—and the fight has ended until another child is born. But Shanae is the Apex of Dark. She can*not* sway. She has to bring harmony. She will be able to embody Dark and physically control it as an element in a way no other being ever has. Sayena will also embody Light and control it as an element, but Light does not fight against Illusion. They peacefully work together. Until Shanae can create that harmony where Dark and Nature blend and coexist, they will tug from both directions and make her struggle to breathe."

"It's not *right*." His golden eyes snapped with the familiar sparks of the formidable Delphinium temper on the rise. "Why Shanae? Why does she have to be the one with this burden? She doesn't deserve it!" he added heatedly. "It gives her nightmares!"

She stopped walking quickly. "It does?" He said nothing, and she turned him to face her. "Robert, how do you know it gives her nightmares?" At his further silence, she prompted gently, "Did you share them?"

". . . Yes."

Only a lover soul mate could share the dreams of one connected to the Ephemeral Plane. The role of Ruler would be split between Evan and Shanae for their generation—Shanae would fight, Evan would defend—but that did not change either heir's powerful connection to the Plane. Robert could only have shared Shanae's dreams and nightmares if he had a soul meant to interlock with hers. "Robert," she asked softly as she cupped his cheek, "do you love Shanae?"

It would have been easy to simply say 'of course' because he loved all of his fellow princesses greatly. Yet, he knew what Liena really asked, and he knew it was serious. "Yes," he admitted very softly. "I don't love anyone more than Shanae. I love her as much as my sister."

It was a telling admission. The princes and their sisters shared bonds so deep and powerful that they might as well have been twin souls, too. No one could understand how or why, but there was no disputing the evidence. If something happened to Shanae or Sayena, Evan and Robert felt it as instantly as Arista and Asheria did—in some cases, they felt it faster. "I knew you would," she told him simply.

It made him feel better. "Then, it's okay?"

She smiled. "It's Destiny." She dropped a kiss on his forehead and then took his hand again. "It will make more sense the older you get." She led him toward the gardens, and partway there, they encountered the familiar figure of Evan. He had been about to go out as well, but when Liena saw him, she held out her other hand and called, "Evan, come with us. We're already looking."

Evan waited for them to catch up and then took her offered hand. "I think," he said softly, "that there's something different happening. I can feel something inside Shanae. It feels like the other princesses, but I don't know how."

Robert nodded. "I feel it in Sayena, too."

"And so you should." Liena took them into the gardens and moved toward the shadowy areas where the black protea flowers grew. "Shanae," she called, her voice soft and beguiling, "come out now! You're not alone in this."

There was no response, which was telling. Among Liena's many gifts was the gift of a voice so beautiful that she could compel others. She was known as a Virtuosa, and the music inside her brimmed hotly enough to become additional power. The only two people she had never been able to successfully compel were Shanae and Sayena—but only if they deliberately ignored her summon.

"Shanae?" Robert called. "Sayena? Please?"

Again, silence. Then, finally, Sayena responded, "Over here."

The boys rustled into the bushes and made a path for Liena to use. On the other side, surrounded by a ring of blossoms, sat Sayena and Shanae. Or rather, Sayena sat. Shanae lay slumped in her arms as if she had passed out. The Delphinium princess was quite a bit smaller than her counterpart—Shanae had a height closer to eight years in age—but she held onto her friend with no less fierceness than if she had been bigger.

An odd pinkness clung to Shanae's skin as if she had been sunburned; that in and of itself seemed an oddity for Proteans neither tanned nor burned. They always kept their normal tone no matter how the sun shined upon them. Liena started to reach for her princess but hands closed over her wrists. Her head swung around, and she found herself looking at the familiar face of her husband. "Lieu?"

"Careful," he warned her. "Right now, only Sayena or Evan dares touch her. I've been watching Shanae for a bit now, keeping an eye on her whenever she ran off. Don't," he started to add sharply to Robert, only to break off as Robert touched Shanae's arm without danger. In fact, Dark power swirled around his hands in a nearly caressing gesture. "Ah," he murmured. "So that's what you meant."

"Told you so," his wife murmured back. She knelt down but took care not to touch any of the children. "Sayena, what happened?"

Sayena looked at her with solemn gold eyes. "She's been hurting. We came here to make her feel better. She suddenly got too hot and fell over. I don't want her alone!" she whispered fiercely, her arms tightening around her friend. "She feels alone!"

A low rumble made everyone look around, but Evan realized first where it originated. "Shanae!" He scooted closer to his sister and touched her arm. "Shanae, we're here. You're safe! Liena!" He looked at the priestess pleadingly. "Make her better!"

"I can't. I'm so sorry."

Power welled up hotly inside Shanae and then spilled into the air. The familiar pink of Protea's Flower Element of Nature, but also the rich black of the Core element of Dark. They seemed to spark off each other violently like two armies at war, and the pained expression on Shanae's face implied the war truly raged inside her soul. And then . . . harmony came. Her eyes opened, and the pink had gone black. The two elements in the air rushed at each other and then abruptly fused into a swirl of gradated color. The pink receded from Shanae's skin as she pushed out of Sayena's arms and gingerly sat up. Her arm muscles trembled as if she had truly fought a war as physical as spiritual.

She looked at Sayena, and Sayena at her. They slowly reached out their hands toward one another with palms facing. The power around Shanae swirled down to her hands, and a matching white/gold gradient swirled up around Sayena's hands. The powers began to coalesce, and finally formed into two tiny Masks. Through the sheer material of Sayena's left sleeve, and under the open petals of Shanae's, a second crowned Flower Mark appeared.

Defender Cultivator marks. The High Princesses were Dual Cultivators.

They took their Masks from the air, but Sayena hastily dropped hers on a cry to catch Shanae as the other girl fell unconscious once more. This time, Liena felt safe to touch her, and gently pressed a hand to Shanae's forehead. She let out a relieved breath. "She will be fine," she promised. "She just needs rest. Lieu, carry her."

Feet came stampeding through the gardens, and Genevieve and Matthew burst around the bushes only to come to an abrupt halt as they beheld the scene. Hannah and Quint, right on their heels, stopped sharply in turn. All eyes riveted to the Masks in their daughters' possession. "So that's it," Quint whispered. "They are Defenders."

Close behind the Rulers came the Elder Defenders and Dual Cultivators, and all also stopped short in surprise. The princesses recovered first and scrambled forward to cluster around their friends. Lieu scooped up Shanae and found himself with several figures hovering at his elbow anxiously. "Calm down," he told them. "She will be fine. She needs rest. Asheria, bring Sayena."

"I'm fine," Sayena tried to protest, only to sigh deeply as Asheria picked her up. "Ashe," she complained, "I can walk!"

"Shush. Captain says you don't, so you don't."

"Aww!"

Lieu headed into the castle with the four High children as well as Arista and Asheria, and the others turned to look at the two High Queens. Genevieve was almost not breathing, and Tessa had to force her to sit down. "Don't pass out!" the Daffodil Defender ordered. "She will be fine."

"I can't help it." Genevieve buried her face in her hands, and barely noticed when Matthew sat beside her and wrapped an arm around her waist. "You *saw* it! She's the one of harmony. She . . . she somehow brought harmony to Nature and Dark after millions of years of refusing to coexist. She and Sayena . . . the Apexes are Defenders as well. Protea and Delphinium have chosen Defenders at last." Her lips trembled as she looked at her husband. "Our baby will have to fight and destroy Nemesis."

"And we will fight beside her!" Veronica vowed fiercely. The mantle of Lead Defender had settled naturally and comfortably on her shoulders. She took command whenever the team worked as a whole unit. Even Claret bowed to her order. "We will aid her and Sayena alike in whatever it is that they have to do! We will help them learn to be Defenders, and we will ensure that they never have to don their

Masks unless truly necessary." She looked at her partners. "Let us go see them. It will make Shanae feel better to wake with us around."

Hannah watched the princesses run into the castle and then took a long breath. "This will remain a secret," she told everyone. "No one will know that the High Princesses have become Defender Cultivators. Flower Marks can be hidden at will, and they shall keep theirs hidden at all times. We will release a statement saying only that the Apexes of Dark and Light have come into their power and begun to prepare for their destined battles."

Matthew looked sharply at Hannah and Quint alike. "You know what Sayena may face?"

Quint nodded. "You know we had been watching for Famine. She has been creeping in, gathering worshippers from all worlds. Her evil slowly poisons all that lives. We planted a spy among her worshippers on Iris. He reported to us that when Sayena was born, Famine reacted with utter horror. Famine is born of the purest disgust and disease rendered when evil sloughs into the physical world. What else would oppose her but the pure power of healing inside the Apex of Light?"

"Sayena is a healer?" Melissa asked, and then shook her head. "Silly question, I suppose. She's always acted like one, so it makes sense her powers would go that way."

"They go both ways," Liena spoke up. She rested her hands over her belly. "She is the Apex, as you said. The Apex of Light represents all that is magical in existence. She is both healer and conjuror, and her skills in battle will create either salvation or destruction. Shanae, being Apex of Dark, represents all that is physical in existence. She will soon come into a strength and skill in combat that will make her, literally, unrivaled. Light and Dark cores have always gone in such a way, and Ruler Cultivators of the two worlds have represented it themselves in a lesser fashion. In its purest form, it cannot be hidden."

"I suppose it makes sense in another fashion," Sandra said slowly. "Shanae has always struggled with nightmares, which is evidence of her being the Apex of Dark who will face Nemesis. Sayena has always struggled with illness. Cultivators shouldn't get sick at all, but she seems to get every sniffle that passes through. That's why. Because of Famine. Only when Shanae and Sayena destroy their destined enemy will they finally no longer struggle with that which opposes them."

"To some extent," Liena agreed.

"Interesting about Robert, though," Jessie decided. "Because of what you said about Light cores, and Delphinium. Robert has certainly chosen an interesting route by becoming quite strong within his own right."

Liena hid a smile. "It is actually to be expected, given his destiny."

She instantly had everyone's attention. "What destiny?" Sandra asked. She then aimed a finger at the priestess. "Don't give us that wide-eyed 'I don't know what you're talking about' look. We've known you too long to fall for that one again!"

"Damn it." Liena snapped her fingers lightly. She smiled. "Robert will be the lover soul mate to the Apex of Dark. He must, by the demand of such a role, be capable of pushing her physically in battle in order to keep her happy by meeting her at least halfway."

"Huh. You know," Quint mused, "I wondered about that. And, really, I honestly expected Sayena and Evan to be lover soul mates too. They show signs of it as well."

"I didn't say they wouldn't be."

A pause, and then Genevieve murmured, "No wonder Evan has pushed to learn magic in a way our lineage usually doesn't. He also needs to be capable of meeting the Apex of Light at least halfway so she does not feel so alone. And yet, because he is physically gifted still, and Robert magically gifted, they can also support their sister." She slowly shook her head. "I found it curious enough that a Ruler Cultivator would find a Caretaker in another Ruler Cultivator the way Matt and I acted as Caretaker to one another until he became Deactivated and became the only Caretaker of us two. This is far more curious still."

Slowly, Tessa said, "I feel as if the sheer fact that Evan and Robert are Activated Ruler Cultivators is *why* they are perfect for

Sayena and Shanae. The Apexes possess the rawest form of Dark and Light cores. They balance each other, yes, but there needs to be further balance inside their souls. To make Dark ever darker, and to make Light ever lighter, they have to be joined to their opposite. So . . . Shanae needs the strongest Light core, and Sayena needs the strongest Dark core, in their soul mates. They can't mate to one another, not when they *must* produce children to carry on the lineages, so their brothers are the next closest thing. And the boys would not have those powerful cores if they were not Activated."

"A reason for everyone's birth," Matthew murmured. "And with Shanae and Evan being the product of a Cultivator/Cultivator pairing, it makes them much hardier to endure the future—and their future children with Robert and Sayena will be even more so." It made him more than a bit curious as to why such inner strength would be needed, though.

"At the least," Amanda decided dryly, "we can be reassured that we won't have to fuss with suitor lists for the High Princes and Princesses!"

"Don't be so sure," Genevieve reminded her dryly. "Evan and Shanae are of the Dark, and we tend to be a bit blind. Sayena and Robert may have some work to do to claim their soul mates, and that could include the lists! There are plenty of laws for a Cultivator to take advantage of to get the one their soul needs."

Time, as she was wont to do, passed quickly. Shanae proved Liena to be right in short order. The moment she recovered from her internal battle, she launched herself fiercely into training. She tagged at the heels of every Elder Defender to demand they train her in whatever weapon they used. That covered quite a bit of ground, but none of them turned her away. She also unnerved them all as she not only picked up the weapon skills quickly, but mastered them within a very short time of starting.

She could not be satisfied by that, and so she dogged Lieu's heels until he taught her how to use a claymore instead of a short sword. The weapon had to be custom-made for her, but she picked it up just as easily despite the heavier weight and larger stature. Her need for armory appeased, she went right into hand-to-hand training. That proved trickier for her to learn since none of the Defenders had exceptional skills. Minimal ones, to be sure, but not the sort she craved.

Luck turned out to be in her favor. Not long after her ninth birthday, after she had mastered every other style, Matthew caught word of an exceptionally talented hand-to-hand fighter in one of their cities. Jayden Takata was young himself, not yet twenty, but his skills could not be disputed. He also responded immediately to the royal request and came out to train not just Shanae, but also Evan, Arista, and Robert. They four wanted terribly to keep up as much as they could with their Apex of Dark. Veronica and Asheria, given their own particularly special roles, also began to train though perhaps not as feverishly. Sayena benefited from all of the training, too; she had plenty of opportunities to practice her healing by cleaning up behind her loved ones.

Jayden's presence had a much bigger reach than he expected. He and Evan bonded rather swiftly despite the age gap, and he showed a surprisingly protective side toward the prince. Genevieve felt a little moment of clarity as she saw them, and it dawned on her that perhaps the search for guardians for Evan might be easier than anticipated. The sorts of people she needed would surely stand out in a crowd for they would have to be capable of keeping up with an exceptionally powerful and stubborn Ruler Cultivator.

With that in mind, she and Matthew turned their attention to the ranks of their own Royal Knights that made up the bulk of the Protea Army. Lieu more than willingly aided them, and they shortly uncovered three more young men that had exceptional skill and the potential of magical gifts themselves. All were roughly Jayden's age, and by the time the search ended and Genevieve had made her choices, the four men in question would be turning twenty-one. Evan had just passed sixteen himself.

You could be no younger than eighteen to enlist in the army, and once accepted in the ranks, you were considered an adult even if not yet twenty-five—and it was rather rare for anyone under adulthood to make it in anyway. These three young men who had enlisted had proven to be more than exceptional in many ways.

The only real problem for Genevieve and Matthew was that their son rather did not want guardians of his own. He felt perfectly fine to share Arista and Kacey with his sister. "Why do I need personal protectors?" he asked in exasperation as he walked with his parents toward the throne room.

Both mother and son wore the Ruler outfits denoting their ranks, as most Cultivators did when on castle grounds, and they also wore their crowns as demanded by such an important meeting. Matthew had a suit of his own, designed to mark him as the king yet make it clear he came of non-Protean lineage. As a homage to his bloodline, he always wore a forget-me-not on his lapel. He, too, wore his crown as protocol demanded.

"Because." Genevieve scrubbed her hands over her face. "Damn it, Evan. I want your hide to remain intact, and you are too inclined to go charging after Shanae and Sayena if you even *think* that they need help. Future charging will involve charging right into war thanks to the High Princesses being Defenders, and I want to be sure that there is someone to keep you alive because you will have only your sword and an ability to harmonize with Nature on your side! Do not mistake me; you have proven quite skilled with magic, but it is not *attack* magic. Rulers do not get such a thing because we have no need. If you were a Dual, we would not be having this conversation. But because you are not, we are, and the Defenders need to focus on the High Princesses and not you!"

"Breathe," Matthew told her dryly.

"I don't see you helping," she shot back.

Evan could only sigh. He found it hard to argue with his mother's logic, much as he might wish otherwise. "I reserve the right to tell these guardians to get lost if I don't like them or they don't suit me."

"And *we* reserve the right to start the search over again if so." Matthew tweaked his nose. "There is no getting out of this, Evan. We have already promoted them to the rank of Commander, as high as one can go within the Royal Knights, surpassing even that of Lieu as

Captain."

"Alright," he sighed again. "Who are they exactly?"

"Well, obviously, you know Jayden with his Light core and affinity for the Fire element," Genevieve said. "He has been joined by Maxim Montague, who uses a mace, has a Dark core, and an affinity for the Glass element; Navidan Arkwood, who uses a broad sword, has Light core, and an affinity for the Thunder element; and Dane Etudele, who uses a lance, has a Dark core, and an affinity for the Ice element. Maxim had already been moving up rapidly in our ranks, and Dane had been on Liena's radar since they both have musical gifts. Navidan is a quiet sort, but he still stood out quite a bit when compared to others."

They sounded interesting enough, though Evan still felt a bit ambivalent. It just seemed like such a useless exercise; he could keep himself safe and help his sister and Sayena at the same time. Robert as well. What possible benefit could there be to adding these newcomers?

Genevieve opened the throne room doors and led her two males inside. Standing partway through the room was the familiar figure of Jayden and three unfamiliar figures. All wore uniforms of black and pink; it marked them as being the highest rank in the Royal Knights. Only those in the highest echelon got to wear the colors of Protea herself.

They made something of an interesting collection. Maxim had silver eyes, opal hair, and brown skin distributed over a height only a few inches taller than Evan's five-nine. Jayden, of course, had emerald eyes and lavender hair paired with fair skin and a height barely less than Maxim. Dane had peridot eyes, yellow-blond hair, and tanned skin across the same height as Jayden. Navidan was the tallest of the lot by an inch or two, and had onyx eyes, auburn hair, and burnished coal skin.

Evan had never been the shy type. He walked forward calmly and told the Commanders, "I won't make your life easy."

The four men grinned in turn, and Maxim naturally stepped forward since the other three had asked him to be lead. He started to speak, but then he looked into the protea pink eyes watching him. A sudden and searing wave of powerful love welled up inside his soul before he could stop it. He had never even imagined it could be there. Evan *needed* him, and he needed Evan. They two had souls that overlapped. "If we wanted easy," he said softly, "we would not be here, my prince."

Evan looked into the silver eyes facing him, and the wrenching tore through his soul in a familiar tangle. Love that rivaled what he felt for Shanae and Sayena. He had a twin soul. That one special person who would love him most. He hesitated for a moment before walking closer to Maxim. There he paused, not sure of his actions.

His twin made it easy on him by reaching out to hug him tight. The tension left Evan as he held on in turn. It was not always easy for Dark elements to express themselves, especially the more deeply they loved. He turned his head to smile at the other Commanders, and he could feel a sense of happiness that the Dual Defenders had never given him. The princesses were only his friends. The Commanders were his companions and brothers. "I'm glad to meet you," he said simply.

Genevieve could only let out a breath of relief that her Sight had not led her wrong. She and Matthew had been hoping Maxim would be Evan's twin! The two High Princes deserved that sort of love, too. And at least Maxim would find his task easier than whatever may befall Robert's twin! "Welcome aboard, gentlemen," she said dryly, "and may Destiny help you all."

* * * * *

On Delphinium, things were not any more harmonious. They might well have been *less* harmonious thanks to the temperament running through the royal family. Robert felt both cranky and annoyed at the entire thing, and his mood did not improve when he discovered *how* his parents had gone about making their final selections. "You did *what*?" he demanded.

Hannah leaned in the doorway to his suit of rooms and purposely blocked her taller son from escaping. He had already cleared six feet by a couple inches; she blamed his father for that one. Quint hovered behind her as a backup defense, though she hoped it did not come to that. "We set up a contest of combat skills. Really, what else could we do? We needed to find you Commanders that could be strong enough to take you down physically to remove you from danger as will inevitably be needed."

"Is this really necessary? Julianna and Ashe said they would be happy to be my bodyguards as needed. I'm not as valuable as Sayena. I'll be fine."

Quint's eyes narrowed over Hannah's head. "Robert, I *never* want to hear you call yourself less valuable than your sister!"

Robert gave him an exasperated look. "But it's *true*. She's the heir to Delphinium. She will have the next Ruler Cultivator of our world. I won't, and I'm fine with that. I really am. If something happens to me, it won't upset the universe the way it would with Sayena." In a mutter he added, "And someone has to go through me, too, to get to her!"

Hannah sighed and shook her head fondly. "Alright, you troublemaker. I understand your point, but I also know you are wrong. There is something only you can do. Something that you are here specifically to do. You and Evan . . . your births are as deliberate as that of our Apexes. And you could be such an easy target for Nemesis and Famine. As they strike out at Shanae and Sayena, who do you think will be the first that they go after?"

His stomach clenched painfully and his hands curled into fists. He was far from a fool, and his Light core had finally done what it had tried to do for eons in his lineage: it had given him Future Sight. He had an ability to see things so clearly that he *literally* saw them happen. Truly, only Shanae surpassed his strength, and Sayena ran him a close third. She, too, had developed Sight from her exceptionally strong Light core as Apex of Light, though hers remained limited to present events.

That meant that Robert could easily see how anyone close to the High Defenders, especially their brothers, would be potential collateral. He needed to step up his training further, and he needed his own guardians so the Defenders could focus on Shanae and Sayena.

On a deep sigh, he gave in. "Alright."

"Gracious of you, my dear." She bit back a smile as he glared at her. Nothing made her happier than to have a little version of her soul mate running around. They kept her on her toes! And, too, Sayena was far from the peaceful little girl she had once lamented wanting—and she could have asked for nothing better. Turns out Destiny had known better than she did just want she needed. "I think you will be pleased by my choice, though there is a bit of a choice left to be made."

He followed her into the hall and then he and Quint automatically adjusted their strides to keep up with hers. "So who have you chosen to babysit me?"

"The three we are certain in are Sabin Fitzgerald, Talon Kensington, and Ulyen Nolte," Quint offered. "They are all turning twenty-one this year, and had been among the ranks of the army already. Sabin led the pack as being the most powerful thanks to his sword skills, and he has a Light core paired with a rather unusual element of Time."

Robert's brows shot up. The element of Time was something called a secondary element, which meant it had been born of a whole Flower Element: Memory, in this case, which only belonged to Claret. A secondary functioned not unlike a primary, though in much more limited scope. The Time Flower Element allowed for time-space related abilities such as paralyzing of enemies, creating portal gateways, and the like. Sabin likely did not have *actual* magic, but he would still be on the different side. Robert could not recall ever meeting anyone with a Time element; Sabin clearly had something important in his destiny. "Interesting. The other two?"

"Talon uses dual scimitars, has a Dark core, and a Metal element affinity. Ulyen uses a bow, has a Dark core, and a Water affinity." Hannah sighed. "I have already promoted all three of them to Commander, of course. But for the fourth, there is some debate. You see, two equally talented young men made the cut and tied for ranking. Diego Santiago uses claws, has a Light core, and an affinity for Air. Vermillion Chance has a Dark core, also uses claws, and also has an affinity for Air."

"Hmm. So you want to see which I get along with better?"

"So to speak."

At least they all sounded as if they would be fun to spar with. Robert braced his shoulders as he followed his parents into the throne room, and he couldn't help but tense slightly as he saw unfamiliar faces. Three wore uniforms of the white and gold belonging only to Delphinium's highest ranks. One other wore a more common Royal Knight uniform, and the last, the youngest, wore more common clothing typically found on farmers.

"Gentlemen," Hannah said calmly, "I would like to introduce High Prince Robert Delphinium, the eldest child and the second heir to the throne of the kingdom. Robert, these are Sabin, Talon, Ulyen, Vermillion, and Diego."

Robert studied them intently and found similarities and differences alike. Talon was the shortest at only five and a half feet but still looked powerful. He had gray eyes, cornflower blue hair, and fair skin. Sabin stood the tallest, taller than even Robert by two inches, and had bright green eyes paired to gray hair and fair skin. Ulyen stood slightly under six feet, had hazel eyes, and peach hair set against golden tanned skin. Vermillion was a bit taller, had crystal blue eyes and ruby red hair, and darker brown skin. Diego was roughly Ulyen's height or a bit more, had strawberry red eyes, and pale blond hair set against tanned skin. He also looked a bit younger than the others.

Robert felt butterflies in his stomach that he couldn't ignore. He made friends with relative ease, and he was an extrovert, but he sometimes butted up against the shyness he had inherited from his maternal lineage. "I . . ."

Sabin looked at him, into his golden eyes, and felt a painful wrenching deep inside his soul. Love. It boiled up violently without warning. Robert *needed* him, and he needed Robert. They were more complete together than not. Because he had always been a natural leader, he took the lead then when his prince needed it of him. He stepped forward and said with a hint of humor, "I understand someone causes so much trouble they need a babysitter."

The nerves began to ease, and Robert began to smile. "You must be mistaken. I'm a paragon of good graces." He looked into Sabin's eyes, and the wrenching ripped inside his soul as well. A wellspring of love just as powerful as what he felt for Sayena and Shanae. His lips trembled as he realized what it meant. Realized the gift he had been given. A twin soul. He *did* have one. He slowly walked forward, looked at Sabin for a moment, and then hugged him tightly.

Sabin could only sigh as he hugged the slightly shorter male just as tight. "You are going to make my life hell, aren't you?"

"Only a little." Robert grinned at him and then let go so he could look at the other two Commanders. They just . . . fit. Felt right. He felt a love for them that was not at all like what he felt for the Dual Defenders. Maybe his mother had been right all along. Not that he would tell *her* that. "Sorry I'm taller than some of you," he told them a bit impishly.

Ulyen snorted softly. "Sorry in advance if that means one of us has to bodily tackle you flat and sit on you to make you hold still."

Robert snorted back. "You're in good company. Veronica and Delilah do that to me already." He sighed deeply and looked at the five before him. "So I have to pick one of you?" he asked of Diego and Vermillion alike. He looked between them intently and then narrowed his eyes a bit on Diego. He really did look a bit young comparatively to the others. "How old are you?" he asked. The answer was quite important to him for it was Diego he felt most happy to see between him and Vermillion. He did like Vermillion, but Diego felt more like the other three did.

Diego winced visibly. "Uhm." An elbow in the side from Sabin made him sigh. "Sixteen, sire."

Hannah and Quint alike stopped dead in their tracks, and only Robert and Sabin did not stare in shock. "You're only sixteen?" the queen echoed. She sighed deeply. "Damn it all, Diego! We can't appoint you, and you know it! You would have to be at least eighteen. What made you apply anyway?"

"I want to protect my prince!" he vowed fervently. "I know he needs me, Your Majesty! I want to help keep him safe and happy!" He shook his head and made his short hair fly. "Please let me protect

Prince Robert!"

Hannah felt a bit helpless. "Now what do we do?" she muttered at her husband.

Robert pursed his lips for a moment and then asked, "How old can a companion-at-arms be?"

Quint began to grin. "Conveniently, the same age as the royal in question. It worked for me and Matt, to be sure."

"Oh!" Hannah brightened. "Of course! That is the perfect solution!" She turned to the five waiting patiently. "Alright then. Diego is too young to be appointed as a Commander; however, out of respect for his desire to protect his prince, and Robert's clear wish to have him close, I will instead appoint Diego as Robert's companion-at-arms, meaning he will be squire and personal attendant alike to the prince—but one with rather effective skills in defense should the Commanders not be available. That leaves me open to appoint Vermillion as the fourth Commander, and he will join Ulyen and Talon in following Sabin's role as lead. Is this acceptable to you, gentlemen?"

"Yes, Your Majesty," all five chorused.

Robert immediately grabbed Diego's hand. "Well, you can't look like this! You're a part of the kingdom now. You need new clothes. You're not a farm boy anymore." He began to haul his new friend toward the door. "Come along with me!"

"Do I have a choice?" Diego groused.

"No," Sabin told him dryly as he and the other three also followed. "And I hate to say it, but you did literally ask for it."

Hannah bit her lip as they all disappeared out the door, but she still giggled anyway. Quint also could not help laughing. It was one less worry off their minds to finally have companions for their son, but they had to feel a bit grateful to Destiny for the ones selected. Hannah just hoped they realized quickly what they had gotten into by agreeing to hitch their futures to her temperamental son!

7

The appointment of the Commanders had far more reaching effects than initially anticipated. It took less than a month before it became somewhat clear that there existed a *distinct* compatibility between six of the Commanders and six of the Dual Cultivators. If a Commander wasn't eyeing a Crown Princess with interest, then she was certainly eyeing him! Much to the immense humor of the royal kingdoms, the one not being eyed tended to not even realize they were being eyed at all! Without fail, every last queen and king wholeheartedly approved of the very real probability that the Commanders were, in fact, the soul mates and future Caretakers of their daughters.

One of the exceptions to the rule lay in Vermillion. He liked the princesses well enough, but he certainly had no interest in any of them in that way. For their part, neither Arista nor Claret felt any interest in him either. Instead, Arista developed a rather strong friendship with Diego that smacked of a developing bond itself. She didn't realize, however, that Diego had already decided that he was perfect for her. At least, not until he took advantage of a visit with Robert to Hyacinth to talk to Skyla and Phillip and tell them rather firmly that he would court their daughter as soon as they were both legal. Skyla looked at him, looked at Arista, back to Diego, and then at her own husband, and only started laughing. Hyacinth Ruler Cultivators needed mates of *very* specific qualities, and Diego had all of them. Arista huffed, puffed, and then threw her hands up and gave in. At least she wouldn't need to fuss with her suitor list!

The other exception to the rule lay in Sabin, but not for the same reason as Vermillion. Rather, the Lead Commander—Maxim had ceded to him as the overall lead for all of their rank—had set his eye a bit firmly on Claret herself! Sabin had always known his Time element would be important, and once he met Claret, he knew at last why. On top of his element, he actually *did* have a sole magical skill—a sure sign of a Caretaker. All Caretakers could receive a single magical gift related to their element that came from either Ruler or Defender side, depending on the need their Cultivator would have of them. Even Deactivated, Matthew had maintained a Nature-based Ruler skill to support Genevieve. Sabin could use his magic to open portals between locations by utilizing time-space; a vastly different skill from transporting, and suitable for the role he would hold. He kept his mouth shut due to only being twenty-one, though. He instead did everything within his power to stay close to her side, and if she still didn't notice by the time he hit twenty-five, he would say something.

The very significance of seven Commanders paired to seven princesses, with the too-young-to-be-appointed Diego pairing to the last princess, was missed by no one. Robert did love Vermillion, but it could not be ignored that he was far closer to Diego. It could not be blamed on Diego spending more time with him—more than even Sabin did as his twin. Robert treated Diego *exactly* the way he treated Talon and Ulyen, and that was what people picked up on. Vermillion took it with a good enough nature, though some thought they spied resentment in his eyes now and then.

Happy years continued to pass. But then, not long after the seven Crown Princesses and two High Princes turned twenty, events took a turn for the worst. An encroaching wave of evil from outside the galaxy swept in and joined forces with Famine to create an immense, monstrous, onslaught. The Elder Defenders ordered the younger Defenders and Commanders to take the High Princesses and Princes away to the safety bunker, and then rushed into battle. The Elder Ruler Cultivators remained in their castles, for if the worst came, as it had with their own mothers, then they and their Caretakers needed to make the sacrifice for their children.

It did not usually happen that way. Usually only the Defenders would fall, and the younger generation would step up to defend the Elder Cultivators in their stead until either the Elders abdicated in their daughters' ascension, or something else happened to take their lives; as Melody had painfully noted so many decades before, Cultivators never made it to a normal lifespan despite their immortality. It made many wonder why they were even immortal at all, but all understood there *had* to be a reason not yet revealed.

Those in the bunker prayed for the Elder Defenders to survive, but braced for the worst. They also deeply believed that this would be one of those instances where, if the Defenders fell, the Rulers would survive. Shanae and Sayena were not the only ones too young to take the throne at fourteen; the Crown Princesses, even at twenty or twenty-one, were also still just too young. That final, last ditch effort of a Ruler Cultivator to save her world could *not* happen this time. It had been demanded only a handful of times across history; Defenders normally handled anything in their way. But with the changes wrought on Blossom Field in this generation, who knew what the next may be?

Shanae, especially, felt her stomach churning as she sat against the wall with her face buried in her knees. She was the only one of her generation to truly know and understand what her birth meant. Only she knew that the kingdoms had to fall in order for her to defeat Nemesis. Her immensely powerful Sight had told her everything. Nearly from birth, she had been tormented by nightmares of what would *have* to happen. She had said nothing. She would keep that knowledge with her to the bitter end; she would do anything to ensure her loved ones continued to believe in an easy happy ending.

Masks sat beside the hands of every Defender, even the High Princesses. The two youngest Defenders had never donned them, but they kept them near at all times. In the utter gloom of the few lamps of the bunker, the sparkling edge to the Flower Marks on Sayena and Shanae's arms just seemed even starker.

As it had happened a million times in the past, the first sign of the inevitable events came in Claret's arrival. Again, unceremonious, and she landed hard on the ground. Her armor and Mask alike showed damage, and she had been grievously wounded. Sabin cleared the room in almost a single leap and eased her off the floor into his arms. "Damn it, Claret!" he said raggedly. "I told you I needed to be there with the rest of the Caretakers!"

Also not uncommon. Caretakers for Defender Cultivators were even more carefully chosen by Destiny than the ones for Ruler Cultivators. They often came equipped with skills in combat, or healing, to make them capable of entering battle at their Defender's side. That fact alone had led to no surprise at seeing the Commanders be potential Caretakers to the Dual Cultivator princesses.

Claret let her head lay on Sabin's shoulder and drew on the ready strength inside his soul. She had never before had anyone to hold her after battle; had never realized how terribly she might need it. She found the strength to remove her Mask and her armor disappeared to her casual uniform as a Defender. Pain slowly lessened as both Kacey and Sayena worked on healing her. "You needed to be here, for Robert," she told her fiancé softly. "And I knew I would be forced to retreat before I was in too much danger." Her eyes went to Shanae. "Someone still needs me."

"They don't expect to survive, do they?" Veronica asked quietly.

The answer came in a way unwelcome but not unexpected. A shockwave tore through the bunker with the familiar sting of Flower Element magic. The Flower Mark on the arm of each Defender began to take on a sparkling edge. The last to appear was on Kacey, for Tessa had been Lead Defender.

There was no time to mourn. Every Defender, including Claret, leapt to their feet and rushed from the bunker to find the fight and ensure that the evil had been defeated and the Elders had not fallen in vain. Shanae and Sayena would have rushed out too, but Evan and Robert grabbed them and prevented them from following. Holding Sayena proved no difficulty for Robert, but Evan could not keep a grip on his sister for her strength surpassed his. She had also already surpassed his height, and would no doubt get even taller before she finished maturing. It took Sabin and Navidan alike to help hold her back, and even then, she dragged them a few steps.

Painfully long moments ticked by before Arista and Asheria returned. They immediately moved to hold their twins. "It's done," Asheria said tiredly. She tightened her grip on Sayena as the other girl burrowed closer. "They won. So to speak."

Shanae clung tighter to Arista for a moment and then let go. "We should all return to our kingdoms," she said quietly. "We must evaluate the damage, and we need to support Mother and Aunt Hannah in this. They have lost their twin souls."

All of the kingdoms grieved at losing the Elder Defenders, but none grieved harder than Genevieve and Hannah. They locked themselves into their rooms and forbade any but their husbands from entering. The Commanders took that order to heart and literally kept any and every one out of the private wings, except for the High Priestess and four High heirs. Shanae and Sayena briefly stepped up to issue any orders needed in the meanwhile.

The Dual Cultivators were left at a bit of a loss themselves. They were fully trained, in their second tiers, and not far from being fully-grown adults. That made it no less difficult to now find their way without an older voice to give advice. Veronica took it the hardest for she no longer had Tessa to turn to in aid for how to be Lead Defender. But, it was that very nature of being Lead that finally had her stepping up to the task and doing what was needed.

Unfortunately, stepping up to the task meant stepping toe-to-toe with Maxim. They two had been striking sparks hot enough to melt the Glass of their shared element, and only Veronica suspected the real reason why. She tried not to dwell on it; she refused to believe Destiny would give her a soul mate so utterly untenable! Really, they were just far too much alike, and she knew full well her own personality, so had no desire to butt heads with herself, so to speak.

They butted heads anew after Liena had been to visit Hannah on Delphinium and help the queen heal; a spiritual healer could not remove the wounds gouged by losing a soul mate, but could at least ease the pain. Veronica and the other Light Defenders had accompanied her back to Protea in order to help support Genevieve as well, but Maxim had blocked them from entering the private suites.

The Commander had seven inches of height and at least eighty pounds of weight on the Lead Defender, but she merely squared her shoulders and went onto her toes to warn him, "Get out of my face. I have right to be here!"

He lifted a brow. Somehow he kept his arms crossed and his hands to himself. She could always churn up his emotions in volatile ways, and lately she had begun to churn up his hormones as well. The closer she drew to adulthood, the more she got to him, and that bugged him on many levels. He refused to get entangled with any princess, especially not one just as stubborn as he was! "Princess," he told her as dryly as he could, "my orders are to let *no one* in."

He had bodily blocked the stairs to the next floor, and perched on the steps behind him sat Shanae, Evan, and Dane. The latter studied the way Veronica's face steadily turned as red as her hair, and he winced. Shanae and Evan propped their chins on their hands, and the princess told Dane in a soft voice, "Bet she slugs him."

"No bet," he snorted softly.

Two minutes later, she said, "You really should have bet. I'm saving up for Arista's birthday gift."

Maxim pinched his bleeding nose and shot a glare at his princess. More than his nose stung; his very pride had taken the shot directly. Veronica's smaller frame had in no way hampered her from at least cracking his nose bone. It had been a literally painful reminder that she was, above all, Lead Defender. "Don't help," he muttered at Shanae. He shot a second glare at Dane as his partner snorted. "You shut up as well, Dane!"

Shanae got to her feet with a heavily put-upon sigh. "You are *such* an idiot sometimes, Max!" She aimed a finger at him. "With Mother indisposed, I give the orders, and therefore I say stop being an ass and let the Dual Cultivators have full access!" She turned on her heel and went upstairs with a swish of black hair. The long locks hung to her hips in back, and had stayed at that length for years. Oddly, hers and Sayena's hair had never grown normally. It grew in fits and starts on the basis of how their power moved. Most could only assume it had to do with them being Apexes, somehow.

Veronica shot a smirk at Maxim and then tossed her hair back as she went up the stairs behind her princess, and her partners followed her. She barely kept from rolling her eyes as Dane all but leapt to escort them. The man was *not* subtle about his interest in Yvette—not subtle to anyone except the princess in question, that is.

Maxim glared at them all as they disappeared up the stairs. "Why does she get under my skin so fast?" he muttered.

"Because you like her." Evan was grinning as he joined his twin. "Really, Max. We all noticed it. Do you honestly find it so surprising? Dane and Navidan have been very unsubtle about their interest in Yvette and Julianna, and we *all* know that Jayden had better give into Ashe before she plays dirty, so why shouldn't you and Nica be the same? You both just don't like it because you won't be able to get away with anything."

"Don't be ridiculous," Maxim muttered. "Excuse me while I find Kacey." He stalked away, but his mood was not at all aided when he had to go to Delphinium to find Kacey, and he found her with Robert and his set of Commanders. Talon and Sabin nearly bust a gut laughing at him, and Robert and Ulyen both had smart things to say. Maxim heaped all the indignity at Veronica's feet and began to plot revenge.

* * * * *

The best laid plans of mice and men—and Commanders—could often go awry. Maxim laid the groundwork over almost four years to get his revenge, only to have it backfire *spectacularly*. Veronica had come to accept that they were soul mates, and she simply would not accept less than everything. A few subtle machinations of her own, and she finally got him to see what they had all seen all along. And since she had turned twenty-five, that meant she could completely dismiss her suitor list and have the only suitor she wanted.

The epidemic spread quickly! Those who had been eyeing their suspected soul mate, or had been not so subtly waiting for said soul mate, finally got their reward as the one who had remained blind got their eyes opened—and most of them in outright humorous if not nearly comical ways. Asheria and Jayden ran a close second to Veronica and Maxim for keeping their kingdoms in stitches, and all four looked forward to relating the tales to their future daughters.

Almost as soon as Diego and Arista made formal their engagement, eyes turned toward Protea and Delphinium. Diego had been the last to turn twenty-five before Evan and Robert, and that meant the two High Princes would soon be adults as well, and have to view their lists. Most Ruler Cultivators at least *peeked* at their lists before adulthood, but neither male had at all bothered. Rumor had it that both lists had reached rather epic lengths, yet no one had confirmed it just yet. It would be seen soon enough on their birthdays.

Becoming an adult was a Big Deal. Every Ruler Cultivator received an epic gala birthday party where she—or he—would meet all of their suitors, dance with each, and begin their search. All of the Crown Princesses had still had their galas even if they had known who they wanted; only Julianna, Delilah, and Arista had accepted suits on the day of their birthday. The rest had come around shortly thereafter. The biggest parties of all were always held for Protea and Delphinium for those heirs had the biggest kingdoms to celebrate them.

With birthdays barely a month apart, the two princes found themselves called into a meeting with their parents only a week before Robert's birthday so that both parties could be discussed. Neither looked forward to the meeting, though for differing reasons. They also did not bother to dress for the occasion and merely wore their more casual royal wear rather than their formal Ruler suits. The sight of the two handsome princes walking down the hall together made more than one servant sigh gustily and wistfully.

Maxim and Sabin waited outside the Delphinium throne room doors, and Sabin intoned softly, "Dun dun dun."

"Shut up," Robert muttered back.

Maxim hid a grin. "In you go. We'll mop up the blood they spill. Promise."

"Oh, *very* funny." Evan rolled his eyes as he pushed the throne room doors open and walked inside with Robert at his side. "Really, is this necessary?" he demanded of his parents. "Can't I have another month before I think about this madness?"

"No, not really," Matthew said politely, but with humor. "Right,

Hannah?"

Hannah grinned a bit cheekily. "Trust us, Evan, you very much want to look at your list *now*."

Robert snorted. "She did what she threatened to do, didn't she?"

"Well, of course. She's also her father's child."

"And there's nothing wrong with that," Quint said staunchly. A grin tugged at his lips. "I doubt it will do him any harm in the long run."

"Hasn't hurt me any," his wife quipped back.

Evan eyed them all and then reluctantly took the rolled up paper Genevieve had in her hand. He let it unroll and winced as the rather lengthy list of names revealed itself. He very nearly chucked the entire thing over his shoulder, but one name near the bottom leapt out at him. "What!" He looked closer, but there was no mistaking it. "Why is *Sayena* on here?" he demanded. "She's just turned nineteen! She shouldn't even be able to state interest for another year!"

"Well, we decided to exercise our parental judgment and let her make her intentions plain early," Hannah told him innocently. "She can't actually court you until she is twenty-five, but she said she's waited this long, she can wait longer."

Evan looked so absolutely flummoxed that Genevieve and Matthew alike started laughing at him. "Oh, Evan!" Genevieve shook her head. "You are *so* my son! Your Dark core has blinded you as terribly as it always blinds us Protean Rulers! My love, you are the only one who had no idea that Sayena has had her eye on you since you were children."

Matthew smiled. "And you are also the only one who did not realize *you* are in love with her as deeply. Who is the one you always wish to love and protect? The one whose hand you hold when you are hurt, or sad? The one you turn to when you don't turn to your sister or Max? You love Sayena as deeply as you love your twin soul and soul-sister, and there can only be one reason why."

Evan could only stand there, feeling a bit punched in the heart and gut alike. He had never realized. Never even thought of why Sayena felt like such another part of his soul. Only over the last few months had he even realized that he found her attractive, and now he realized that itself should have been a clue. That attraction would grow and deepen as she herself matured, and only when *she* was twenty-five and could meet him as an equal would they both feel the full glory of being lover soul mates. "Well." It was all he could say.

"Do you accept her suit?" Robert teased his friend. "Just think: you won't have to fuss with your list at all by tentatively accepting her until she is an adult."

"Of course I accept her!" Evan shook his head. "I just feel a little foolish, I think. *How* did I miss it? Not her feelings. *Mine.*"

"Characteristic of a Dark core, really," Matthew reminded him. "And the more powerful that aspect of Dark is, the more blind you can be. Just as the more powerful the aspect of Light, the more clearly you can see. You are the brother to Apex of Dark. You are far more Dark than any other may be. Sayena is, of course, the Apex of Light. No one will see clearer than she does."

"Although . . ." Genevieve slid a smiling look at Robert, "her brother is far more Light than any other may be, so he runs her a close second."

"On a related note," Robert told her politely, "I don't suppose you'd be willing to bend the rules as well to let me place myself on Shanae's list even though she's only turning nineteen in a month?"

"Not that we didn't expect this question, but I feel it only fair to ask why should I bend the rules for you where I've bent them for no others—and others have indeed asked?"

He looked her dead in the eye. "Because we all know that I am the one meant to be Caretaker to Shanae, that I am the only one who could be her soul mate. All of the reasons that make Evan the perfect soul mate for Sayena are the reasons that make me perfect for Shanae. I have known all of my life that I would love no other, and as she blossoms before me like the protea flowers in her castle, I find that I want nothing more than to be by her side forever. With or without Destiny, I would be with her."

"Oh damn you." Hannah buried her face in her hands and bit back a sob. "And here I said I wouldn't cry!" She snatched Quint's handkerchief when he offered it. "Damn it."

Genevieve thought back over the years, and she could pinpoint where she had seen Evan and Sayena fall in love. She could not pinpoint Robert and Shanae. Even soul mates still fell in love. They still got to feel that beautiful moment of falling into the arms made perfectly to hold them. "When did it happen?" she asked softly.

He knew what she asked. He looked at her, and he smiled a bit whimsically. "There was no fall, Aunt Genevieve. Not for either of us. I saw it. I was *born* to love her. Born loving her. She was born to love me. Born loving me. There will never be a fall. That happened in Life's garden when our souls first formed."

Matthew took a long breath. "Robert. You must be warned. Shanae made it very clear to Genevieve that she would make her mother force her hand. She refuses to wed unless and until she destroys Nemesis. She will not drag anyone, let alone a Caretaker, into her fight. She does not even intend to take the Defenders with her! Not hers, not Sayena's! She will *never* easily accept you, Robert. Perhaps *especially* not you. She is blinded to you as her soul mate, but not blinded to her deep love."

He arched an arrogant brow. "She has until she is twenty-five before I get ruthless. Place me on her list of suitors, but do not tell anyone that I am there." He looked at Hannah and Quint. "Maintain my list for the time. I will play the part. I'll make it seem as if I am looking for my mate but have not yet found her. If Shanae's twenty-fifth birthday comes and she has not realized I'm the best thing that could happen to her, then I will play dirty, and Aunt Genevieve can force her hand."

After a moment of thought, Genevieve told Evan, "Are we allowed to be terrified for when you four give us granddaughters? I'm not sure what will happen when opposites attract, mate, and produce offspring! What if Shanae and Robert have a child that is perfectly half of each parent?"

Evan grinned wickedly. "It will be amusing, that is for certain."

Evan tentatively accepted Sayena's tentative offer to be his suitor—though there was nothing actually tentative about it—and he enjoyed his birthday party in peace without concern for dealing with all of his now brokenhearted suitors. Sayena equally enjoyed the tentative process for it meant that she did not even *need* a list. A Ruler Cultivator could completely dismiss their own list by making an offer to court someone, and they would not get a new one unless their offer was fully declined.

Her offer was fully accepted when her twenty-fifth birthday arrived. In the middle of the grand gala celebrating her birthday, she brought Evan to the center of the dance floor and asked for him to be her Caretaker, and for him to let her be his. The cheers that resulted when he accepted could have been heard from the other planets.

That left only two Rulers remaining. Robert, now thirty-one, had played the part well enough that he had not yet found his soul mate, but even his own suitors knew the truth—they just played along! Shanae, the beloved Apex of Dark, remained completely and adorably oblivious to the reality of things. Every last court, every last Cultivator, every last Commander, kept their mouths shut if only for the sheer humor of it all.

The week before Shanae's twenty-fifth birthday, her parents tried to call her in to look at her suitor list for the first time. The High Princess outright refused and dug in her stubborn heels. Genevieve could have pulled rank, but found it far too hilarious to bother. If her child would just *look* at her list, she would notice the name at the top and figure things out. Then again, perhaps Robert's plans banked on her not looking. Delphinium Cultivators were good at planning complicated things.

The birthday woman's 'big day' arrived, and the guest of honor felt absolutely no happiness or joy for the event. Her introverted tendencies made parties a terrible bore at best and a painful headache at worst. All of her attempts to beg off for a small ordeal fell on deaf ears, and she found herself vexed and frustrated and generally pissed off at the world in general—an impressive feat for the seemingly eternally even-tempered Apex. She was nearly stomping her feet as she went to the small manor on palace grounds where Liena and Lieu lived with their three children. The eldest would soon be twenty, and the youngest had just turned ten.

Liena heard the door slam and bit back a smile. "Hello, Shanae," she called.

Shanae stepped into the doorway to the kitchen and then plopped down on a chair at the counter. "My parents hate me."

"Huh-oh." Liena leaned on the counter. "Do tell."

The tirade poured out of Shanae before she could control it. There was no one other than Liena that she could turn to for counsel. "My mother has invited all of my suitors to the gala tonight so that they can vie for my now adult hand! I'm going to have to dance with all of the ones that attend, and it's expected that I'm going to have to have some sort of short list made by the end of it! Damn it, Liena, none of my suitors suit me!"

"How can you be so sure before meeting them, or even knowing who is on your list?"

"Because I don't have to look at my list to know who is on it, because all of them have made a point of sending me gifts!" came the retort. "And I know all of them well enough to know they will *not* suit me!" She ticked off the points. "My Caretaker needs to be a warrior type who is willing to let me take the lead in battle, someone tenderhearted but strong-willed, and someone who is big enough to protect me yet comfortable with me being stronger!"

Somehow, Liena kept her grin inside. "Shanae, my love, I believe you just described the High Prince of Delphinium. I'm afraid that you might be comparing all of those eager suitors vying for your hand to the most eligible bachelor in the universe."

Shanae groaned and put her head on her arms on the counter. "Oh, gods, I am! I try not to, I really do, but I find flaws in every suitor!"

Liena tucked her tongue in her cheek. "Robert has no flaws?"

A glare was the response to that. "He has flaws enough to make me want to kick him, but every single one of those flaws is only a flaw to *me* because it means I can't make him back down in a fight and he can out stubborn me and he matches me wit for wit and why is it him?!" she finished on a half-wail. "He can't be my soul mate!"

Liena gave up and laughed outright. "Oh, Shanae!" She crossed around the counter to hug the taller female. Shanae had finished growing and would only continue to delicately age until even that stopped at forty as immortality fully kicked in. She had a warrior physique paired with a rather curvy figure, and she was a strikingly tall six-foot even in height. Really, her height alone underscored why Robert suited her; he, like Arista, was big enough to bodily remove her from danger as needed. Arista had capped out at six-one. "Why do you fight the idea so hard? What is wrong with loving a man like Robert? I think I can say with relative certainty that he is one of the *easiest* people to love."

A little shudder went through Shanae's body. "My destiny." Her lips trembled. "I already face knowing he will die," she whispered. "That he may die in vain, trying to protect me from a future we cannot stop . . ."

Liena's gaze lowered. "Shanae, *nothing* will keep him from fighting at your side." She walked a few steps away with her arms crossed around herself. "No matter what you have told yourself, you know, and I know, that Robert is your lover soul mate. I knew from your birth that he would be."

"You did?" Somehow it made Shanae feel a little better.

"I did." She turned to face her princess, and something haunted and agonized filled her eyes as if to imply her soul wept. "Please. Do not throw away a chance to be with him. Do not sacrifice a chance to be with the one who completes your soul. There is nothing more bitterly painful."

Shanae took a sharp breath as she realized something she had suspected without understanding. "Lieu isn't . . . Lieu isn't your soul mate," she whispered.

A sad smile curved Liena's lips. "No. I love him with all of my heart, and I do desire him deeply, but he is not the holder of my soul. He knows, Shanae. I told him in the beginning. And, well . . . he does not *have* a soul mate. He does not have the sort of power that would allow it. I did not think he could make me happy, but he does. I am happy through my heart, but not to my soul. You always know the difference, always feel that yearning for more." Her lips twisted. "If only Lieu had my soul mate's soul, or my soul mate had Lieu's heart, I could be perfectly happy. I suppose it was not my destiny."

"Why . . . ?"

She sighed. "He was blind and I was proud. But that's a different story entirely. Learn from my lesson, love. Please don't throw away a chance at happiness that permeates your soul. It is a precious gift."

Shanae took a long breath. "Liena . . . I don't think you're right. You can't be. He's older than I. Surely, if we were soul mates, he would have noticed by now and said or done something. Look what Sayena did to Evan! She and her brother are too much alike, really."

Liena bit her lip. Hard. "Well, it's hard to dispute that."

She shook her head and made her hair dance. It had gone through another spurt and now hung to her knees; Sayena's had actually hit floor length after she and Evan became engaged. Or rather, after she and Evan had become lovers after becoming engaged. Either sharing their power in such a way had caused her to hit a new peak, or it had just stabilized her power, but the result could be seen. "I'll figure things out," Shanae decided. "I know there are things you can't tell me." In a mutter as she went to the door, she added, "It just doesn't seem fair that I be so attracted to him. I wish he suffered the same as I!"

Somehow, Liena held back her laughter until Shanae had gotten out of range. Lieu's arms slid around her waist, and she laced their fingers together contently. "If Robert doesn't tear through her blindness by the end of the party, I'll eat my cloak. He's been remarkably patient, especially for one of Delphinium blood."

Her husband chuckled softly. "Speaking from personal experience, even the even-tempered can be pushed to the limit when trying to wait for love. Do you suppose he'll do what I did to you and seduce her in the maid's closet?"

She snorted delicately. "I do hope at least *he* remembers to lock the door."

* * * * *

Shanae's mood had not improved by late afternoon when her handmaidens descended on her to help her bathe and get dressed. They had brought the black skirts and corset that would go under her Ruler gown to turn it into the more formal version demanded of this occasion. They also had the crown jewels that were hers by rights as heir to the throne.

She scowled at her reflection as a maid brushed out her hair, but she brightened when her door opened and one of her favorite people walked in. "Arista!"

The Hyacinth Cultivator winced wryly. "Don't be happy to see me, honey. I am not the bearer of good news."

Her eyes closed. "Now what?"

"Well . . . let's just say that tonight is going to have a lot in common with an auction block."

"Not *all* of them," she groaned.

"*All* of them," Arista confirmed wryly. "I looked twice to be sure. All of your suitors have confirmed attendance."

"Would screaming and ripping out my hair make a difference?" It was bitten off between her teeth.

The maid tugged on her hair. "It'd make my job easier."

It made Shanae laugh. "Well, *you* volunteered because Delilah was busy getting herself ready, so you can only blame yourself." The smile faded and she scowled at Arista. "How is this fair?"

Arista made a vague gesture. "All of the laws around Cultivators, especially Ruler ones, are designed solely to ensure our happiness. Suitor lists? Of course we have them; how many Rulers in history would have missed meeting their soul mate if said soul mate hadn't had an excuse to get close? Sleep with someone willingly and have to marry them? Look at Nica and Ashe for why that one is in place. We don't actually feel sexual desire strong enough to act on with anyone except our soul mate, though we might feel a mild thrill here and there, and sometimes we need that sort of leverage to get said soul mate to accept more than a physical relationship—and sometimes they need it on us!"

"Like you and Diego."

"Oh, very funny. I'll have you know that was mutual on both sides, and we're lucky we were alone when hormones fully kicked in." She shook her head, bemused as always as to how her relationship with her now husband had progressed. His role as Robert's companion-at-arms had not changed any more than her role as Defender; they spent days with their Ruler Cultivator and then returned to Hyacinth together. "You get my point, however. And, well, the fact that your list has officially reached record lengths can only be blamed on you."

"Me!" Shanae scowled.

"You're personable, smart, powerful, beautiful, and you are the High Princess to one of the biggest kingdoms in the *universe*. Anyone worth their salt will at least *try* to catch your eye and hope to be your soul mate."

"I just feel as if I'm being pressured more than anyone else," she muttered. "Which is not fair. Robert's not being pressured, and he's six years past his birthday!"

Arista kept her mouth shut on *that* one. She said only, "He *is* being pressured. Hannah and Quint are being lenient because they truly want him to find happiness, but Delphinium is a bit desperate to see him settle down. Robert has managed to buy himself time by talking fast, and getting Hannah to agree to let him take his time so long as he is actively looking, but both of his parents are definitely getting anxious." None of which was a lie, blessedly. "Shanae. *Please.* Try to enjoy tonight, for me and the ones who love you most. We hate seeing you miserable."

"On one condition." Shanae grinned at her. "*You* have to wear your hair in curls."

Arista scowled as the maids giggled. The Hyacinth Crown Princess' intense dislike of fancy hairdos had been a source of amusement for everyone. She deliberately kept her hair short enough it couldn't be put up or curled, but distractions over preparing for Shanae's birthday meant it hadn't been trimmed in three months, and it now hung just long enough to be curled. "If you suffer, I suffer?"

"Misery loves company."

She snorted. "Alright, fine. You win. I'll let Delilah make me prettier for you."

Shanae beamed. "I love you!" The smile faded as she added in a mutter, "*Sixty-three* suitors to dance with? For the love of the gods."

Arista hid a smile as she left the room. Technically, she was off by one. There were actually sixty-four names on the list. The one at the top of the list had, in fact, started the list, and he had every intention of claiming the dance he was owed. Whether or not he told Shanae *why* he claimed said dance could be left for debate. Sabin had cheerfully confirmed to Arista that Robert had finalized his plans and would be putting them in effect during the gala, but the Lead Commander had not specified what those plans entailed. Arista didn't really need to know; she already knew she would be entertained.

A note waited for her when she opened the door to the rooms she and Diego shared when in residence, and she recognized Julianna's handwriting. It read only, *I'm bringing the cake.* Pleased, Arista tossed the note on her table. Shanae had only wanted a small, personal, party with the Defenders, and they would give it to her. There was no duty more important to a Defender than the happiness of their High Princess.

* * * * *

The gala began before sundown and was attended by literally thousands of people. Shanae endured the throng for as long as possible, but two hours in, she felt a desperate need for fresh air and escaped to the balcony off the grand ballroom. It overlooked the glorious natural pool in the gardens, and more than one Cultivator— child or adult—had jumped off it into the deep end during hot summer months. Shanae felt damn near tempted right then, just as an excuse to leave. She had danced every dance, yet never with the same person twice. She was only partway through her list of suitors, and the line did *not* seem to be getting smaller. It was not flattering. Truthfully, it was a pain in the ass.

The clock had ticked over into the twenty-first hour of the day, yet she did not need to see a clock to know such a thing. Delphinium hung beautifully in the sky, and she could see the glittering palace on the surface. The two worlds rotated on opposing axis over the same twenty-four period, and so everyone on each world saw the other at some point over the day. Always between twenty-one and twenty-two hours, the two kingdoms would face one another.

It actually happened that all worlds could see at least one other, if not two in nearly all cases. Only Iris and Statice, at the end of the lines, saw only the sole planet ahead of them. The rest saw those before and after, and Protea and Delphinium, being large enough and close enough, saw each other to the side as well. Shanae could see Hyacinth as a small sphere in the sky from the same balcony during the mid-morning.

If only it were mid-morning *then* and the madness behind her. She leaned on the balcony and looked down into the reflective surface of the pool. The wavy refraction of the other kingdom seemed apt when the palace over there was nearly empty. Shanae had seen the two High ruling couples holding court together, and of course Evan and Sayena had been blissfully dancing together in the way only the newly engaged could. Strangely, Shanae had not yet seen Robert. But, then again, it was hard to see around the insane line of suitors waiting to dance with her. They blocked one of the doors entirely.

"Your Highness?" a male voice asked behind her.

Annoyance simmered inside her as she straightened. It did not show on her face as she turned, though, as her Dark core ability to hide her emotions served her well. Nothing except cool disdain could be seen. The suitor standing behind her surely had to be her least favorite of them all. No amount of fair looks and easy charm could hide the fact that he was a greasy serpent just slithering along at her feet in the hopes of marrying into one of the two most powerful of all kingdoms. Marry Tevlan? She would sooner drink poison.

"May I help you?" she asked politely. "You have had your dance. I owe you nothing."

"I merely wished to see you." He stepped closer and smoothly placed his hand over hers on the rail. "The light of Delphinium is becoming to you."

"We tend to flatter each other, yes." She removed her hand from his grasp. "You have not been given permission to touch me, my lord. Do not presume to assume you have rights no other does."

"The Sun Goddess," he countered mockingly. "Wanted by all, but refusing to be possessed by any. Do you enjoy the chase?"

"When I feel like a beast being scented and hunted by bloodhounds?" she countered curtly. "In fact, I do not. I like even less the hounds who will not take no for an answer. I have told you repeatedly to remove your name from my list. It will be a burning day on Iris before I *ever* marry you."

His hands shot out and closed around her upper arms. A blend of disgust and insult filled her eyes. He would *dare* attempt to get physical with the Apex of Dark? Moreover, he would *dare* touch her hidden Flower Mark as a Defender? He may not have known of its presence, but he would have felt her magic as soon as he touched her — and he had not let go. She grabbed his wrists, twisted lithely, and dumped him over the side of the balcony. The resounding splash he made as he hit the pool had several people in the garden stop and look up at her in surprise. "He needed to cool off," she said breezily. She sashayed back into the ballroom and left appreciative laughter behind her. No one else liked Tevlan either.

Maxim and Navidan materialized at her side out of seemingly nowhere, and the former asked her politely, "Can I get rid of him? Please, pretty please? I promise not to break anything that can't heal quickly."

"Have fun." She grinned a bit as the two Commanders zipped off toward the doors. She didn't feel *at all* guilty, either. She turned around to move further into the room, and she barely hid a wince as the next cluster of eager suitors descended on her. She grit her teeth and forced herself to smile. It was time for drastic measures. The rules said she had to dance with all of them before she could leave for a while and take a real break. Well, no one had ever said *what* dance, now had they?

The Dual Cultivators had strategically placed themselves around the ballroom in ways that meant they could react quickly should danger arrive that the Royal Knights could not handle. Evil did so like to interrupt what should be happy moments, and the final Ruler Cultivator's moment of adulthood certainly seemed like a prime choice. However, as they all heard the music change, they all began to disperse, and more than one was giggling. Shanae would get her escape soon enough.

The most basic of all gala dances was known simply as a three-note. A three-note was often considered a romantic dance since many musicians could pack quite a bit of emotion into just three notes per measure. Protea, like all worlds, had its own cultural dances; most infamously, Protea had developed a variant of the three-note known appropriately as a nine-note. Very, *very* few ever managed to master it since it took exceptional physical strength and stamina. Shanae, and Evan for that matter, had made it into a nearly artistic expression.

As the nine-note melody continued to merrily play, Delilah and Kacey stood with Ulyen and Talon and watched as the High Princess twirled elegantly away from a suitor halfway through a bar and left him gasping for air in the middle of the floor. The next suitor stepped forward, tried heroically to keep up, but only tripped herself and landed flat on the floor. The pattern kept on repeating as the nearly gleeful musicians played their hearts and souls out. A nine-note could be murder to dance, but spectacular fun to play.

Arista walked up to them with a scowl on her face that did not at all detract from her beauty; much as she hated them, curls truly flattered her face. "I'm not happy," she muttered.

"The curls are not that bad," Kacey assured her friend. "Delilah did a nice job on them."

"Yes, she did, but that wasn't what I was talking about." Arista crossed her arms. "We need to talk to Genevieve and Matthew. Lord Tevlan overstepped himself. Shanae had to dump him over the balcony into the pool."

Ulyen coughed before he laughed. "That's our Shanae! Is he still in the water, or do we get to fish him out?"

"Please?" Talon asked hopefully.

A decidedly devilish smile crossed Arista's face. "Let's just say that Max and Navi already took *great* delight in escorting him out."

Diego joined them at that moment, and he was not alone. Julianna and Asheria had also wandered over. "You really need to be watching the floor," Julianna told them all on a laugh. "It just keeps getting better. It looks like the aftermath of a war!"

Heads turned, and more than one person snorted out a laugh. Suitors littered the floor like soldiers lost in battle. Shanae, as collected as ever, just kept on dancing. The *only* sign of her exertion lay in her hair starting to escape its pins; not even her skin looked flushed, and she had not broken a sweat. The message seemed clear: if you could not keep up with the Protea Princess, you could not keep her attention.

"Hmm." Asheria tapped a finger on her lips. "I think the band needs a break after this, don't you? Perhaps I and Dane, and maybe Liena, should take over things, don't you all agree?" Her eyes lingered on where she could see a familiar tall figure now visible at the end of the line of suitors. "Why, I think it's the perfect time for two Shamans and a Virtuosa to bring some extra, hmm, *punch* to events."

Shamans existed only one level lower than Virtuosas. They had been born with a power capable of resonating musically, which contrasted to their higher ranked friends who had so much music it *became* power. Shamans could also summon emotions or powers already existing inside people, but not actually awaken them if they had not been found; that skill lay only with Virtuosas. Shamans could not actually compel people either, but they could certainly use their voices to strongly influence. Dane and Asheria alike held Shaman power, and pairing to Liena's Virtuosa power always created something both beautiful and memorable.

Diego grinned a bit as he watched Asheria head off to find her musical partners-in-crime. "I'm so glad they're on our side." He lifted a brow at Delilah. "Where are the others?"

"The High Queens and Kings are watching the dancers from the thrones, and Sayena is with Yvette and Veronica to get things ready in Shanae's room," Delilah offered. "Evan is helping to usher the defeated candidates off the floor after they collapse. Robert, well." She grinned. "You know where he is."

They all grinned at that, and they turned back to the scene. It had not gotten better; in fact, it looked worse as all other dancers had abandoned the floor and left only Shanae and her desperate suitors. Only a few remained, and if she had noticed the man at the end of the line, it did not show on her face. She looked wholly focused on ending what she clearly saw as an inane courtesy.

Navidan and Jayden joined their friends on the side, and the former said dryly, "I still don't know why anyone thought nine beats per second was reasonable."

Kacey glanced at his hands and asked only, "Do you need a heal?"

"Oh, it's minor. And worth it. Also, Jayden promised to teach me how to avoid hurting my knuckles for next time."

Jayden just shook his head fondly as he watched the floor. "Someone remind me again that I'm glad I never had to go through that."

Julianna smirked. "You're glad you never had to go through that because Ashe took the direct approach and seduced you. But even if she hadn't, she would have kept the dance easy for you. She set her eye on you pretty much the day you arrived."

Sabin sauntered up and offered a bag of popcorn. "Thought I'd share before the show really begins." He grinned wickedly. "And here we all thought we might be bored."

Arista glanced at the floor and saw only one suitor valiantly trying to keep up with Shanae. The last of the line stood patiently at the edges of the floor as if merely watching, but a sort of waiting tension in his body resembled that of a predator circling prey. If *anyone* could keep up with Shanae in a nine-note, it was the only one who made her work for a win in battle. "Battle stations," she murmured as she saw Asheria, Dane, and Liena waiting to take over for the band finally approaching the rousing end of the song.

Shanae had no idea of the musical coup de tat on the cusp. She could barely hide her glee as she left the last suitor panting in her dust. She gave the boy credit; he had managed to not trip during most of his round. He could still barely catch a breath, and she twirled away from his grip without remorse. Too slow, too bad. And too long overdue to be done! She could not resist finishing the dance by herself, if only because she really did love a good nine-note for making her feel alive.

Much to her utter shock, hands grabbed hers and twirled her with casual expertise right back into a couples' version. She landed against a maddeningly familiar chest, and the height alone told her who held her. She looked upward swiftly, and her heart began to pound with both nerves and frustrating desire as she found herself staring into Robert's rich golden eyes. "What are you doing?" she demanded.

"Dancing with a willful princess," he retorted calmly as he continued to lead her across the floor. The sheer fact that he could even *speak* while moving to the nine-note really said it all about his own skill.

The music came to a rousing end, and cheers went up as people saw he still had her in his grip, and looked no more or less affected by the dance than she did. In fact, he looked a bit better off since his curly hair continued to sit tamely under his royal coronet, and her hair had finally escaped some pins under her own. She blew a lock of her hair out of her face, and his lips kicked up into a devastating smile. "Let me help."

He plucked a single pin from her hair, and like removing a keystone, the entire coil unraveled swiftly into a black curtain. More than one person gasped or sighed with delight. Little was more beautiful than the shimmering veil of their princess' hair. Yet, there was a little hint of forbidden to the action that added to the gasp; Robert's casual gesture looked incredibly intimate. He had taken a right that no other would dare ask.

Yet, it was a right she had given him; she hated wearing her hair up, and she had always told her friends that if ever she had her hair up willingly, it meant she felt bound by Destiny. Robert had taken that to mean that bound hair equaled the pressure of her birth, so he resolved to remove the pressure by removing the pins. Strangely . . . it worked. "Thank you," she muttered. "Are we done now?"

"I don't know. Are we? I wouldn't mind dancing with my best friend." He played the card without batting a lash. "And wouldn't you like to at least enjoy *one* dance on your birthday? Really, I am almost beginning to think you're afraid of me. You haven't even said hello to me for several days." The music had ended, and he released her only slowly. The ball was in her court. The challenge had been issued.

She glanced to the side and saw the band taking a well-earned rest. There was no escape in saying they had no music, however. Dane had already seated himself at the piano, and Asheria was tuning her flute. Liena sat perched gracefully on the top of the piano. Shanae very nearly panicked right then and there. She did *not* want to dance with Robert to that lethal combination of musical talent, but walking away would prove him correct. She would have to take the risk that the music wouldn't tear her open in a way she could not hide from. On a little breath, she listened for the first chord and sank into a curtsey.

As if they had rehearsed it, Robert bowed in the same moment. His fingers lightly cupped her chin and drew her effortlessly to her feet as the three-note music curled around them. The drugging romance of the piano and flute only seemed to underscore Liena's voice as it lifted in haunting melody.

> *In this town I keep on walking*
> *Searching for the beginning of the end*
> *In this heart I keep on waiting*
> *Searching for the end of the beginning*

A Virtuosa could compel others to feel the emotions she did, or she could play upon the emotions of others and force them to awaken.

Shanae was lost before she knew she was being led. She sank almost unconsciously into Robert's arms as he moved her across the floor. Trust. There was no one she could trust more. She loved to dance with him. She didn't need to worry she was too tall or too skilled. All that kept her from enjoying every moment was the way her body heated with sheer lust every time she looked up at him. It was *not* fair of the man to look every bit like her secret fantasy lover.

> *In your eyes, in your arms, everything comes to a stop*
> *And the gods have decreed that time will repeat*

> *In a never-ending dance, the music plays on*
> *And we twirl, laughing and dreaming around the floor*
> *In a never-ending dance, the stars whirl overhead*
> *And my love for you is the beginning and end of everything*

Robert nearly smiled at the words. Liena was not subtle sometimes. He let his eyes move over Shanae's face and savored the way light from Delphinium in the skylights overhead made her glow. He loved nothing more than to dance with her for their skills there matched as perfectly as anywhere else. "You're beautiful," he told her softly, sincerely.

She shrugged one shoulder as he spun her in a long sweeping arc. "I look like Shanta." In fact, many had mistaken the painting of the first High Queen of Protea for a painting of the current High Princess.

"Enough to be her twin," he agreed. "However," he added softer, "I'd always know the difference between you. I'd still think you were more beautiful. There is no one more beautiful to me than you, Shanae. I love how you look in the light of my Mother."

> *In this town, nothing is as it seems*
> *Sadness is permeating every shadow*
> *And in this town, I keep on dancing*
> *Through the endless night holding onto you*

She looked up quickly and felt the room spinning around her head in a way that had nothing to do with the dance. She fell into his golden eyes as the song tempted her with things she could not have. His eyes. Always his eyes in her soul. The eyes that promised happily ever after and a willingness to share her burden. He truly was her soul mate. How could he be anything else? But knowing and accepting he was her soul mate in no way changed her destiny. Even if he somehow figured it out himself, she needed to keep him away for his sake. His death could not be in vain; too terrible already lay the thought that he *would* die. "Thank you." It was all she could say.

In your eyes, in your arms, everything begins anew
And the gods have decreed that time will hold still for us

It was time for him to be a bit less subtle. Subtlety could so often be lost on those of Protean blood; goddess knows he and his sister had mutually smacked their foreheads over their Dark companions for *years*. "So you've never looked at your suitor list, eh? I assume that means you've never bothered to let anyone actually court you. No secret kisses where no one is looking, to see if sparks exist?"

A hint of pink to match her eyes began to climb her neck and face. "That's none of your business!" she hissed. If he knew it was true, she would never hear the end of it. It was more than a bit unheard of to reach adulthood and not even experiment once. Like *hell* she would admit it was his fault for ruining her!

In a never-ending dance, this world is changing
And we are standing on the threshold
In a never-ending dance, the stars are bright
And your love for me is the beginning and end

A soft laugh rumbled in his chest. "Uh-oh. Don't tell me you spent so much time training that you forgot to go experimenting with a suitor or two." Nothing could have delighted him more. Erasing competition would be much easier if there was nothing for him to compete against.

In a never-ending dance, the music plays on
And we twirl laughing and dreaming around the floor
In a never-ending dance, the stars whirl overhead
And my love for you is the beginning and end of everything

Liena's voice trailed off on the last note and so too did the piano and flute stop caressing the sky as they faded into the night. The release from the song was a blessing, for Shanae had *no* answer to give

Robert. Amid the wild applause of the room, she curtsied swiftly and hurried off the dance floor as fast as she could without running. She could hear Robert clucking his tongue at her softly, but she absolutely refused to accept the new dare. A smart warrior knew when to throw a fight.

Shanae very nearly ran through the halls as she tried to get to her rooms to escape for at least an hour or two. The party would run until the first hour of the morning, and she would have to return for that, but she could at least have a breather now that she had obliged protocol by dancing with all her suitors.

The hallways leading to her rooms had been kept mostly dark, which came as no surprise even though maids would have surely guessed she might escape. Shanae, being Apex of Dark and fully a Dark element, could see in absolute dark let alone minimal light; she actually saw *better* in it. Sayena could do the same to absolute brightness.

She did not notice anything at all unusual until she started to reach for her door handle. No light could be seen under the bottom edge. *That* was not normal; she had left a lamp on personally. She listened at the door, and heard nothing except silence. Rather deliberate silence, as if someone had tried to muffle every noise. Her mood improved significantly as she realized what might be happening, and she opened her door to step inside.

The lights promptly came on, and there was a resounding cheer of 'surprise!' as all of her closest female friends came out of hiding. Only Claret was not present, but Shanae did not at all feel abandoned. Claret had already taken an entire day off from the Hall of Records to spend it with Shanae. She had begun to emerge more now that she and Sabin had married, but she still felt duty-bound to remain within the Hall of Records to maintain events and only emerged as needed by her queens, princesses, and planet. Sabin could now travel to the Hall of Records himself at will thanks to his own Time magic being enhanced by her Memory one, and he ensured she did not wholly shut herself away as she had for so many millions of years.

Shanae smiled at all of her friends and then held her hands out to Sayena as she walked forward. Their fingers meshed easily, making sparks fly as their opposing powers teased each other, and then Sayena leaned up to kiss her cheek. "Happy birthday," she said. Her golden eyes twinkling, she added, "Arista and I put our heads together over this one."

Arista grinned. "I still have a bump where the connection was made."

"With your hard head?" Shanae retorted. "I'm impressed you felt anything." A bit belatedly, she looked around her room and realized that they had been hard at work. Ribbons, streamers, bubbles, and all manner of things decorated her sitting room to make it sparkle and glitter cheerfully.

A laugh caught in her throat as she walked over to the punch bowl; it had a little fountain turning in the middle. She tasted the punch and immediately grinned. It was spiked with fermented juice. Lucky for her that she didn't get drunk easily. Unlucky for her friends who kept trying. It had happened only once, but since she and Julianna had shared the hangover, neither had minded.

"Bring out the presents!" Sayena called into the bedroom where several of the other Cultivators had disappeared.

Shanae lifted her brows and watched as Julianna carefully pushed out a cart with a large and beautiful cake on it. The confection was elaborately decorated with fudge and strawberries, and the cake itself had been made of more chocolate. Shanae's mouth watered just looking at it. "I'm going to go into a sugar induced coma."

"And you'll go happily," Julianna countered teasingly as she began to cut slices. "Next!"

Next proved to be Veronica, and she handed Shanae a brightly wrapped gold box. The birthday girl shook it suspiciously, and Veronica grinned. "Your brother was fair game. You are not. *You* would hit me for it!"

Evan's twenty-fifth birthday had been celebrated by a cheerfully wrapped present loaded with a devious contraption that had fired a cream pie into his face. Even Maxim hadn't been able to stop laughing at the sight. It was one of Shanae's fondest memories, too. "Alright, I trust you." She opened the top and found an adorable toy ferret wearing a fancy ascot and hat. "Ee!" She clutched it close, entirely uncaring how childish she had sounded. "I love him!"

The next couple of gifts came from the other Light Defenders: Asheria gave her a leather-bound diary with high quality pages, Yvette gave her a crystal clock that actually worked and had an alarm, and Sayena gave her bottle of perfume that had been specially made just for her. It consisted of proteas and sunflowers.

Delilah went next and offered a box that Shanae tore into with a glee that made everyone laugh. Inside was a handmade set of brush and mirror, the former of which had specially crafted spines that could get through Shanae's fine hair without damage. Shanae had expected it—Sayena had gotten one for her *very* fluffy and curly hair—but she still loved the beautiful design Delilah had picked.

Kacey produced two silken lace ribbons that she tied around separate locks of Shanae's hair. It would make her feel as if she were held, and not bound, to wear something made by one of her Defenders. "Also handmade," she promised. "Talon grumbled at me working so hard on weaving, but he didn't complain much when I made him get me the silk I needed. I think he dotes on you as much as he does me."

"Probably because I'm Sayena's future sister-in-law," Shanae countered dryly, "and she is to Robert's Commanders what I am to Evan's set."

Sayena pounced on that as the perfect segue. "Speaking of marriages, I suppose we may as well get the terrible part over. Can you make a short list of your top ten suitors?"

"*Ugh.*"

Her friends struggled to hide smiles. "Can't you even name a few?" Asheria pressed. "You danced with sixty-three different people, Shanae."

"Sixty-*four*," Yvette corrected on a little smile. "She danced with Robert, too."

A hint of pink began to climb Shanae's face. "He doesn't count.

He's not one of my suitors."

It was not their place to correct her, but the blush seemed very telling that perhaps their Dark princess was beginning to, literally, see the Light. "Mm-hmm." It was all that Kacey said. "What did Arista give you? You always get her gift early, along with Evan's. What did he get you as well?"

Shanae's eyes softened as she looked at her twin soul. "She gave me a protea blossom. One of the ones growing on the plant in the shade of her favorite tree on her kingdom. She had tended it all these years just to return to me as an adult." She snuggled closer when Arista hugged her tight. "As for Evan, he gave me a locket that has a small painting of our family within. He had it replicated from the one in the grand hall. Now I can know I always carry the love of my family wherever I go."

"So that's all the gifts then!" Yvette decided, and then paused. "Wait. Robert. Didn't he give you a gift?"

Shanae paused as she dipped up punch. "How odd. No, he hasn't. He's normally first in line to try to outdo Evan or Arista." She scowled. "Not that I'm happy with him right now. He asked me something far too personal during that dance."

There was motion out of the corner of her eye, and she turned her head to see Julianna and Arista shaking hands solemnly while Asheria watched on. It looked like some sort of deal had been made. "What are you doing?" she asked suspiciously.

"Nothing." Arista winked at her. "Now let's have some cake and see who goes into a coma first."

"Can we get Sayena drunk while we're at it?"

"Oh, *very* funny," her sister-in-law grumbled. It wasn't *her* fault that she couldn't handle fermented beverages very well.

By the second hour of the morning, all guests had been sent home and the disaster of the grand dining hall and ballroom would be cleaned up the next day. Shanae could finally relax alone in her room. She had made the obligatory additional appearance, but to her sheer delight and disbelief, none of her suitors had gone near her again. She should have *started* the night with the nine-note!

She hummed anew Liena's song under her breath as she wandered through her sitting room and into her bedroom. Her handmaidens had come and gone, and her formal under clothes now hung up once more. She'd had her bath, and she had wrapped herself in her favorite silk nightgown and robe. She just couldn't wind down for sleep, though. It was terribly unfair.

Someone knocked softly on her door, and she arched a brow. "It's very late—or early, as the case may be. Who is it?"

"I bring a belated gift, princess," an elderly man's voice called back.

The voice wasn't entirely familiar, but it wasn't entirely unfamiliar either. Staff from the Delphinium and Hyacinth Kingdoms alike were in residence to help with cleanup, so it wasn't impossible that he belonged with them. She opened the door only slightly and looked into the hall. An old man stood hunched over a cane, and a cloak covered most of his figure. She hesitated before opening the door further. There was just something about this person that threw her off, and she didn't know what. It didn't feel *dangerous* though. "Who sends the gift?"

"High Prince Robert Delphinium."

"Ha!" She snorted rudely. "Late as ever. It isn't even my birthday anymore! I hope it includes an apology."

He said nothing and offered a single black protea. Her heart fluttered as she reached out to touch the petals and discovered it had not come from the kingdom's gardens, or even from Hyacinth. Robert had taken seeds from her palace's garden and very carefully cultivated this blossom on his own world, and for at least a decade at that, so he could give her a blossom she did not know. He and Arista. They were no good for her heart, really.

She reached out to take the flower, and her eyes focused on the hand holding it. Belatedly, she realized the hand was far too young and strong to belong to an old man. In fact, it was a familiar hand that spent more time in her dreams than she cared to admit. "Damn you!" She snatched her hand back and whirled to dash into her room.

Robert had always been just as fast. The cloak fluttered to the floor as he snagged her around the waist and carried her into the bedroom. He kicked the door shut behind them without concern. If someone came knocking and caught him with her in her room, even while she was in her nightclothes, it wouldn't immediately be held against them. Frankly, they would have to be caught in the *act* of something before someone couldn't simply dismiss it as part of their friendship, and while he very much intended to marry her, he would play *that* particular card as only a last resort.

Shanae glared down at his arm as she seethed in silence for a moment. No wonder she had sensed something off! She had been subconsciously sensing his magic. His Light called to her Dark in a way that she had never encountered with anyone else, even others with Light cores. "I hate you."

"If you did," he murmured in her ear, "you wouldn't be so pissed." He put her down and turned her around gently. Much to his amusement, but not his surprise, she immediately took a swing at him. He blocked the first punch, dodged the second, and ended the half-hearted tussle by catching her wrists and pinning her against the wall.

Her heart began to beat overtime. She hated being so aware of him. She hated more that his body perfectly molded to hers as if they were two halves to a whole. His lips skimmed her ear, and she couldn't fight a shiver of delight. His soft laugh just sent more heat rioting through her body with gleeful desire. It had gone into absolute *overtime* ever since she had seen him in the ballroom, as if her age had literally unlocked the floodgates.

"Ah ha." His lips curved triumphantly. "You little liar. Pretending all this time that you're not as attracted to me as I am to you."

She shot a glare at him. "Since when have you been attracted to me?"

"Since shortly after you turned eighteen, given you're an early bloomer," he admitted candidly. And it had leapt into a full-fledged *inferno* when he had looked at her across a dance floor and seen her in the glory of fully blossomed maturity.

"Don't joke!"

He caught her chin and lifted it until their eyes met. Her height was only one of the many things he loved about her. "Do I look like I'm joking, Shanae?"

"No." Her eyes measured his, but she could not read what lurked behind the gold. "What brought this on so suddenly?"

He had planned out a big and romantic confession of love, but could see now that she would not accept such a thing—yet. He would have to fall back to Plan C instead. "Well, I've been suspecting a mutual attraction for a while now. And I certainly care about you more than I care for nearly anyone else. When you said you had never been kissed, it worried me. I don't want you to risk what happened to me; my first kiss was *not* the right kind of memorable."

Her brow slowly lifted. "You're offering to be my first kiss out of the goodness of your heart?"

"You missed the part about the mutual attraction." He smiled. "What have you got to lose? We're sure to feel at least a little thrill."

"Fair enough. And nearly all Cultivators get to feel little thrills before finding a soul mate, even if the thrills don't go anywhere. Go ahead and thrill me." He already owned her heart and soul, and she had just made her body's interest patently clear. She literally had nothing to lose except a chance at something spectacularly wonderful.

He slowly slid one hand up to cover her still hidden Defender Flower Mark, and her eyes widened at realizing how . . . intimate it suddenly seemed. Cultivators touched each other's Marks with common frequency as casually as they may hug one another, but just like a hug, it could change greatly depending on *who* did the touching. This time, for the first time, Robert touching her Mark felt *incredibly* intimate. And welcoming. His magic seared through her Mark into her body and sank like a wave of heat into where she had always felt so . . . cold inside. His gesture, too, carried unspoken respect for her strength and role as a Defender, and a feeling of utter safety swept over her. Security. Only he could protect her heart and soul and give her a place to rest. Her Caretaker who tended to her when she could not tend to herself.

His head lowered and his lips lightly brushed over hers. She stopped breathing. His lips brushed a second time, then a third. Each made her lips tingle more with need for the pressure of his. The fourth time his lips came back to hers, he lingered and let the kiss deepen one breath at a time.

She had no idea how long they stood there. Had no idea that his control was threadbare and only her unconscious trust held him in line. That one kiss was devastating in a way she had never dared imagine could be possible. When he finally lifted his head, she very nearly dragged him back in for another. She didn't want him to stop. In fact, she was half-tempted to ask *him* to marry *her* just so she had a legitimate excuse to seduce him.

The thought felt not unlike a slap of cold water. "Oh hell." The door was unlocked. Anyone could have walked in right in the middle of that. *How* long had he kissed her? She barely remembered her own name, let alone noticed the passage of time.

"No one knows I'm here." He could only be grateful for the distraction. It kept him from kissing her again, and again, and perhaps not stopping. Imagination and frustrated fantasies had been burned away by that single embrace. The matching, aching, desire in her eyes did not help his self-control any, either. He could feel her magic pulsing into his blood from where he touched her Mark, and it seemed wickedly erotic somehow.

"Good." She took a swift breath and opened the door as he stepped away. She peeked in the hall and saw it was clear. Relieved, she smiled and stepped into the doorway to let him out as if he had just stopped by to talk. A need for revenge for the trickery had her saying innocently, "Thanks for being my first kiss. That was a nice little thrill."

Much to her delight, a flicker of temper flashed in his eyes. "Little?"

"Naturally. It gives me a benchmark for evaluating any future suitors. Wasn't that your intent?" she asked politely. "You wanted to make sure I had a good first kiss and allow us to indulge our mutual attraction. Indulgence achieved, and that was a nice first kiss." Her eyes widened when he yanked her off her feet and into his arms. "H-hey!"

That was as far as she got before his mouth claimed hers with none of the tenderness he had shown before. Raw hunger poured out of him as he devoured her, and she lost all will for resistance. A whimper seared her throat as she met his passion headlong. He had her arms trapped. She couldn't even hold him. The sensation of being helpless was oddly thrilling. Someone who was big enough to hold her. Someone who could keep her safe. The thoughts tumbled again and again through what was left of her brain. Cold? There was no such thing.

He released her just as abruptly, and she staggered a step as if drunk. She grabbed the door to maintain her balance and stared at him. "Uhm." For the life of her, she could find nothing else short of *'take me, I'm yours!'* and even half-drunk on desire, she refused to let those words past her lips.

His fingers caught her chin. "Little thrill? *Nice?*" His voice came as little more than a soft growl, and his eyes burned brilliantly with a complex tangle of lust and temper and something even hotter that she felt terrified to name. "You know that what exists between us is neither little nor nice. We will never burn for anyone else the way we burn for one another! Deep down, even your stubborn Dark soul knows that!"

As he stalked down the hall, she didn't have to look deep down to know he was right. He was her *soul mate*. The hunger produced between two souls meant to interlock was a more wonderful and powerful desire than any that a body alone could produce. It was the place where Love, Life, and Destiny met, mingled, had a party, and got everyone drunk. She had *no idea* how Liena and her soul mate had resisted. "I'm in such trouble," she muttered as she went back into her room.

Despite evidence to the contrary, there *were* observers to the scene, and they would hold what they had seen as blackmail to help Robert. Julianna sighed and slapped a gold coin into Arista's hand, and Sabin grinned. "You know him almost as well as I do. Good call, Arista."

"It was a good hunch." Arista held up a finger in the air. "I understand him. And I understand Shanae. It was easy to assume that he would bulldoze past her Dark blindness and erase any chance of a miscommunication. You can't be subtle with the Protea Kingdom. You really can't. Really, if Evan hadn't been more easy-going about things, we would have absolutely seen Sayena pull this on him as well. And it's almost a shame that didn't happen, because it would have been hilarious."

Vermillion and Talon were also present, and the former muttered, "I don't like this."

"Well, Robert does, and all that matters is his happiness." Talon elbowed Julianna lightly. "I can't believe you accepted that bet."

"I didn't think he'd have the nerve to do it, or the skill to get her to open the door," she admitted.

"He has the nerve of a thief," Sabin said dryly. "Why do you think we love him?" His smile faded into a frown as he watched Vermillion stalk off down the hall. Vermillion had . . . changed. He had grown to hate Proteans with a fiery passion, though none of them really knew why. He had more than once shown a hate for Diego as well. He did love Robert, though, and the other Commanders could only pray that that would continue to override everything else. If it didn't, then things could get ugly.

* * * * *

Shortly into the next month, the first of the new year, Sayena and Evan's engagement party would be held. The two weeks leading up to the event were filled with all manner of things, and both Shanae and Robert remained busy as they helped their siblings with logistics and organization. Engagement parties were always planned by the according couple, held on the kingdom of the one holding highest rank. That meant the party would be on Delphinium, but it did not mean Protea didn't have work to do!

Most suspected that Shanae had thrown herself whole-heartedly into helping her brother in an effort to avoid scrutiny about her own lack of a suitor. Her list had cleared itself dramatically; only a few names remained, though she did not know whose since she *still* refused to look at it. Genevieve and Matthew, at their wits' end over their youngest, finally decided it was time to play dirty. Unfortunately for Evan, he drew the short stick to be the one to tell Shanae.

He found his sister in the library, and she was going over the historical tomes about previous engagement parties to see if they had missed any traditions. He winced a bit and then squared his shoulders. "Shanae?"

"Did you know you're supposed to put a black protea blossom in her shoe, and a white delphinium in yours?" she asked without looking up. "It's good luck for the betrothed of a Ruler Cultivator to have a blossom of said Cultivator's patron flower in their shoe. Why the shoe? Seems silly, but we could all use luck!"

Well, there would be no better segue. "So then you can plan on putting a black protea blossom in someone's shoe very soon."

Her head jerked up. "What?!" It dawned, and she dropped her face into her hands. "Damn it, Mother! Now how did I know she was going to force my hand when I couldn't give her and Father a short list?"

One of the other laws in place to protect an heir stipulated that a queen could force her daughter's hand by personally narrowing the suitor list down to two candidates, and the princess *had* to choose one of them to marry. It only came up when a queen feared outside forces influencing events . . . or she worried her daughter might not have noticed her soul mate. In Shanae's case, both applied.

"I *told* you that you should have just lied and kept them happy." Evan grinned as his sister sighed heavily. "Well, on one hand, it's not as bad as you think. On the other hand, it might be worse."

She closed her eyes. "Alright. Let me have it. Who's the first choice?"

"Tevlan."

She gagged. "I know our parents do not hate me, and they are also not stupid. They have decided they know exactly who they think is my soul mate and they want me to marry, and they are bound and determined I fall in line. They ensure me choosing the other candidate by giving me an absolute ass for a second option."

"That about sums it up."

"So? Just who is it that I'm to be the blushing bride for?"

He watched her intently. "Robert." And with over two decades of knowing his sister inside him, he lifted his fingers and plugged his ears.

She didn't notice. "WHAT?!" The shriek echoed off the walls and was audible even on the other side of the castle. She grabbed her shorter yet elder brother's shirt and gave him a shake. "Robert isn't one of my suitors! How can he be one of my choices?!"

He coughed. "Technically, he was your first suitor. He sort of put his name on your list even before you were nineteen. We always assumed you would eventually look at your list and see him there, but you never did. You really have only yourself to blame for being surprised, honey. Literally everyone knew but you."

"I don't want to marry him!"

A black brow slowly lifted. "Yet you let him kiss you."

She had been wondering if word had gotten to him. Sayena had accidentally dropped the news that she knew, and Shanae had expected her to tell Evan eventually. "I did," she sighed. "And very deeply enjoyed it, as I'm sure you may guess. I love him so stupidly, Evan. He's my soul mate."

"Then *why* are you resisting?" he asked in frustration. "I hate seeing you so miserable!"

"Because I will not let him die for me!" she shouted at him. Her hands curled into fists. "He sees his life as less important than Sayena's, just as you see yours as less than mine. You two . . . you would act as Caretakers first and Cultivators second. You would protect us at the cost of your lives, the same way the other princesses act as Defenders first and Rulers second." She shook her head hard. "I won't let him die for me, Evan!" No sacrifices would be made in vain; she would not be able to bear it.

"You honestly think that being betrothed will make a difference?" he asked her with all seriousness. "Do you honestly think that Robert would not, right here and now, sacrifice himself to save you? Whether you two wear rings on your thumbs or not, he would not hesitate. He loves you, Shanae. He knows he is your soul mate. He knew long before you did. And can you honestly tell me you're at all surprised by this turn of events?"

She sighed deeply as she sat down on a chair. "I admit that he said some things that made me suspect he knew even before I did. I just didn't realize he had been on my list even before it officially started, though I do suppose that explains the dance he coerced on my birthday. Why maintain a farce of having his own list?"

"To keep you from taking his head off." He smiled when she snorted. "Don't worry about it too much. You have two weeks until you have to decide. Your decision is to be announced at the engagement party."

She groaned. "Don't worry he says!"

Two weeks later, at the height of the party, Robert walked into the ballroom after giving Evan an obligatory yet unnecessary tour of the castle and found his eyes immediately finding Shanae. She stood talking to a visiting delegate from Ranunculus, and she clearly had the older woman charmed. Because it was not her party, she had not worn her Ruler gown; instead, she wore a slim dress of black and pink that flattered her coloring. Her hair had stayed down, and crystal-lined lace ribbons wove within the locks. Only the coronet on her head and the Flower Mark visible over the low edge of her bodice were markers of her royal blood, but she looked every inch the princess regardless.

He wandered over to where she stood and gave her a mock scowl. "Are you flirting with Yura again?"

She grinned at him. "She asked me to marry her. I'm considering it."

Lady Yura was old enough to be their grandmother, and she had known both since before their births; Ranunculus and the two High planets had been trying to hammer out an alliance for at least that long. She could only chuckle softly at their antics. "Well, if Prince Robert is my competition, I'm afraid I must back down. I think he would win."

"Faint hearts never won fair ladies," Robert quipped. "And speaking of fair ladies, I don't suppose I might steal this one for a dance?"

"Of course, my dear." Yura covered a smile as she watched them head onto the dance floor. She certainly hoped they invited her to the wedding. If she had ever seen two more perfectly matched people, she could not recall it.

"Let's try to keep this to under nine beats per second, please," Robert teased as he swung Shanae into his arms and they merged seamlessly with the other dancers on the floor.

She grinned up at him. "You have proven to keep up with me even if I don't." As he twirled her and brought her back, she slid her hand down to rest on his chest instead of his shoulder. The gesture was deliberately intimate for her hand covered his hidden Flower Mark. "When were you going to tell me you were one of my suitors?" It came out as nearly a purr of menace.

He just smiled. "Today, in fact. I gave you six years to realize you and I were soul mates, and it didn't happen, so I decided to be more ruthless on your birthday."

"Ah, so that *was* a line of bullshit about worrying for my first kiss."

"Not *technically*," he countered judiciously. "I really was worried. I just also saw it as perfectly convenient. I had other plans formed depending on the route you took."

And that right there was why he and his sister so often terrified her and her brother. They really liked to have their own way. "Which plan was that one?"

"C."

"Dare I ask what A and B were?" she asked dryly.

"Probably not. There was a Plan D as well." He grinned. "Shanae, I truly did intend to tell you tonight. I intended to formally ask to be on your list and for you to sincerely consider me as your choice of husband. I *suspected* your parents might force your choice, but I didn't know for fact that they would until I got the message it was done." He cocked his head. "Out of curiosity, who is my 'competition'?" She scowled, and his brows shot up. Only one possible person could have provoked *that* level of distaste. "Lord Tevlan? Well, I suppose I should be looking into having a Delphinium wedding suit made, shouldn't I?"

"It doesn't bother you that you're winning by default?" She looked up at him, and her eyes memorized his beloved face. She could hardly believe this man would be her husband. Now if she could only keep him out of her fight!

"I'd have won anyway."

The utter arrogance of the statement made her laugh out loud, and the sound drew several smiling glances. Nothing made any court happier than to hear their Ruler Cultivators be truly happy.

Tevlan walked in the door on the heels of the laughter, and the slight swagger to his steps had several disgusted eyes turning toward him. He paid no heed. He had been informed of the forced decision and he couldn't have been happier. He had yet to find out who his competition was, but he felt confident that he could beat anyone.

His eyes fell on Shanae and a frown darkened his face as he saw how intimately she danced with her partner. The man holding her wore a coronet of some sort and a white and gold formal uniform, but Tevlan had never bothered to learn the intricacies of the galaxy and didn't know what they signified, or if they even signified anything. It only irked him to realize the man looked every bit Shanae's perfect opposite and therefore, curiously, her perfect match. Temper simmering, Tevlan started across the floor.

Shanae's entire body tensed, and Robert looked down at her. The look on her face said it all. He glanced toward the door, saw Tevlan approaching, and protectively pulled Shanae closer as they stopped dancing.

Tevlan stopped before them and barely spared Robert a glance. "I want to talk to you," he told Shanae.

"I was under the impression," Robert said softly, "that one greets a princess with more respect. Particularly a princess of a rank such as Shanae's."

Tevlan's eyes flashed with fury. "Who are you to talk to me of rank?"

A cool smile was the answer. Robert calmly tugged aside the slightly open collar of his dress shirt to reveal the Delphinium Flower Mark on his chest. "I think I know more than you, *lord*."

Shanae barely kept from laughing wickedly in delight. Leave it to Robert to give her what she could not get for herself: sweet revenge! "Tevlan, meet His Royal Highness the High Prince Robert Delphinium of the Delphinium Kingdom, second heir to the throne and eldest child of High Queen Hannah Delphinium and her husband, High King Quint Delphinium. Oh," she added smoothly, "he's also my future husband."

Shock froze Tevlan's voice for many moments before finally he managed, "That's impossible!"

"How so?" She swept one brow upward. "He's been one of my suitors since I was nineteen. My parents narrowed my choice to you and to him. As I had been intending to choose him all along, there was no real decision to be made." She sighed. "Honestly, Mother is just too impatient. I only turned twenty-five a few weeks ago. I'm the baby of the galaxy, after all," she added cheerfully.

Robert smirked. "I trust we have your well wishes?"

"Why him?" Tevlan demanded. "Is that what you were looking for all along? A high rank to pad your position?"

Shanae's eyes flashed black, and the ground trembled slightly in warning. Even the land of Delphinium could respond to the deadly fury of her Nature power. No land anywhere could ignore her call. "I wanted," she said softly, "someone that saw *me* and not a rank. One who loved me despite the burden my existence brings. I wanted someone I could trust. Robert is the only one who has ever given me that. Please remove yourself, Tevlan. This party is for my brother and future sister-in-law. If I have to, I will call for the Commanders to remove you—again. I am quite sure Sabin and Ulyen would be *happy* to take the honors this time."

Knowing he had been defeated, Tevlan turned on his heel and stalked from the ballroom.

Shanae took a deep breath and glanced around the room. An

excited buzz had quickly spread as the entire conversation got repeated verbatim. "All we need now," she told her betrothed dryly, "is for word of a certain unmentionable event to get out and my plan to make a scene will be complete."

"Well," he said smoothly, "if it's a scene my princess wants, I suppose I could go to Plan D after all." A light tug on the hand he still held had her tumbling into his arms. His other hand lifted to frame her face, and he lowered his head to kiss her soundly with a lover's casual intimacy.

The crowd burst into cheers and laughter. Over it, somewhere, she heard Veronica shout, "Go Shanae! Hook him good!"

What the hell. She freed her arms and threw them around his neck. The cheers grew in volume and so did laughter. When he finally eased back, she kept her grip on him for fear that her trembling knees would not hold her weight. "You certainly do intend to marry me," she said huskily, "if only because I've just scared off every other suitor in the universe."

"You're the only one I have ever wanted." He kept her close as they left the dance floor and headed toward where their parents sat. All of the Dual Cultivators were present, even Claret, and all of them wore matching grins. Evan and Sayena looked especially smug. "I *told* you I'd handle things," Robert scolded them lightly. "You act as if it was in doubt."

"Well, it *took* you long enough," Quint scolded equally.

"She's a Dark element, Father. What did you expect?" He tugged Shanae closer when she made a motion as if to get away. "I'll leave it to you lot to make the proclamation that you've been holding onto for the last few years. Shanae and I need to have a long overdue talk."

"We do?" His fiancée lifted a brow but amiably followed as he led her out of the ballroom and into the gardens. It was comfortably between twenty-one and twenty-two hours, and she could see Protea hovering in the sky before them. Just looking at it made her heart ache. "I love my world," she said softly, lifting her free hand as if to touch it. "There's no one who loves it more."

In that moment, he knew he had never loved *her* more.

Enveloped in the glow of Protea, she had a raw radiance that consumed him. He knew she was the Apex of Dark, that she possessed arcanery as an ultimate being, but he had never realized what it truly meant until that moment when he felt her power reaching out to find his Light.

She turned her head to say something but the words caught in her throat as she saw the way he looked at her. Her heart began to beat harder. "Robert . . ."

His hands lifted and framed her face. "I love you," he said quietly, intensely. "I never said it before because I wasn't sure you'd believe me. I'm still not sure why I was born. I'm sure there is a reason for everything changing as it has, but I don't know yet what it is. It still doesn't change that I live for *you*. I never fell in love with you, Shanae. You had my heart and soul the day I was born."

She closed her eyes on a wave of emotion so strong and powerful that it blinded her. "If you'd said something sooner, I wouldn't have waited this long either." What did it matter? Liena and Evan were both right: Robert would fight by her side whether or not he knew she loved him as terribly as she did. She could find the strength to tell him the truth before the end came, and there would be no vain sacrifice. She *deserved* to be happy before that end arrived. "I've always resented my destiny." Her eyes opened. "But if Destiny gave you to me, I don't resent it anymore. I was born loving you. I'll never stop loving you."

He swept her up into his arms and held onto her fiercely as he buried his face in her hair. She could feel the hammering of his heart against her chest. It beat with the same rhythm of her own; they could never fall out of sync. *Had* never fallen out of sync from the day she had been born. If that wasn't a mark of Destiny, she didn't know what was. The answer had been there all along.

Genevieve and Matthew's reason for forcing their daughter's hand became clear only a month after Shanae and Robert celebrated their engagement party, as a new wave of evil began to sweep through Blossom Field. It came in with a potency unseen before in the waves that had taken the lives of prior Defenders. Only Shanae and the four High Queens and Kings knew why, and none of them spoke of the oncoming end of the kingdoms. The other queens of the Flower Kingdoms, however, suspected *something*. All of them had made it into their fifties in age, and a very near future held another generation of Cultivators, whether Dual or not.

The first real sign of the severity of the events came when the sun disappeared briefly from the skies of all worlds that currently saw it. A low sound like a cry of the planets' Cores echoed across the ears of all Cultivators. Shanae felt suddenly sick to her stomach and went glassy pale. Power whipped around her body as she stood on her balcony and stared at the sunless sky. "Nemesis."

The sun returned as the power ebbed, but she knew what had happened. Nemesis had finally gotten free. He would gather those he could corrupt, would amass an army of evil Nightmayres, and he would feed on the terror of the populace until—gorged and bloated—he came directly after Shanae herself.

He was not the only problem. Famine had gained in strength as well. Her corrupted worshippers had spread out across the worlds. When she felt Nemesis, she did not see a rival. She saw a potential ally. She deliberately sought out the source of all evil and they joined forces. Now, when evil flared, it flared twice as hard.

Battles began to dot the daytime. All Defenders carried Masks at all times, and though Shanae and Sayena carried theirs as well, Veronica still forbade them from entering battle unless there would be no other recourse. They conceded to her willingly enough, but she knew they did so only at their own choice.

Defenders naturally deferred to the strongest in the ranks, which *usually* was the Lead Defender. However, Shanae and Sayena were technically more powerful than Veronica, and so she would defer to them should they exercise their right to lead. When she had asked Claret why it would happen that she be Lead Defender when the position, by rights, should belong to Shanae, Claret had gently reminded her that, no matter the reasons why both High Princesses were Defenders, there would be a day they hung up their Masks in order to rule. Destiny had known of that, and so had planned for that.

Veronica fervently hoped to have them hang up their Masks before ever donning them, yet she knew it a hopeless wish. They could all feel the oppressive weight of events set in stone, and those with Sight could barely sleep at night.

Two days after Nemesis had awakened, Shanae knew *something* terrible had happened. She could feel it as a painful jolt into her soul from her fiancé, even while they were still on two different worlds. She immediately transported herself to Delphinium's castle. Her sense of anguish from her soul mate only doubled in proximity, and her racing heart, she knew, did not actually belong to her.

She opened the door to his rooms just in time to hear him demand raggedly, "Am I to lose you, too, Diego?"

She moved to the doorway of the sitting room and found a tear-streaked Robert facing down Diego and a man both familiar and yet unfamiliar. He bore a striking resemblance to Vermillion yet was not the Commander in question. It took her only a moment to place him: Rubeo Chance, Vermillion's brother. He was two years younger than his brother, and therefore two older than Robert. He had been a frequent enough sight in the Delphinium Kingdom after Vermillion's appointment, and despite his rather aloof nature, had become endeared to all Cultivators—perhaps more so than his brother. "What happened?" she asked quietly, and drew all eyes.

Robert took a long breath and focused on her steady heartbeat trying to calm his own. "Vermillion disappeared. We don't know where. He had gone to investigate a flare-up, but he never returned. Chance and Diego want to go look for him. Chance for obvious reasons, and Diego because he has the skills to help protect them both."

Chance nodded a bit at Shanae. "I don't feel my brother is dead. He had not been himself lately, though, and I worry for what trouble he may have bitten off in an effort to prove himself better than Diego."

Diego grimaced. "And as that is *no* secret, I am going because I'm guilty of aiding in that feeling Vermillion had." He looked at Robert. "If Vermillion is dead, his position as Commander will become mine; Hannah has already made that clear. I hope, for your sake, he is alive. I know you don't love him the way you love me, but I do know you love him. That is enough for me, and should be enough for him!"

"The Chance brothers have trouble understanding love," Robert said a bit tiredly. He buried his face briefly in Shanae's hair when she moved to hold him. "They don't really *get* the different levels that can exist."

Chance did not deny the charge. "Let us go, Robert. You know I care for your well-being as well." Though his calm and somewhat cool voice did not change, the softer edge to his crystal blue eyes seemed to underscore the words.

Robert let his fingers tangle with Shanae's. "Very well. You have my permission. Do not *dare* give your lives! I can't lose you as well, especially not you, Diego." He watched both men hurry from the room and then let his head drop onto Shanae's shoulder. "Why must this happen?" he asked painfully.

"Because of me," she admitted softly.

His head jerked up. "Never say that!" he shouted at her. "You are not at fault for the whims of Destiny!"

"But I am the *result* of her whims," she reminded him. "For me to do what I must, our kingdoms must fall. And that means all of us within them must fall. There must be a rebirth. A restart. I can only destroy Nemesis in a time that has forgotten him for that will take away his greatest power. I'm so sorry." She rose up to kiss him tenderly. "I hate it more than you do."

No one need ask what came of the events; though no one could determine the specifics, Arista felt the moment her husband was torn out of her soul. She poured all of her grief into the will to endure for Shanae's sake, but she began to deeply hold suspicion for the future. She and Diego had not yet borne a child, and as both had entered their thirties, that alone had been an oddity—as much as her mother and father's continued existence. None of the Dual Cultivators had yet had their own children. All had assumed it lay in Shanae and Sayena's younger ages and wanting to keep generations the same age, but now they suspected Destiny had something else up her sleeve.

When the next wave came, it came brutally. Statice and Iris were nearly wiped out as Famine targeted the Light planets and Nemesis pursued the Dark. Dane lost his life in an effort to send Yvette to safety by accessing transport magic he did not naturally possess, and Sabin lost his by physically barring the time-space portal he had opened for Claret to escape through. The two Dual Cultivators only bore up under the loss for the same reason as Arista: someone still needed them. People fled from the ravaged worlds to Carnation and Daffodil beyond, and at last Tokala knew of only one way to salvage what remained of Iris. She tore out her own Seed and used it to freeze the Core until a time when the world could recover. Such an action took her and Taben alike, and Yvette arrived on Delphinium to the news that she was, effectively, now a queen.

Claret did not dare risk her Seed to freeze Statice for recovery. Instead, she used her very power over Time to do the same. Her world, too, would sleep, and someday it would awaken—just as someday her soul mate would return. Knowing such a thing in no way eased the tears that fell at feeling where he had been torn out of her.

Robert suffered just as deeply in losing Sabin for he had lost his twin soul. Sayena and Shanae clung onto him tighter in order to help. There would be no reprieve for anyone. Famine and Nemesis did not stop where they had started. Carnation and Daffodil became their next target. The pattern repeated. Maxim and Talon sacrificed themselves to send Veronica and Kacey to safety, and by the time the two princesses landed, their worlds had been frozen by their mothers' sacrifices, and they had become queens.

It continued to spread. Gladiolus and Orchid repeated the pattern. Navidan and Ulyen lost, Julianna and Delilah sent away to defend the High Princesses and Princes, and the Ruler Cultivators giving of their Seeds to freeze their worlds' Cores and buy more time to stop the evil. Hyacinth and Aster fell next in the same way. Diego had already been lost, however; Skyla herself ordered Arista to flee for Shanae needed her most. Jayden fell on Aster to save Asheria. The two twin souls to the High Princesses landed nearly at the feet of the one they loved most, and before the hour passed, they were queens.

Other worlds beyond tried to send aid to no avail. Other Defenders could not even *enter* Blossom Field. Vicious storms in space had cut off the center of the universe. Nemesis and Famine, bloated and gorged on blood and terror, reveled in what they had wrought. They parted forces and turned their malevolent eyes on that which they hated most: the legendary Apexes of Dark and Light prophesized to destroy them.

They did not go right for the palaces. Instead, they crept in from the edges of Protea and Delphinium and slowly moved toward the center. Delphinium suffered the hardest for Famine's disease power began to poison the very land itself, and everything began to wither and die. It was the people on Protea to suffer, and not the land, for Nemesis needed people to *live* in order for them to produce the terrible dreams he fed upon.

Pallas could not keep the Ephemeral Plane stable any longer, and without a Knight, no one could police the terrible dreams. Shanae tried desperately to siphon them off personally, yet never seemed to make a dent. Those of the Faith, led by Liena, did their best to aid the Plane as well, but they only drew Nemesis' gaze directly onto themselves. Rising hate and unbalance among the populace found them turning on the easiest target to find a way to save themselves, and that meant they turned on the witches of the Faith. Thousands were burned or drowned before all others went so deep into hiding that they seemed to disappear entirely.

Liena was among the first to fall, for her position made her the prime target. Lieu fought until his last breath for her life, and his, but to no avail. The royal family searched a bit feverishly for their three children, but Protea herself refused to tell any of them what had happened to the High Priestess' lineage. Only time would reveal if Liena had spoken truly of the descendants to come.

The Defenders had aligned themselves along the borders of the two remaining kingdoms. Shanae and Sayena, against any and all protests, journeyed to visit them every day. Another week ticked by as the two evil armies kept creeping in. Shanae had just woken to a blood red sunrise when she felt . . . something. She scrambled into her clothes and grabbed her Mask before transporting herself directly to where her Defenders stood grimly confronting what could truly only be called a nightmare.

Thousands. Thousands and thousands of monstrous creatures that bore the moniker of Nightmayre.

"I will fight," Shanae told Arista.

"You will not." Arista turned narrowed eyes on her twin. "What do you think to accomplish here? Nemesis is not here. If he was here, I would put the Mask on you personally. He is not, and therefore you cannot risk yourself. You must survive to face Nemesis and destroy him, and then we can all be reborn together."

That Arista had half-guessed the reality did not surprise Shanae. She also did not correct the assumption. She *did* have to survive to face Nemesis, if only to seal him away until that moment of rebirth. "You try so hard to protect me from what you know you can't stop, and I love you, but let me be with you!" Shanae pleaded.

"Our decision is final," Kacey told her softly, her tone as hard as the Metal of her element. "Claret, remove our princess for her own safety."

"No!" A bubble of time-space magic surrounded her, and she beat her hands on it uselessly. It was this very sacrifice she had so desperately not wanted to see, yet she had caused it by going to her friends' aid as her soul demanded. "Damn you!" she shouted, and it could have been at Arista, Claret, or even Destiny herself.

The last thing she saw before the magic forcefully removed her from the scene was the sight of the four Defenders beginning to glow brightly with magic. Shanae landed hard in the safety bunker, much to her lack of surprise. Only a Lead Defender could force the retreat of a fellow Defender, but *any* Defender could force the retreat of a High heir in the case of extreme emergency. Either way, the one being sent away always landed in the bunker. Shanae found it bitterly ironic that the one person who had always before been sent away had been the one to send *her*.

Only a few moments after she arrived, Sayena landed with even less grace in a heap beside her. "Ashe?" Shanae asked tiredly.

"Nica, as a Lead is wont to do." Tears choked Sayena for a moment as she curled her hands into fists. "They wouldn't listen to me! I *tried* to tell them that it didn't matter, but they were convinced they did the only thing they could!"

Though no shockwave went through the bunker this time, they knew exactly when the Defenders fell for they each felt their twin soul torn violently from them. Nothing could have kept them inside that bunker this time. They rushed out and used their power to take them to the place where the Defenders had been. No sign of them remained, and thousands of monsters had been decimated.

Sight stirred inside both High Princesses, and they just *knew*. They rushed back to their palaces, only to find the new onslaught had begun there. Yet, neither Nemesis nor Famine had appeared. Shanae's claymore allowed her to cut her way through to where Evan, Genevieve, and Matthew fought as well.

It's terrible! Sayena's voice echoed across Shanae's mind. As Apexes with arcanery, they could not only enter any mind they chose, they could also communicate across any distance with one another. The telepathic skill had stayed on the down low because it unnerved even their loved ones, but it now became a vital tool.

It's terrible here too, Shanae countered. *We can't fall yet, Sayena! We have to endure! We have to seal Nemesis and Famine, and they are taking their sweet time, hoping we fall before they arrive!*

Then what should we do? Tell me, and I will follow.

Shanae did not have a chance to answer. Genevieve and Hannah had already reached much the same conclusion, and more than even the Defenders, understood how absolutely critical it be that the two Apexes engage their destined enemy. Almost as if they too could read one another's mind, the two High Queens tore out their Seeds.

It was the glow that alerted Evan and Shanae as to Genevieve's action. "No!" Evan tried to lunge toward her, but Matthew knocked him flat to the floor.

The Seed glowed brighter and brighter and then simply blew apart. The shockwave it released rattled the entirety of the world and obliterated every bit of the attacking enemy. Eerie silence fell on both worlds as both High Queens fell.

Matthew, Evan, and Shanae scrambled to Genevieve's side even as Robert and Sayena scrambled to Hannah's. Two worlds, so different, yet so alike, bound by matching destinies. Events unfolded as if Destiny played the same melody with two different hands—an encore of the long forgotten past.

Genevieve felt only peace as her blurry eyes tried to focus on the faces of those she loved. She had done what had been needed, and she had fulfilled her duty. Someday, she would see her children live freely without fear. "Shanae?" she managed to ask softly.

"I'm here." Shanae pressed her mother's hand to her cheek. Somehow this hurt less than losing the Defenders; perhaps because her mother had not made a sacrifice at all. This was her moment to be free. The Defenders *had* to someday return to carry on the lineages of their worlds, but Genevieve had already done her part, and everyone else of her generation had already been lost. Now she could be with them forever. "I love you, Mother. I am so proud to be your child."

Genevieve's lips trembled a bit. "I am more proud to be your mother." She shifted her gaze to Evan. "Evan. How lucky I was to be your mother as well. To be given *two* such wonderful gifts . . . I am glad." Her eyes began to close. "I will always watch over you," she murmured softly as her breath sighed out. "Always."

The Mark on her chest faded away, and her body dissolved into shimmers of color. It took only moments before she no longer existed on the physical plane. Black-pink power swirled around Shanae's body and then up toward her head. It coalesced into a familiar crown whose weight felt as if it had been carried since birth. Protea had claimed its new High Queen.

Shanae.

The grief in Sayena's voice only made tears well in Shanae's eyes. She fought them fiercely. *I know.* She slowly stood and crossed her arms as she stared out into the now-empty distance. Nemesis would come for her directly soon enough. A day, at most. Perhaps that very night. "Father?" she asked quietly.

Matthew took a long breath. Though gaping wounds had been torn into his soul, and the pain nearly felt unbearable, he did not actually feel *grief*. The tangible effects of losing his soul mate could not be stopped, but his mind and heart had long before accepted just what would very probably happen. "I think . . . my time is here as well. We both know that here or later, my time is done. I have no reason to be here without my Cultivator."

Evan nodded and then slowly stood to move to Shanae's side. "Then go. We will handle the rest." Somehow, he found a smile. "Maybe . . . that is why you are also a Ruler Cultivator, Father. You can burn your Seed as well."

Matthew looked at his children and felt his heart ache no less than Genevieve's had. He reached inside to pull out his Seed, and it materialized in the air before him. Deactivated, it did not glow. Yet it existed. And he could burn what remained in it to follow his mate to the Realm. "Remember," he told Evan and Shanae alike as he began to glow, "that I regret nothing that brought me here. I love you both more than anything. I will be your guiding hand when you need it."

Evan very nearly reached out as Matthew began to dissolve, but Shanae caught his wrists. The two siblings stood watching until the last, until their father no longer existed on that plane and had moved beyond to find not just their mother, but the beloved other members of his generation. *Uncle Quint?* She asked it of Sayena.

Gone, came the tired response. *Before Mother. He threw himself over me before Robert got close. He . . . knew Mother would make her sacrifice if needed. I feel as if I have no control over anything, Shanae!*

We always have some level of control. We just have to choose to exercise it. Shanae took a deep breath. "Evan. Go to Sayena. She needs you more than I do."

He nodded, though it bothered him. It did not seem fair that he have to choose between the two he loved most. "Robert will come in my stead, whether you like it or not." He hugged her fiercely for a moment. He cared not that she was both taller and stronger; she was his beloved baby sister, and he would always protect her when she needed it.

She hugged him back and then let go so he could use his magic to transport to Delphinium. She moved silently through the castle toward her rooms, and she only barely acknowledged the servants who bowed in her passing. None of them said a word about what had happened, nor did they try to pierce the invisible barrier she had wrapped herself within. They simply moved quickly to do what they could to pretend, if only for a bit, that things could ever be normal again.

Shanae had just stepped onto her balcony when she felt a familiar presence behind her. Strong arms curled around her waist, and Robert buried his face in her hair. The tears brimmed anew but would not fall. She would not let them. "I made choices leading to this moment," she murmured. "Not everything that happened was beyond my control. Yet the one thing I wanted most, that literally was mine for the taking, I feared to reach out for. I knew that to take what had been offered would bring worse."

"What do we discuss this time?" he asked softly. He let go when she pulled away, and he turned with a bit of a frown as she walked into her bedroom. "Shanae?" He stopped breathing entirely as she began to calmly remove her clothes until she stood before him beautifully nude. How did such a perfect creature want *him*? "Shanae."

"Just once," she told him softly, fiercely, "I want to be selfish. I want to be unafraid. I'm always so afraid! How do you all think I am so courageous when I want nothing more than to hide? It is not courage; it is only bravery."

"It is both," he told her huskily, "because you have learned to not be afraid of some things and are therefore courageous, and you are also brave because you choose to move forward even though you are afraid." And that she would choose him as her selfish moment was beyond humbling. He crossed to her and skimmed a gentle finger over her lips. "I want everything you do," he said softly. "I have only one condition."

"And that is?" she asked.

Her eyes, as she looked up at him, were so deep that he felt as if he could drown in them. There, right there, lurked his entire existence and the reason for his being. His voice grew huskier with a need as emotional as it was physical. "This becomes our wedding night. Vows or no vows, you'll be my wife in every sense of the word and I will be your husband. It won't change, no matter how much time passes, or what our names change to. No matter what lives we live, how different our worlds are."

She slid her arms around his waist and pressed closer. There was no hesitation in her heart and therefore none in her voice as she said, "I think it's always been that way. Even if you hadn't asked, it would have been that way. If my destiny is to die, I want to die knowing what it was to truly live." A tremulous smile curved her lips. "It wouldn't be fair if we were the only ones to die without ever once knowing our soul mate's touch."

He tilted her chin up and kissed her deeply as he held her closer. He felt shaken all the way through his soul by the gift Destiny had given him by choosing him for the Apex of Dark. If it was literally the last thing he did, his lover would feel nothing but joy and pleasure until the end of everything. She had earned this, and so had he.

As his hands slid warmly down her bare flesh, he murmured against her lips, "Someday you need to let me undress you. I've dreamed about that." He released her long enough to strip his shirt off and then caught a breath as her fingers skimmed down his Flower Mark. He ran a knuckle down her left arm in intimate retaliation. "Let me see."

Her Defender Flower Mark, always before hidden, appeared anew on her arm. The sparkling edges only shimmered more when he bent his head to press his lips there. A quiver ran through her entire body of desire that consumed her soul and body alike. He was her gift, her reward, for obeying Destiny's commands. If she regretted only one thing, it would be to have not taken him for herself sooner.

Their lips met in another kiss that slowly unraveled. Time could wait for them. She took a step back, then another, bringing him with her. When she felt the bed touch her hips, she sat down and pulled him down with her. His hands beside her hips kept his balance and he released her from the kiss only to nibble at her neck. "You're overdressed," she teased him huskily.

"Am I?"

"Just a bit." She tugged at his pants waistband and then let it snap back teasingly. He released her and straightened, and she leaned back on her hands to watch with love and desire as he finished removing his clothes. How could he seem so utterly perfect to her? If he had flaws, her eyes simply did not see them. She loved most how he could have the soft edges of his magical lineage yet have defined muscle from his decades of trying to keep up with her. At least, *that* also made sense at last. He had truly made himself into her perfect Caretaker.

"What are you smiling at?" He lifted her into his arms and then dropped her onto the middle of the bed to make her laugh. It wasn't the first time they had jumped on a bed together, but the antics of childhood existed on a separate plane from adulthood.

"Maybe you make me happy." She rose to her knees as he knelt beside her, and her hands began to move over his body to memorize all that she could. His hands moved over her in turn, and though hungry desire stirred, it simply could not take away the deeper hunger of their souls to simply *know*.

Desire did have to be appeased, and it finally began to burn hotter and hotter until fingers trembled. Until breathless sounds were as much a gasp as a sigh. They rolled over the covers in a teasing trade of strength until she finally won and held him pinned beneath her. She stared down into his nearly white eyes and could not find the words for how she felt. There were none in existence that could compare.

She took him slowly, savoring every moment, and felt him

trembling beneath her as he fought to let her have her way. His fingers bit into her hips, thrilling her with the reminder that maybe, just maybe, he could be the stronger one. "Next time," she promised against his lips. "You can have your wicked way with me next time."

He buried one hand in her hair and held her closer for a devouring kiss. "Promise?" he asked thickly when he released her a bit. His hand slid down her body in a burning caress before curving around her hip again. He twisted beneath her slowly, tormenting them both, and loving how her pink eyes had turned to black with her power.

She followed his urging and took the lead, taking him again and again until ecstasy finally claimed them as surely as they had claimed each other. Inside that moment of pleasure that radiated as deeply through her soul as her heart, her universe aligned itself and was, at least for a time, perfect.

She lay draped across his chest, her cheek over his Mark, and felt no need to move anywhere anytime soon. When his arms slid around her waist and tightened in a fierce hug, she lifted her head enough to see his face. A smile tugged at her lips as she saw the trace of tears in his eyes that she knew came only from joy. "You Light sorts are always crying."

"It's not our fault that you Dark types make us emotional. Wouldn't do you or Evan any harm to cry now and then, you know." He tugged her up for another kiss and tasted her sigh of happiness as it breathed into his lips. He shifted and rolled over to tumble her onto the bed beside him. "Next time?" he asked huskily. "I don't think we're done yet."

"Not yet," she agreed. Against his lips as she drew him close anew, she whispered, "Not ever."

Some hours later, after the sun had set, and Delphinium had finally begun to appear on the horizon, he thought to ask, "What do you want for a wedding band?"

The covers had been haphazardly tugged over them both, and their empty dinner tray sat on the table. She had been lying in his arms, no desire inside her to be anywhere else even though she could feel her destined enemy finally beginning his approach. Not even an hour remained. "Hmm. We never did get around to discussing that."

"You kept putting it off, which I understood once you finally told me everything. But because I know there will be another time for us, we may as well discuss it now. We exchanged rings of common stone borne of our worlds as an engaged couple, and so now we need wedding bands for our wrists, made of whatever we choose for the other to find. I'm thinking amber for me."

Only Protea's Nature-rich world had trees that produced sap that could harden into the rare gemstone. All worlds had such an item. For Delphinium, it was opal. Only the Illusory word could produce opals from the dew drops of its flowers. The crown jewels of all lineages possessed the coveted stones belonging to their world.

Shanae already wore a ring of common stone from Delphinium, and Robert wore one of common stone from Protea; common meant the type of stone was standard across all worlds, but this piece had specifically oriented on their home world. Thinking of balance, she nodded a bit firmly at her husband. If they had common, they as well have the uncommon found nowhere else but the world of the one they loved. "Then I want opal." She smiled as his fingers played with her hair. In the course of the few hours from when they had become lovers to that moment, it had grown significantly. It now touched the floor where before it had only reached her knees.

"Definitely must be an Apex thing," he decided as he twirled a lock between his fingers. "And it feels . . . stronger, if that makes sense. I think perhaps it truly is that I and Evan stabilize you and Sayena. You are ever more Dark, and she is ever more Light, if we are there to make you so."

"I don't mind, really. I rather like the long hair. And at least *my* hair is fine and straight." She winced wryly. "You and Sayena do not have my envy as much as my sympathy." She reached up to ruffle his thick hair. "Much as I like to play with it, I don't want to own it." She reluctantly sat up and took a breath. Their time, in that life, had reached its end. "Promise me something?"

He watched her slide from the bed and begin gathering her

clothes, and he reluctantly did the same. He could also feel the end drawing near, but, like her, he didn't feel fear for it. Someday, no matter how far in the future, they would be together again. "What, Tash?"

The nickname tightened her heart with emotion. It was his secret name for her. Their secret words, whispered in a darkened bedroom where only love could enter. "When we find each other again, you won't let me get away with pretending I don't love you. If somehow I am too blind, give me the light to see." She smiled as she slipped her shoes on her feet. "You're good at that, you know." She watched as he finished dressing as well and then went into his arms and held onto him tightly.

He held her just as tightly and let out a ragged breath. How had she been able to stand this foreknowledge? How had she been able to continue to smile and laugh? She was stronger than even he had known, and it made him love her all the more. "It's a promise."

They headed through the silent castle to the gardens and then to the fields beyond. The encroaching army approached as a force of the condemned, and moving at the front was a figure that had literally haunted Shanae's dreams. Nemesis.

He resembled little more than a writhing mass of . . . something. Some might have called him shadows, but he truly bore no resemblance to the real shadows born where Light and Dark overlapped. He could not be called darkness. He simply . . . was. An ominous figure who loomed over the nighttime and turned natural nightmares into something to be feared and loathed. Who fed on the worst of emotions inside all souls. Evil itself.

Shanae looked at the Mask in her hand and then calmly lifted it to put it on. Black-pink power swept down her body to form armor her planet had never before needed to form. It as strongly resembled her world's flower as her Ruler gown did. She took a long breath to evaluate how she felt for she had never worn it before. "It feels . . . comfortable. Inside and out. I don't feel it. No weight. Now I understand why Arista always said I did not need to train to wear my armor in battle. It conforms to me, not the other way around." She held out a hand, and Dark power swirled down her arm to form into a powerful claymore. A bit of amber in the hilt held a protea blossom. The black blade did not resemble the sword she had always before used for this had been solely born of her Apex arcanery. "So be it," she said softly.

On Delphinium, Sayena and Evan had also spent the entire day together. Sayena barely noticed the crown on her head; she had carried the weight inside all of her life. She stood on the balcony of her room and watched as Protea became bigger on the horizon. "Mother and Aunt Genevieve were crowned as High Queen in a ceremony," she murmured, mostly to herself. "Why did it fall this way for Shanae and me?"

Evan sat on the swing of the balcony and lightly moved it back and forth as he watched his lover. When she was ready to be held, she would come to him. She so rarely pulled back that he always let her go when she did. "Maybe something worse is happening than we think, 'ena. I always felt as if . . . there was something Shanae did not tell us. Perhaps our worlds knew that it needed to crown the High Queens now lest it never happen at all."

Sayena's fingers tightened on her arms and then she went to Evan and curled up on his lap to burrow close. Tears slid down her cheeks. "She would never tell me!" she whispered fiercely. She hiccupped back a sob. "I kept asking her, kept begging her to tell me, to let me share the burden. She never did!"

"Well, when the dust settles, we'll make her tell us everything she kept inside."

Her head suddenly jerked up. "It comes." She shoved out of his arms and grabbed her Mask off the table as she ran toward the doors. Her lover kept pace as she scrambled through the castle as fast as she could, and he caught her each time her own feet tried to trip her. She had always called it a part of his special magic that he could know even before she did when her clumsiness would rear its head.

They stopped just beyond the castle grounds to watch as the army approached. The figure at the front had been a menacing presence looming in Sayena's life since her birth. Famine.

She bore no resemblance to any living being, carried nothing in her appearance to make her tolerable to look upon. Disease ate away her flesh to reveal bone beneath, and putrid color clung to the nettles that made her hair. She left poisonous slime in the wake of her feet, as if it simply could not be contained within her skin.

Sayena looked at her Mask, and her fingers trembled. Yet, she did not hesitate as she put it on. White-gold swept over her and at last produced the armor her lineage had never before made. It as strongly matched her planet's flower as her Ruler gown did, and felt just as comfortable. It had, perhaps, a bit more actual metal armoring than most, but that could be a result of her lesser physical gifts. It usually fell that way.

She held out her hands, and Light swept down her arms to form into a long white magical rod topped with an opal holding a delphinium blossom in the center. If she felt any oddity, at all, it lay in her hair suddenly being braided where it had been loose. She often wore a braid for she liked the complicated plaits, but this braid had been made purely for keeping her hair back and therefore tightly confined even her curly hair. All Defenders who had long enough hair found that hair automatically entering into the bound form as soon as they donned their Mask. Thinking it, she looked at Evan. "Our destinies bind all of us, not just Shanae. I wonder if she is the only one who ever really knew."

Nemesis moved forward of his army and crept steadily closer to Shanae. She held her ground, and even held an arm in front of Robert to keep him back when he would have moved to her side. Pink sunlight rippled over her body as if her Nature power had just kissed her skin. Black darkness flowed in its wake. The combination was promise and warning alike.

"So. We meet at last," Nemesis told her, his guttural voice barely able to pierce the air. Hate and greed churned through his shell as he stared at the High Queen before him. Even he could feel déjà vu for it felt like confronting Shanta anew, but . . . different. His obsession with the first Cultivator of Protea paled now before his obsession with this one. She represented everything he wanted: the Dark power to bolster his own, and the Nature power that kept him from claiming the day. "You are not strong enough to destroy me!"

Shanae did not deny the charge. He had been gorged and bloated on the chaotic emotions of those without hope, and because of it, she simply could not awaken into her true form as an Apex and release the Whisper of Hope inside her soul with enough force to destroy him—yet. "In that," she said softly, "we agree." She looked to the sky, and she could see Delphinium in its full force. She could see the palace, and she thought she might just be able to see Sayena, too.

Somehow Sayena kept her trembling legs from showing as Famine approached. She wanted to run, yet did not want to run because running would doom too many people. Her hands tightened on her rod as she watched her destined enemy move in. Evan started to step forward, and she immediately swung her rod around to block him.

Famine's eyes burned with decrepit flames as she stared at Sayena. "So you're the legendary Apex of Light that is supposed to defeat me," she mocked. "What hope is there left for you to find, Your Majesty? I've eaten all the hope these pitiful lives have to offer."

Sayena knew it was no empty boast, and fear bubbled. If she could not defeat Famine, then what would that do to her world, and the galaxy? To the *universe*, for Famine would not stop there. She would only spread out and consume the rest. Sayena looked to where Protea hung in the sky in its fullest form. Somehow she just felt as if she could see Shanae standing before her castle, too. *Shanae. Lead me. What do I need to do to win?*

We can't win, Sayena. Not here. Not yet. She opened her mind and let her voice touch both Robert and Evan as well. They deserved to know. *We can only buy time. We must ensure a long enough time for people to forget them. To believe, perhaps, that we have won. To let them be nothing but a legend to scare children. To allow hope to blossom anew, to give us the strength we need.*

Delphinium is so terribly poisoned, Shanae! I have sent all who lived upon its surface to Protea. My world cannot support life any more than the frozen worlds can. It needs to be frozen, too, to heal. I can't do this alone. I don't think Robert and I together could, even with burning out our Seeds.

No, but you and Evan together could. If you and Evan burn your Seeds together, you will be able to banish and seal Famine, and freeze Delphinium until it can recover. If Robert and I burn our Seeds together, we will be able to banish and seal Nemesis, and give Protea's Core the strength it will need to bear up until its Ruler Cultivators can be reborn. Only the combination of our opposing elements will do such a thing.

A long silence met her, and then, softly, Sayena said, *I believe anything you tell me. Evan agrees. We will do what we must here, and someday we will all be together again. I love you, Shanae. I'm not sure I told you enough.*

Somehow Shanae smiled. *You told me every day of our lives, you silly girl.*

Well, you are of the Dark. You sorts need to be told those things. We Light sorts just always know.

Robert slipped his hand into Shanae's free one, and she looked up at him for a moment. She released her claymore from her other hand and reached up to touch her Flower Mark hidden by her armor. He mimicked her gesture, and their Seeds appeared under their fingers. A black glow radiated around Shanae's hand that could be seen from the other world, and she could see the white glow of Sayena.

Without guilt or hesitation, the four Ruler Cultivators tore open their Seeds and burned the raw potential within. Shockwaves of power ripped across the surface of both worlds that rattled buildings and knocked anyone standing off their feet. Where it was night, it suddenly lit like the day, and where it was day, it suddenly went as dark as the night.

Nemesis and Famine saw the danger too late to escape. They fought and they screamed and they railed against the unfairness, but they could not stop the power from flinging them away from the physical plane. They entered into the Ephemeral Plane, and then they descended below it, down to the deepest and most bitter reaches reserved only for the truly terrible of existences. There they would stay until, inevitably, they found the strength to break free anew.

The Masks fell off Shanae and Sayena and shattered on the ground, and their armor disappeared again. They and their lovers alike fell to the ground behind them. Robert and Evan were already gone, their bodies dissolving into shimmers of color. The two Apexes looked with blurry eyes at the empty lands before them and then let go of their last breath. They, too, dissolved into shimmers of color that flowed up into the skies and then beyond to the Realm of the Gods.

Only their crowns remained behind as a symbol of what had been lost, and what would someday again be reclaimed once more.

(Realm of the Gods)

Orion went looking for his wife, and he found her and Enaya sitting together under a tree. The First Defenders had gathered around them in comfort and solidarity. Lycander stood nearby as an additional support. Orion raked a hand through his hair tiredly and then just outright said it. "It's done."

Shanta's hands clenched together. "As you knew it would be done?"

"As much as I could know, yes. They made a few choices I did not wholly anticipate, but I assume my mother did."

"Did Claret sacrifice herself for her princess—I mean queen?" Tarveel asked him quietly. "It shocked all of us when we saw she had not been forced to retreat. But then, I suppose Shanae is different in many ways. I hope we figure that significance out soon enough."

"She actually intended to," Orion admitted readily, "but Pallas retreated her to the Hall of Records against her will at the last moment."

"He can do that?" Eriline, the First Defender of Gladiolus asked curiously.

"He can. Surprised me as well, I admit. He says he requested the skill from our grandmother as soon as Shanae was born and he saw how much Claret loved her. I can hardly blame him, nor be surprised the request was granted." He took a long breath. "Claret is recovering. Slowly, but still recovering. I went to see her, to see how she would possibly endure millennia without Sabin, but . . . I discovered a curious presence."

"Who?"

"Time and Love. Grandmother has blunted Claret's memories and removed aspects of Sabin's presence. Love blunted the wounds of

pg. 178

his absence and has effectively returned Claret to a state not far from what she had been in before meeting him."

Enaya's mouth opened and then closed. "Then Claret won't have to suffer until his rebirth?" She let out a breath of relief and leaned her head on Shanta's shoulder as much to give as receive comfort. "That is something, then."

"Is there anything else?" Shanta asked softly. "I need something to hold onto, Orion. I can't bear to look at Protea!"

Her husband walked closer and held his list of names out where they could all see it. "Here is the promise of the future you need, my love."

Many familiar names had been crossed out through the list, but that was not the significance. The significance lay in what names were *not* lined out on the list: the names of the other nine Dual Cultivators, Robert, Evan, the eight Commanders, and Diego had not been marked as complete. Their time had not ended. Their souls had arrived, but they had been rejected.

"How long?" Lycander asked.

"That I cannot say," his brother-in-law sighed. "The Apexes minimized the damage to their Seeds by joining with their lovers, but that does not change the fact that they all burned themselves out. Well, Robert and Evan burned out. Shanae and Sayena, by nature of their infinite power, cannot actually burn out. It is more accurate to say they tore their Seeds into pieces to unleash the full force of their power as unawakened Apexes."

"If they had been awakened . . .?" Enaya trailed off.

He nodded. "The outcome would have been *very* different. However, given the state of the universe, their awakening now was simply an impossibility. Not enough hope for them to utilize. They could not awaken, therefore they could not destroy their destined enemy, therefore . . . they did what they had to in order to ensure the future." His Sight stirred, and he gazed into that very future in a way only he could see. "It will take millennia," he murmured. "At least five. That will be enough for their Seeds to recover to where they can be reborn, and it will be more than enough for people to, as Shanae so accurately put it, believe that they won. Nemesis and Famine will have nothing to feed on when they return, and what little they will muster before the Apexes awaken and destroy them will not be enough."

"What will happen to Protea in the meanwhile?" Tarveel asked of him and Shanta alike. She squeezed her twin soul's hands tighter in support. "The other worlds are frozen; they will breathe without living until their Rulers return. Protea both breathes and lives still. What will become of a world not frozen who does not have a Ruler?"

Shanta got to her feet and walked a few steps away with her arms crossed tightly around her body. "Under normal circumstances, terrible things would happen. Slowly, bitterly, painfully, Protea would become just like the other worlds. Barely breathing. Not living. Everything decaying and dying. Eventually it would completely collapse into itself and cease to exist entirely. But . . . Shanae took the effort to plan for such a thing, to prevent it from happening. She bolstered the Core of Protea by using Robert's Illusion magic to . . . mimic, I suppose is the word, her own power of Nature and create a false Seed that should be just enough to help Protea endure. It will fade when either she or Evan are reborn and bring back a Ruler to the land." She drew a long breath. "As to the general state of Protea, I just do not know. I suppose we will learn that as time passes." She turned around and at last found a smile. "Are Genevieve and Hannah reunited with the others?"

"They are." Orion smiled in return and moved to tug her into his arms. "But they are not strong enough to take yours and Enaya's places, either. They can take their mothers' places as the Goddesses assigned specifically to Protea and Delphinium, but you two will just have to stay in charge of the entire Realm for a while longer until Shanae and Sayena finally come to the Realm of the Gods to stay."

"Lucky us," Enaya grumbled.

S.J. Garrett

The Redemption Wars

Time passed. Years became decades that became centuries that became millenniums. In the days following the end of the Royal War—as most called it—Protea struggled hard to endure. It finally broke into smaller countries with nominated interim leaders who would govern over the world jointly until the day when the kingdoms could be reborn. That they would, they all knew. The brave souls who had approached the ruined Protea Kingdom palace had found the High Queen's abandoned crown hovering in the center of the grand throne room, protected by a column of darkness. The message seemed clear: the queen would return.

Losing the Ruler Cultivator had even further reaching effects for the magic that came with them had evaporated. Portalpads ceased all functionality, and so did any other device that ran on the magic pulled from the planet through its Ruler. Society did not collapse, but it certainly tripped flat and had to find new ways to recover and to do through other means what had once been done with magic.

Lucky for one and all, Protea had always been abundant with natural resources from its Flower Element of Nature. The sun itself could be harnessed as power, and so could water. Once a few enterprising souls discovered that lightning could be created in controlled ways, electricity became a thing and slowly began to improve lives to at least where they had been before the Royal War—but without space travel.

Traveling through space had too heavily relied on magic to be recovered easily, if ever. Worlds beyond Blossom Field could finally enter again, but they could not do anything to help for they also relied heavily on magic. All alliances remained as status quo, and people from beyond the galaxy did still visit, but the numbers dropped dramatically for few ships had the strength to return home again without a magical boost from Protea. Within a thousand years, the visits stopped entirely, and alliances entered into suspension until Ruler Cultivators returned once more.

As more millenniums began to pass, technology began to progress further. Science flourished. Lives changed significantly, but with such slowness that it sometimes took a few generations before people truly noticed the changes. By the time the sixth millennium of the Royal Era began, life had settled into a rhythm wholly different from the one of the first millennium, yet one that held peace.

No one at all believed any longer that Nemesis or Famine could ever return; some even doubted they had ever existed! Even the Cultivators themselves and the former kingdoms became little more than a myth or legend. Only the interim leaders of the world held onto the knowledge of exactly what had happened, and they passed from generation to generation the needed facts of what had once been and what would once be again. When the Ruler Cultivators of the worlds returned, and the worlds awoke from their frozen sleep, the leaders would willingly give control back to the ones it rightfully belonged to, and the descendants of those who had fled the other worlds would finally get to go home.

In December of Royal Era 5079, Protea finally took a real breath again, and the false Seed disappeared as magic welled. The magic was picked up by sensors as a quake of sorts, and while no one really knew *why* it had happened, the leaders figured it out quickly: a Ruler Cultivator had been born anew. Two weeks shy of a year later, a second quake occurred, but it came much more powerfully than the first. The other Ruler Cultivator of Protea had been born anew as well. A quiet search was made, yet no one ever found these two children of the planet. And so it happened that life continued on like normal, as if literally life-changing events had not been set into motion again.

Almost five years passed from the day of the second quake without much to show for it other than the perhaps not-unexpected sudden overabundance of Nature power that particularly effused the city of Lux on the largest landmass of Protea that had once held the capitol of the world. It had been known enough for its quantity of parks, but one park in particular really took off. The section of the garden where the namesake protea blossoms grew went a little crazy, and they took over most every surface. Gardeners just worked around them, and visitors were all but begged to cut some and take them home.

Little Siobhan Toulume loved the protea flowers almost as much as she loved delphinium ones. She approached her fifth birthday very soon, and so had asked her mother to take her and her only slightly elder brother to the park to see the flowers. There happened to be a delphinium section butted right up against the protea one, which made Siobhan very happy. It made her brother happy, too, and their own presence made others happy as well—they looked a bit like a white delphinium personally!

Both brother and sister had fluffy, curly, white hair matched to pale gold eyes. Siobhan had a bit of plumpness to her body that her brother mostly shared; his higher activity levels meant he had a bit more streamlined look. The two could easily be mistaken for twins despite Rocky being rather taller than his sister; she had a petite height contrasted to his taller than average one. There was, in fact, a whole month of the year where they were the same age, so even their mother would often just call them twins and skip the explanations. She and her late husband had never figured it out either.

Siobhan saw Rocky and their mother gathering flowers in a basket and so wandered off on her own toward the protea section. She knew that as long as she did not leave the park, she could wander most anywhere. She found what she wanted and started gathering up an armful of the pretty black protea flowers into a bouquet. At the sound of a low growl, her eyes slowly widened and she hastily swung around.

A large dog—larger than herself—had planted himself in the path and watched her menacingly. His low growls vibrated on the air. Siobhan's eyes began to well with tears as she clutched her flowers and pressed back against the bush. She could not find her voice to yell for help, and while she knew her brother just always knew if she needed help, she felt afraid for him to come running and get hurt.

Her eyes slammed shut as the dog started to lunge, but when she heard a surprising whine instead of a growl, she cautiously opened her eyes again. They then widened even further as she realized another girl almost her brother's height had planted herself in the path between dog and victim. Siobhan could only stare. The other girl looked like the very protea blossoms she held! Long, fine black hair with a glossy sheen, and the look she sent over her shoulder came from pretty pink eyes. "Uhm." It was all she could manage.

The other girl nodded at her firmly. "It's okay." She walked fearlessly to the dog who whined again and then sniffed at her. His ears came up and his tail thumped happily on the ground as she patted his head. All hints of danger evaporated. "See?" the girl said. She turned a smile on Siobhan as bright as the sun. "He's okay. He just got scared, too. Come here."

Siobhan felt a surge of bravery as if this girl had just given it to her. "Okay." She walked over to the dog and got sniffed in turn. He then licked her face, and she giggled. "He's nice!" She hugged the dog with her free arm. "You're a good puppy. I'm not mad." He scampered off merrily, and she turned to her new friend. After a moment, she held out the bouquet. "I'm Siobhan!"

Shana Chivanti looked at the smaller girl and then the bouquet, and then smiled. "Shana." She took the bouquet happily. She loved protea flowers best, though she loved *all* plants and flowers and animals almost equally. Delphiniums did sort of run a close second, so she liked how this other girl looked. She thought they might be the same age, but couldn't be sure because the girl looked very small. "I'm almost five."

Siobhan brightened. "I'm almost five!" She threw her arms around Shana's neck in a happy hug that made her new friend look at her a bit wide-eyed. "Oh. No hug?"

Shana shook her head. "I don't mind." She just wasn't quite used to spontaneous emotion from strangers, even though, strangely, this girl really did not feel like a stranger at all. She felt a little like a sister. She would know; she had an only slightly elder brother to judge by.

Speaking of. The bushes rustled and a boy who looked enough

like her to be a twin, if shorter, came hurrying onto the scene. He was not alone. Rocky came scooting around the bushes from the other direction, and both boys skidded to a stop in sheer relief at seeing their sisters just fine.

"Rocky!" Siobhan ran to her brother and held his hand. "That's Shana! A dog scared me, and she made it a friend!"

Edgar Chivanti sighed as he took Shana's hand. "Again?"

She smiled at him. "All doggies are puppies to me. He was just scared." She hugged his arm and then looked at the boy beside Siobhan. He looked very like his sister, yet . . . just seemed more beautiful to her. She felt oddly happy just being around him. Like Siobhan, he did not feel *new*. She glanced at Edgar's face to see him looking at Siobhan much the same way, and decided maybe it was just because of the flowers they liked.

For their own part, Siobhan had been utterly enchanted by Edgar, as much as if not more than she had with Shana. Rocky liked Edgar enough, to be sure, but his eyes could not quite move from the tall girl beside him. She looked . . . a little haunted, maybe. Like something in her eyes hurt. He wanted to hug her, and after a brief thought, he walked over and did so.

Shana's eyes went slowly wide. Like brother, like sister, but Rocky's hug made her feel . . . much safer. Even more than if her mom or dad or brother hugged her. "Hi?"

He let go and grinned at her. "Hi. You needed a hug." He then hugged Edgar, who looked just as surprised. "You too."

The two Chivanti siblings looked at one another and then started laughing. Siobhan giggled in turn and then, not to be left out, she hurried over to hug Edgar as well. He looked as flummoxed as his sister for a moment and then hugged her back.

By the time Octavia Toulume found the four, they had sat down on the ground near the blossoms and were talking animatedly. Siobhan finished making a wreath of protea blossoms and plopped it on top of Shana's head; Edgar already wore one. Octavia could only sigh. Leave it to her kids to make new friends *anywhere*. "Found you!"

Siobhan and Rocky alike brightened and scrambled up to run

over and hug her. Shana and Edgar studied her curiously and then smiled because she reminded them of their mom, except she looked like her kids, and Shana and Edgar looked like their father. "Hi," Edgar said. "I'm Edgar. My sister is Shana."

Octavia knelt down to be closer to their height. "Hello to you both!" she said warmly. She fought an urge to pick them up and snuggle, if only because they had just met. "I'm Octavia. Where are your parents, young ones?" She almost said 'little ones' but with Shana almost the same height as her own very tall son, she refrained.

"Not far," Shana promised her. She got to her feet and then tugged Edgar up as those same parents started calling their names. She hesitated, as did her brother, as both looked at Rocky and Siobhan. The other two already had tears in their eyes at saying goodbye. Finally, both dark haired siblings ran off to find their parents.

As the first tears rolled down Siobhan's face, Octavia wiped at them. "Baby. What's wrong?"

"I don't wanna say goodbye," Siobhan sniffled. "I wanna see them again!"

Rocky looked just as miserable, so Octavia scooped up Siobhan before taking his hand to go see if she could find the other family. Unfortunately, she found nothing. They had moved pretty quickly. With both of her children now crying, she felt a little upset herself. "I'll keep looking," she promised. "There was something oddly familiar about them, actually, so maybe I know their parents already."

A month ticked by, however, without anything coming of her search. Siobhan had her fifth birthday, and very clearly did not enjoy it as much as she might have had her two new friends been in attendance. She and Rocky tried very hard not to pester their mother, and asked all they met about 'the boy and girl with protea eyes', yet nothing worked.

Only a few days after Siobhan's birthday, she and Rocky were playing in the backyard of their house when Siobhan felt . . . *something* surge inside her body. Something hot and wonderful and yet odd but not foreign. She tripped over her own feet and landed smack on the ground. Rocky tripped over his own feet in his haste to get to her side, but when he finally knelt beside her, she looked fine. "Siobhan?"

She slowly held up her hands and whorls of gradated white-gold color began to move down her arms to her palms where they coalesced into the form of a white mask. It looked somehow familiar to both children, and it resembled their beloved white delphinium flower as well. As Rocky reached out to touch it, something stirred inside both their minds. Something that felt like memories. Flashes and snippets of sound and color and emotion flew past their eyes. Another world. Another time. A kingdom. And amid all of it, others around them. Ten others, but two stood out most: two other royal children . . . with protea eyes.

"What is it?" Siobhan whispered.

"I don't know," Rocky whispered back.

Another month ticked by, and Shana likewise had her fifth birthday. Luckily for the introverted child, her parents abided by her wishes and kept the party extremely low-key and small. Shana and Edgar badly wanted to have Siobhan and Rocky there, but their father had been unable to figure out who the two children were or where they lived. Even having their mother's name did not help, since neither Shana nor Edgar seemed to be able to say it right, and each time they tried, it came out different.

A week went by before Shana found herself playing in the large gardens of her family's home. They lived in the very large manor in the mountains just outside of Lux, and her father traveled to and from his company nearly every day. Sometimes the two siblings could go in with him, other times they stayed home. Because of Shana's extremely advanced intelligence, she and her brother got to have tutoring at home rather than go to normal school. She had a capacity to learn and remember that baffled more than one person, which lent itself to why people were so surprised she could not remember the name of that mysterious mother and children she had met. It felt strangely deliberate somehow.

As she sat on a bench to watch fauna wander by—they could not be kept out of the gardens or away from either child, so no one even tried—she felt a stirring inside her body. A surge of something that felt familiar yet different, but not at all foreign. Even as she noticed it, her brother came running up to her side. He had just felt *something* from her. She slowly lifted her hands and a gradated black-pink color swirled down her arms to form into a mask. It felt, and looked, familiar, and it resembled their favorite black protea flower.

Something flashed through their minds equally. Snippets and sounds and color, memories of a distant time. A kingdom. Others around them, protecting them. Two in particular stood out: two children with delphinium eyes. Shana looked at Edgar, and him at her, and they both frowned. They did not understand, and they had no way of finding the other two to ask if they did.

"Shana! Edgar!" came their mother's voice. "Time to go with your dad to town!"

Shana had no idea what to do with the mask, but to her surprise, it seemed to disappear *somewhere*. She shook it off and ran with Edgar through the gardens and then the manor to the front outside. Their father was already in the electric carriage—EC or carriage for short—and their mother waited to help get them fastened in.

Electric carriages ran on solar or electrical power and were vehicular devices people could ride to travel long distances. Models came in single, double, or up to five-person versions. They were normally very safe—as much as anything a few thousand pounds moving at top speeds could be—but accidents still happened from either sheer foolishness or just terrible timing. For that reason, they actually had their own lanes separate of cycles or pedestrians. Some streets separated them by wide painted lines, and others by outright fences or barriers. Housing spaces, by nature of the laws requiring slow speeds, tended to be more likely to just paint out lines.

Their father happened to be one of the very good drivers, and both kids felt comfortable riding in the backseat. Shana watched out the windows as trees and the like zipped by. It felt a bit like flying, which she had always wanted to do.

For all of time thereafter, she would legitimately be able to say she did not remember what happened next. Something made a horrific screeching noise, and she heard her mother scream. Edgar cried out.

Metal crunched, and suddenly she just didn't see anything at all. But things hurt. She could feel them hurting even in her unconsciousness. She stirred only enough to hear loud whistles and people yelling, and maybe the sound of fire, and she felt unfamiliar arms carrying her. She could hear Edgar calling her name. She tried to open her eyes but just could not.

Something jostled her, and everything hurt fresh with blinding pain. She instantly went under anew. There would be no relief in her sleep, however. There never was. Always under the surface lurked the nightmares that plagued her short life. Why could she never escape them? And would whatever had just happened become a new one? She didn't know.

The paramedics on the scene of the horrific accident found very fast that Edgar could not be separated from his sister. Somehow he had escaped with little more than a minor concussion and a fractured forearm, but Shana had been hurt *far* worse. Edgar could not be pried from her side, so finally the paramedics put them onto the same medical carriage together. They even put them on the adult-sized stretcher so he could lay next to her. She looked a bit horrific herself, covered from head to toe in bloody bandages, and her arm and leg alike splinted. No one had told Edgar that their parents hadn't survived; his focus had so narrowed to just his sister that they doubted he would notice. Perhaps, in a way, that could be a blessing. They could delay the inevitable terrible news.

At the hospital, the two were given the same room. Shana had not actually woken, but because her vital signs were as stable as could be expected, none of the nurses or doctors tried to bring her around. Edgar had his own bed, but almost as soon as the temporary nurse left the room, he crawled out of it and instead into the bed with his sister. He hugged her tight with his good arm. Her pain seemed to be stabbing inside his own body and he couldn't bear it. Desperate longing to make it all better rose hotly inside him, and suddenly he hurt a *lot* more—but she didn't. The pain he felt became more his own and less from her. Her breathing even sounded better. He tightened his grip briefly and then closed his eyes. She couldn't leave him. Never

ever. They needed each other, and now more than ever. They had no one else left.

Octavia worked as a pediatric nurse, and served as an on-call emergency one with it. She would get called in to be assigned to particular children in need of personalized and direct care. When she got the call that an EC accident had killed two parents and both children had been badly hurt—especially the daughter—she immediately threw down everything she had been doing, dropped Siobhan and Rocky at their babysitter, and rushed to the hospital. She was still fastening on her badge as she walked through the doors of the pediatric intensive care. "Tell me everything," she said briskly as she took the offered clipboard.

The male nurse nodded swiftly. "Two kids. Both five, but not twins. The boy turns six in a week. Names are Shana and Edgar Chivanti."

Her head came up quickly. "Chivanti?"

He nodded again. "Yeah. Chivanti Corporation is about to go into a nosedive unless the board of trustees grabs hold fast and efficiently. Randall Chivanti and his wife were in that car, and they died on scene. The kids are theirs."

Sudden dots began to connect for Octavia. A brother and sister of the right age, named Edgar and Shana, who had looked familiar to her. Of course they had; few didn't know the Chivanti Corporation since they all but ran not just Lux but most of the landmass. Randall himself had black hair and pink eyes, which must have been what had stuck in her mind. "What room?"

"P-9."

She hurried down the hall a bit faster than she might have normally, and when she peeked into the room, tears welled in her eyes. Sure enough, two familiar children awaited her inside, though both looked in *far* worse shape than she remembered. Edgar seemed intact enough, but Shana looked particularly miserable. She always hated seeing children hurt, which was why she had gone into her field of work, but these two . . . they got to her as much as her own did.

Edgar's eyes opened at hearing the door, and when he looked at her a bit defiantly, she walked further into the lamplight. "Hello, Edgar," she said softly. "Remember me? I'm Octavia Toulume, Siobhan and Rocky's mother. I'm your nurse now. You can stay by Shana as long as you're not hurting yourself, okay?"

The sheer relief he felt at seeing a familiar, and welcome, face made tears briefly sting his eyes that he blinked away. "She hurts," he whispered. "Can you make it better?"

"Well, I can do my best." She walked over and moved him to the other bed briefly so she could check on Shana. As she pressed a hand to the girl's forehead, groggy pink eyes opened. She smiled. "Hi there, sweetheart. Remember me?" She got a little nod in response, and her heart ached as Shana turned her face into her hand. "I'm going to take care of you and Edgar now. Everything will be okay."

She administered medicine as needed, read stories, and held both when she finally had to deliver the news about their parents. They did not cry as much as she had expected, but it had not taken long to realize both had as much a propensity to keep that inside as her own two had to just be open.

She got home after the first day and found Siobhan and Rocky waiting for her. They always rushed to hug her after she got home from an emergency call, because they knew she needed it. She did not always get to save all of the children she cared about. "Are they okay?" Siobhan whispered against her mother's neck.

"Well, I think they will be. But . . . would you two like to see them?" She had made the decision on the way home to ask. Shana and Edgar felt so damn *alone*, and they had literally been left alone. No other family members could be found. Yet they knew Siobhan and Rocky, and if they felt anything like her children did, they would be happy at the reunion.

"Can we?" Rocky asked.

"Of course. It's not against the rules. And it might be good for Siobhan to visit the hospital as something other than a patient." A terribly sad but true statement as her little girl had a horrific immune system and seemed to catch literally every passing disease. She had spent almost as much time in the hospital as she had anywhere else, which had also lent itself toward Octavia's job choice. Oddly, Rocky himself literally never got sick *ever*, so perhaps he had inherited his sister's share. Either way, the hospital would not be unfamiliar territory to them, though the circumstances would. She took one of their hands in each of hers. "Siobhan . . . Rocky . . . the two children . . . it's Shana and Edgar."

Tears immediately welled in both sets of gold eyes, and then Siobhan fiercely and adamantly shook them off. "Take us tomorrow!" she demanded. "We'll help! They need us! Shana needs me to save her, 'cause she saved me! I wanna see Edgar!"

Rocky nodded just as fiercely. "We can help them! We make them happy, too! We can be their family! They'll be okay, because we'll be there to make sure!"

Octavia gathered them both close on a smile. "My little eternal optimists. If willpower alone can make things happen, they'll both be healed in no time."

She took them the very next day, and she knew her instincts had been spot on, as the moment Shana and Edgar saw the two in the doorway, they visibly brightened. "I brought someone special to see you," she said warmly.

Siobhan dashed across the room and climbed up onto the bed beside Shana. Tears welled and spilled down her face as she looked at the myriad of bruises and bandages covering the other girl as well as the sling on her broken left arm, and the cast on her broken left leg. Gently, carefully, she hugged Shana around the neck. "Does it hurt?" she asked softly.

Shana shook her head a bit. "Not a lot."

"You're lying." Edgar frowned as he said it from where he sat in his own bed. Rocky had climbed up to sit beside him. Unlike his sister, Edgar had already begun to heal quickly. His broken forearm had just a splint rather than a cast. "You hurt. I can feel it."

Octavia found no surprise in that, actually. Rocky and Siobhan often shared their pain between them as well. She chalked it up to the oddity of them being so close and all but literal twins. "Well," she said, looking at the charts," she can have more medicine now. I'll get it."

"No, it doesn't hurt that much anymore," Shana reiterated. She smiled, almost hesitantly. "It doesn't hurt when Siobhan is hugging me. I think she's magic."

Siobhan nodded firmly. "Then I'll keep hugging you!" She looked at Octavia fretfully. "Can we stay with them?"

"Please?" Rocky added. He itched to hug Shana as well, but instead held onto Edgar's hand because Shana, clearly, needed Siobhan more right then. Edgar didn't look nearly as bad, and didn't feel as bad either. He and Siobhan could just take turns hugging and cuddling the other two, making sure both would get better faster. As he watched Shana, however, he could just feel as if he couldn't breathe deep enough. It looked a bit like maybe she couldn't either, so he took a long breath that steadied him anew. Curiously . . . Shana almost immediately started doing the same.

Octavia looked at Shana, at Rocky, and then back again. She then looked at one of the few visible marks on Shana, and she could actually see it seeming to fade before her eyes. Magic? Maybe it was, though magic had been lost for millennia. As a nurse and a born caregiver, she didn't really mind how it happened. Just that it did. "Alright," she said firmly. "You can stay. I'll be on call almost all day anyway, in case Shana or Edgar need me."

It took less than a day for the doctors and other nurses who would stop by to check on the children to realize that both Siobhan and Rocky alike had a *powerful* impact on Shana, and that trying to make either of them sleep in the cot brought in was a futile effort. They took turns snuggling up against either Chivanti sibling while they slept, always staying very close by. If Siobhan was the one doing the snuggling, Shana quickly and almost visibly healed faster. If Rocky was the one doing the snuggling instead, Shana's entire system stabilized and she didn't struggle to get air through her bruised lungs and ribs.

It took only two days for her to be in such good condition that she and Edgar moved out of intensive care into a normal room. Octavia couldn't bear to part with them, and they very badly didn't want anyone else caring for them, so she requested and received the assignment to continue serving as their nurse. As far as the hospital was concerned, the health and well-being of their patients mattered most. If the Toulume family as a whole could ensure these two children healed entirely and could move on with their lives, anything was on the table.

Octavia, though, did start doing some other rounds since the more the two children healed, the less direct observation they needed. She instead set them up with games and a Visuality so they had entertainment on demand. Visualities were large devices that ran on electrical and solar power to get audio and visual signals from varying studios that produced episodic shows and full-length theatrical productions for entertainment. Over a hundred channels existed in the Lux area, not including the fifty that were world-wide, and at least one always had on something suitably fun for children.

A smaller device called a Personal Phone System, or PPS for short, worked almost the same way but allowed direct communication between people who had shared their personal codes. Octavia always had hers on hand for obvious reasons, and she found herself glad there was no limit on the number of calls she could make or receive since she shortly discovered she needed to make a *lot*.

She had fallen head over heels in love with Shana and Edgar, and she could not stand the idea of watching them go into the children's Care House. They would be well-provided for, obviously, but they would not get the same sort of love she could give. She had noticed very quickly that they *craved* love as deeply as they could give it, rather like her own kids, and she wanted to give them a new home together.

Unfortunately . . . as soon as she contacted the government to start the process, she encountered an unexpected blockage. The board of trustees from the Chivanti Corporation had put a request in as a sort of stop-order to any potential adoption of the Chivanti heirs, claiming that they would be better off in the Care House.

"What sort of bullshit is that?" Octavia muttered as she stared at her PPS. She had gone outside to the break area to take the call, and her shoulders slumped as she dropped her head onto her arms on the table in front of her. Tears burned her eyes. "What is *wrong* with them?" she whispered. "Why would they possibly think the Care House better than a loving home? Don't take it personally, they said. I'm a great parent, they said. But I'm not 'good enough'? How?!"

Someone sat down at the table across from her, and she looked up quickly. A somewhat taller than average woman had joined her, and her lavender eyes held warmth as they sparkled against her bronze skin. Pink hair the color of delicate statice blossoms fell over her shoulder in a loose braid. She wore relatively casual clothes, yet she exuded an air that felt nearly royal. She also looked very unfamiliar.

"I'm sorry, was I too loud?" Octavia asked hesitantly.

The woman shook her head. "Not at all. I came looking for you. My name is Clara Memoria. I caught wind of the events, Octavia, and I would like to help."

Octavia just sighed. "How can you possibly help, Clara? I'm up against some people who have a lot more money and a lot more power than I do. If I want to fight that stop-order, I need to prove that I am the best choice for Shana and Edgar. But I can't do that alone, and I just don't have the money to hire a legal advisor with the bravery to confront the Corporation!"

Clara smiled. "What would you say if I told you that I myself am a legal advisor, and that not only do I have more than enough courage, but also the skill and sheer stubbornness to make anything happen as I want it to."

"I'd say I probably can't afford you."

"No charge." She shook her head as she received a surprised look. "This is . . . personal to me, Octavia. Those children you love . . . I might love them more than you do. Let me help you help them. I want nothing more than to see them be happy."

The note Octavia heard in her voice was one she had honestly never heard before. A powerful chord of love so deep and true that perhaps nothing could ever remove it. Her lips trembled as she smiled. "Then I'll accept whatever help you can give." She hesitated, and then went with her instincts. "Clara . . . *is* Siobhan healing Shana?"

"Oh, to be sure. Love and hope make great healing forces."

Octavia had a feeling she had not actually gotten the real answer she had sought, yet she had gotten more than enough of one to appease her. "Would you like to see them?"

"I'd love that."

Oddly, Octavia did not at all feel surprised to see all four children, especially the girls, react to Clara as if they had been reunited with a long-lost friend. She also felt no surprise that Shana's introverted don't-touch-me-unless-I-say-so personality effectively evaporated and she wanted to be cuddled by Clara as much as, if not more, than Octavia. Her future mother felt no jealousy over such a thing, though. She could see they had a special bond, and she treasured it. Anything that could make her four children happy was fine by her.

Clara took over the fight against the stop-order and the board, and in less than a few days, she had removed the former and unexpectedly cowed the latter. They backed off so quickly and immediately that it felt almost suspect, but Octavia refused to dismiss her change of luck. Clara also stepped in to take care of anything else needed for the two Chivanti heirs, including handling the details of their parents' estate, getting the trust fund their parents had made for them active and operational, and putting together a hefty package of information that held all details of their father's will that would not be effective until both turned twenty-five.

In regards to that last item, she sat down for a lengthy conversation with the siblings that Octavia did not attend, and after it, both seemed to have a renewed energy and positive outlook. Unusual for the little pessimists, but not unwelcome. They took the package of information and had Octavia put it away in her home security box, and she did not ask any questions. If they did not want to tell her, she would not ask. She also made sure they knew that if they wanted to keep quiet on their connection to the Corporation, she would stand by that decision. That turned out to be their preference, so even Siobhan and Rocky did not get told the real facts. They just knew their new family members had money from their parents, and that was it.

One month after the accident, Octavia got to take Shana and Edgar home with her. Edgar's arm had entirely healed, and he looked no different than before the accident. Shana's arm had healed up entirely, and nearly all her wounds had gone away, but a few that had needed stitches still had some healing left to do, and she had to use crutches because her leg needed a cast for another month. She proved unexpectedly dexterous on them, and navigated fast and confidently. Watching her scoot up the steps, Octavia said dryly, "You and Edgar are as graceful as Siobhan and Rocky are clumsy! It's like you four are completely polar opposites, not just in appearance but in personality and physically too."

"That's why we're friends!" Siobhan said cheerfully. She knew better than to run up the stairs so moved slowly. She got to the top and tried to run up to meet Shana, but only tripped over her own feet. Edgar seemed to appear from out of nowhere, and he caught her safely. She couldn't help but happily hug him in turn. She did really love Shana lots and lots, but she really loved Edgar more. As much as she loved her brother, actually, but somehow . . . different. She did not mind that since she knew Rocky felt the same about Shana. They could figure it out eventually.

Octavia led the way down the hall toward the bedrooms. "Siobhan and Rocky have their own rooms, and the room I had been using as a study could be a bedroom. It's up to you four how you want to split things."

A look exchanged among the four kids. Siobhan really wanted to ask Shana to share her room, but felt shy about pushing for it when she knew Shana deserved to choose for herself. Likewise, Rocky felt the same about Edgar. Oddly, the two Toulumes might have been the extroverts, but they could be painfully shy sometimes. The two Chivantis were introverts without a shy bone in their body, though they *did* hesitate if they felt something too strongly.

Shana looked at Siobhan's face and then took her new sister's hand, nimbly balancing on just one crutch. "Can I stay with you?" she asked with a smile.

Edgar nodded at Rocky. "I'll stay with you, okay?"

Siobhan and Rocky visibly brightened. "Okay!" both said in almost the same voice. Siobhan then frowned at her mother. "But . . . Shana and Edgar need clothes." And it went without saying that Shana would assuredly *not* be able to share Siobhan's, nor would Edgar be able to share Rocky's.

"That's covered," Octavia promised. She grinned. "Most of their things will be delivered from their home very soon, and we can go shopping for anything else." She knelt down to everyone's height, and her heart ached as all four moved to hold onto her tightly. "Welcome home," she murmured as she kissed first Edgar and then Shana's foreheads. "Welcome home." She really owed Clara more than could be repaid, but the advisor had all but disappeared from the face of the world. Magic, she thought again. Maybe it really had come back to Protea after all.

Shana had fully healed and recovered from the ordeal within another month. She almost immediately began pestering her new mother to take training and classes in all manner of physical sports. Varying types of hand or foot combat, dance of different styles, and even weaponry. Octavia felt utterly flabbergasted by the requests but gave in and let Shana try out a few. She took to them instantly, with a born skill that rattled even her instructors. She would master just about anything within a year if given a chance. She *craved* learning, and like a sponge absorbed everything thrown at her.

Not to be left out, Edgar and Rocky immediately began demanding to take the same classes. That actually did not surprise Octavia since she had expected the two boys, on basis of personality, to want to keep up with Shana. Edgar proved nearly as naturally skilled as his sister, and while Rocky did not have the same natural skill, his sheer stubborn determination and hard work meant he kept pace anyway. Siobhan had no desire to learn to fight, and she instead tagged along with a first aid kit. Her most important job was to patch them together when they inevitably got hurt.

War never happened on Protea, but people could still do terrible things to each other, so combat training was not *that* unheard of, even for children. Additionally, the further away from a city you got, the more likely you would be to start encountering very dangerous wildlife. Some could be dangerous enough that not even the most skilled trackers sought their footprints as trophies.

It took barely a year for Shana to start mastering things and begin moving on to more. No one could stop her, so even her instructors kept on pushing her toward more in an effort to find her limits. Quite simply . . . she had none. She would be a walking weapon before adulthood, and not even Octavia actually felt bothered by it. It just seemed to fit her, somehow.

Even after a year of living together, the four kids had not actually told one another about the masks the girls had found, or the fact that all four of them had started discovering they had magic. Real magic. It just did not occur to mention it, or to bring up those odd maybe-memories all had shared. They just loved too much being around each other to spare it a thought.

Things changed not long after Shana and Siobhan turned six. Very shortly after Edgar's subsequent seventh birthday, the young prince accidentally fell out of a tree in the park while trying to retrieve Siobhan's wayward kite. He landed hard, and wrong, and did more than a bit of damage to his ankle along the way. As the other three scrambled to his side, he bit back a wince of pain and held out the kite. "Got it!"

"You're hurt!" Siobhan shouted at him. "I didn't want you to get hurt!" She looked at his red and swelling ankle, and agony welled up inside her. She couldn't handle it. She couldn't handle her most important people being hurt. Her fingers touched the swelling gingerly, and a swirl of white-gold magic swept down her arm. The healing power lessened the swelling instantly and mended all damage underneath.

Edgar stared at his ankle and then at Siobhan. "Magic," he said softly. "You have it too?"

"Too?" Rocky echoed. A vine suddenly climbed down the tree and offered a delphinium blossom to him. His head jerked around toward Shana and he found black-pink swirling around her hand. It looked warm and safe, and somehow made her more beautiful. "You have it, Shana?"

She nodded, and then smiled. "But I'm not that good. That's all I can really do right now. Edgar has magic, too. More than me, but not a super lot. Mostly we can do things with plants, and animals. Him plants, me animals. I mean, I can do stuff with plants, too, but he's *much* better than me. Can you?"

Rocky reached out, and white and pink magic moved over his fingers to form an illusion of a protea blossom. He offered it to Shana, and when she took it, it dissolved into little pink fireflies that flew around her head almost like a crown. "Not as much as Siobhan," he admitted, "but I can make things. Sometimes if I make them enough, they become real." He brightened visibly. "So we all have magic! We're all alike!"

Edgar nodded firmly. "We can practice together!"

Shana and Siobhan, though happy enough about all of them sharing magic, still exchanged a quick look. They just felt . . . uneasy, for some reason.

Red and gold magic suddenly swirled around all of them and left little glass balls in their hands that held either protea or delphinium blossoms in the very center. All four heads turned quickly, and they found a girl not much older than either boy standing just a few feet away. Short red hair framed a face set with yellow-gold eyes and ivory skin, and she just felt *familiar*. More importantly, however, not only did she have magic, but in her hands she held a mask as well. A red and gold one that resembled a carnation as strongly as she did.

Virginia Tungsten could see the familiarity in their eyes, so walked forward and said, "I'm Virginia. And . . . I need to explain to you about your magic, your Masks, and some . . . really amazing stuff."

The explanation could not be brief, though she tried to keep it to the most important things. She had been given intact memories the moment she found her Mask, and she had known that, as Lead Defender, it would be her duty to guide her princes and queens. It did surprise her a bit that they would have such utterly fuzzy memories of their own, yet she did not feel bad for it. There were a lot of things she would happily put off Siobhan and Shana knowing until absolutely necessary. Other things could be revealed as years passed.

"So we're . . . Apexes and queens." Siobhan looked at the sky. Though Delphinium could not be seen at that moment, she would be able to see it in the evening. The frozen world no one really knew anything about, and the ruined kingdom on its surface. A kingdom so very like the ruins of the one on Protea. She and Rocky always felt a pain and a longing when they saw Delphinium, and now she knew why.

Virginia nodded. "The lost High Queens that people don't think really existed. But you do. And the other worlds, the other kingdoms, are still frozen and healing. My own of Carnation follows behind Delphinium." She stepped closer and smiled. "I want to show you something." She tugged down the collar of her shirt to reveal the softly glowing carnation blossom on her chest over her heart. Another shimmered into appearance on her arm. The one on her chest had a single blossom while the one on her arm had two blossoms, and all had sparkling edges. "These are my Flower Marks. You have them too, just hiding."

Ever fearless, Shana reached out not unlike how she had reached for her Mask, and her own Flower Marks appeared. Unlike Virginia, both her Marks only had one blossom, and they also had a crown wrapped around the middle. Only the one on her arm had a sparkling edge, yet only around the blossom itself and not the crown. The other three reached out as well and found other differences. Siobhan's Marks matched to Shana's perfectly other than being a delphinium and her crowns being white instead of black, but their brothers only had normal Flower Marks on their chest.

"You're only Ruler Cultivators," Virginia told the two princes. "And those Marks don't sparkle because there's more than one of you. Siobhan and Shana have crowns because they are Apexes." She shook her head. "We can talk about that much later. Not important now." She nodded firmly. "But the Masks? They and the Mark on your left arm mean you are also Defender Cultivators like me. We fight evil when it comes, just like they say in legends. And it will come. Because we exist, it will come. So we will train and work hard and be ready." She took a breath and braced her shoulders. Memory told her a fight was inevitable at the immediate moment. "I am Lead Defender. That means I'm the strongest of us eight who protect the High Queens and High Princes. I am the leader. And as leader, I say that I don't want either of you to put on your Masks without a choice."

Siobhan thought a moment and then nodded. "Okay. Because you mean well."

Shana, however, narrowed her eyes ever so slightly. "If evil comes, I'll fight."

Despite being several inches shorter, Virginia immediately went toe-to-toe with the other girl. "No, you won't." Her chin set and her eyes narrowed as she saw Shana scowl. "I said no."

"And I don't have to do what you say. You're not stronger than me, or Siobhan. I am a Defender, right, so I will help."

The feeling of frustration seemed quite familiar to Virginia. Torn between the urge to defer to the stronger Cultivator, yet driven to protect her queen at all costs. "*Only* if there is something *only* you can do. You're stronger, okay, but I'm supposed to protect you."

Shana hesitated, thought, and then nodded. "Okay. I know you need to protect me, and that's okay even if I don't need it."

Edgar and Rocky shared a brief, almost wry, smile as they felt as much déjà vu as Virginia did. Strange how those words sounded so familiar. Maybe some things just could not change no matter what. After a moment, all wished away their Marks, and the two Masks got stuck into backpacks. Calling was easy; sending back not so much.

"Where can we find the others?" Siobhan asked Virginia eagerly. "Can we look for them?"

Virginia shook her head on a smile and then took one of Shana and Siobhan's hands in each of hers. "I found them! Come with me, okay? There's someone you really need to see first." She tugged them along deeper into the park, and called, "Sherry! Lexie! Look who I found!"

Two other girls, one as tall as Shana and the other slightly taller than Siobhan, looked over from where they had been sitting on a bench. The shorter had long orange hair, fiery yellow eyes, and light brown skin. The taller had fair skin covered with freckles, short blue hair, and cloudy white eyes. Sherry Darnigan and Alexandria Urias looked first at Virginia calling their names and then at the four other children she had brought. Pain and love and loneliness welled inside their hearts and souls before it could be stopped.

Shana and Siobhan alike stopped dead in their tracks as they looked at the other two. Love. It consumed them wholly. As much as they felt for the boys in their lives. Tears began to run down Siobhan's face and she dashed forward to jump onto Sherry to hug her fiercely. Shana couldn't move, visibly hesitating, so Alexandria walked over to hug her instead. At the feel of her arms, Shana's lower lip quivered and then she burrowed closer against her twin soul.

Virginia felt very happy with the scene. Nothing made her happier than to make her queens or princes happy, so reuniting them with their twin souls had been her first priority. "We know the other Cultivators, too," she promised. "And we'll meet them soon, okay?"

The others turned out to be Desiree Rikavet, Yvonne Kingfisher, Juliet Dario, Kellie Yu . . . and Clara Memoria. Shana and Siobhan did not feel surprised by Clara being the Statice Dual Cultivator. It made lots of sense, especially since she, just like all the others, physically resembled her patron flower. They both looked and felt familiar to all four High heirs, burned deeply into even their fuzziest memories of the past. Strangely, oddly, they actually remembered the other Cultivators far better than they remembered each other, but Virginia adamantly refused to tell them why that would be, instead insisting again that they would get more answers when they were older, and some of them they might figure out on their own.

Octavia did not get clued in to any of the life-changing events, or the reality of the existences of her children and their new friends. She just accepted the fact that there were suddenly seven big sisters to help keep an eye on the younger four and shook her head. Younger seemed a misnomer as the seven girls were technically all born the same year as Rocky and Edgar, but they just acted like protective big sisters, so the boys conceded to being the 'baby brothers.' At least they had their own little sisters. Shana, the overall youngest, took her role with good enough nature since she was and probably would always be the tallest other than Alexandria and Rocky. Seemed fair enough to her.

Happy years went by. Shana continued to merrily master anything she wanted to learn, and Alexandria and Virginia tagged along to many of her classes as well. Sherry did, too, and Juliet did on occasion. Siobhan got plenty of practice with her healing magic thanks to them, and on the down low where no one could see, she and brother alike practiced with their expansive range—her especially. She seemed to be everything magical in existence, almost as if to balance how Shana had come to embody everything physical. Edgar also proved a surprising fluency in magic despite being Protean, and could actually create plants rather than just control or influence them. It would do him no good in battle—which Virginia *repeatedly* mentioned—but he just felt happy to share his magic with Siobhan the way Rocky loved sharing his physical strength with Shana. It helped them understand these most important people in their lives.

By age ten, some of those unanswered questions started to answer themselves. Siobhan and Rocky were helping Octavia set the table for dinner when Siobhan chimed up, "I'm going to marry Edgar, and Rocky will marry Shana."

The statement came as no surprise to their mother. "Of course you will." She hid a smile as she put down a basket of biscuits. "Do *they* know that?"

Rocky shook his head. "Not yet." He cocked his head. "I don't think they've noticed," he decided. "They don't notice stuff like that. I mean, I know they love us like we love them, but maybe they just don't know what it means. Ginny said that there are two types of soul mates. Twins and lovers. Sherry and Lexie are twins for Siobhan and Shana, so that means Edgar and I are their other soul mate."

Octavia did her best to not laugh. When hormones started kicking in when the kids got closer to twenty-one, things would get only more entertaining. Especially if her two Dark ones still remained adorably oblivious. "I promise not to tell." She winked. "That'll be your job someday. Go fetch them for dinner."

After they had all sat down and started eating, Octavia finally brought up something she had been putting off. "Shana, the accelerated study program on Axium finally got back to me. They've accepted you as a full-time student."

Shana looked over quickly. "Really, Mom?"

"What program?" Siobhan asked.

Octavia sighed. "As you and Rocky know, Shana has been

utterly miserable in school because she can't learn enough fast enough, and I haven't been able to find a suitable tutor for her to learn on her own. One of Alexandria's fathers brought Axium's program to my attention. It is specifically designed for children like Shana who just aren't suited for a normal school setting. She would be able to learn anything and everything she desires." She looked down. "However, it means she'll need to move to Axium for at least ten years to complete the program. She could be there even longer if she decides to attend their university."

"B-but!" Tears welled in Siobhan's eyes. "That's so long!"

"I know, but it may be for the best for Shana. It's her decision." She looked at her other daughter. "You have the final call on this, love."

Shana was still thinking about it a week later, and her family did not help much. Edgar badly did not want his sister to leave, but he kept his mouth shut and didn't give an opinion either way. On the other hand, Rocky and Siobhan could not stop themselves from pleading and begging Shana not to leave. They knew she felt terrible in school, yet neither could really bear the idea of not having her always there by their side.

Shana said nothing of her internal turmoil, but Alexandria knew her twin all too well. She finally managed to pry the entire thing out of Shana, and immediately cornered the two Delphinium Cultivators at school the following day. "Stop," she told them both very firmly. "You're making Shana sad."

Fresh tears ran down Siobhan's cheeks, and matching ones filled Rocky's eyes. "But she *needs* us," Rocky said fiercely. "She'll be alone over there! She's always so alone. Lexie, come *on*. You don't want her to go, right?"

Alexandria shook her head. "I'll go with her. So will Desiree and Kellie. Clara said she would make sure. She can come home to visit, you know, and maybe you can go out there. Axium is only on the next landmass. Just a few days away by ship. It'll be okay." She took each of their hands and squeezed gently. "Let her go," she urged. "She needs this. Things need to happen, okay?"

It was the hardest thing that either sibling had ever done, but they knew Alexandria to be right. Swallowing their own sadness, they fought back tears and instead began to encourage Shana to go. She was startled initially, and then deeply grateful. All of her guilt evaporated entirely, enough that she began to be excited at the coming adventure. She tried to keep it hidden, but Rocky spied it without any effort and found he could no longer be sad when she looked and felt so happy.

Almost a month later, Octavia took all four kids to the southern dock beyond Lux to put Shana on the ship that would sail to Axium. Most of her luggage had already been shipped, so she only brought a bag with the things she needed for the next week. She felt no fear at all for doing the voyage alone. She had insisted on it because she knew she needed to be used to doing things for herself.

At the port entrance, Octavia hugged her fiercely and then slowly let go. Even only just over ten years old, already Shana had gotten taller than her adopted mother. "You have fun, alright?" Octavia told her softly. "And call us a lot. Every summer, you can either come home to visit, or Edgar will come see you."

Shana nodded and smiled. "Okay." She then turned and hugged Siobhan fiercely. "No crying!" she scolded. "I'm not going away forever." She rubbed at the tears in Siobhan's eyes and then hugged Edgar. For a moment, she almost could not let go. Only knowing that she would see him again soon and that they could call each other any time finally made her release him. She turned toward Rocky and found him offering a hand. She frowned.

He shook his head. "I want to walk you to the dock. We can say goodbye there."

"Oh." She paused and then took his hand. Refusing to let herself look back, she walked beside him through the busy port. "Why?" she asked him softly. "I won't change my mind now. I know you're still upset. I can feel it."

"I know. I'm not going to ask you to stay." He stopped walking and smiled as a hint of pink touched his cheeks. "I want to ask you to keep me in your heart. I don't have to be first, but I want to be someone the most special to you, like you are to me. Someday, I want to be your boyfriend. I think . . . we're soul mates. I really love you, Shana. Not *like* I do Siobhan, but as *much* as I do."

She could only stare at him for a few moments. She had missed that one entirely, though hindsight made her feel a bit silly that she had not at all noticed his feelings. It took barely a minute to evaluate her own feelings. "You *are* my most special person," she admitted softly. "I love you as much as I love Edgar or Alexandria, just differently. I think . . . you're right. We're soul mates." She smiled, and her pink eyes glowed like the protea blossoms growing down the walls. "I want to be your girlfriend someday, too. So . . ." She rose up the small distance in their heights and kissed his cheek. "Someday, when I come home for good, we'll be each other's mate."

He touched his cheek as he watched her walk away and kept back the tears determined to well up. He managed only until he got back to where the other three waited, and then he let his mother hold him as the tears came free. "I smiled when I said goodbye," he whispered against her neck.

"Then you'll smile when you say hello again," she promised. She gathered Siobhan and Edgar close as well. "Let's go home."

Siobhan discovered very quickly that she did not like having her room back to herself after so long, so both Rocky and Edgar took turns spending the night with her for the first month until she settled. Even then, they all still spent more time together, and would gather each time Shana called.

Any worry about Shana being alone in Axium alleviated itself quickly as well. Clara, rather guiltlessly, pulled strings both literal and magical and arranged for one of Alexandria's fathers to get a transfer to Axium that moved the entire family. Shana had been all but adopted by her twin soul's parents, so they immediately offered to house her rather than her live in the school's dorms. In very short order thereafter, both Desiree and Kellie's families also *conveniently* made a move to Axium that allowed the other two Dark Defenders to be near to their queen. Virginia instead promised to protect Edgar as needed, and she and Alexandria exchanged contact information to make sure they were both kept up-to-date.

Clara would be the first to say time could not be stopped, and it continued to pass through peaceful years. Edgar visited Shana every summer, yet she never managed to come home for her own visit—and neither Siobhan nor Rocky could get to see her. Something always happened. By the time twentieth birthdays approached, Rocky had decided it must surely be the whim of Destiny, so he continued to practice patience no matter how difficult. Reuniting would be only sweeter after so many years. At least he could still talk to her when she called.

At age twenty, teenagers began the transition into adulthood and could begin gaining independence. One of the first things they could do was move out of their parents' home, though it did have to be to someplace close by. Octavia helped by offering her opinion on the different apartments they perused, but she trusted their judgment. Honestly, all of them had been acting much like adults since their mid-teens anyway.

Once Siobhan had turned twenty and the two males twenty-one, they got more serious about their planning. Rocky and Siobhan expected to get an apartment with Edgar, but they found themselves surprised when he responded to the idea with an empathic negative. "Huh." Rocky crossed his arms on the kitchen table and studied his future brother-in-law. "What gives with that? You tired of us finally?"

Edgar grinned, taking it as it was meant. "Well, you *do* get on my nerves sometimes, but mostly because I feel as if I'm always chasing you with a dustpan to sweep up your broken hearts."

"We're not that bad!" Siobhan said in exasperation. She bonked him lightly in the head with a rolled up periodical newspaper.

"I beg to differ, and Gin would be the first to agree!" He hooked an arm over the back of his chair. "Actually . . . I just really want my own place."

Siobhan studied his face, and her eyes softened. "Because of Shana," she murmured. "You want to save a place just for you two for when she finally comes home. This summer, right?"

He shook his head. "Actually, no. She decided to start her university classes out there for now. She wants to do the first two-thirds of her university degree there and then do the last out here. So

. . . she won't be home until maybe April of 5104."

It was currently February of 5100. "Four years!" Rocky sulked a bit. "Destiny better make it worth it," he muttered. "It's very obvious that some sort of celestial shenanigans are happening. What is it she wants from us?"

"Not you," Siobhan corrected. "Me. And Shana. Destiny expects something from *us*." She scowled. "Which our Defenders definitely know and aren't telling! They all know a lot they haven't told us. Comes with the territory, I guess. They're so determined to be our bodyguards and protect us from *everything* that they forget sometimes to be our friends first!" She scowled. "I tried yelling at Ginny over that. Didn't go over well."

Rocky winced. "Probably about as well as the time *I* tried yelling at her over it." In a grumble, he added, "Not fair to make a Lead Defender be a Glass element."

Siobhan had to grin. "At least she can keep us in line."

They finally decided on two apartment buildings not far from one another. Edgar, still receiving monthly stipends from his parents' trust, got a larger one with two master suites. Siobhan and Rocky got one a bit smaller, but still with enough space for them both. They knew Octavia would support them as needed, and they refused to take more than necessary. Siobhan had gotten a scholarship for her living expenses to attend the university to study medicine, and Rocky had started working at a ranch outside Lux. He made more than enough to cover his own expenses, though he still waffled a bit on exactly what to pursue in his studies. He would start with basics for now.

Later that year, both Rocky and Edgar turned twenty-one and caught up with the other Cultivators. The very next year, Siobhan (and Shana) also turned twenty-one. A lot could happen at or after hitting that age, especially where hormones were concerned. Most people started to get the full presence of them, though others skipped them entirely, and others as yet only found them after getting to know someone. The whole force and fury wouldn't be in swing until after finishing maturity by twenty-five.

Usually.

Siobhan got a little bit of a shock a few months after her birthday by looking at Edgar one day and suddenly feeling a wave of such powerful desire that she almost pounced on him right then and there. She refrained, if only because they happened to be in public. If *that* was the starting shot, she almost worried about how much stronger it could get in four years. How did something that already consumed her heart and soul as much as her body possibly get stronger? Well, Sherry had warned her that if she and Edgar really were lover soul mates, it would happen.

To her frustration and amusement, however, Edgar seemed to be still oblivious. Not unusual for him, really, and a vague feeling of the distant past told her that something very like this may have happened already. She considered her options for getting him to look at her as a nearly-grown woman rather than just a dear friend and then decided the blunt tactic really had to be the best choice. You could *not* be subtle with Proteans. Ever. She didn't envy her brother's future at all.

Still, she knew how to bide her time. After catching dinner together, she asked Edgar, "Can I come back with you to your apartment? I'm not feeling like leaving you right now."

He snuggled her closer. "Sure." He all too often felt starved for her presence as well, so did not object any time she wanted to visit. It had just been getting more frustrating lately because each time she looked at him with her soft gold eyes, he felt an unmistakable urge to kiss her. Damned if he would scare this most important person to him!

He let them into the apartment and then headed for the kitchen. "Bubbly water?" he called.

"That'd be nice." She wandered over to the window to watch the setting sun. She heard him return and turned around to watch him sit down on the couch. The sunset seemed to caress his hair and skin, drawing out the Dark inside him with such force that she felt an almost magnetic pull. He did not use Dark as an element—supposedly only Shana could—but that made him no less a child of Protea and therefore deeply, powerfully, of the darkness. From dawn until sunset, Proteans exuded raw sunlight, and from sunset to dawn, they poured out pure darkness.

He glanced over to ask what she was thinking, and he stopped breathing. She *glowed*. Radiantly, beautifully, as if the Light inside her soul could not be contained. She illuminated everything around her, and her light spilled into his own soul with an almost seductive lure. She was the Apex of Light, everything magical in existence, and a glorious blend of Light and Illusion elements. "Siobhan?"

She calmly walked across the room, and she stripped off her sweater as she went. Before he could blink, she slid onto his lap facing him. "Hi," she said huskily. She trapped him there with her hands on the couch beside his head. "You know what Juli told me? A Cultivator's Caretaker considers it their sworn duty to seduce their Cultivator at the earliest opportunity. Since we're each other's Caretaker, I hope you don't mind that I decided to take care of that duty."

His mouth went dry. Of course he had seen her unclothed before, but suddenly it felt so very different. She looked soft, warm, and utterly perfect. Petite yet plump, and he ached to feel her under his hands. "What do you mean by Caretakers?" he managed to ask.

"Oh you." She pressed her forehead against his, unable to stop a smile despite the knots of frustration. "Edgar, really. Haven't you noticed we're soul mates?"

He opened his mouth and then closed it. A sheepish smile began to cross his face. "Uhm."

She nipped at his lower lip. He really did have a terribly kissable mouth. "Are we feeling silly for not noticing?" She cupped his beloved face in one hand. "You are of the Dark, my prince. I knew when we were ten that we would end up here."

"Half naked on my couch?"

"Okay, maybe not that specific, but I knew we were soul mates. We had to be." A beautiful glow moved over her skin, and her two Flower Marks appeared. Her breath hitched as he took that for an invitation and pressed his lips to the Mark just over her breasts. "Edgar?" She caught his face again and tilted his head back. Her lips trembled. "I love you. More than anything. As much as my twin soul and soul-brother. Be mine. Be my king someday when my world is healed."

He tugged on her long and fluffy hair until she leaned closer and their lips finally met. Hunger welled potently, and the sweet marshmallow taste of her power teased his tongue. "Yes," he whispered. "To all of it." He kissed her again, slowly, savoring her, and then added huskier, "You can go home tomorrow. Want to share my bed?"

Her lips curved. "I even promise not to kick you this time."

That sort of change in status quo could not be hidden, not that they had any desire to try. They instead officially announced an engagement that would last until after both had turned twenty-five and could legally marry. All of their closest friends took the news happily, especially Octavia and Rocky. Their mother had been expecting this to happen, and she was not disappointed with the story when Siobhan guiltlessly gushed the details.

Rocky felt perfectly content with things, and he had no problems with Siobhan spending as many nights with Edgar as she did at their own apartment. He couldn't feel neglected or abandoned by his sister, not when this almost literally changed nothing about their lives other than shifting hers and Edgar's relationship from one of children to one of adults.

As he hung out with Yvonne for lunch on a rare day without classes, however, she asked him, "Are you lonely?"

He thought about it sincerely and then admitted, "Yes. Every year not getting to see Shana makes me want to see her more, and having it so very clearly confirmed that Siobhan and Edgar are soul mates, I know all the more that I and Shana are. It's almost impossible to bear just talking to her once a month because I want so much more. I want to be her Caretaker, Yvonne. You lot won't tell us what's in the future that we know has to exist, but I know it won't be good. I want to be there, to shelter her heart and fight by her side."

"Yeah, don't hold your breath on the fighting part." She poked him in the nose. "Virginia will never allow it."

"I'm a Caretaker," he muttered. "I have rights, too."

"You're also a Ruler Cultivator of Delphinium, and *we* Defenders have rights."

"You're Rulers too!"

"We have armor."

He glared at her and then had to laugh. "Okay. I guess that's fair. We can have this fight again later when it's more important." He swung their hands between them. Just being with the Light Defenders always made him happy, though he just got the oddest feeling that, somehow, maybe, he might be missing something more. He shrugged it off as always and instead let his mind think of the future. Only a few years more, and the one he loved most would come home, and then everything would be as it should be.

For that, he could continue to wait.

As February of 5104 rolled around, life had become nearly idyllic. Lux continued to thrive as the biggest city on the landmass, and the one with the strangest overabundance of natural energy. After nearly twenty-five years, still no one could figure out how even things that should not have been suited for the warm climate thrived no matter who planted them, or where. You could not have a brown thumb if you lived in Lux.

Although, Siobhan thought wryly as she stared at the miserable potted plant on her kitchen counter, you could certainly *try*. She sighed as she poked at the drooping leaves. Her eyes held humor as she looked to where her brother was walking into the kitchen as well. "I think maybe Edgar needs to look at this poor thing. I'm pretty sure it's alive only by sheer stubbornness."

Rocky snorted softly as he went to get coffee. Right on the edge of adulthood for both with Rocky at twenty-four and Siobhan at twenty-three, the two siblings still looked enough alike to pass for twins, despite a rather significant difference in height. Siobhan had settled barely at five-two, and her brother had beaten her by an entire foot. She had never lost her beautifully plump shape, though maturity had added a delicately curved bust and hips. Rocky had also not lost his softness, though his continued love of physical training meant he had earned himself quite a bit of defined muscle to go with it.

Siobhan's fluffy and curly hair also now reached the floor in length, while her brother's stayed short. She had *tried* to cut her hair, but it had never grown in a normal way to begin with. If she lopped it off, it took only a few *minutes* to grow right back out. Shana had been like that, too, actually, so at least she had never been alone in her oddness. She had finally given up trying, and now just enjoyed experimenting with different sorts of braids.

Rocky bent a bit to look at the miserable plant and then decided dryly, "You're right. Invite Edgar over under the auspices of seducing him and then make him play gardener."

Siobhan bit her lip but still giggled. "It would serve you right if I did! We try to pander to your sensibilities by never spending the night together here. It's terribly unfair of me to parade my lover under your nose while you still don't have yours!"

"Soon," he intoned, almost like a mantra. "As in literally months now. And I swear to all that's holy and divine, including Destiny, if Shana does not come home in April, I will god damned *swim* to Axium!"

Siobhan bit back more giggles. "I don't think anyone will appreciate your efforts, and Desiree would be pretty vexed to have to use her Water magic to go save you from drowning." Thinking of the varying gifts of the Cultivators, she ran her hands lightly over her arms and looked to where a trunk sat under a large window. Inside that trunk was only a single object: her Mask. She had never actually worn her Mask, at least not that she could recall from either life. She kept it safely locked away as she had promised, and there had been no need to get it out. Yet, she could not shake the feeling that that time would come *soon*.

"Hey." Rocky tugged her close and kissed the top of her head. "I'm here. My Sight has not seen anything yet, and it usually keeps me up to date on the trouble you'll be in."

It made her smile as intended. "Lucky you, having Future Sight. I just have Present Sight, so I only know if you're in trouble once you're actually in it!" She glanced at the clock over the stove and then groaned as she realized how late they would be to class. "Damn it."

All of the Cultivators, including Siobhan, attended the same Chivanti University within their city. Everyone suspected a connection to Edgar and Shana, but they had never said one way or another whether they held any relation to the former owners of the Chivanti Corporation that owned the university. Octavia obviously knew, but she had been no more forthcoming about the details.

Rocky followed Siobhan's gaze to the clock and sighed. "Oh,

hell. Edgar will not let us live this down." He snagged up his backpack and stayed close on his sister's heels as she ran out of the apartment and down through the complex. He kept one hand free to grab her arm each time she tripped, which happened frequently enough since she had solely magical gifts and no physical ones. He had countered their lineage by training, but he still could be tripped up on occasion.

Which inevitably happened as they reached the pedestrian lane where Edgar stood patiently waiting for them. Rocky's shoe caught the edge of the cement and down he went. He landed right at his brother's feet, and the other male said dryly, "I give it a nine for not taking me down with you."

"I endeavor to try," Rocky muttered. "Damn it all." He accepted his giggling sister's hand and got nimbly back up. "Besides, I would probably do damage if I took you down, unlike Siobhan."

Edgar grinned a bit. He had also all but finished growing and stood at an average enough five-nine in height. And while he certainly possessed a strong frame of his own that seemed pure physical strength, he still wouldn't escape unscathed if the bigger of the two Toulumes decided to trip right onto him. His black hair, which he had normally worn short, now stayed in a neat ponytail at the base of his neck. "I can usually catch us both if she does that."

"Or just let us fall," his lover teased.

"Depends on whether we're alone or not," he teased back as they began to walk down the street together. The university sat only a few blocks away, and they always walked to their first classes together. Rocky and Edgar, and the four Defenders, had roughly a year of classes left. Siobhan had two thanks to being younger.

"Do you mind?" Rocky complained. "I'm still here."

"So walk faster," his sister retorted, sticking out her tongue a bit.

He returned the gesture. "See if I save you the next time you trip. Sheesh." He walked a bit faster to leave the conversation, but not far enough that he left them behind. He actually did not mind when they got to flirting; mostly, he kept hoping that they would finally just decide to move in together and make things simpler. Siobhan practically lived over at Edgar's anyway.

Siobhan studied his back and then looked at Edgar. Solemnly, she said, "I can't wait to see him wrapped around *someone's* finger the way you've got me wrapped around yours." She hugged his arm playfully. "I mean, since we're so much alike, and you and Shana are so much alike . . ."

Edgar's grin looked a bit wicked. "To say the least! I'm looking forward to it too, and having her share again the frustration of keeping you two from breaking your hearts over every little thing. And, yes, we're still on for two months from now. The process is going so smoothly that I have no doubts it will happen."

"No need for Rocky to swim the ocean?" she asked dryly.

"Thankfully for the heart rate of the Defenders, no."

She rested her cheek against his arm. "You're so strong inside. Stronger than me maybe. I don't think I could handle not having Rocky for most of the time. And as hard as it was for me and Rocky to let her go, you had it just as bad, yet you never once complained. You could have. Maybe not to her, but to us at least."

"You know I try not to burden you."

She narrowed her eyes at him. "One of these days, I will finally teach you that it is *not* burdening me or my brother when you are bothered by something and need someone to tell."

"Just as one of these days, I will teach the two of you to think before acting?" came the polite, yet amused, retort.

She just sighed. "Got me there. Oh well."

None of the Cultivators shared classes, and they did not all have classes on the same days, but they had staggered schedules for the days they did share so that they could all have lunch together. By the time Siobhan got to the table they had commandeered, she was the last one to arrive. She plopped down between Sherry and Edgar and cracked open her lunchbox. "I'm starving!" she said cheerfully.

"Bottomless pit," her twin soul teased her affectionately. She shot an equally teasing look at Rocky. Maturity had given her a nearly sultry beauty that her custom designed clothes always flattered perfectly. She rather enjoyed making clothes that best suited an individual person. "I sometimes wonder if either of you eat at home."

"We do, thank you!" Rocky scooped up dip with a chip. "Our metabolisms would just be happier if we could snack in class. I haven't dared that since the last time I got crumbs in a keyboard and my computational sciences teacher almost chucked me out."

Juliet looked up from the cookbook she had been reading, and her green eyes sparkled merrily in her olive toned face. Her yellow hair had been tucked under a net where it would stay out of her way in culinary classes. "You have to pass my advanced pastry class on your way to your second classes. We always offer the visually impaired yet tasty food things to hungry students. Pop in for a popover or something!"

"You will never get rid of them again," Virginia noted dryly as she added dressing lavishly to her salad. She always carefully watched her food intake since she had to keep up with her own strength as Lead. Her beautiful features and vibrant coloring had become paired to a strong body proportioned with curves in such a way that she could wear *anything*, so she had become popular as a model among the artists of all trades on campus. She was actually studying art as well, so she alternated between being in front of and behind canvases. It was for that reason that she aimed her fork at Yvonne and said, "You lost the bet. You owe me a nude study."

"What the hell did you bet that involved being naked?" Edgar asked Yvonne a bit incredulously. Of all of them, she had the most modesty, so it seemed far more a jump than anyone else.

A bit of pink climbed her fair skin, and her golden yellow eyes held sheepishness. Her long hair made of purple ombre shades had been clipped up out of her face in a way that reflected her lack of concern for being stylish. "Let's just say that I learned my lesson and will never doubt her again, okay?" In a grumble, she added, "Why are she and Sherry so obsessed with making me look more fashionable than I am? I save my style for designing the interiors of houses."

Juliet lightly hit her on the top of the head with a napkin. "Because you always entertain us with your ability to literally not give a damn and yet somehow command attention. Making you deliberately command attention, either via Gin's art or Sherry's clothes, always creates a suitably spectacular show."

"One of these days I'll start caring and then you'll need a new target."

"Bet you won't," Virginia said slyly.

"Oh, no you don't! I'm not falling for *that* again."

Siobhan couldn't help but giggle. Nothing made her happier than to be with these people. They perfectly completed her life, and yet . . . something just felt *missing*. The other four Defender Cultivators, and her beloved sister. They *needed* to be there to complete the set. It just didn't seem right without all ten Dual Cultivators, though Siobhan could give some allowance for Clara's need to stay in the Hall of Records. *Some*. She shook it off as she looked at the large clock affixed to the highest tower of the main university building. It could be seen from any location on grounds. "I have a political sciences class I better not be late for *again*." She hopped up to her feet, stopped to kiss everyone, and then hurried off.

Rocky and Edgar also had classes quickly approaching and so finished up and headed off after kissing everyone goodbye. The four Dual Cultivators left at the table shared a long look between them before sighing deeply. Yvonne ran her hands over her arms to combat a chill. "I still really don't like that they don't remember each other that well. Alright, they've proven to not need to remember, but . . . they deserve to have all of those wonderful memories."

"With the good comes the bad," Juliet murmured. "What about on the other side? Still extremely fuzzy?"

"To be sure." Virginia sighed. "Our other queen is doing just fine, all things considered. Remembers snippets of Protea, next to nothing of Delphinium and the others. And, like Siobhan, she absolutely remembers *nothing* of what it means to be an Apex. Yet . . . she has never stopped being obsessively driven to hone her body into the penultimate weapon."

"Which is likely why Rocky's near obsession with continued training hasn't tapered either, nor Edgar's." Sherry drummed her fingers on the top of the table and then went very still. Her eyes unfocused as she stared into the distance, and her friends tensed. Her eyes finally cleared, and her fingertips quivered. "Damn it," she whispered.

"What did you See?" Virginia demanded.

Sherry slowly turned to look at her friends, and a somewhat sad and almost bitter smile curved her lips. "The end of the innocence of Light."

* * * * *

The Ephemeral Plane had become somewhat unknown as far as the general populace was concerned. In the height of the Royal Era, it had been a very well-known location due to being under the guardianship of the Protea Kingdom, as well as the quantity of members of the Faith of the Goddess who had used it for all manner of things, up to and including astrally walking the Immortal Fields or contacting the Hall of Records to uncover information about past lives.

In the five thousand years since the fall of the kingdoms, those of the Faith had not truly re-emerged into the open. Only a handful were known across the surface of the world though their population did still number at least a few hundred. Curiously, while those of the Faith only numbered a few hundred, those with majik numbered higher. Far too many witches had been forced to abandon the Path of the Goddess for their own safety, and that meant their children and further down the lines had either not even known they had majik in their blood, or if they did, they didn't truly know what it meant. Meeting someone with majik who was not of the Faith guaranteed that, at some point, someone in their lineage *had* been of the Faith.

The Ephemeral Plane had depended on those of the Faith far more than anyone had realized. The diminished presence of good majik within the Immortal Fields lent itself to a lingering and steadily rising unbalance not aided by the lack of a Ruler Cultivator for Protea to provide Nature magic. The unbalance could, to some level, be controlled by Pallas, yet even he could not do it all alone.

Eventually, that unbalance began to creep down through the

Plane to the deeper reaches. It disturbed that which had been contained, and it began to make locks and safeties far less safe. Down there, buried amid the most terrible of existences, lurked the two worst of all.

Famine had been pushing at her seals for millennia, and finally, at last, she felt something give way. Savage satisfaction filled her as she pushed harder. Seals cracked, and a shudder tore through the Plane. With a surge of necrotic power, she burst free and tore through the Plane and toward physicality. She broke out into the skies of Delphinium and found a suitably desolate landscape. It had barely recovered at all in the five millennia since she had poisoned it. How perfect.

She flew toward the castle, intent on claiming it as her own, but she came to an abrupt halt as she discovered it had been covered in a protective barrier of some sort. She raged against it, battered her decrepit hands, until something broke and she could enter. A bright glow drew her toward the center, to the grand throne room, and even she felt mesmerized by what she saw within.

The crown of the High Queen. It hovered within a column of light inside the center of the room. Famine rushed to claim it and plunged her hands into the column. Ripe agony made her scream, and she tore away to discover her hands had rendered down to bone, all flesh melted away. "So be it!" she snarled. "When she is dead, this will be mine!"

She turned her gaze toward the sky through the broken ceiling. She could see Protea in the night sky. Where else would all those disgusting creatures have been reborn except on the world of Dark? It could take in and support their power in a way no other world could. She reached out with power to look, and she swept her eyes across the surface of the planet.

Two hotspots lit up as being positively saturated with Cultivator magic. The one they called Axium looked as if it had been cloaked in darkness. Famine made a disgusted noise; as if she cared about the Dark Defenders and their precious Apex of Dark. She would bother herself with them once she had removed the only real threat to her existence: the Apex of Light. She could only be within the city called Lux, for the city of 'light' indeed looked as if it had been bathed in its namesake. The Apex and the Light Defenders surely lived there.

Finding them would not be hard. Cultivators, Ruler and Defender alike, had exceptionally high resistance to disease. Few ever got sick. Perhaps that was one of the reasons she hated them so terribly. She pulled a face and then spat onto the floor. The disgusting ooze began to bubble and then metamorphed into the putrid and monstrous form of a creature she had affectionately named a 'Germ.' It would find her target without any difficulty.

* * * * *

Plagues were so rare that it sometimes took ages for people to even realize that the few cases of sickness were highly contagious. This time, when sickness swept through Lux, no one could mistake it. It infected everyone of every age in any form of health, and those with weaker immune systems got hit the hardest.

Siobhan, unfortunately, still fell into the latter category. Her tendency to be a sickly child had carried over to being a sickly teenager and now a sickly adult. Every passing disease could knock her down for days. She had grown to accept that disease was merely a part of her life, and she would forever spend at least two-thirds of her life suffering in some form or another, so she had learned to carry on as best she could. She also accepted that she would be hospitalized with regretful frequency; at least she took advantage of it by asking all of the professionals who worked with her mother about their jobs, since she wanted to go that direction as well.

The moment the plague hit the city, she shut herself away in the apartment and wore the filtered face mask she had been custom made in order to protect her. Rocky, and anyone who visited, took the full effort to completely change clothes in the laundry room before they approached her—and she stayed away from the laundry room at all times.

It took only two days, however, before every precaution proved ineffective. She woke one morning and felt as if she had been beaten with a stick. Everything hurt. She could barely breathe, and her entire body shook with chills from fever. She could not bite back a whimper as she tried to sit up.

Her brother appeared in her bedroom doorway, a dark look on his handsome face. "Honey." He moved closer and eased onto the side of the bed. She fell forward against his chest, and he wrapped his arms around her tenderly. It always abraded against him, deeply, when he could not protect her. "We tried."

"I know." She closed her eyes and let him be her strength. "At least I can't get you sick? I'm the only weird Cultivator who doesn't have any resistance," she managed to tease.

Edgar and Octavia alike still affectionately called the Toulume siblings the 'eternal optimists', and neither had bothered denying it. Rocky smiled and smoothed Siobhan's messy hair out of her eyes. "Let's get you into a cool bath to temper that fever, and then I'll braid your hair and feed you. Okay?"

"'kay." She never really tried to argue when he babied her. It balanced itself since he didn't argue when she babied him. One of the benefits to being so much alike was that they pretty much understood that if one of them *had* to do something—like nurture and care for a loved one—the other did too.

By the time she had suffered through the painful bath, gotten her hair braided, and managed to eat some mild soup, their closest friends had shown up. They didn't bother with the switching of clothes this time as it was already too late. Sherry sat down next to Siobhan on the couch and had to smile when her twin automatically snuggled close. "I'm the last person you want to cuddle right now. I run a higher temperature as a Fire element. Snuggle Yvonne. She's always colder."

"I wanna snuggle you. No offense, Yvonne."

Yvonne smiled. "None at all taken! But I can probably still help." She blew on her hands, and cold air puffed from her lips to create a fog of tiny ice crystals. She walked over to Siobhan and gently placed her foggy hands on the other woman's neck. She winced as Siobhan yelped. "I know. It hurts. But it *will* help. One of my gifts as a Ruler lets me regulate temperatures of places *and* people."

Siobhan didn't argue, but she did tuck her face against Sherry's neck for comfort. Tears ran down her cheeks that she ignored. She *knew* it would help. It always did. That didn't make it suck any less.

Rocky sat down in one of the other chairs, arms crossed and chin set, and Juliet sat on the arm to hug him comfortingly. "She'll get better," she promised. She rested her chin on his head. "She always does. I know you don't like seeing her sick. None of us do."

"I'm just so frustrated by it!" he told her. "It just does *not* make sense. Not just that she always gets sick, but that this new plague has come at all! It doesn't seem to be missing anyone! I think maybe five people at school, Edgar, and the lot of us have been spared. That's *it*. Also, those five? Pretty sure they were getting it when I saw them yesterday. Even Mom is really feeling it, and she's built up a high resistance to most everything from working in the hospital so long."

Juliet looked at the others over his head, and all four Defenders collectively nodded in agreement. They had run out of time to protect Siobhan. "Be that as it may," Virginia finally said, "the fact remains that Siobhan's state is . . . expected." She sighed as that drew both siblings' glares. "I know, I should have said something sooner, but I honestly wanted to keep it quiet as long as possible. Unless she remembered the price of being an Apex, I didn't want to be the one to tell her!"

Siobhan felt better now that her fever had diminished, so she sat up. She tucked up her knees and wrapped her arms around them. "You're saying that this is because I'm an Apex?"

"More specifically, it's because you're unawakened as an Apex." Virginia shot to her feet to pace off her agitation. "Siobhan . . . damn it. I don't know how to tell you this!" She raked her hands through her hair and swung around. "There is a price to be paid for an Apex to exist. The price of your birth lays in the creature known as Famine. She's as terrible as she sounds, and in a way, I'm kind of glad you *don't* remember. Sure as hell most of us wish we didn't."

"So Famine has finally come after me?" Siobhan asked with a calm at odds with her clenched hands.

"The plague is proof of it. And once you finally pay the price and awaken, your immunities will build properly and you should never get sick again." Yvonne made a vague gesture. "We always assumed the price is fighting and destroying Famine. Which, since you get sick easily, kind of does make sense how it would be classified as a 'price.' In the time of the kingdoms, you got sick with relative frequency, too. Perhaps not as terribly as now, but the illnesses back then were not as terrible as they can be these days. Evolution, I suppose."

"And it has to be me?" she whispered.

"It can't be anyone else," Sherry sighed. "You are the Apex of Light, the epitome of all that is magical, and you possess the greatest of all healing powers. Ironic, I suppose, in these circumstances, but it is what makes you the only being capable of destroying Famine. You can heal disease, Siobhan, and not even Kellie can do that. No other healer can. Famine directly targeted the Delphinium Kingdom specifically because of you."

"Then so be it," Siobhan decided. She shook her head. "You can't keep me cooped up any longer. If I'm going to get sick, then I'll just deal with it. I've already dealt with it all of my life. Now I will confront it face-to-face." Her smile looked a bit sad. "You can't fear what you have always lived with."

Keeping her cooped up no longer did not actually mean she returned to classes. All classes had been canceled for the entire university. In fact, almost the entirety of Lux had come to a dead halt. People with more minor cases of the illness kept running what absolutely had to stay running, but the streets more closely resembled a ghost town. Siobhan knew it could not get better unless and until she confronted Famine, and she could not confront Famine unless they knew where she had hidden herself. They would not figure that out unless they could get Famine to attack directly, and she would not do that unless they revealed themselves. So, despite the protests of her four guardians, Siobhan insisted on going out. Never alone, however. All four Defender Cultivators and her brother alike always accompanied her. She hardly minded that.

The six of them had just settled into a favored park to have a quiet lunch together when the air went biting cold. Sherry's head jerked up as her Sight stirred and told her that danger approached the two Delphinium heirs she lived to protect. Virginia recognized the signal and leapt to her feet. "Masks!" she ordered sharply.

Masks could be shrunk to make transportation easier, especially since calling for a Mask to hand only worked for the two Apexes—and then only if the Mask hadn't been locked away. Virginia and Sherry wore theirs as a charm on an earring; the matching communications mask that allowed them to contact any other Defender made up the other earring. Yvonne and Juliet wore both versions of their Mask as charms on a bracelet. All four pulled off their Mask, and it grew to full size.

Vile ooze bubbled up out of ground and then took shape into the form of the Germ. It did not need to see the Masks to know it had found its targets. Their very immunity bespoke of their identity. It went not after the four with Masks, however. It immediately lunged toward the two without, vicious claws arced to kill.

Siobhan threw her arms over her head on a little shriek that doubled when her brother grabbed her and knocked her down to the ground safely. He very badly wanted to fight, too, but he knew better than that. He stayed low with Siobhan and made them a much harder target to reach through the four Defenders that moved to stand in front of them.

The four exchanged a glance and then put on their Masks. Magic colored the same as their Flower Element swept down their bodies and called up their armor. Each reflected their world's flower in some manner, and literally suited them in an elemental fashion. Virginia took a step forward with a hand held out, and a halberd appeared in her grip. Anyone with strong enough magic could use whatever magic they did have to hold objects of particular importance, and Defenders in particular preferred to use it to hold their weapons. Juliet and Sherry followed suit, and it was a wooden staff to the former and a short sword to the latter. Yvonne, of Iris and purely defensive magic, had no weapon. She instead stayed back a step to cover the others with her skills.

The Germ saw uneven odds not in its favor and began to rip off pieces of flesh. Each that fell became another Germ. In only moments, a dozen confronted the four Defenders. It did not stop them from rushing in and going on the attack with weapons and magic alike. Siobhan very nearly cried out but Rocky hastily clamped a hand over her mouth. "Don't!" he whispered in her ear. "Let them concentrate!"

She yanked his hand off her mouth. "I have to help them! I'm a Defender Cultivator, too! Delphinium chose me! I have to get my Mask!" She shook her head hard. "I'm not feeling well enough to transport alone, not while Delphinium is sick as well. Help me, please!"

He laced his hands with hers and accessed the transport magic his by right of birth as a Ruler Cultivator. It had significantly diminished as well thanks to their world being poisoned, but it *did* still work within at least a few miles. They tried not to use it unless in dire circumstances, and this counted! He got them safely to the interior of their apartment and then followed his sister as she ran over to the trunk. A part of him, naturally, resented that this burden rode on her shoulders. He resented it on the shoulders of the other women as well. He had to resent it for he loved them and it put them in danger. That did not mean he doubted why they had been chosen, or that there was need.

Siobhan opened the trunk and looked at the white and gold mask within. Its delicate design echoed to the Flower Mark on her chest and arm, both of which appeared anew as she looked at the Mask and felt her Sight stir. Though her Sight had always before been limited to the present time, for once it offered a glimpse of the future. She knew, felt *positive,* that to put on the Mask would lead to her death. Her fingers trembled only briefly before she picked up the Mask and put it on. White-gold power swirled around her and formed her armor. It felt . . . familiar. Comfortable. Despite her foggy memories, she knew she had indeed worn it before.

She shot to her feet and then wobbled as her illness made her less-than-stellar grace more pronounced. "I have to help the others!"

"I'm going." Rocky stood as well.

"No, you're not," she told him on a scowl.

He matched her scowl equally. "Yes, I am!"

"No, you're not!"

"Yes, I am! And the more we argue about it, the worse things are at the fight!"

Her eyes went wide. "Oh, damn it all!" She grabbed her bigger brother's shirt and dragged him down closer to her height. "You will sit out of the way or I *swear* I will put you to sleep so you have no choice!"

He seethed a bit. He knew damned well she would do it, and without guilt. "Unless you're in trouble and the other four can't get to you fast enough."

"Fine." Activating her Mask had bolstered her own magic, and she could use the transport herself this time. They landed in the middle of the fight, and she shoved her brother out of the way of a stray blast. It hit her instead and knocked her flat on her butt. "Owie!"

"Damn it, Siobhan!" Virginia knelt beside her and helped her stand. "We had it handled!"

"It's my fight!" Siobhan shouted at her in turn. "Stop trying to protect me from doing what I was born to do! Wah!" The last added as Juliet bodily lifted her and carted her over to Yvonne. Siobhan kicked her feet. "Put me down!"

"Fine!" Juliet plopped her down beside the Iris Defender. "Stay here where you're better off! Defenders solely of magic orientation stay at the back. These are the rules, and you abide by them or else!" She aimed a finger at Rocky. "You! Over here as well. If you're going to be here, stand behind the people who can make shields!"

He nearly stomped his feet over to Siobhan and Yvonne. The Iris Defender wisely hid a smile to the best of her ability. She snapped off a quick ice shield to protect Virginia and then turned to her prince. "Rocky, let me see if I can at least help you to some extent. If we can re-unlock your ability to call up your Ruler suit, it will provide at least some measure of defense. Our Ruler outfits *do* have some magical aspects to them, else we wouldn't be able to just conjure them up at will. It might give you a few more defenses so that if you continue to insist on being present, at least you will not be such an easy target." She smiled. "Rocky, we fully respect that you are, in fact, physically stronger and more skilled than Gin. However, you must respect that we live to protect you and Siobhan, and we love you enough to give our lives willingly."

"Will you let me fight if I can get a proper weapon?" he muttered.

"Yes," Virginia shot over her shoulder as she stabbed a Germ with her halberd and then ripped it apart. "Until then, behave yourself!"

While Siobhan called up her rod and used it to start sending off magical blasts of her own, Yvonne turned her attention to Rocky. "Shirt," she ordered. After he had removed it so she could see his Flower Mark, she studied the blossom intently. It looked perfectly normal, all things considered, and as he had been playing with and studying his own magical gifts for almost two decades as best he could under secretive conditions, it really should not have been hard for him to access his Ruler suit. She called shenanigans of an ultimate being sort, and most probably Destiny oriented.

She lightly touched the Mark with her fingers and used her own magic to find his. It welled as a swirl of white and gold Illusion Flower Element, and she saw his eyes widen as if he had just somehow figured something out. The magic swept over his body, and his normal clothes immediately disappeared to be replaced by the familiar suit of a male Delphinium Ruler Cultivator. "There!" she said in satisfaction.

"Duck!"

She hastily grabbed Rocky by his lapel and yanked him down with her as she dropped flat. Siobhan had already dropped down as well, and the stray blast went harmlessly over their heads. Rocky, smart man that he was, stayed down. The two Defenders leapt back up, and Siobhan swung her rod high. "Please work!" she muttered under her breath.

Under normal circumstances, casting healing magic on an enemy fell under 'not smart' as far as tactics went. But because the Germs had been made of disease power, and were almost effectively undead, healing power could actually be detrimental. The pure white Light from Siobhan's magic became positively corrosive under those circumstances, and rather than merely damage the Germs as she had hoped, she ended up obliterating them entirely.

The additional benefit came in the backwash of the magic hitting Virginia, Juliet, and Sherry, and healing whatever injuries that they had sustained. Virginia, in the process of trying to cut a Germ in half, found herself applying force to nothing and her halberd smacked into the ground so hard it sank in half a foot. She let it stay there as she turned to look at Siobhan. "Why the hell didn't you do that sooner?"

"I didn't know it'd work." Siobhan gave in to her trembling knees and sank down to sit on the ground. "I'm scared," she admitted shakily. "Okay, I'm really scared. But I have to be here. I have to do this. Delphinium made me her Defender Cultivator as fully as she made me one of her Ruler Cultivators. You can't keep me out. I love you for trying, but you can't. I would rather be here with all of you than anywhere else."

Sherry removed her Mask to send away her armor and then knelt in front of her twin soul. "We accept that, just as long as you accept that we will, of course, not ever be happy with Delphinium's choice." She smiled and held on tight when Siobhan threw her arms around her. "I love you too, Siobhan."

Siobhan let go and then sent away her weapon before removing her Mask to send away her armor. The others did likewise, and Rocky went back to normal. At a lifted brow from Juliet, he also put his shirt back on. "Since when do you have modesty?" he grumbled.

"I'm more concerned with you getting cold and tempting Destiny into finally making you get sick."

"Yes, Mother."

Siobhan huffed out a breath. "Famine will now know who I am and where I am." She paused briefly to sneeze. "We can probably expect her to come after me directly now, right?"

"Maybe and maybe not," Virginia disagreed. "She might want to try to handle things via her minions. Why would she expend effort where it isn't needed? We'll just have to hold up until she finally does come after you, and then we'll help you do whatever it is you have to do."

Siobhan nodded. "Which means this could last a while."

"Very probably."

She sighed. "In that case, I'm going to go talk to Edgar. He needs to know what's happening so he can be prepared for any potential fallout." She added in a mutter, "Knowing him, he'll be as bad as Rocky and want to get into things."

Yvonne fought to hide a smile. "He *does* have less of a temper, Siobhan, so perhaps not. Still, yes, he should be told. If only because he is your Caretaker as much as a Cultivator, and he deserves to know *why* you will be in danger."

Siobhan smiled. "No Cultivator chooses an inferior mate, right? Guess Shana and I just decided to choose especially special ones."

"Indeed," Virginia murmured.

Edgar had just finished washing dishes when his doorbell rang. He quirked a brow as he felt a familiar presence, and he walked over to open the door. "You should be resting!" he scolded her. "Get in here and warm up!"

"I have a fever. I'm warm enough." Siobhan still hustled into the apartment. "We really, really need to talk, Edgar."

"I assume this is related to you being in danger earlier that I could feel?"

Her eyes went wide. "You felt that? But-but . . . Ginny said that only Defenders could feel their Caretaker in danger, not Rulers, and you're *only* a Ruler and not a Dual like me. Okay, though, because you're *my* Caretaker, maybe that's why you felt it because Caretakers to Defenders always do feel if their Defender needs them." She began to frown. "Wait. That still doesn't explain anything else about how Rocky feels me in danger, or me sensing him, or you and Shana, so maybe it's because we have special gifts we don't even know about, and okay this going to be so much more trouble because evil is here and I have to fight!"

He could only stare at her in a combination of shock and unintentional amusement. He had *long* before learned how to keep up when she or her brother entered into one of their tirades, but they still could stir his sense of humor. "Breathe." He smoothed wisps of hair out of her face. "Remember, we all knew this surely had to be inevitable because Defenders don't exist without need. Did Virginia finally explain *why*?"

Her shoulders relaxed a little at his touch. "Yeah, more than we had really gotten out of her before. As an Apex, I'm . . . I'm sort of an ultimate being, right? The epitome of all that is magical. Well . . . that means I have to fight and destroy something called Famine." She deliberately said nothing of what she had seen through her Sight, but she did tell him what Virginia had explained. "She really wouldn't explain more than that, though, and I definitely know there has to be more. Something terrible about the fall of the kingdoms, I think."

He slowly nodded. "Alright. At least we have some sense of things for now. Anything else we need to know, I guess we will figure it out on our own. I will try to stay out of things, I promise, but if you need me as your Caretaker . . ."

Her fingers smoothed across his beloved face. "Nothing would stop you, I know." Humor lightened her gold eyes. "Now teach that sort of patience to my brother, will you?"

He snorted. "You don't ask for much, do you? I'll be glad when Shana is here to divert him, and I can focus solely on being your Caretaker." Black and pink magic swirled down his arm and formed into a delicate black protea blossom. He tucked it over her ear. "I've always thought that I had magic just for you, so I can understand you."

She sighed softly and deeply with contentment as his lips teased hers. Her Caretaker. How perfect he was just for her. She could be his Caretaker in turn, putting him back together each time his need to get physical inevitably got him hurt. They worked so well together. "What if you manage to finally get sick if you kiss me, you silly man?"

"That's alright. I know a healer."

* * * * *

Things seemed to settle a bit for the next day though all remained on edge. Being among the only healthy people in town, the four Dual Cultivators picked up whatever spare jobs they could do. They refused all pay, however. None of them really needed the funds; they either received support from their family—Sherry and Yvonne— or had scholarships that covered living expenses—Juliet and Virginia. Juliet also worked part-time in the campus bakery as a paid internship as part of her degree, so, like Rocky, she had additional income from a job. He still worked part-time on the horse ranch just outside of town just because he enjoyed the work.

Edgar had no need to work a paying job unless he wanted, thanks to the trust fund's inability to run out of money because it came directly from the company. Being unable to get sick himself, he also picked up a few jobs just to help as needed.

At all times, at least one Defender accompanied Siobhan and Rocky. They *really* wanted to slap a guard on Edgar, but that would split their ranks too much for safety. Virginia had to trust that he would continue to behave himself and stay out of things, though she did not expect it to last forever. While he *was* a Ruler Cultivator, he had always seen himself as Siobhan's Caretaker first and foremost. She did not look forward to when Shana awoke as the Protea Defender Cultivator. Rocky was already enough trouble where his sister was concerned, let alone adding his soul mate!

The third day out from the first attack, all five Defenders were together with Rocky to walk home from some jobs they had done when Sherry stopped dead in her tracks as a chill swept over her body. They all knew the signal this time and grabbed their Masks. Siobhan wore hers along with its communication counterpart on a necklace now.

Slime oozed up out of the ground and became the familiar, putrid, shape of a Germ. It again tore off pieces of itself to make more, and this time it shortly created a horde of a hundred that swarmed in to surround the six Cultivators. In a low voice, Virginia told Rocky, "I will make you a path. Take it, get to a safe corner, and *stay* there. Are we clear, Robert?"

The use of his Ruler name made him wince. "Yes'm."

The five Defenders donned their Masks and called their armor, and Virginia summoned her halberd. She lunged forward on a shout and immediately drew the ire of many Germs as she cut down a set with a single attack. Even Yvonne ducked right into the middle, choosing to take direct damage if only to serve as a distraction. As soon as a path formed, and Rocky ran out of the way, Yvonne dropped back with Siobhan to resume her role as a magical defense.

The fight should have been lopsided in favor of the Germs, yet it actually swung to the side of the Defenders. Siobhan proved positively lethal as she began firing off blasts of Light magic and Illusory deceptions. Five thousand years of waited destiny rode on her armored shoulders, and she would be *damned* if she let anything stop her! None of them could tolerate the idea of losing, and it made them especially potent.

When the bodies and the dust finally settled, all Defenders looked more than a little ragged at the edges once they took their Masks off and sent away their armor, but Siobhan took care of healing everything except her own minor injuries. She tugged off her Mask and put it on top of her head, and the injuries revealed themselves as a minor constellation of cuts on her outer right leg where a Germ had managed to get past her guard and pierce the armor. Even cloth armor portions to Defender armor were *exceptionally* strong, but they had limitations.

"Can you heal that?" Yvonne asked after quickly checking the severity of the wound. "You usually don't get injured, so we've never had this problem."

"And you wouldn't have been injured if I hadn't been distracted," Juliet groused.

"Don't worry about it, Juli! And I can't do anything for it in either case," Siobhan sighed. "Healers can't heal themselves, sorry. We heal by taking in the wounds of others and mending them. Kinda can't do that to yourself. I mean, someone *probably* could if they had a way of making their magic do the same task twice at the same time, but I've never heard of it." She half winced as her brother moved closer and hovered a hand over the wound. "Which means Rocky gets to practice healing. Fun. Please don't mess up this time. It's a strange thing to have you heal me and then I have to heal you where you couldn't mend what you took from me!"

Rocky shot her a dirty look but couldn't say much. Much to his relief, he could remove the wounds and mended them safely on his side without damage. "Healing isn't really my specialty," he apologized.

"No surprise," Sherry told him. "Your gifts as a Ruler usually fall in line with the normal Delphinium ones where you basically act like a magical battery and can boost the gifts of those around you, or making an illusion so strong that it eventually becomes real. How did you unlock healing?"

"That thing about making illusions that become real?" He smiled wryly. "I kept trying so hard to use healing magic that I basically created it inside myself over time. I just really worried about Siobhan because she was our only healer without Kellie present. So, I just kept at it until I could do at least the most basic of things."

It underscored his great gift for magic that he had actually conjured an illusion of a *skill* and made it real. It had taken years, certainly, where his other illusions would take days to months of constant maintenance, but he had still done it. "Not bad, kid," Virginia told him.

He scowled. "I'm barely a year younger."

"Still applies. And you're still not allowed to jump in fights. No weapon, no fight."

"Do my hands and feet count?" he asked hopefully.

"Nope."

"Come *on*, Ginny!" Siobhan threw her hands in the air. "You know he's just as good at weaponless combat as he is with a weapon!"

She did, in fact, know such a thing. She also knew that until he had full memory of *all* of his past life, including the ability to use what magic he did have to enhance his physical skill, he would actually be at a disadvantage without a weapon in hand. He was still of Delphinium. He needed that edge. "My word is final as Lead Defender."

Two sets of gold eyes started to turn white with temper. Sherry smoothly stepped forward and linked elbows with both of them. "Let's go to my place and get ice cream! I'll make your favorite chocolate chip kind." She hid a smile as they both looked at her with interest. Leave it to their nearly bottomless bellies to divert them from being mad at Virginia! "Come on."

Virginia watched them walk off and then tugged her PPS out of her back pocket. "Kellie Yu," she ordered her phone. It beeped in response and she waited. When the other side clicked over, she said without preamble, "It's Gin. Roust Clara to be courier. Our prince needs your services."

Kellie just laughed. "I'll take care of things, promise."

* * * * *

Things did not improve over the next week. The illness had begun to spread beyond Lux, and the world leaders issued a lockdown. No one could enter or leave the city, and those in the worst stages of the disease had to be quarantined. Siobhan had not gotten worse personally, but she had certainly not gotten better. She spent her time curled up on the couch at either her own home, or Edgar's. What few part-time jobs had been available were ceased as the entire town went into lockdown. Only the hospitals remained active, but even they moved slower.

The four Defenders opted to spend more time with Rocky and Siobhan at their apartment, if only to keep Siobhan from being too stressed. Edgar came over frequently enough as well, and after he had left one day, Siobhan grumbled, "I swear he's finally going to get sick if he keeps kissing me."

Juliet didn't look up from the stew she had commandeered the kitchen to make. "I'm fairly sure the threat of death won't make him stop kissing you, which is really how it should be."

"Eh, you know he's safe enough." Virginia was flopped in one of the overstuffed bean bags and had control of the remote that controlled the Visuality in the place. Over two hundred channels and yet there often still seemed to be nothing interesting on. "Besides, Juli is right. You really wouldn't stop him even if he didn't have Cultivator immunity." She found one of the world-wide channels showing a musical film theatrical debuting a new actor and stopped there. He was quite attractive, and he had a hell of a set of vocal skills. "Ah, better."

"Oh he's good!" Yvonne noted. She stretched and then leaned back against the couch. "Sounds like a Virtuoso. He should go far." She tilted her head back to look at Siobhan. "The waiting is eating us too.

Famine should not wait much longer. She's trying to weaken you but it isn't working. She just can't override a Cultivator's immunity entirely, not even your compromised one."

"Just how does that work anyway?" Rocky asked as he looked up from the book he had been reading. "I've never really understood, and it's not in our few memories."

"It's a byproduct of having a Seed," Yvonne explained. "We're kind of like gardens, so we're supposed to be able to treat disease like something biodegradable and break it down. Siobhan basically has weeds in her garden throwing her off."

"Makes me wish I had a lawn clipper for my inner garden," Siobhan grumbled. "Or a sword. I'd settle for a sword."

"The idea of you with a sword gives me a chill. But on a related note!" Virginia rolled lazily up to her feet. "Rocky, I have a present for you." She walked over to him and held out her hands. Red and gold magic flowed over her fingers and materialized a beautiful scimitar of supreme craftsmanship. "Here you go!" She handed it over.

He could only stare at the blade. "It's gorgeous." He held it up to the light and watched as the sunlight passed right through the blade. Testing, he called up his magic and watched it also pass through the blade in a swirl of white and gold. His head swung back to Virginia. "This was made by a Metal Flower Element, so it's got to be from Kellie!"

"It is," she agreed. She sat down again on her bag and lifted a brow. "I know you all too well, Rocky. With or without my order, you would be trying to charge in. It's just how you are. And since I know I can't entirely stop you, I decided to make sure that at least you have some more level of defense and therefore called Kellie. She made this and had Clara deliver it to save time."

He felt a bit humbled to be reminded that Virginia fully respected his skills in battle despite her driving need to protect him. "Thanks, Ginny," he said softly. He thought about things and then asked, "Does Shana know what's happening?"

"No. She has no need to know for now, *especially* if you and Edgar behave yourselves."

Siobhan couldn't help but giggle. Later, after everyone else had gone home, she told her brother, "Speaking of Edgar, I'm going over to see him. It keeps him happy because he's trying so hard to stay out of things, and he's driven by a need to help me if needed."

"Fair enough," Rocky said. "Spending the night?"

"Very probably. I want to live my life as much as I can, you know?" She grabbed her coat and keys and hurried out of the apartment. It felt so frustrating to have no control over her life! She did respect the four other Defenders' need to protect her and her brother, but they needed to have a bit more respect for *her* need to know what was going on around them. She, like the two men, chaffed more than a bit at the restrictions.

Later snuggled together on the couch with her lover, she rested her head on his shoulder and asked, "I'm not sure I ever asked when you and Shana figured out you had magic. You two were very not surprised when I used mine to heal you up after that fall. I and Rocky found ours out very quickly after I found my Mask. You?"

"We were still in the hospital. Weird things were happening." Edgar thought back to those painful days. "The very day she found her Mask was the day of the accident. We'd both been sensitive to nature before, and after I turned five, I discovered I could enhance and influence flora and fauna alike, though more specifically flora. Didn't really see it as being magic until after the accident. Shana started talking to the birds that would fly in our window. We got curious and started experimenting when you two were away for whatever reason."

She still felt a little awed by both Chivanti siblings and their utter bravery. Despite losing their parents in a terrible accident, they didn't run in complete fear from the vehicles that had caused it. To be sure, Edgar couldn't handle the idea of driving a carriage and had never bothered to learn, but he still allowed for them to be in his life. If he couldn't walk or take the common public transportation versions, he just asked someone else to drive. Usually Siobhan volunteered. She still wondered how he managed to get into a carriage at all. Shana could drive single-person ECs, but anything beyond that, she had the same issues as her brother. "I wonder why we never mentioned the magic to each other."

"Probably just never crossed our minds. And if you weren't so driven to heal all that moves, it might have been ignored for longer."

She teased back, "If *someone* didn't have a propensity for getting hurt, maybe I wouldn't have that driving need." She smoothed a hand across his chest and felt his Flower Mark tingling her skin. They never hid their Marks from one another when alone. "It bothers you. Staying out of things."

"Of course it does."

"So why are you doing it? Let's be honest, Virginia might growl and snarl at you and Rocky, but she *does* understand your feelings."

Frustration eked into his tone. "I want to help, Siobhan. More than anything. But I know that I am not supposed to interfere. I knew that as soon as you told me the why's of your existence. This is a matter of Delphinium Royal House, and I am Protean. Besides," he muttered, "Gin scares me, whether she understands or not!"

She was still turning over those words when she went home the next morning. She walked into the apartment and found Rocky in the sitting room with his Personal Computational Machine. He had both a love for and a knack with anything related to the machines, and deciding to study it at university had only taken it a step further. PCMs did just about anything and everything imaginable that could be possibly electronically related, and they had helped create the culture of the last two centuries by introducing the ability to store data electronically. People affectionately called that data storage the 'spider' since the hubs that maintained it tended to make a spider-web shape when viewed from above.

The spider allowed for people to communicate, share, and connect with others across the world. Siobhan liked to follow mini-webs run by people who did art things because then she could admire their hard work. Really, the only downside to the spider was that people with exceptional skills—her brother included—could sometimes find ways to get into other PCMs and mess with the settings. She usually pretended she didn't know what he was doing; he normally used his powers only for good.

"I was looking up information on that new actor," he told her when he saw her enter the apartment. "His name is Byron Rancul." He grinned. "Big following starting up. His official mini-web is only just started. Sherry wants to meet him since she's a Shaman and he's a Virtuoso. His sort is even rarer than hers!"

"Well, she's 'only' one in ten thousand. He's more like one in one hundred thousand." She sat down on the couch beside him. "Last night, Edgar said something that was very true and got me thinking about everything happening. About why he strives so hard to stay out, and maybe why you're so driven to get in. This is a matter of our Royal House, not his."

Rocky put his PCM aside and turned to face his sister. He gently laced their fingers together. "Then," he said quietly, "we should handle this ourselves. When Famine finally makes a move, we'll make one back. In fact, I think I might already have an idea. I noticed something at the last fight." He smiled wryly. "The benefit of standing back is seeing what those in the thick might miss."

Her brows lifted. "This ought to be interesting."

* * * * *

Famine stared malevolently into her scrying mirror and fought the screams of rage welling inside. Why wouldn't that cursed queen die?! Hatred swelled as she shifted her gaze toward the figure of Edgar walking home from somewhere. The Caretaker of the Apex of Light and a Ruler Cultivator of Protea. *He* could not evolve. *He* did not have armor. Moreover, he was endeared to not just Siobhan, but also Rocky, and Famine hated the High Prince of Delphinium nearly as much as she hated the High Queen. Perhaps it was time to weaken the Royal House by striking at someone empowering them both. If she could take down the Delphinium Defender Cultivator's soul mate, then she increased her odds of winning.

Nothing would stop her from claiming what was rightfully hers! This 'destiny' would never come to pass.

* * * * *

Edgar of course had Sight thanks to his Protean lineage as a descendant of Orion. It was Present Sight, like what Siobhan possessed. The only people he knew with All Sight—seeing past, present, and future alike—were his sister and Clara, and Rocky and Sherry were the only ones with Future Sight.

Present Sight meant he could see things happening in real-time in other locations, or things happening invisibly in his own. He stopped dead in his tracks as his Sight stirred and his eyes unfocused while he watched inside his mind as ooze crept down the walls of the buildings near him. He swung around and leapt backwards just as the ooze materialized and a Germ lunged toward him with hooked claws. Black and pink swept over him to put him into his Ruler suit, giving him additional defenses, but his hand flexed in frustration at his lack of a weapon. He would have to get hands on, which he had plenty of skills in.

It would just hurt a lot without armor.

Siobhan and Rocky had just met up with the four Defenders when Siobhan went deathly white and clutched at the hidden Mark on her chest. Rocky and Sherry grabbed her arms when she staggered and kept her on her feet. "Siobhan?" Sherry asked. "What's wrong?"

"Edgar," she managed to say. "He's in trouble!" Fury turned her eyes from gold to white in a blink. Only those of the strongest internal Light cores could have their eyes turn white in temper. Likewise, the strongest Dark cores went black. "How dare she?!" she snarled.

She ripped away from her brother and twin and ran off down the street as quickly as she could manage. If she cared that she tripped more than once, no one noticed. They had enough trouble keeping up! And, truly, their fury went just as deep. Virginia took the attack almost as personally as Siobhan did.

They skidded around a corner to discover Edgar more than a bit bloodied but still holding the Germs at bay with skill. "Thank goddess for him being Protean!" Virginia muttered. If he had been from a magically oriented world rather than a physically oriented world, he could have already been killed; Rulers just did not get to use magic the same way Defenders did. Edgar certainly did use magic in ways Proteans normally could not—he could actually conjure up plants of all types—but he still did not use magic in a way that could produce attacks or shields.

Sherry's hand shot up and snapped off a powerful fireball that incinerated the Germ lunging for Edgar. He wisely took the chance to dive back out of the way so the Defenders could move in. All five donned their Masks and armor and got to work, though Siobhan scrambled to her lover's side to heal him. She didn't bother to ask if he was alright; the answer seemed obvious in the dark red blood staining his skin and clothes. She asked only, "Is there anything I *can't* see?"

"Sore ribs, but otherwise everything is rather visible." He let out a breath as her magic erased the wounds and took away pain. He regained his feet and sighed. "I really did not intend for this to happen. I'm sorry, Siobhan."

She shook her head. "It's fine. Just stay here!" she ordered him. "I mean it!" She hurried over to join Yvonne, but she glanced briefly at her brother before doing so.

The look had Edgar on his guard. "Do I want to know what you two are planning?" he muttered at his friend.

"Very probably not," Rocky muttered back. "I'm going to help as best I can. Siobhan's right. Stay here." He called up his Ruler suit and scimitar and moved forward to help cover the two magically oriented Defenders when anything got too close. They could spend less time dodging and more time casting that way.

Edgar felt frustration bubble and looked down at his hands briefly. He looked up again when he heard a yelp and saw Juliet kicking a Germ away from Sherry. Juliet had minimal hand and foot skills herself; maybe she would let him teach her some more advanced things. She had never really gone to those classes with them, but it couldn't hurt her to pick the skills up.

He felt a sudden presence behind him and froze. Familiar power touched him, and his shoulders relaxed again. "Why are you here?" he asked softly.

"I'm just a courier," the figure behind him said in amusement. "Try not to get hurt again. Alexandria and Kellie had a devil of a time distracting your sister."

He felt something put in his hand and looked down to discover he had just been handed a weapon. The long sword showed remarkable, and familiar, Metal skills. Some of the tension left his soul. He turned to say thank you, but discovered the 'courier' had already disappeared. A smile touched his lips. She literally never changed.

The Germs not only numbered more, but they had been made stronger. Famine fed on the illness in the people, and it made her creations extra potent. Even just destroying one of the Germs had hazards as they released a backwash that could also do damage. It also seemed to evaporate loose debris in the area.

When Yvonne moved a few steps away, Rocky said in a low voice to Siobhan, "You think you can use that?"

"I've been watching," she whispered back. "You were right about her yanking back the bits of the Germs not entirely destroyed so she doesn't have to spend extra energy making new. That backwash isn't evaporating things. It's transporting them.

"So if we jump in, you can absolutely use your magic to transport us to wherever she is."

"I'm sure of it. You were right about everything else, so I trust this too."

"Someone," he did not name names, "will kill us even if we survive."

"Yeah, well, I'm literally sick of this." She caught his sleeve when she saw a Germ about to go down only a few feet in front of them. "Move!" She ran forward and threw out Light power that struck the backwash and opened an oddly colored sphere that vaguely resembled a time-space portal. Before the others could react, both Siobhan and Rocky dove through it.

"Damn it!" Virginia snarled. "I should have realized they were too complacent! We're going after them!"

"I'm going too," Edgar demanded as he walked closer.

"The hell you will! Same rules apply to you as your cohort, kid: no weapon, no fight!" Her eyes narrowed as he pointedly held up his new sword and she recognized the skill that had made it. "*Some* people should most want you to stay safe."

"*Some* people," he countered politely, "know I would go with or without a weapon. We Dark types don't usually sit on the sidelines, Gin. You know that." He smiled. "If I promise to do what I'm told, will you feel better?"

"Only a bit," she muttered. "As you said, I know Dark types!"

The two Delphinium siblings found themselves stumbling out the other side of the portal where they tripped over their own feet and landed flat on the ground. Everything felt . . . odd. Familiar and yet not. Distorted from what they thought they should see. Some sort of ash covered everything in sight, including the dirt that had broken their fall.

Siobhan slowly pushed herself up onto her knees and looked around. Even the very air felt dead. Thick. Near impossible to breathe. The sky overhead looked a disturbing shade of acidic yellow. A chill roughened her skin, even through the armor. *Death.* It clung to everything around her.

Rocky gingerly sat up as well. "Where are we?" he asked in a low voice. He turned to look behind them and went very still. Pain welled inside his heart and soul as tears filled his eyes. "Siobhan."

She turned to look as well. A little cry caught in her chest. Pain. Protest. Behind them loomed the once impressive structure of a castle that must have surely looked glorious in its day. A castle she could see inside her fuzzy memories of her last life. The Delphinium Castle. They had landed not in another dimension, but on the frozen and still infected world of Delphinium.

She put her hands on the ground and her fingers trembled as she felt how sick and tired her Mother was. The world breathed still, but only barely. "How did you even have the strength to bring back our Seeds?" she whispered. Her head lowered, and her shoulders shook. "Who was here to love you? There was no one to make everything right." Tears slid down her face under her Mask and then dripped to the land. Dust puffed into the air. Another tear fell, and the land shimmered softly. A beautiful white delphinium began to sprout, and its glow reflected across her armor.

"We can save our Mother," Rocky told her fiercely. He got to his feet and then drew her up as well. "If we remove Famine, then you can heal Delphinium. It may take ages for her to recover, but we can wait." He caught her gloved fingers in his. "I'm here."

She held on tight for a moment. "I'm not alone. I know." She drew a deep breath and began to walk toward the ruins. Her rod appeared in her hand as she went. Where else would Famine hide except inside the one place she could not claim? Only a true heir of Delphinium, one of its chosen Ruler Cultivators, could ever take the throne. Siobhan had already claimed it, and until she died—permanently—or willingly gave it away to her own future child, it would remain hers.

A hundred feet from the doors, Germs surged out in a violent wave, packed so tightly they moved almost like water across the ground. Rocky shot around in front of Siobhan with his scimitar at ready. "Keep me as healed as you can!" he snapped. "I'll cut through! I can buy you time if you cover me with magic!"

She swung her rod up in answer and sent balls of Light power flying at the Germs. The concentrated elemental power blew the monstrous creatures apart. Seeing it, Rocky for the first time in his exceptionally long existence finally realized why Light had never before been controlled as a physical element. It was positively unstoppable in the right hands. If he *ever* met someone who could outcast his sister, the universe would change.

The pair of siblings made a perfect combination as they forced their way deeper through the horde. Rocky had the physical skills needed to keep enemies away from himself and Siobhan alike, and she was small enough to stay close enough to him to either heal anything too terrible or simply fire off shields to protect him. When he looked at least remotely healthy, considering he wore no armor, she focused on attacking magic. His own magic channeled through his weapon also added punch.

The Germs just kept on coming like an incurable infection. Rocky gauged the distance to the castle doors and took a quick breath. "I'll hold the field. You have to go straight for Famine!" he told

Siobhan.

Her hands tightened on her rod. The idea of leaving him alone made her stomach churn. Yet, unless she did, they stood no chance. She had to place her faith in his skill, and the hope that the other Defenders would be coming after them. "Don't die," she whispered. "I can't lose you."

"Hey." He paused enough to tug on her tightly bound braid. "I'm not going anywhere. Promise."

She gulped a quick breath and then nodded. To aid in the efforts of her brother, she slammed the bottom of her rod onto the ground. A shockwave of Illusion magic rose up and created exceptionally realistic impressions of herself and her brother alike. Confused, the Germs went after the mirages and could not tell real from fake. Rocky took immediate advantage of the confusion to start removing high quantities of the enemy before they realized he was real.

Siobhan kept her head low and ran as fast as she dared toward the castle doors as soon as she saw a pathway open. She made it past the Germs and scrambled into the castle only to slide on the dust covered marble floor and go tumbling to the ground. Now aware of the danger, she more carefully got to her feet and fought the urge to run back outside to help Rocky. Nothing hurt more than to leave him behind when he was neither a Defender nor had armor.

She knew where to go. Just, somehow, knew. She moved as if by memory through the castle toward the grand throne room. The doors hung from their hinges but still mostly stayed in place, so she shoved them open. The first thing she saw was the column of light holding her crown. The second was Famine herself.

Memory stirred anew. A vignette of the past. She stood before the castle with Edgar, in his Ruler suit, beside her. No sign of her brother. Where had he been? She shook it off fiercely and moved slowly across the room toward the crown. The entire room looked as sickly as the sky, proof that Famine had begun to corrupt the entire structure. "Surprise!" she mocked the evil entity. "I found you!"

Hatred glowed from out of Famine's haggard face. "So you did," she bit out. "You think you can destroy me? You're not even awakened!"

"And you are bluffing about your power!" Siobhan shot back. "If you were as powerful as you think you are, I would already be dead!" Light glowed through her eyes and then down her Mask and armor. "It's time this ended!"

Famine laughed at her. "You? You can't even move and cast at the same time, and you have no physical skills!" She gave a sudden yelp as Siobhan abruptly appeared in front of her and smashed the end of her rod into her face so hard that it sent her stumbling.

"Maybe not," Siobhan smirked, "but I can move at the speed of Light, and I can still swing my weapon pretty hard!" She swallowed a yelp and scrambled back as Famine came after her with skeletal hands hooked like claws. She ran desperately to one side of the room and swung around to fire off a blast of magic. It missed when Famine dodged and then came in again.

The pattern repeated, making the fight into almost a non-fight. Siobhan could not run and attack, and if she held still, Famine had time to dodge. Yet, Famine could not get close either for Siobhan could make herself invisible and blink across a room.

One of Siobhan's blinks made her slip and fall on the ground. She looked up sharply as Famine closed in, but the creature never reached her. A scimitar whipped through the air like a boomerang, driving Famine back before she could get close. The blade swung back the way it had been thrown, and Siobhan's head jerked around to find Rocky in the doorway.

He looked ragged and bloody, but he still had plenty of strength, and he proved it by rushing across the floor toward Famine. "Let's see how you do with two of us!" he snarled. Over his shoulder, he added, "I'll distract her! Do whatever you have to, Siobhan!"

Siobhan scrambled up to her feet and started firing off healing blasts. The magic had double duty; it had to pass through Rocky to get to Famine, and that meant it healed him on its way to harm her. Not needing to dodge meant that Siobhan had more than enough time to start casting the biggest abilities in her arsenal.

It did not take long before Famine looked as ragged as Rocky.

She could not break through the Delphinium High Prince's impressive sword skills. He also had far more grace than his sister and did not seem to even notice the dusty floor. His blade swung around as she tried to move past him, and it hacked entirely through her arm. She screamed shrilly as the limb fell to the ground and decayed.

Ugly power began to move through her body. "So be it!" she screeched. Her only remaining hand shot out and closed around Rocky's neck before he could dodge. Disease power blasted into him at pointblank range in a way even his Cultivator immunity could not stop. He went a sickly shade and sagged in her grip.

"*Rocky!!*" His name tore from Siobhan as a pained cry, and she scrambled across the ground toward him. When Famine dropped him to the ground, he did not move. "No no no no!" Siobhan slid to her knees beside him as tears ran down her face. He breathed only shallowly, and he had been brutally sickened. Nearly as terribly as their world. His pain churned so hotly that she felt it echo into her own body. Her skin actually burned from his fever, even through her gloves, when she pressed her hand to his forehead to desperately pour healing magic into him. Nothing happened.

"I can't do this," she whispered. She cradled her brother's head against her chest and ignored Famine cackling as the entity flew around them in mocking circles. "I can't."

Softly, across her mind, she heard an oddly familiar voice say, *Siobhan. You can do this. If you reach for the Whisper of Hope inside your soul, and embrace who you are as an Apex, you can create a miracle.*

She looked up sharply. "Clara?"

Yes. The world has forgotten Famine. There is hope in the people. Reach out, gather it, and whisper it to the sky. Unleash the Whisper of Hope that only an Apex can and fulfill your destiny. But be warned, Siobhan, that your destiny carries a price. The birth of an Apex always does. A healer heals by taking in that which afflicts others. If you take in that much disease, you will lose your life, and possibly permanently.

"Will my brother live?" she asked softly. If he could live, if perhaps he could carry the promise of future children for Delphinium, then she could be willing to let go.

Only you will not.

"Then so be it." She looked up toward Famine, and her eyes turned white as she reached toward that glowing Light deep in her soul. She let go of every restraint, stopped fighting what bubbled inside her. Her Mask disappeared as her armor began to dissolve until nothing but Light and white-gold delphinium blossoms surrounded her. Her Flower Marks started glowing with more and more force until the one on her arm suddenly took on a second blossom and the crowns of both began to sparkle. Wings of glowing white burst from her back as the crown on her Marks also appeared on her right cheek.

Famine could not move, could not breathe, as she stared at the Apex of Light. Siobhan looked at her for a long moment and then looked down at her brother. She tenderly cupped his cheek and let her magic pour into him. Disease evaporated and the color came back to his skin. She put him down gently on the floor and got to her feet. Her unbound hair fluttered in the force of the power around her as she looked once more at Famine.

Rocky's eyes opened just in time to see Siobhan flying across the ground toward Famine. A sudden realization of her intent made his heart freeze. "No!" He scrambled up to try to stop her, but he only made it a foot before Juliet and Virginia tackled him back down to the ground. He could only watch in horror as Siobhan literally plunged into Famine and disappeared. The scream of primal anguish from Famine made all of them flinch.

The other three ran over to join Rocky and the two Defenders, but no one could say a word. Only Yvonne and Sherry restraining Edgar kept him from trying to go after Siobhan as well. "I can't feel her!" Edgar managed to say. "She's being torn out of me!" A quick look at Sherry and Rocky confirmed they felt it too, yet there was nothing to be done to stop an Apex once unleashed.

"It burns!" Famine raged. She began to release maniacal blasts of necrotic power through the air. "Make it stop!"

Yvonne put up a hasty shield around everyone. "What do we do now?" she asked.

"Wait for a miracle," Virginia admitted quietly.

Siobhan continued to dive deeper and deeper through the disgusting muck that made up Famine's essence. She consumed the disease that tried to force her back and released it behind her as a trail of pure healing energy. When she suddenly could go no deeper, she knew she had reached the very center of her enemy's core. She looked at her hands and then curled them into fists. "Let the Light," she whispered, "shine out with Hope."

A soft voice welled on the air around her as if to repeat the Whisper. The evil power in the area diverted and flooded right at her. It poured into her body and she calmly began to release it as the purest light of healing hope.

No one knew what had happened. Famine had grabbed her head in agony and continued to scream. Her skin began to split and peel to release the light swelling inside her. Her screams spiraled louder and louder until they abruptly cut off as she blew apart and the force inside broke free. It exploded away as a blinding shockwave that seared everyone's eyes briefly. The wave consumed Delphinium entirely, pierced into the frozen Core, and purged it of all illness. Like a prism, the Core then released the wave across the entire Blossom Field galaxy.

The Cores of Aster, Gladiolus, Carnation, and Iris unfroze and healed of illness. Protea herself healed, and all those who had been sick were just, suddenly, *not*. Any illness. Any injury. Anything not permanent. Gone as if it had never been. The planets that had been healed may take millennia to fully recover and be capable of supporting life again, but now they *could*.

The light drew back in and revealed Siobhan hovering in the air where Famine had once been. She was still in her Apex form, and her eyes were closed. The power holding her began to release her, and Rocky and Edgar lunged across the ground. She landed safely in Edgar's arms, and he knelt to put her on the ground. He could not speak or breathe around the gaping wounds inside his soul where she had been torn free. Tears ran unchecked down Rocky's face, and Sherry had hunched into herself.

"She's smiling," Virginia managed to say. "Damn you, Siobhan!"

She buried her face in her hands. "What price is this?" she asked raggedly. "It should have been our lives, not yours!"

"Can't she come back?" Rocky demanded thickly. "Her time can't be up!! She hasn't had a child for Delphinium!" The others looked at him, and his gut clenched. "But I could?" he whispered. He shook his head hard. "That's not right! It can't be right! My children will be with *Shana*! They will be Protean! Won't they?" It came out ragged as a sob caught in his chest. "We couldn't have both Protean and Delphinian children! Siobhan *has* to come back!"

Softly, from the eaves, came Clara's familiar voice, "You are not wrong, Rocky. Your children with Shana will be Protean. Siobhan must come back to salvage Delphinium's future, but she cannot do it alone. Her body—her soul's garden—has been too terribly damaged. But you . . . her *Activated* brother, you could save her. If you pour magic from your Seed into hers, her body will be able to mend itself as a healer normally does. It has to be your Seed. No other could do this."

"So why can *he*?" Sherry's voice was thick with tears and pain. "Why not me, or Edgar?"

"That, too, will only be revealed with time." As silently as she had appeared, her presence faded once more.

Rocky took a breath and lifted a hand to cover his Mark. His Mark began to glow hotly, and he reached out with his free hand to touch Siobhan's Ruler Flower Mark. It also began to glow. Without any hesitation, he opened the conduit between them to give her his energy and magic. Such a thing, normally, was done to Activate a previously Deactivated Ruler Cultivator; that was why it made a Cultivator so very weak to do.

Siobhan suddenly took a powerful breath and her heart began to beat. A hint of color returned to her skin. Rocky had no more color than she did. Both Marks stopped glowing, and he began to fall. Juliet hastily caught him and then sighed as she held him in her arms. "Too much alike for our sanity," she groused.

Virginia could only smile wryly. "Lucky us. Stuck with *two* Delphinium children. One of us is going to either have a heart attack or lose our hair."

Yvonne had to smile toward Edgar as he cradled Siobhan. "Honestly, I feel more sorry for our partners. They have it worse with two *Protea* children!"

Edgar found a smile and then buried his face in Siobhan's hair. "Honestly, I do too." His arms tightened against his will. He could feel her again, interlocked with his soul where she belonged. Maybe things wouldn't get more powerful after their birthdays. They already felt . . . cemented. Perhaps they had carried over their souls' maturity from their last lives. Maybe that was one of the things that had saved them all.

Unknown to any of them, Siobhan had been conscious just under the surface and able to hear them. She said nothing, but her mind turned over the ramifications of everything said, and everything she had endured.

Only two days later, life had returned to normal for everyone. Very few people knew what had actually happened. Virginia, in full Mask and armor, presented herself to the world leaders on behalf of High Queen Sayena Delphinium and told them that they would not live to see the galaxy restored, but that it *would* happen eventually. The High Queen had no need nor desire to act as a queen again until her world could once more support life, and so things would remain status quo at least until the High Queen of Protea returned as well and decided how things would proceed. It was accepted as given, and things stayed as they were.

Siobhan bided her time until a week had passed and she could go somewhere without either her brother, lover, or twin needing to be with her at all times. She did not begrudge them that need, but what she needed to do did not need others. After securing some alone time, she took herself on a solitary transport to the ruins of the Protea Castle and walked calmly within. She had known of the ruins, of course, since they sat on the other side of the mountains around Lux, but she had never visited. Most people in her time knew little to nothing of the events from five thousand years before as more than a myth. Which, perhaps, truly was best for all involved.

She moved to the grand throne room and stopped to look at the crown hovering in the center. It looked nearly identical to her own, barring the different metals and gemstones used. Where hers had opals, this had amber. Her own crown sat in the trunk at home where her Mask had once been kept. It would stay there until needed.

She turned around and lifted a hand. Light flashed invisibly across the sky. Only a moment later, a time-space portal opened and Clara walked out. She looked the same as always, of course, but she wore clothes more in line with the common sort of the current time period. It matched to her choice to use a new name. Her two Masks hung from a charm bracelet along with the hourglass that marked her position as Librarian. "Hello, Siobhan," she said on a smile. "I was expecting you to call me."

Siobhan looked at her a moment and then her eyes narrowed. "I need answers, Claret."

The Statice Cultivator sighed, knowing what the use of her real name meant. "I know what answers you want, but I cannot give them. You will not like them."

Siobhan shook her head a bit sharply. "I don't care! I need to know!"

"Your answers will come, Sayena. You know well that there is another who was born with a price to be paid."

A bit of a bitter smile twisted her lips. "Will she have to die, too?" She met Clara's eyes. "The others do not know. I will *never* let them know. How that feels. To kill your body before your soul is freed, rather than your body fade away by your soul's departure. I remember how that felt at the end of the kingdoms. Dying by the destruction of your Seed . . . that death is *peaceful. Painless.* What I felt recently was the entire opposite. It felt like being trapped within a dying garden and knowing you will wither all too soon. It hurts unlike anything else." She shook her head hard. "I will *never* tolerate Shana suffering that!"

Clara's fingers clenched briefly together in an unusual and surprising display of agitation. "You do not speak wrong, but . . . hers . . . I suppose you could call it a fate worse than death."

It made Siobhan feel sick in a different way to hear such a thing. What could be *worse* than that terrible experience? "I *will* help her."

At that, a smile returned to Clara's face. "Of course you will. But she won't like that."

Siobhan smiled in turn. "I've handled her and her brother for two decades now. I think I can figure out how to break through any arguments she makes."

Clara thought about things past, and present, and future and just chuckled softly. "I suppose you're right."

(Axium)

Shana woke on a near scream and muffled the sound by pressing her hand hard against her mouth. The walls were just thin enough in her apartment that she could wake her roommates up. She turned over and buried her face in her pillow as she struggled to fight the nausea and pain gripping her internal organs. She never remembered her nightmares clearly, but she always remembered the way they made her feel.

She finally shoved her covers back and walked across the room to her door. She eased it open and looked out. It was silent and dark, and she headed down the hall to the bathing room quickly. Once she was in the small room, she shut the door and turned the light on.

Her own reflection greeted her, and she winced at the sight of the pallor to her normally golden brown skin. She ran water in the sink and splashed it onto her face. "I'm stronger than nightmares," she muttered softly to herself. "I won't be defeated by them."

Oddly enough, the nausea faded away with her words and she felt something in her heart relax. She took a long breath and dried her hands and face. Something loomed in her future. Something terrible. She had always known that, had always known the nightmares tied to it.

She just didn't know what, or why.

(Lux, two months later)

April had arrived in Lux, and the naturally warm climate of Protea had begun to shift toward the familiar surge of spring life. Color saturated everything. Siobhan had expected to see such a thing, but things suddenly looked . . . more intense. She noticed it for sure as she headed to her first class of the day; Rocky had none other than a gym period much later, so she was on her own for once.

Nature power had gone into *overdrive*. From just the day before to right then, everything had exploded into bloom as if someone had given the city a boost. Her eyes narrowed ever so slightly as she thought about timing and the whys of how such a thing may have happened. She bided her time until after class and then went toward where she knew Edgar had just finished a Business Operations class. She had always teased him over such a blasé degree to pursue, but she did suspect he had ulterior motives of *some* sort. He certainly did seem passionate about it. She let it be for now; she would nag later if she sensed something important happening that she did not know about.

As soon as Edgar walked out of his class, he winced at seeing his lover glaring at him. "Siobhan."

"Something you want to tell me?" she asked politely. "Because, wow, how *interesting*, but I got asked by maybe half a dozen people on my way over if the new student is related to you because she looks enough like you to be your taller twin! And, hmm, isn't the Nature lovely this time of year, Edgar?"

He coughed as much to hide a laugh as in sheepishness. He tucked her under his arm and moved her away from the door so they would be less likely to be overheard. "Alright, busted. Yes, Shana is already home. She started her first classes today. I wanted to surprise you two and Mom, and bring her home tonight for dinner."

She scowled. "Darn it, Edgar! That's not good enough and you know it! I want to see my sister, and I sure want to see her and Rocky finally be together! I want my brother as wrapped around her finger as I am around yours!" She crossed her arms and thought with such force that Edgar looked at her a bit warily. "Okay," she said. "What's her schedule?"

Rightfully amused and wary alike—he never trusted either Toulume when they wanted something—he said, "One photography class right now followed by an open gym workout for physical education."

She pursed her lips. "Rocky has the open gym after that." She nodded. "Okay. That's what we do." She pulled out her phone and said, "Rocky Toulume." When her brother answered, she said cheerfully, "Hi! I just got told that the gym is going to get closed during your normal time, so you should probably come take this open gym period instead. I mean, you don't want to skip it. You get cranky if that happens."

Rocky audibly paused. "Uh, okay. Thank you. Guess I'll head over?"

"Okay, have fun!" She closed and stuck the phone back into her pocket with a satisfied sort of flourish. To Edgar, she said, "I give them an hour before I march in, and damn it all, they had *better* look suitably together as soul mates!"

Edgar fought back a laugh. "Have I mentioned how glad I am you and your brother are on the side of good?"

She grinned. "Repeatedly."

Rocky rightfully knew he was being set up, though he genuinely had no clue just why or for what. He simply grabbed his gym bag and left the apartment. It took less than half the distance to the university for him to notice the significant change to the city. His heart began to beat much harder as longing welled hotly.

The deeper he moved through campus toward the gyms, the less he could breathe for painful hope. His fingers trembled as he reached for the knob of the door, but then froze as his Sight stirred. The powerful premonition rose up and briefly blinded him as it whispered through his soul. His life was about to change forever. To enter that door would be to enter past the point of no return. If he was smart, if he did not want his life to change, he should walk away. Just walk away and not open the door.

As if he could ever walk away! He opened the door swiftly, and he felt his entire existence tilt on its axis as he stared at the tall warrior goddess dressed with casual grace in workout wear. Nothing had changed. She still looked every bit his sister's perfect opposite: lean and fit with a powerful physique offset by a surprisingly defined bust and hips. He wistfully studied her long legs. Toned and tempting alike. And, as ever, she also looked very much exactly like a female version of Edgar, right down to the sassy curve of her lips and protea pink eyes.

Shana felt a sudden powerful Light sweeping across her soul, and her breath caught. Longing welled as she turned sharply, and there in the doorway she found the one she had missed the most. He looked exactly how Edgar had described, exactly as she had always imagined, and a potent blend of emotions, some she couldn't quite name, seemed to spill over inside her soul. Familiar emotions, somehow. Her soul mate. He had been right so long ago. Even though they were not yet twenty-five, she just *knew*. "Rocky."

He shut the door behind him and walked closer. "I missed you," he said softly. He slowly reached out to cup her cheek, and her skin felt familiar to his fingers. He could nearly taste her kiss on his lips. His soul mate. He had always known she would be. An ache swelled for the memories he did not have of the past. He *needed* to remember this most important person. Needed to know what *she* needed from him as a Caretaker.

"I think I'm going to possibly lose my mind if you don't kiss me," she whispered as he drew her closer. "Get on with it, damn it."

He dragged her in and claimed the kiss he had craved for years. For a lifetime. Perhaps for millennia. She tasted like wonderful dark chocolate and felt impossibly perfect in his arms. The rising tide of desire seemed too damn forceful and untamed to possibly get stronger in less than two years, and he very nearly tumbled her right down onto the padded floor.

She would not have argued or stopped him, frankly. In fact, when they finally parted a bit, she could only manage to whisper, "Thank goodness we're alone in here. If we'd met at the port, we might have embarrassed some folks, including our siblings. And as much as it feels damn tempting to just say 'who has an empty apartment we can borrow', we are still on the university's time."

He grinned. "Still not a shy bone in your body."

"Please. Shyness just makes things take longer." She caught his shirt and tugged him back down for another quick kiss. "I don't mind when you're right," she told him softly. "And you were right, Rocky.

We have to be soul mates. There's no other reason for me to feel the way I do. You're . . . my everything."

Rocky slowly and reluctantly released her and then stepped back to look at her. "You are unfairly gorgeous," he finally told her. "Edgar never told me much, just that you two still looked like twins. Damn him."

She grinned a bit wickedly. "He told me all about you, so I didn't feel that surprised to see you—other than the fact that, wow, I didn't know I would have such a thing for softness *and* muscle." She swung away with a grace nearly elemental, her entire body moving in precise control as if she could command every muscle she owned. "I look forward to being much closer, to be sure. Tell me, do you still strip off most everything as soon as you get home?"

"I temper that some living with my sister, but for you, I could make an exception." He moved slowly to flank her on the floor in a deliberately challenging gesture. Sun from the skylights seemed to melt across her golden brown skin. "You always look as if the sun has kissed your skin. I wonder what other Light doing the same might do to you."

She watched him from under her lashes. "You'll find out soon enough. Are you actually *challenging* me, Your Highness? You would dare try that with someone to be the Apex of Dark? Lexie says I embody everything physical in the universe. That's pretty ballsy of you. Aren't you Delphinium types supposed to be magical?"

He planted his feet and slowly lifted his hands. A nearly sensual smile tugged at his lips. "I'm magical enough, but I fought to make myself into your perfect Caretaker. I would think the Apex of Dark might not accept a suitor she can run roughshod over in battle. We used to spar plenty as children, and I could push you as no one else did. You'll win here, of course, but you'll need to work for it—and you love that."

A thrill curled through her body that wasn't entirely just lust. His strength truly appealed to her *more* than his handsome face and strong form, and appealed all the way to her soul. No, he could not beat her. No one could. She accepted that as much as she had accepted everything else in her life. But the idea that he could push her, make her stretch herself, made her deeply happy.

She lifted her hands in a mimicry of his pose. "No rules," she told him. A smile as sensual as his own filled her face and made her radiantly beautiful. "Give me everything you have."

"Maybe later. We're on university time." He shot toward her on a shout, willing to take the first strike and see how she responded.

The fight turned violent and furious in short order as kicks, blocks, punches, and more were fired off and countered faster than most eyes could track. He threw his full weight against her, fought fiercely and powerfully to drive her higher, and she simply adjusted and kept on pushing back. They traded back and forth on being the aggressor, and when he managed to get her to the ground, she fought free and flipped him over so that strikes were replaced by grappling. Time seemed to lose meaning until, finally, she got him pinned and held him there in a way he could not break free.

They both breathed heavily, looked as sweaty and disheveled as they felt. He smacked a hand on the ground in a gesture of yielding, and she shot at him a bit breathlessly, "Is that for real, or are you still ready to fight?"

"I'm dead, Your Majesty," he told her tiredly, but still dryly. He knew full well she could go another few rounds, could dig deep for strength and stamina he could never match, and he simply had nothing left to give. "You win." He found the strength to reach up and tangle his fingers in her messy black hair. It hung to past her hips, as it had for years. Yet it never got in her way. He had always thought it might be a different sort of magic. "Happy?"

She released her grip so he could get free if he wanted, but he didn't bother to move and let her continue to pin him to the floor. Not that she minded the position herself. He made a positively delightful place to rest. "Very." She lowered her forehead to his and smiled. "We once said we'd be each other's girl or boyfriend, but, is it just me or . . . does it feel like maybe we *skipped* that somehow?"

"You mean it feels as much to you as it does to me that we're already married, which is really sort of illegal for almost two years?"

He watched her hair slide through his fingers and then reached up to push more out of her face. "So maybe we skip to being engaged and get married as soon as we can to put things on a proper keel."

"I could be convinced." She couldn't resist stealing a quick and hungry kiss. "I don't have a bed at home yet."

Hungry heat flushed his body at the obvious invitation. "I do. Is that an offer to share it?"

She started to answer, and the doors to the gym swung open. They both turned their heads and found their siblings standing in the doorway. Neither looked at all surprised by the scene, and after a moment, Edgar told Siobhan. "Okay, fine. You win. More than an hour would mean we wouldn't see them again for a day or two."

Shana had to laugh at that. "Damn it, Siobhan! Sadist." She rolled lithely free of Rocky and gained her feet before offering a hand to help him up as well. "You set us up, didn't you? Well see if I argue with that!" She walked forward quickly with her hands held out.

Siobhan ran forward to meet her, and their hands meshed together like two magnets connecting. Their Light and Dark cores came into contact anew and, for the first time in their life, sparks literally flew between their hands. They both pulled their hands apart in surprise and stared at one another. Then, laughing, they clasped hands again and let the sparks flare as they wanted until their cores had evaluated the other and come to an accord. The sparks faded, and Siobhan laced their fingers tighter. "Maybe it's because we're matured fully."

Shana thought about it. "You're probably right. You mean we *all* feel old somehow?"

"And how!" Siobhan released her hands only to hug her tight around the waist. "I missed you," she whispered. "So much! It was never the same without you around. And I know I should completely let go and back off and let you and Rocky be together, but I just can't let go right now, okay?"

Shana held onto her sister just as tightly and smiled. "Hey, Rocky and I have plenty of time. We can share. Besides, I should probably get furniture for my room before I bring him home to it, right? I came here from Axium without much since I wanted to start anew."

Siobhan had to giggle at that. "Based on recent evidence, the floor seemed good enough for you two."

"Yeah but I'm not coming to you to ask you to heal rug burns," Rocky retorted dryly. "Bad enough I had to heal some for *you* once."

"Well *that's* awkward." Shana eyed him. "You can heal? Since when?"

"I'll tell you later," Edgar promised her dryly. "When I tell you also what's been going on around here. As you said, there's time enough for everything. Let's go get some dinner and then take you home to see Mom. I called her while we were waiting for you and Rocky and I told her you're home. Be glad you two are holding off. She would have seriously marched into the room and broken things up. She missed you, too."

By the time they had finished dinner and were enjoying dessert, it almost felt a bit as if Shana had never actually left home at all. Nothing important had changed. "What made you decide to do the split university thing?" Siobhan asked her as they shared a sundae at the diner. Their brothers were dueling with spoons over their own, and the women let them be. "Especially at this time. University switching in the middle of a quarter is odd enough."

"It normally is, but I'm on a different scheduling program because of my advanced placement, so what is halfway to you is actually starting for me. And while Axium's university had perfect introductory and intermediary classes, Lux has the better advanced ones I want to take in order to graduate with my best possible skills. I'm sort of getting two degrees," she admitted. "Photography and Business Operations alike."

Siobhan studied her, thought again about Edgar, but said nothing. She could bide her time until she felt it the right moment to push for answers. She didn't expect them to be outright forthcoming, of course. Not when they were so ridiculously of the Dark. They tried to do everything by themselves! "Okay, well that does make sense! Were you living with Alexandria the entire time over there?"

"I was, though once I turned twenty, her and I, and Kellie and Desiree all got an apartment together. Which means, of course, that now I miss *them* terribly." She sighed. "However, Lexie promised me that she and the others would transfer, too, so I should see them very soon and we can all be together as a team again. It's so hard, only being able to have just a few of the people who complete you. I missed the Light Defenders too."

"I missed the Dark ones," Siobhan admitted softly. "And so did Edgar and Rocky. It was hard here, too." She shook it off. "It's in the past! What're you up to this weekend? And tell me about being a photographer! You use a camera, right? It kind of doesn't surprise me, really. You always showed interest in it."

"What can I say? I got lucky in knowing what I wanted. I take pretty photos of people mostly, but sometimes I play with landscape images. I'm mostly keen on fashion and theatrical sorts of photography. It's fun working with actors and models. As for this weekend, I really need to go shopping. In addition to the aforementioned furniture, I sort of need clothes and the like. I literally donated everything except some bare essentials before coming home. So I'll be spending the weekend shopping."

"I'll help!" Siobhan promised. She grinned. "And I'll call up the others! We'll make it a big event and a sort of welcome-home type thing."

Shana's eyes warmed. "Absolutely, I would love to have all of you help me tackle some shopping needs. You may kidnap me at your will this weekend." She grimaced. "Just as long as someone else does the driving."

Siobhan immediately covered her hand soothingly. "Just call me or Rocky," she promised gently. "That's our deal with Edgar, too. You don't have to face something you're afraid of alone, okay? If you can't use an electric bike, then you've got us to take you in our carriage."

Shana smiled. "Thanks, Siobhan."

"S'what sisters are for! And I definitely think we're almost sisters twice or three times at this point."

"Is that good or bad?"

"Maybe both?"

Shana laughed. "Fair enough, I guess."

With dessert done, they paid for their meal and then headed for the house sitting only blocks away from the Toulume apartment. It looked the same as Shana remembered, and she felt nostalgia and loneliness well. She had only gotten to see Octavia once or twice over the last thirteen years, though she had called her adopted mother frequently enough. Just hearing her voice could make Shana feel better.

The door opened, and Shana saw Octavia in the doorway. She looked almost the same, too, just now with some gray beginning to stripe her white hair. Shana stopped dead in her tracks, which made the other three stop as well. Rocky took one look at her face and knew she had smacked into that innate Dark difficulty with emotion. He caught her hand in his and pulled her down the pathway to the steps where Octavia waited. "Look what I found!" he said cheerfully. "And she says I can keep her."

Standing on the second step, Octavia actually reached eye level with her youngest. She could not fight back tears as she reached out to hug Shana tightly and rock her gently. "Welcome home, baby. Come inside and tell me *everything*. Anything new I don't know."

Shana smiled and held onto Octavia's hand as they entered the house. "I'm apparently going to marry Rocky. Is that new?"

"Ha! No, not really. You'll need to try harder. He told me that intent when he was ten. And, to be fair, I just sort of had this feeling all along, really." Octavia poured out the tea she had already been brewing, and she added a single sugar to Shana's for she remembered still everything about what her four kids did and did not like. "Try again."

"Hmm. I might be on call to get a newly famous actor naked on photographic print?"

"Okay, *that* is new. Do tell."

Shana bunked that night in her old shared room with Siobhan, and her sister stayed as well. The men shared their old room. That just, somehow, made things feel more as if they had become normal anew.

None of them had classes on the following day so simply spent the time together as much as they could. Rocky had to leave early, though, for work, and he lingered over kissing Shana goodbye. "Maybe some time soon," he whispered, "after you get that new bed. I can help you test it."

"Maybe you can," she whispered back. "Get out of here." She shoved him out the door, but she was smiling.

The weekend arrived only a day later, and Shana braced her shoulders for the inevitable crowds in the shopping center. She had told Edgar not to bother getting anything before her arrival because she wanted the fun of picking out her own. He hadn't minded, nor had he minded sharing his bed for a night or two. Unlike someone *else* he often shared a bed with, she didn't kick him in the middle of the night.

Bright and early on Saturday, Shana heard the doorbell and went to answer. She found a familiar face on the other side, though she had not seen the other woman in over a decade—in this life. She brightened. "Juliet!"

"Shana!" Juliet happily hugged the taller female and felt a fresh spurt of amusement. At least protecting Shana would be a familiar exercise; she had grown used to tackling down those bigger than her in order to keep them safe! "Welcome home, hon. Siobhan said you needed to get some shopping done! My cousin owns a furniture shop. I can wrangle you a great deal on some pieces. I'll even drive you there."

"Deal!" Shana grabbed her shoes and jacket and contently followed along behind Juliet. "It really does feel good to be home," she decided. "Glad I missed out on that plague, though. That would have been no fun, even if I don't seem to ever get sick."

"No kidding," Juliet murmured.

They tackled the furniture store, and Shana fell in love with a hand-carved bed and dresser set. Juliet's cousin cheerfully offered a discount on a matching nightstand as well, and Shana couldn't turn it down. After arranging for delivery that afternoon, she followed Juliet back outside to her carriage. "I don't normally spend lots of money," she confessed. "I've always been a frugal sort, even though my parents' trust for me means I could live more than comfortably. It's just not my style to be extravagant. Weird, maybe, for a queen."

Juliet smiled at her as she navigated toward the cluster of shops that made up the main center of shopping for Lux. "Not necessarily. I seem to recall you being a bit on the less-than-extravagant side back then, too. You raised such a ruckus over handmaidens putting amber in your hair that your mother finally let you use crystals."

Shana snorted softly. "The more things change, as they say."

They met up with Sherry and Virginia at the shopping center, and Shana was just as happy to see them as she had been to see Juliet. Once Yvonne joined them, it felt even better. Having the four Light Defenders helped fill the gap inside her heart where she terribly missed her Dark Defender guardians. She had gotten used to missing Clara—the Statice Cultivator visited only once or twice a year—but the other three had been a semi-permanent presence in her life.

Siobhan also caught up with them in short order, and the six had incredible fun scouring the shops to find all of the things Shana might possibly need. Along the way, Sherry borrowed a shop's tape measure in order to jot down Shana's measurements for herself. "So I can make you things as well!" the seamstress said cheerfully. "I like designing things for the ones I love. We'll glamorize you so that Virginia has to paint you."

"Only if I get to do figure studies of everyone," Shana countered, sticking her tongue out a bit. "If I'm going to be everyone's dressmaker doll, you all have to play nice and let me make you look amazing too!"

"Naked again," Yvonne grumbled.

"Again?" Shana lifted a brow.

Virginia grinned wickedly. "She lost a bet."

It made Shana laugh. "Being with you all is almost like being with the other Cultivators. I miss them," she added softer. "I hope they come here soon. They promised they would."

Siobhan could barely imagine what it would be like to not see her four Defenders whenever she wanted. All over again, she marveled at the strength inside her sister. She slipped her hand into Shana's and held on in support. "You have us now, too," she promised.

"You're not alone, okay?" She leaned her head against Shana's shoulder. "You and Edgar. You always think you have to handle your own burdens. But you have us. Lean on us."

"If I can," Shana promised. "It's hard for me, sorry."

"Well, you wouldn't be you if you weren't that sort of person," Sherry agreed with a smile. "And we love you anyway."

It proved a good thing that all of them had driven their own carriages. The quantity of bags Shana accumulated shortly hit rather impressive numbers. She had not just clothes, but many of the little things that she had never before indulged in obtaining. Copious books, knickknacks she wanted to display, and even her own PCM—which she had always wanted but had never been able to justify. Once she upgraded her current physical plate-system camera to the more modern electrical sort that used digital plates, she could use the machine to do all of her processing.

The loot was hauled back to her apartment, and champion flirting from Virginia got several other people in the apartment lobby to help bring everything upstairs. Shana shooed them all off after that; she wanted the fun of putting it all away to herself. In another humorous contrast, the Chivanti apartment often looked a bit impeccable while the Toulume one always appeared scattered. Order versus disorder. Perhaps another reason they worked well together.

She had just finished putting clothes away in her closet when she heard the door. She wandered out to see who had arrived, and she slowly lifted a brow as she saw deliverymen. All of her furniture had already arrived. "What did you order?" she asked Edgar as he signed off on papers.

"I didn't. I had nothing to do with this. Well, other than the fact that I might have blabbed to someone about you having the second master suite with the balcony."

Her brows shot up as the men carried in pieces of furniture she could not identify, and a small box that looked, weirdly, as if might have been *wiggling*. She did not need to ask to know who Edgar referenced. "What in the name of the gods did that man do?"

She had to wait patiently, however. She bided her time by

putting away books on the shelves in the sitting room. As soon as the deliverymen left with cheerful farewells, she dashed down the hall toward her bedroom. The balcony doors stood wide open, and she stepped out slowly to discover a cozy swing had been installed. It looked perfect for curling up with a book—or a person.

The formerly wiggling box sat on the swing, and it wiggled more as she approached. A note had been pinned to the top. Out loud, she read, "You would never have asked for this, but I know you always wanted it. Invite me over to snuggle you both sometime." She blinked. "Both?" She dropped the note and tore open the box to discover an adorable black baby ferret sitting inside. It made a sweet little 'dook' noise and then scampered out to climb up her arm to her shoulder.

"Well, hello!" Enchanted, she scooped the fuzzy creature up and nuzzled his fur. "Aren't you sweet!" She had always wanted a pet, but Octavia's allergies and her own lack of feeling actually settled anywhere had prevented it. This one felt perfect. She sensed her brother and turned to look at him with a trembling smile. "Those two are more dangerous than ever. How do they always know what other people need?"

He began to grin. "I have no clue. And they're not any better where their eternal optimism and belief in the greater good of mankind is concerned. I've banged my head on a wall over both of them more than once." He wanted to tell her everything else that had been going on recently, but, at the same, he desperately did not. He wanted to keep her world as normal as he could until he had to tell her that there was a price to her birth. A price! How could any life carry such a thing? He could understand it was the result of an Apex having arcanery, but he did not like it.

"I'll keep that in mind," she decided. She put the ferret down and grinned as he scampered into the apartment to explore. "Sebastian," she decided. "That's his name. Or Bastian for short. It fits him." She sighed. "He read my mind. I swear he did."

Edgar knew who she meant, but he still asked, "Rocky?"

"Who else? Every time we see each other, we just . . . I have no words for how we click together. There is *no one* that I feel closer to. I never imagined having a lover soul mate could feel that way." She looked at her brother and smiled whimsically. "I just can't imagine my life without him and Lexie and you. You as much as them. All three of you . . . help complete me. I don't think I could handle losing you anymore than I could losing my two soul mates."

Her words did not surprise him. He had watched the same bond between Siobhan and Rocky *literally* devastate Rocky when Siobhan had died. Looking anew at how deeply Siobhan and Shana seemed bonded, much as Rocky and Edgar had, he thought he could safely assume that whatever bound the four siblings together truly was near identical to what bound soul mates. Reciprocity happened quite a bit between people who shared soul mates, and it clearly applied here as well. But the why? Well, that still remained unknown. They would just have to wait for those answers along with the rest.

Whether they *wanted* those answers could be left for debate, though.

18

Classes began anew on Monday, and Shana found herself a bit irked as the day progressed. People seemed insistent on calling her Edgar's 'baby sister', and that chaffed. She was not only less than a year younger, she was bigger! She would have to start knocking teeth down throats if they didn't cut that crap out.

"That's a scary look," Siobhan said solemnly as Shana walked up to where she stood. They were the only two who had afternoon Monday classes, and so they walked at least partway home together.

"I feel scary. I'm going make you a widow before you're wed."

Siobhan bit her lower lip to hide a smile. "In his defense, he tried all Friday to correct people on things, but, you know. Everyone likes the idea of a 'baby' sibling of some sort. I gave up on arguing about being Rocky's 'baby' sister *ages* ago. Speaking of my brother, put him out of my misery *soon*. He's driving me nuts."

Shana started laughing. "It's not any easier over here, I promise! It's just one of those timing things, and he's been trying to be nice about letting me get lots of time with Edgar before he starts stealing some of it for himself. I have *plenty* of time though." She shook her head wryly. "I'm still getting settled in. I've only got two classes right now. I'll pick up a full schedule next quarter. I kept this one light because I knew I'd be coming home."

"Which we're all glad you did!" Siobhan gave her a quick hug as they stopped outside the complex where Shana and Edgar lived. "See you soon! Should I bring Rocky with me when I come over during this week?" she teased. "I've tried to not come over as often as I used to now that you're there."

Shana snorted. "Don't worry about my delicate sensibilities any! You keep my brother distracted and I'll keep *yours* distracted as well. If not directly, I can tempt him with my PCM. He promised to work on it anyway." She grinned a bit as she watched Siobhan hurry off. While she deeply loved and appreciated both Toulume siblings, she still felt more than a bit vexed by their incredibly generous natures. She had a feeling she might have to clean up behind someone's broken heart eventually, and she had a whole new sympathy for her brother. She had left him to handle this by himself for too long. Oh well.

"Ah! There you are!"

Shana glanced over and saw a carriage pulling up beside the pedestrian lane. Virginia sat in the driver seat. "Hi to you too! Where *else* would I be? I'm not a socialite who goes to events right after school."

Virginia grinned. "Alright, that's fair. What are you up to right now?"

"Going home."

"After that."

"Changing clothes."

"It's like prying teeth with you and Edgar!" Virginia said in exasperation. "Allow me to be more specific: what *activities* have you got planned?"

Shana laughed. "You make it so irresistible! Other than doing a bit of homework, I have no activities planned. What is it you want me to do, and will it humiliate me in any shape or fashion?"

"I'm a lonely extrovert whose friends are busy," Virginia lamented dramatically with a hand to her heart. "I am stuck asking the introvert if she is willing to go with me to the horse ranch just beyond town." She felt no guilt for lying and never had. Rocky worked at that ranch, and she disliked as much as Siobhan did to see him and Shana be frustrated and miserable. She had already pulled other strings with some help, and she would make sure her prince and queen got the time together that they deserved. She needed them to be happy, damn it. "You in?"

"I love horses, so why not?" She walked around and climbed into the front passenger seat. "I can be the social battery for my lonely extroverts. Just return me home to let me recharge when we're done!"

Virginia just laughed.

* * * * *

The Springwood Ranch that covered a fairly vast stretch of land outside of Lux was a favored spot for many people. It had picnic grounds, beautiful areas of flowers, a lovely spring, and a large pasture where horses ran freely. It also had stables and a corral where the expert staff members would teach visitors how to ride, or even show off some more expert skills of their own.

Almost as soon as they had arrived in the city, Alexandria and her two partners had been drawn to visit the place. They had literally just gotten a house in the city, had barely unpacked, and they had just *needed* to go to the ranch. Alexandria's eyes moved a bit restlessly over the corral as a wind ruffled her short hair. Her freckles nearly glowed in the afternoon sun, almost as proof of her being so special to the ones with Nature power. "What drew us here?" she murmured.

Kellie shook her head a bit and made her long peach hair sparkle. Copper eyes and brown skin rounded out her coloring, and caught more than one passing eye. "Well, we'll know soon enough. I know you want to see Shana, Lex," she soothed. "But if we need to be here, then here is where we will be. She doesn't even know we're here yet, so she won't mind a detour."

Desiree leaned against the fence beside them and sighed deeply. Curly ultramarine hair and intense purple eyes stood out powerfully against her light brown skin and underscored her lineage as they always had. "It *is* curious though." She took a sudden breath and straightened as she saw a familiar figure on horseback. "Or not. Look."

The other two followed her gaze and saw someone they had not seen in years. The last time they had seen him in this life, they had all been children. The last time they had seen him as an adult had been in another life. "Ah," Alexandria murmured. "So that's it." She smiled as he rode up to the fence. "It's been a long time, hasn't it?"

Rocky stared down at all three Dual Cultivators for a long moment, not necessarily surprised to see them so much as to see them *there*. "You three must have taken the fastest ship! I knew you were going to come home very soon, but maybe not *that* soon." He grinned and felt something inside relax a bit. It felt a little as if some holes inside his heart had filled to have all of his beloved Defender friends near once more. And, too, he had happiness for Shana as well. "Kellie, thank you for making Edgar's and my weapons."

She smiled. "Of course! If we couldn't be there to protect you when you got in over your head, at least we could feel better knowing I had at least armed you." She scowled. "Gin has already filled us in on some of the events. No more of that out of you!"

He winced. The only downside to having more Defenders around was that many more people to try to protect him. He would rather they focus on his sister and soul mate, really. Thinking it, his frowned deepened. "What do I need to know to help Shana?"

"I'm glad you two have already met again!" Alexandria said only. "Saves us the effort of trying to put you back together. Have you seduced her yet, as a Caretaker nearly always does their best to do?"

"It's an effort on both sides, trust me." His eyes narrowed. "Lex. Come *on*. You more than anyone else know what I feel! I watched what happened to Siobhan; I know Shana will suffer! Let me know what I need to know in order to help her suffer less!"

"Answers will come, Robert," Desiree said softly, and firmly. "And they are not pleasant answers. We hesitate only for the sake of our queen. We will put off the day where she must don her Mask for as long as we can, just as our Light partners put off the day as long as they could for Siobhan."

Understanding their position in no way made him like the situation, and he rode off before he started asking more questions and getting less answers. He just got the sick feeling in his stomach that something possibly more terrible loomed in Shana's future compared to Siobhan's. What price was worse to pay than wrongful death?

Alexandria watched him ride off and just sighed. Nothing felt worse than having to resist the urge to give her princes or queens the things they asked. They asked for so little to begin with, and it only felt worse when they asked for things to help others.

She took a sudden quick breath as she felt a familiar Nature power tease her soul. Her head swung around, and she spotted her twin soul walking down the dirt road from the parking lot with a familiar red-haired figure beside her. It had only been less than a week since last seeing her, but it had hurt almost as much as a year apart. "Of course," she murmured. "She would be drawn here as well."

Desiree and Kellie followed her gaze and also felt something relax. "Tell me not to go running to her and grab on," Kellie groused. "I always want to bundle her up in cotton somewhere and make sure no one can find her!"

"No help from me," Alexandria groused back. "I want that more than you do."

"Both of you behave," Desiree scolded mildly. She smiled as she caught Virginia's eye, and her smile widened as Virginia took Shana's chin and turned her head toward the three Dark Defenders. "I really do love Gin. I had missed having her boss all of us around. And seeing her butt heads with Shana over such a thing."

Shana felt only a moment of confusion when Virginia grabbed her, and as she saw her three beloved Defenders, her heart ached powerfully as her lips trembled. She almost hit the ground running and rushed over to throw her arms around Alexandria. She clung on with all of her considerable strength and hid her face against her twin's shoulder.

"Easy." Alexandria buried her face for a moment in Shana's hair. "I'm here now. We all are. We're only a block from you at all times, just as we always promised. You're not alone." She looked up to smile as Virginia reached them. "Hello, Gin. Thank you."

"You're welcome, though you were not technically my target. Welcome home." She hugged Desiree and Kellie alike and then kept an arm around the latter's waist companionably. She could hug Alexandria once Shana finally let go. "We've already been in contact, and I've kept you updated, but there's some things we could only discuss in person."

"I imagine so," Desiree agreed wryly.

Shana finally let go of Alexandria and hugged her other two friends nearly as tightly. She mostly ignored what they had said; she had known for ages that Alexandria had stayed in contact with Virginia, and that had never bugged her. She had liked knowing that some of the Defenders had been on hand to protect her brother. Especially since he had *clearly* been in *some* sort of trouble a few months earlier. She would pester for her own answers later. She knew how to wait for what she needed.

She hopped up to sit on the side of the fence and smiled. "I guess I don't mind so much being dragged out of my quiet apartment for this. Thanks, Ginny!"

Only Siobhan, Shana, and Rocky could get away with calling Virginia by the affectionate version of her name. Edgar could, though he rarely did, but no one else. She stuck to her full name or just Gin with everyone else. Only her beloved queens and princes could be so informal. "You're very welcome!"

The thunder of hooves sounded behind them, and everyone turned to watch as Rocky sent his horse over an obstacle without touching the bar. With casual skill, he put the white horse through a few other paces to the cheers of some observers and then rode over to where the five Dual Cultivators stood.

Shana's Sight suddenly stirred, and it almost seemed to overlap past and present together. For just a moment, she saw Rocky wearing an outfit that looked a lot like a Ruler suit of some sort, and a coronet sat upon his white hair. She blinked and the vision evaporated to reveal he had stopped in front of her and had a hand held out. "Uhm. Sorry." She shook her head quickly. Where had that come from? Were her fuzzy memories now starting to unfuzz themselves? But *why?* "I think I just zoned out for a moment. Did you say something?"

He had recognized the reaction of someone with Sight and wanted to ask what she had seen, but something told him to leave it alone. "I asked if you wanted a ride," he said only. He smiled. "I promise to keep my hands to myself."

She arched a brow. "Somehow I don't trust you."

"Damn." He snapped his fingers and then grinned at the others as he swung down out of the saddle. "I'm supposed to give a speech about the Ranch to newcomers, but the rest of you have already heard it from the staff."

"Tch!" Shana shook her head in mock dismay. "You mean I don't warrant the speech? I demand equal treatment, sir!"

He slowly lifted a white brow. "Well, if it's equality my lady wants . . ." He reached out with unexpected speed, caught her around the waist, and lifted her bodily into the corral with him.

She glared at him as her feet hit the ground. It was not fair that he still be enough bigger than her to manhandle her as if she were his sister's size. It seemed even more unfair that she *liked* such a thing. However, "I would like to make it clear that I still tolerate *very* few people moving me anywhere against my will, and the next time you do that, my size ten boot will find its way to a sensitive portion of your anatomy."

He did *not* envy Alexandria's duty to protect her, and the wry smile on the Defender in question's face implied she did not either. "You wanted equality," he told Shana reasonably. "Therefore you get to put your smart ass in a saddle and I'll give you the speech while I teach you to ride."

"*Teach* me?" A black brow just as arrogant as his lifted in turn. "I've been riding for over a decade now, and I'm damned good at it. I could outride you *blindfolded*." She looked around and spotted a black stallion only a few feet away. "Is he available?"

"Yes, but he's named Whirlwind for a reason. He has a hell of a personality conflict. I have yet to see him let anyone but me stay in the saddle for long." He offered the reigns to the white mare contently standing beside him. "Borrow my horse. Coral is as sweet as a dove."

"No, I like Whirlwind." She took a step forward with her hands held up, and the stallion glanced at her curiously. "Hi there," she said softly, gently. "Come here, pretty boy." She stood still as Whirlwind immediately walked over and started sniffing at her intently. When he pressed his head against her chest on a sigh, she smiled and ran her hands over his head to scratch under the itchy tack he wore. "There you are. You're not a troublemaker at all, are you? Aren't you beautiful?" She laughed when he tried to nibble her hair. "I'm not edible!"

More than one jaw dropped in the area. Rocky's wasn't one of them, though. He had of course known that Shana's particular Nature gift lay primarily in fauna, and this just proved more evidence of it. He honestly did not remember her ever meeting any animal that she had not instantly befriended. "Want a saddle for him?" he asked dryly.

She shot him a grin. "Why bother?" She caught a handful of Whirlwind's mane and swung with casual grace up onto his back. She scooped up the reins and tugged to tell him to turn and start walking. "I can outride my brother, by the way. Drove him nuts when we would race every summer. We tend to be more competitive with each other than others, actually. Go figure."

Rocky quirked a brow. Edgar was his emergency backup trainer when a new horse arrived that was simply too stubborn for even him to work with. "I'll remember that the next time I'm having trouble. I'll put your number on my list of trainers with your brother's."

"Will you pay me?"

"Absolutely."

She grinned. "Deal." She turned Whirlwind toward the beaten path around the large corral and sighed contentedly. She had missed riding. And since there was a nice incentive to visit, she would probably get back into it. Turn down a chance to see Rocky on horseback? She wasn't stupid. The man hit a godlike level of sexiness.

She moved with such fluid grace that it almost seemed as if she had become an extension of the horse beneath her. "She never stops impressing me," Alexandria admitted. "She would go for a walk and come home with a menagerie following her. Good thing my dads had a sense of humor over it!"

Rocky grinned a bit. "That sounds familiar! She did her best to keep them out of the house when we were kids because of Mom's allergies, but if we had windows open and screens down, birds would absolutely fly in and perch on her head or shoulders. That's why I decided to get her a pet once she came home. I thought she might like having a semi-permanent animal friend to keep her company. Wait until you meet Bastian, her ferret." He eyed Virginia. "And I appreciate your attempts to put her under my nose, Ginny, but we really are getting there at a perfectly decent speed."

"I want you happy," she reminded him gently. "And that means I want you to be with your soul mate." She smiled. "I'll back off for now, though."

"Much obliged." He glanced up as Shana stopped beside him on Whirlwind. "Having fun?" he asked warmly.

"Lots." She smiled from under her lashes. "Want to join us? He promises not to toss you off."

He took her offered hand and swung easily up behind her on Whirlwind's back. The stallion barely noticed the added weight and merrily trotted off with both royals on his back, almost with a hint of a prance that implied he *knew* them to be royal. Rocky let Shana steer and lightly rested his hands on her waist for balance. Just having her close could be enough for now, and he briefly buried his face against her neck.

"What's that for?" she asked softly.

"Nothing. Just love you."

Virginia watched them and felt her heart ache a little at the way Rocky instinctively seemed to be trying to shelter Shana with his body and soul. Even with the sun behind him, she did not get lost in shadow thanks to her lover's Light. "He and Edgar. Seriously. Always acting like a Caretaker first." She knew it was a bit hypocritical when she and her partners acted as Defenders first and Rulers second, but at least *they* had armor! "We need to get Shana up to speed very soon," she sighed. "She deserves to know what is going on."

"I agree." In a lower voice, Alexandria admitted, "I hope, at the least, Rocky can again give her good things to dream. Her entire life has been a nightmare she cannot escape. I often wonder if she ever sleeps at all."

Virginia's hands clenched together in pain but not in surprise. She had wondered more than once even as children. "Anything I or the other three can do," she vowed, "we will do without hesitation. Shana is as important to us as Siobhan is. You will keep me involved in everything, Alexandria. That's an order as Lead. I need to know what is happening around our queen."

Alexandria nodded. "You have our word."

Oblivious to the conversation, Shana and Rocky continued to enjoy their ride around the large corral. As they began to approach back toward their friends, she said very softly, "Are you free this evening? Edgar called me on the way here, and he's apparently going to be out with Siobhan until very late. I told him to stay at your place so you could stay at ours."

His hands tightened on her waist and then slid around her in a hug. "I can make myself be free. You know I want nothing more than to be yours. But . . . there's fear inside you. I can feel it. What's wrong, Shana?"

She took a long breath. "Destiny and I . . . we have a deal. She will give me what I want at any given moment, and she can demand something of me later. I've wanted to see you, to be with you, for so *long* but never could, and now suddenly I can? I know what she is telling me. I can have you, but there will be a high price to pay." She shook her head a bit. "I don't care. I'll pay anything if it means I can just be happy. For once truly happy. To sleep in your arms where nightmares cannot find me."

He thought back again to Siobhan and the price of her birth, and fear flashed through him that he fiercely shoved down. Whatever Shana needed of him as her Caretaker, he would give. Anything. His life, his soul. If she paid a price, he would try to pay it with her. "I'm yours," he told her softly. He pressed his lips to her cheek for a moment. "Whatever you want from me."

She could not help but smile at that, and it looked a bit wicked. "Ooh. Now that sounds tempting." She pulled Whirlwind to a stop near the fence and smiled as Rocky nimbly got to the ground. She joined him shortly and handed over the reins. "Here you go."

"Take Whirlwind in to the stables," Rocky told a staffer who walked closer. He passed the reins to the other man. "And you get to take over. I'm clocking out a bit early."

The staffer hid a smile. "You got it, boss." He headed off with the grumpy stallion reluctantly following and tugging at the reins he held.

It wasn't the first time Shana had noticed her lover acted as if he was in charge around the place. "Boss?" she asked politely. "*Your* list of trainers?"

Helpfully, Virginia told her, "He's sort of the manager here. And I only say 'sort of' because he's *technically* the co-manager. The other manager is moving toward retirement and has been letting him run the place for the last year. Rumor has it that when Rocky graduates, the manager will turn everything over entirely."

"So nice for him to finally have a *reason* to be bossy." She ignored the way her other three friends were trying not to grin at her. She honestly did not care if anyone knew the plans for the evening. In fact, them knowing would make them less likely to interrupt! "Rental is up on the introvert. Rocky and I are going home."

The others laughed, and Desiree helped her hop over the fence. "Tomorrow we'll have dinner together. That way you can see where we are living and know where to find us when you need us. For now," she rose up and kissed Shana's cheek, "go be happy."

"I intend to." Shana kissed Virginia on the cheek as well in thanks and then took Rocky's hand when he offered it. Their fingers laced together almost intimately, and she leaned against his arm as they walked away from the corral toward where he had his carriage parked. Once in motion, she asked, "Did you really know all along this was our destination?"

"I did." He navigated the streets with easy skill, though slower than normal. If he had either Chivanti in his carriage, he doubled down on safe driving and not alarming them. A memory made him smile. "You know how Siobhan clued Edgar in right?"

"Uh-oh. No."

He told her, and enjoyed listening to her laugh. "I won't lie. I would absolutely have done the same thing to you in her shoes. I just got lucky enough to clue you in long before we needed to get to that point."

"I have no objections to you stripping and pouncing on me any time we're alone. I just want to put that out there." She watched his profile as he drove, and hunger only continued to churn all the harder inside her body. The tightness to his jaw implied he knew she watched him, and she let her gaze slowly drift downward. His own desire seemed an obvious thing even behind denims. The only thing that kept her hands to herself was the need to not distract the person driving a machine she knew for a fact could be lethal.

He had barely parked the carriage before he swung around in his seat and reached for her. She hastily scrambled out her door. "Not out here!" she managed breathlessly as he came around the back of the carriage with a predatory stride that sent her pulse spiking. Things had better not get stronger in a few years. They wouldn't survive it if it did!

He stayed far closer than could be considered polite as they took the stairs to the apartment a bit faster than usual. Her fingers quivered as she unlocked the door. She had barely gotten it closed before he crowded her back against it and kissed her with an edge of desire that had the keys falling from her numb grip. Desperately, greedily, she fisted her hands in his hair and returned the kiss as ravenously as it was given until neither of them could breathe.

She grabbed at him for balance as he snatched her off her feet with a strength that only made her burn more. Nothing truly turned her on more than his strength, perhaps partially because she knew how hard he had worked to earn it. "Bedroom," she managed to say. She hooked her knees around his hips for balance and caught his face in her hands to take another wild kiss. "Down the hall." A little gasp of part laughter and part alarm caught as he tried to turn and almost tripped. "You better not drop me! I'll never let you live it down!"

"I wouldn't." He caught hands full of her hair to drag her into another kiss. His tongue tangled with hers until he stole the little gasp she made that he craved. They bumped into the wall more than once thanks to his lack of balance, but somehow made it safely into her bedroom. Before he tripped them, he tumbled her down onto the carpet.

"Rug burns!" she told him breathlessly.

"I'll heal them." His mouth rushed hotly over her face and then lower. He jerked a bit too hard at her shirt and the buttons popped. "Dammit."

She felt a laugh of sheer delight and desire combined rise. Her head had been spinning all along, and now she felt a bit drunk. Two could play the game, and she dragged at his shirt until he finally stripped it off. She flattened a hand against his chest and felt his heart hammering under her palm with the same crazy rhythm of her own. The pull of her magic tugged at his, and his Flower Mark appeared under her palm. With easy skill, she tumbled him over and pinned him instead. She buried her hands in his hair and bent to kiss him greedily. Would she ever get enough of his marshmallow Light taste? Probably not, and she did not at all mind.

His hands moved a bit roughly over her bare sides and then up to remove the bra she wore. Her Flower Marks glowed darkly as they appeared, and he leaned up to hotly kiss the one right over her breasts. The little moan she made raked dangerously at his self-control. "Touch me," he urged. His mouth moved to caress her breast and then teased the taut nipple. "I need you to touch me." The sudden rasp of calluses on her fingertips over his sensitive skin made his breath catch as desire tightened his body only more. She knew it too. Her pink eyes all but glowed as she walked her fingers down his chest, and darkness swirled inside their depths temptingly.

She shifted and leaned down to taste his Mark as he had done to her, and the shudder that went through his body thrilled her. Her caresses moved lower, and she found his durable work denims in her way. She nearly ripped them in frustration. Only the knowledge that he couldn't leave without them stopped her. "You better remove those or I will."

He nearly gave in to the sensual threat because it sounded sexy as hell, but the same thought had occurred to him. He got free of her half-hearted pin and quickly stripped off what remained of his clothes. Frankly, he had almost forgotten even his shoes. He then reached out and fiercely removed her lingering clothing as well. Naked, there could be no hiding the power she possessed, and his stomach quivered with sheer lust. He could happily spend forever learning and memorizing all of that beautiful muscle.

They reached for each other at the same time in another

desperate kiss and tumbled breathlessly over the rug until she finally let him pin her without breaking free. She had no desire to be anywhere except right there in his arms. He began to kiss and taste her as thoroughly as she had tasted him, and she fought the urge to flip him over and return the favor again. His mouth suddenly buried hotly between her legs, and she could not stop a cry of delight. She could not *breathe* for the greedy need burning inside her body.

She grabbed at him when he rose up and she swiftly reversed their positions to resume her exploration. She had a goal this time, and when she found his arousal, she tasted him as wholly as he had tasted her. His hands bunched briefly in her hair, and she felt a strange surge of power not just through her body but even her scalp. When she slowly slid back up his body, she found her hair had gotten longer. "You have a strange effect on me," she teased him huskily.

Eyes more white than gold flashed up at her. "I'm not done yet." He grabbed her and rolled, and his heart quivered when she again let him pin her. That she *wanted* to let him shelter and protect her only made his desire burn more. He dragged her into another nearly combustible kiss until she was twisting desperately beneath him.

"You had better—" She broke off on a moan as he positioned himself and then drove deep into her heated body. Something more powerful than desire seemed to well, and she felt, all but heard, a powerful *click* inside her soul as they locked together there as they belonged. The emotion he always gave so generously, the magic infusing his soul, seemed to pour into her own soul until she could not ever imagine not feeling him there. Nothing could tear them apart except death—and even death might not dare attempt such a thing.

She threw her arms around his neck and held on with all her strength as he took her again and again. Love and desire fed each other back and forth until her entire body felt like it might well shatter under the pressure, and she could not stop a whimper of sheer desperation. He drove harder, deeper, his own breaths not much less fevered than hers until the tension finally broke into searing waves of ecstasy. She might well have cried out then, but his kiss stole away the sound as they both drowned inside the pleasure. She had no strength left to catch him when his arms gave out, but he felt so perfectly delightful as a blanket that she honestly did not care. Rug burns would absolutely be worth every moment of that interlude.

Some strength eventually did return. Enough so that they managed to get to their feet only to collapse into her bed. She curled into his arms with her head on his shoulder and let herself savor the happiness of being there. She smoothed a hand slowly across his chest and trailed her fingers over his Flower Mark. His fingers covered hers, and she smiled as she tilted her head back to look up at him. "Did that tickle?"

"A bit." His arm around her tightened and then his hand slid up to smooth across the Flower Mark on her arm. "I liked it." His stomach suddenly rumbled, and he felt his cheeks heat as she started laughing. "We skipped dinner."

She sat up and gave a lazy stretch. She had never felt more perfectly content and happy, both emotionally and physically. A roll of her shoulders told her that if she had any burns, she did not really feel them. "Let's find something in the kitchen." She watched him slide out of bed and bit back a sigh of appreciation as fresh desire stirred. She had really gotten first prize in the lover soul mate competition for he had a beauty that truly went through both body and heart. Destiny could never demand anything she would not willingly pay to feel so loved and wanted by this most special person.

He glanced back to see her smiling at him, and the smile brought an instant rush of hunger to taste her lips. "What are you thinking, or do I dare not ask?" The words came out husky despite his best efforts.

The smile widened. "Just thinking about how it feels like we have lost time to make up for." She bit back a giggle as he immediately swung around and leaned down to cage her against the covers. Only he could bring out the silly laughter she so often never felt. "I thought you wanted dinner."

"It can wait. I feel like snacking on chocolate right now."

"Funny, I have a craving for marshmallows. We're a few graham crackers shy of dessert."

"We can do without. Crumbs in the bed would be terribly

uncomfortable."

"Too true."

Down deep within the deepest reaches of the Ephemeral Plane, the oldest of evil, the worst of its sort, had pushed against its bonds for millennia. With every passing year, those bonds had gotten weaker. Finally, at last, the creature known as Nemesis managed to break through and tore out of confinement. He surged across the Plane in a violent surge and then burst back out into the physical plane. He entered into a night sky across Protea and violent hatred churned as he looked down on the sleeping cities. *She* slept down there, and not even Nemesis knew whether he hated her or wanted her more.

He went looking for the perfect place to make his own and he found it in the ruined halls of the forgotten Protea Castle. The moment his essence touched the ground, dirt and grass and even stone began to lose all color save for a bloody hue. He found the throne room but did not dare enter. The glow radiating from the High Queen's crown seemed to cast sunlight into all corners of the room. Nothing could harm him faster than the sunlight buried so naturally within the power of Nature.

He instead moved deeper to the dungeons beneath where neither sunlight nor the light of Delphinium could reach. Only sinister bloody spheres made it even possible to see at all. He reached out with tendrils and grabbed onto that which he had hidden. "You!" he hissed, his guttural voice still unable to pierce the air wholly for all that existed rejected his presence. "You still do my bidding!"

A figure appeared on the floor. The red-haired man had remained unconscious, hidden inside the depths of Nemesis' mired muck within the recesses of Plane, but now he returned to life. He gingerly sat up and looked around. The place was familiar, and a sneer curled his lip. "Protea."

"Do as you promised," Nemesis warned him, "and I will do as I said. Get me what I want, and you will get what you want. Find my enemy and destroy her!"

The man rolled up to his feet and found that his uniform of formerly white and gold had turned bloody red. So be it. "As you command," he said, and reached for the power he had been granted by his master. He would find the one Nemesis wanted, and then he would go after the one he hated most.

Nemesis watched him leave and then let his power burrow down deep into the ground where it festered like an infected wound. He could hear Protea cry out in pain, and it only fueled his power more. The time for reckoning had come. The Apex of Dark would never awaken, and destiny would never be fulfilled.

* * * * *

Shana awoke with a sudden start and dashed into the bathing room and water closet before she became violently ill. The spasms would not seem to pass at first, and eventually left her huddled on the floor beside the basin. Of course, she thought a little sadly. She had gotten one night of happiness, and the very next, misery.

A hand knocked lightly on the door. "Shana?" Edgar asked. "Are you alright?"

"No," she admitted honestly. "Something has happened to Protea. Something that made me sick." She had to break off for another wave of illness. "Obviously," she managed to say. "You?"

"Nothing that terrible, but I'm not a Dual Cultivator. I'll get some bubbly water for you."

Bubbly water, with or without flavorings, had always been good for settling upset stomachs, even those provoked by problems with a planet echoing into its Cultivators. It had happened so very rarely in Shana's life that she could count it on one hand. The other two incidents had involved scientific studies that had *not* been in the best interests of the world. Clara had taken care of nipping those in the bud on Shana's behalf. This, however, was something else entirely.

She finally found the strength to leave the closet and found

Edgar waiting with the water. She accepted it and then sat down on the edge of her bed beside him. Tiredly, she leaned against him and let her head rest on his shoulder. "Just another new nightmare," she murmured. "I wish I knew where they came from."

* * * * *

A week slowly ticked by. Neither Chivanti sibling made any improvement over the course of it. Edgar got by well enough, though everyone knew he was nearly always fighting a queasy stomach, but Shana could not keep anything down at all. Kellie worked hard to try to heal the symptoms, but could only take the edge off briefly. Juliet began to scour her cookbooks for things she might *possibly* be able to make that Shana could consume.

Siobhan could not *stand* it. She felt as if she was watching herself from months before; this had to be the firing shot in whatever would lead to the price of Shana's birth. "I have to make her better!" she whispered fiercely to Sherry as they watched Desiree take both Protea siblings home in the middle of a class. "I'll heal her next time! I know I can give her more relief than even Kellie can."

Shana may have been sick, and she may have been a Dark element, but a tendency toward being blind did *not* make her stupid. After she and Edgar got home, she curled up on the couch with her omnipresent bottle of bubbly water and said, "What haven't I been told yet, Edgar?"

He sat down in the opposing chair with a heavy thump. He let his head fall back and plopped a cool cloth over his eyes. "Please be more specific as I am relatively fried mentally right now and can't figure out what you want to know."

"Siobhan. What happened to her? I *know* she's a full Apex now. So something happened." She watched his shoulders tense ever so slightly and knew she had hit it on the head. "The last week, I've watched the seven Dual Cultivators close ranks around you and I, which is to be expected since it does seem that we're the target of some sort of attack. It's exactly like what happened to Siobhan, right? Some incident that led you to being hurt and in danger—and probably Rocky too, though I can only now sense him because we're officially lovers."

He sighed and did not sit up. "Yes. It wasn't pleasant. It boils down to there apparently being a price to your births as an Apex. I don't know what yours is, Shana, I swear. No one will tell me anything either. But . . . Siobhan had to die a wrongful death."

She tilted her head back and let her eyes close. "There are things worse than death, really."

Another day came and went. Shana really did not want to be cooped up any longer, so some of her friends agreed to take her out—under the condition that if she got sick, she went home immediately. Since Alexandria was one of the friends in question, and she could physically cart Shana over her protests, Shana had no choice but to agree. The others to join them were Kellie, Juliet, and Siobhan. To at least keep things low-key, they went to the local public studio where the latest theatricals could be watched.

Each time sickness reared its head, Siobhan guiltlessly used her magic to help take the edge off. She really could not do much more than that, but at least she knew she could make her sister more comfortable. She also elected herself as 'bubbly retriever' and always made sure Shana had a bottle on hand. A bemused Shana said nothing about it; Light types needed to nurture and care as hard as Dark types needed to protect and defend.

They had just left the studio when Shana stopped dead in her tracks. A chill rippled over her body. Recognizing it as the *exact* same look Sherry would get, Juliet hastily stepped in front of Siobhan even as Alexandria and Kellie bodily blocked Shana. "What did you See?" Juliet demanded.

"I can't be sure. It feels familiar. I don't know why. I didn't even really *see* anything. Just felt it." She crossed her arms tightly to fight the chill.

Someone screamed in the distance, and all five Defender Cultivators looked up sharply. They could just make out the figure of someone firing off magical blasts at people. The blasts looked nothing like elemental magic belonging to Defenders, or Rulers. They looked like evil. The necrotic, bloody, wake they left behind felt far, *far* too familiar to Alexandria and Kellie.

"What's going on?" Siobhan whispered.

"Someone is trying to find Shana," Kellie admitted a bit grimly. "What better way than to just attack indiscriminately? You know how you repel most magical attacks thrown at you because you are pure Light? Well, Dark is the opposite. It absorbs and takes in. Someone lobs something at Shana, even if she can't block it, odds are that she will just absorb it. Which, yes, can be dangerous as well, which is why *neither* of you are allowed to just arbitrarily bounce or eat magical attacks. It can have hazards to you or others."

"We're taking Shana home," Alexandria told Juliet. "Get the others and see if you can't drive this attack off."

Shana set her chin. "I have a Mask, too."

"And you will not wear it unless there is no other choice," her twin shot at her. "Period." Sensing the sheer wave of stubbornness, she stopped bothering with words. She merely picked Shana up and walked away. Kellie followed quickly, and she called Desiree with her communication mask along the way. Alexandria and Kellie wore their two Masks as earrings; Desiree wore a bracelet.

Juliet did not have to call the others. Sherry had Seen the danger as well and already gathered Yvonne and Virginia. The three Cultivators caught up with their two partners and all donned their Masks and armor before they approached the scene. It alarmed them all that the enemy had already gotten so close to pinning Shana's location. Only a block closer, and she would have been in range, and her coloring alone may have given her away before any absorbed blast did.

More alarming still was that, as they approached, they all began to feel as if the man in the bloody uniform was familiar yet they could not determine from where. Siobhan felt less alarmed by that fact than her guardians; their memories had always felt intact, but now they faced evidence that perhaps something had been taken away from even them.

The man swung around, and his crystal blue eyes narrowed. "I figured you might show up eventually," he sniped. He shot a little smirk toward Siobhan. "So they finally let you wear your Mask, Sayena?" His sneer moved to include Virginia. "Yet you won't let Shanae don hers, Veronica?"

Virginia merely hefted her halberd threateningly. "Not with the likes of you running around. You want to tell us who you are? We can guess you work for Nemesis."

A brief confusion and almost disappointment filled his face and then disappeared. "My name is Vermillion Chance," he told them with a mockingly courtly bow. "Shame you don't remember me at all, but I suppose I should have expected that." His face tightened. "I was never important enough to anyone."

"You're not making yourself any more endeared by aiding in trying to destroy one of our queens!" Sherry shot at him in turn. "You won't find her, you bastard."

"Don't be so sure of that!" He began to disappear into a transport. "There's more than one way to draw out the Protea Dual Cultivator!"

Siobhan felt a chill through her soul, and, oddly, a deep sense of grief she could not place. She wanted to yell and rage at this Vermillion, and she could not figure out why—it seemed extreme, even considering the danger he posed to Shana and Edgar alike. "Do we tell Shana?" she asked softly. "How much more time can you possibly buy her, Ginny?"

"Not much," the Defender said tiredly. "Not very much at all."

* * * * *

Shana had not been happy to go home, but she had kept her mouth shut. Instead, she focused on trying to be happy to have her friends over for dinner. She had not gotten to cook for them in a while, and no upset tummy would keep her from feeding the ones she loved! She shared that sort of thing with Juliet, really. She hoped to con or emotionally blackmail the culinary school expert into teaching her new things.

Alexandria and Kellie sat at the high counter that surrounded the kitchen island and watched with smiles as Shana began to competently take over things. "Leave it to Edgar to make sure he picked the apartment with a kitchen almost as big as the one from the castle," Kellie joked.

"It's not *that* big." Though it reflected the apartment as a whole, really. Edgar had not bothered to go for cheap when it had been unnecessary. Hence the double master suites, and the separate sitting and dining rooms from the kitchen. "Besides, we both really love to cook, so it gives us a nice place to work in."

After a moment to watch, Alexandria decided, "You're going to give Juliet a run for her money."

"Nah. She's professional. I'm just a talented amateur. I follow recipes; she invents them!"

The conversation stayed light, and it pointedly stayed away from anything happening outside or with their friends. "You gotten anyone naked yet?" Kellie asked humorously as she was thumbing through some of Shana's recent photos. "Other than Rocky of course, though I'm skeptical if you would be thinking of art in those circumstances."

"Yeah, right now him being naked is definitely a distraction. Give us a little more time to be settled into our relationship and not feel as if we're making up for five thousand years of missed time. As for anyone else, nope, not yet there either. I'm planning out my attacks." She playfully stuck her tongue out at her twin. "I *will* eventually get you to pose nude for me, too."

"I'd give my life for you," Alexandria said mildly, "but my clothes stay *on* in photos."

"Damn shame when you have a nice body," Kellie told her.

"Thank you, but stop helping."

Shana knew that she could absolutely capture the airy and untamed spirit of her twin in photos if given half the chance. She also knew her weapons, and how to use them. Her lower lip began to quiver, and tears shimmered across her eyes. "You don't trust me,

Lexie?"

Alexandria's head hit the counter with a thump. "Alright! You win."

Pleased, Shana went back to her cooking. She didn't use the lip thing or tears very often. She saved them for special occasions. It was amazing how effective they could be on some people.

As she ducked down to rummage in the cabinet for another pot, a warning rumble from her stomach had her covering a grimace. It took all her concentration to pretend that she was fine. There wasn't even anything except water *in* her stomach to reject, yet her body continued to insist that there was something stuck. Something had deeply gripped Protea herself.

The front door opened. "I'm home!" Edgar called.

Glad for the distraction, she snorted softly. He was home, but an hour late. "Do I know you?" she called without standing.

"I'm not *that* late," he laughed as he entered the kitchen, "and I brought a gift."

"Oh really?" She stood up with the pot in her hand and spotted a grinning Rocky standing just to the side of her brother. She put her free hand over her heart and fluttered her lashes. "Gee, I've always wanted one. Is it housebroken?"

"Absolutely," Rocky responded, straight-faced, "and I do windows in a pinch."

"Wow, just think, I'll be the first to own one," she told Kellie and Alexandria. "Once I figure out precisely what he *is*, mind you. For all I know, he's as common as a dandelion."

"No, sadly, I'm original."

"Is *that* what we're calling it this week? You should hear what your enemies call you."

"It can't be worse than what my friends call me."

Edgar started laughing, and that set off the entire room. Over the counter, Rocky exchanged a quick high-five with Shana. They sometimes saved up their banter just to entertain the others. They knew full well it could be a spectator sport, and far be it from them to not keep everyone in good spirits. "I didn't know you were coming over," Shana told him on a smile. She shot him a distinctly flirty look from under her lashes. "I'd have dressed up for you. Or down, as the case may be."

"That would be unfair with polite company around," he groused. He skimmed a knuckle across her cheek. "Actually, I just gave Edgar a lift home from the ranch since he came out to help me today. He usually does on Saturdays, you know. He asked me if I wanted to stay for dinner and I thought I'd stay the night as well. Siobhan and I want to start spending more nights here to support you until this, whatever it is, passes." He leaned down to kiss her and said against her lips, "I even promise to behave myself."

"That's a first for your family," Edgar said dryly.

Shana shook her head in amusement. "I'm thinking of studying genetics. I think there's got to be a reason for the creepy compatibility thing going on, other than the whole Light/Dark aspect." She looked at Alexandria. "Do you think genes can lead to bad taste?"

"Is that a dig at me or Rocky?" Edgar complained.

She grinned. "It was a dig at me and Siobhan."

"Living room," Rocky said firmly, shoving his friend toward the door. "Before she turns the knife on us too."

"That means you too," Shana ordered the two Dual Cultivators. "I need room if I'm feeding a bottomless pit." She watched them file out and then her smile faded as she braced a hand on the counter. It was swelling inside, that thing trying to hurt her, and it made her feel as if she had been covered in the blood of the innocent. She looked at her hands and saw red blood dripping to the floor through her Sight. A new nightmare.

She made it through getting dinner done, but she ate very little. She pushed at the food on her plate silently and let the conversation flow around her. A buzzing in her ears made it hard to concentrate on anything anyone said. Unable to pretend anymore, she got to her feet and picked up her plate to take it into the kitchen.

"Goddess damn it all," Edgar said raggedly. Under his breath he added, "When will this end? I wish I could share how she suffers!"

"Don't even dare think such a thing," Kellie told him sharply.

Rocky and Alexandria suddenly went white, and the color left Edgar's face only moments later. Before Kellie could speak, they all heard a plate shattering on the floor. It was followed by a thump. Alexandria shot to her feet so fast that she jostled the table. "Shana!"

They found Shana lying on the kitchen floor, huddled in a ball of misery with her arms wrapped tight around her body. A power that seemed to be darkness and nature all at the same time seethed over her skin with a black and pink gradient of power. Vines coiled around her legs and slowly climbed her body.

The sight of it stopped Rocky briefly; for the first time in two decades, he had finally realized that Edgar's magic was very different from Shana's. Edgar's magic was black and pink, but the two came as totally separate colors, reflective of how the pink actually produced his Nature magic and the black came as a byproduct of his planet's critical Dark core. Also for the first time, Rocky then realized the very real difference in his own magic from Siobhan's. Hers was also a gradient of white and gold, and his was the two separate colors. He had honestly never actually realized before the differences.

He looked back in his memory and realized also that the other Dual Cultivators may have had two colors as well, but they were not a gradient either. They only had one element, but two colors, because nearly all elements had two sides: attack and defense. Light and Illusion were their own opposite sides, just as Dark and Nature were their own opposite sides. Therefore the gradient could only be a result of the two queens being Apexes. Only the two Apexes utilized Dark and Light as actual elements, and therefore the black and white had fused to their other colors. It felt significant somehow, and his Sight stirred. "Harmony."

"Yeah. It's painful and complicated, and better you remember it yourself later." Alexandria knelt beside Shana but did not touch her. "She's fighting. Damn it, she's fighting where I can't go to save her!"

If Shana heard them, it could not be determined. Her entire body arched as if to escape something, and her eyes flew wide to reveal they had turned solidly black. Another shudder ripped through her body before she went limp in blessed unconsciousness. The vines crept higher up her body.

"Can I touch her?" Rocky asked Kellie and Alexandria alike.

"If anyone can, it's you or Edgar." Kellie let out a rough breath. "Siobhan, too, if she were here. The rest of us? No chance. Not without being badly hurt. We're just not strong enough to touch the raw source of all darkness."

Rocky knelt and eased Shana into his arms, and his eyes flew wide and blind as he abruptly got sucked into a vision. A whirling storm of nightmarish images burned across his gaze and made him bite back a scream of combined terror and anguish. Tears welled in his eyes as he fought to escape, and just as suddenly, he came back to himself. He could barely breathe. "Wha-what just happened?" he managed to ask.

"What did you See?" Alexandria asked in turn.

"Nightmarish things." It dawned. "Did I . . . did I see Shana's nightmares?" He began to feel sick as well. "In my life . . . there have been times . . . I just felt as if I was having nightmares that didn't belong to me . . . were they Shana's?" His voice began to shake. "Has she been having these nightmares all her life and she never told any of us?"

"All her life," Edgar confirmed tiredly. "Every night of her life. A lot of time during the day. You know how Siobhan was always getting sick? Once I learned about Famine and her role in that . . . I began to think the nightmares were Shana's equivalent. I knew about them because it started almost from birth. She made me swear not to tell you or Siobhan or Mom." Softer, he added, "The nights you're here, that you are holding her in sleep . . . she doesn't have nightmares. It's as if they can't find her there, the way that Siobhan always seemed to just get healthier if I held her."

Alexandria nodded a bit. "You are correct about all that, Edgar. And, Rocky, it is not unusual for a lover soul mate to share the dreams of a Protea Ruler Cultivator thanks to them being the Ruler over the Ephemeral Plane as well. Siobhan has probably shared Edgar's dreams often enough but never mentioned it because she didn't realize." She pressed her fingers to her eyes briefly. "We can't buy Shana any more time. She has to awaken. I'll fetch her Mask. We'll take her to the park garden where they have the biggest growth of protea flowers. Kel, call Gin and the others. Everyone needs to meet us there. And that includes Clara!"

Though night had spread rapidly, it took no time at all to get everyone rousted. All had remained on edge anyway, and sleep had been hard to come by for more than just Shana. Word moved quickly from Cultivator to Cultivator, and all made their way directly toward the protea section of the park's garden where, so long before, the four heirs had met for the first time.

Siobhan arrived last, even after Clara. When she spotted her brother and lover standing with Shana in the former's arms, she gave a little cry and rushed over. "Shana?" She took Shana's hand in hers and held on tightly. "I'm here," she whispered fiercely. "I will help you through this!" No answer came, and she abruptly whirled on Clara. "I have had it!" she shouted. Her gold eyes flashed a threatening white. Siobhan and Rocky alike rather quickly went white, but if Edgar or Shana finally got provoked to black, their friends *hid*. "You will tell us everything, Clara! That is an order as your queen! *Give us back our memories!*"

Clara lowered her gaze briefly and then removed the hourglass from her bracelet. It rose up over her palm to become full-size and began to spin rapidly. Waves of pink and lavender spread from the hourglass and swirled around Siobhan, Rocky, and Edgar; she could not help Shana unless the other woman awoke.

What had been fuzzy became as clear as the glass of Virginia's magic. Whole and complete memories of their past lives flooded all three Cultivators. Including memories, all three realized, that the other Cultivators—even Clara—did not possess. Rocky and Edgar could see their beloved Commanders quite clear, and so could Siobhan. She took a sharp and pained little breath of realization for the enemy she had confronted without knowing why he felt familiar. She knew now.

Beyond those memories came the sharp and oppressive memory of the weight on Shana's birth. Of the terrible thing she had to do. The literal pressure of millions of years of waiting and expecting her to fix what someone else had broken. She had spent her entire life *knowing* that life as they knew it had to end in order for her to do what was needed, and that she would just be born *again* with the same weight.

"How do you demand that of someone?" Rocky whispered. "How can we force her to remember that?"

Shana's eyes abruptly opened. "I have to know." She pushed at his shoulders until he reluctantly let her stand on her feet. He had to keep an arm around her, however, and it was only his strength that supported her. All of hers had been stolen. "I have to know. Destiny is my mistress, and she is harsh." Her laughter sounded bitter and empty of all joy. "I obey Destiny," she said flatly, "because I have no choice. But I will not be her slave. Give me my Mask, Alexandria! Let me be what I am supposed to be! I will pay whatever price is needed! Clara, let me remember!"

"It will not be easy," Clara told her. Despite the calm tone, her hands visibly shook where she held her hourglass. Her queen's pain had gouged her as deeply as the rest. The one she loved most. She had never loved any Ruler Cultivator the way she loved Shana, though Siobhan ran a rather close second.

"Do you think it's easy now?" Shana demanded. She took a very cautious step away from Rocky and nearly fell. He caught her again, but she was barely aware of him as more than the light of sanity inside her soul. "I've had nightmares my whole life," she whispered faintly. "He's always been there, a part of me, trying to destroy me. At least let me know who he is!" she shouted.

Siobhan pressed her hands against her mouth before she cried out. Tears poured down her cheeks as she felt the whiplash of pain and fear inside Shana. A tremor went through Edgar's body, and she turned to hold onto him fiercely. She buried her face against his chest. She couldn't stand this. If the Defenders didn't do something, she would find something, anything, to make it better herself.

Alexandria looked at the Mask in her hand and then stepped forward to give it to Shana. With seemingly no hesitation, Shana lifted the Mask and put it on. Black-pink power surged around her body violently and then released a shockwave as the entire world tried to offer its strength to its Daughter. Armor formed on Shana's body, and her now ankle length loose hair bound into the tight braid that came as a default for all Defenders with longer hair. Somehow, seeing it happen to Shana just made unease stir. Being bound to their destinies did not feel as . . . terrible, as hers did.

Clara closed her eyes and held out the hourglass once more. Pink and lavender flowed to Shana, and it released the same memories inside her as had been released inside the other three. Shana's eyes flew wide behind her Mask and then slowly closed. Her gloved hands slowly curled into fists, and only one tear escaped her tight control.

Siobhan surged forward to hug her fiercely. "Cry!" she snapped. "Cry, damn you! It's okay to cry! I'll hold you together." Her best friend since her first birth. Her sister in the heart from two lives. Was it reciprocity from their brothers, or just them? Maybe it was both. They had been inseparable at times, very nearly as close to each other as to their twins. How could she have ever forgotten this person from her past life?

"Maybe later," Shana said softly. "I can't fall apart yet, Siobhan." She drew a breath that still sounded ragged and reached up to remove her Mask once more to send away her armor. Her mind reached for Siobhan's, and she asked, *What is it that I can sense inside you that is so upsetting?*

Siobhan's lower lip quivered. *Vermillion betrayed us, Shana. He— he was the one there the other day, attacking to find you. He sold his soul to Nemesis.*

You can't keep that from Rocky.

Yes, I can!

Well, I can't. Shana released Siobhan and straightened. Everything hurt as her body tried to rebuild defenses against the encroaching evil. Now that she knew him, she knew how to block him. "Vermillion Chance," she said quietly to the Light Defender Cultivators. "You fought him recently."

Rocky's entire body jerked. "What?" he managed to ask. "What? No!" He shook his head sharply. "That can't be!"

"I'm so sorry, Rocky," Siobhan whispered. "It's true. He betrayed us." She moved to hold her brother instead.

Virginia's eyes narrowed sharply. "Who was Vermillion?"

"He was once one of Rocky's personal guards, a member of the elite branch of the Royal Knights who went by the rank of Commander. There were others for him and Edgar alike, but they are not yet important, which is why none of you remember them." Shana crossed her arms tightly around herself. "He hated me," she admitted and did not look at Rocky as his head swung toward her. "As much as he hated someone else, really. I wish I could be surprised by this, but I'm not." Her eyes hardened. "For betraying my soul mate as much as for joining to my enemy, I will destroy him."

"Not if we get there first," Sherry bit out. She gave a little cry and lunged forward as Shana suddenly staggered. "Catch her!"

Shana landed safely in Alexandria's arms and was already asleep even before her twin lifted her properly. Rocky shook off his own pain and moved closer to touch Shana's arm. His breath came out softly as he saw nothing terrible. "No nightmares," he told the others. "Not this time thankfully." When Alexandria handed him Shana, he clutched her closer protectively. If his arms could protect her from nightmares, he would never let go.

"They will diminish for now," Clara agreed. "But they will never leave her fully until Nemesis is gone for good. She lived her entire life in the kingdoms knowing they would fall, and his presence hovered over her the entire time. He hovers still, and only removing him will ease that."

"What?" Alexandria could barely get the word out, and she knew she had to look as horrified as everyone else did at that revelation. "Sh-she *knew*? She knew all along what would happen?" She had always assumed Clara had known, for obvious reasons, but it had *never* occurred to her that Shanae had known as well—though looking back, she wondered how she had missed it. "Why didn't she tell at least me?" she demanded furiously.

Edgar slowly shook his head. "She never told me either, Lex. Or Robert. Or Siobhan. We only knew there at the very end, that the kingdoms had to fall so she could fight Nemesis in a time that had forgotten him." He made a helpless gesture. "It's . . . Shana. It's how she is. We can't change her, even if we wanted."

"For what it's worth, I tried to tell her to let everyone know," Clara said. "She told me that it would change nothing and that all she wanted was to see everyone smiling and laughing until too late. Lex, you noticed there, toward the end. You had mostly guessed right. You more than anyone other than Evan or Robert, she wanted to keep happy. She needed you to be strong for her."

Alexandria curled her hands into fists and let Sherry hug her. The other Defender knew all too well how hard it could be to be willing to sacrifice their life for their twin, yet never want to hurt them in any shape. "Damn it."

Clara let out a tired sigh. For once, she felt as old as she truly was. Every year of her existence sat heavy on her shoulders. She did not want to think of how heavy they sat on Shana's shoulders as well. "We'll all spend the night at your place," she told Edgar. "Shana will rest deeper and easily if the presence of all eight Defender Cultivators are near her in addition to Rocky and Siobhan alike."

Edgar nodded. "We have plenty of room—and blankets." He started to reach out for his transport magic and then paused. "Clara?" he asked. "What price will Shana pay?"

She hesitated a bit and then finally admitted, "I truly do not know. I only know it will be worse than death. Death can be an escape, or a release. Shana . . . I just don't see her receiving that." She churned over things she had always suspected, especially after meeting Shanae and watching her grow. They churned all the stronger now seeing how Shana had evolved. "Not for a very long time, anyway," she murmured.

Deep within the underground of the Protea Castle, Nemesis raged and screamed and tore at the walls. Vermillion stayed clear out of fear for his own life. The evil entity barely remembered his presence. She had awakened! She knew of him, would find him! She would destroy him and he could not stop her!

He stared sightlessly into the distance and listened to the eerie silence. He felt her the way she felt him. It had always been such. The one creature he could not claim. The one creature he wanted most to claim. He would be a nightmare not confined to the night if he could just take her power. "I will not go down easily, Apex."

His voice echoed off the walls as a sinister threat that even his minion flinched to hear. There was no escape for anyone at all as long as this beast lived.

*   *   *   *   *

Shana awoke with an abrupt start as nausea churned in her stomach. She sat up straight and looked around a little wildly. She was in her bedroom, at home, and Bastian slept as a ball of fur on her pillow. On the floor of her room, she spied blankets and sleeping bags holding a few of her friends. She could sense the others in the apartment with her.

She gingerly got out of bed and found someone had put her in her favorite pajamas. The fluffy material felt soothing on her skin as she carefully tiptoed over to her balcony. She eased the door open and went outside to sit on her swing. She could not determine the specific time, but it had to be between twenty-three and twenty-four hours for she could clearly see Delphinium's palace from her window. Not as big as from her own palace two hours earlier, but still there on the edge of what she could see of the other world in the sky.

She did not hear anything, but someone sat down beside her on the swing. Strong arms curled around her waist. On a little sigh, she leaned back against Rocky's chest and closed her eyes. "Isn't it a sign of the end of existence if a Delphinium child wakes easily at midnight?"

He smiled and rocked the swing lightly with one foot. "I sensed you wake up, and that you needed me." He nuzzled his nose into her hair. "I had thought about snuggling you in your bed while you slept, but you were fairly restless for once so I let you be out of worry you'd wake if you didn't have enough room. I'd rather you have restless sleep than no sleep." He laced his fingers with hers and watched his home world in the sky. "Did you sense him?"

"Mm. He's afraid and furious. He'll send some Nightmayres after us next time, of course. He would not dare try to show his face to me." She let the rocking of the swing and her soul mate's warmth comfort her where nothing else ever could. "The sins of our ancestors," she murmured. "It must infuriate him how much I resemble Shanta."

"His obsession with you doesn't seem like Famine's obsession with Siobhan," he admitted. "I feel as if . . . he wants you. Not strictly in a dead sense."

"It's a strange area," she agreed. "You're not far wrong. He wants to claim me and my power. Why wouldn't he? I represent everything he needs. Dark power to make him stronger, and Nature power to destroy him. The conflict of my own elements created him. Protea's elements created Evil. It was our sin, and so I must cleanse it."

"Because you alone created the harmony between Dark and Nature, created a way for the sun to burn even in the middle of darkness."

"Me alone for now." She tilted her head back to smile up at him. "Any child we bear will have a harmony as well. She may not be able to use Dark as an element, only I could do that, but it will still flavor her Nature magic in the way Light will flavor her as it comes from you. It'll take a special Defender Cultivator to be her twin, to be sure. An understanding of both Dark *and* Light."

"Positive of a girl are we?"

"True, we both carry intergalactic blood, so we might get an oddity like you and my brother, but my gut says that we're in for a girl. Maybe because I can only think of girl names. Mother always said that should have been a clue she was carrying Evan; she could not think of his name because she was focused on the wrong gender. She got close though. She had liked Evelyn best. I'm kinda partial to Leslie Ann. You can think up a shorter version for her Ruler name. She'll probably need both. I admit, this thing of pretending to be perfectly normal is appealing."

He nuzzled at her ear again. "I've got plenty of time for that. And I agree. This life is more enjoyable in many ways. More freedoms." His heart ached a bit that she would not get to keep her freedom forever, though. Someday, inevitably, she would have to don her crown and rule as High Queen. Until then, he would do whatever it took to ensure she had the freedom she needed in order to be herself. "How long until this is over?"

"Not very. A day or two at most. I'm not at all afraid." She straightened and turned to smile at him. "I'm not even nervous. I don't know what price I will have to pay, but I accept it. I will survive, Rocky. I have to, if we're going to have that child we just discussed."

He leaned in and kissed her tenderly until she had almost melted against him. His fingers lifted to caress the Flower Mark on her chest under her shirt, and he felt her heart skip a beat inside his own chest. "I love you," he whispered huskily as he eased back. "And whether it's legal or not, whether anyone understands or not, I am your husband. Our vows have not broken. I am yours." He slid his hand around to caress the Flower Mark on her left arm. The touch was deliberate, a gesture of love and respect for her status as a Defender. "I will always be yours. Eternally. My Tash."

The sound of the old, beloved, nickname made her heart tighten with painful love for a moment. Their secret words. "My Caretaker." She drew him down for another kiss, almost unable to find the words she needed to express how terribly she loved him. She eased back and whispered, "I am always yours. Eternally." She looked up at him with trembling lips. "I wish you could learn to be less tenderhearted, though. It terrifies me."

"Well, I wish you wouldn't hide so much inside," he retorted politely. "We're even." He nibbled teasingly on her lip. "You make me tempted to join you in your bed this time. I'd behave myself, though. I need you to rest for once."

"I only rest if you're there. I want to sleep in your arms where nightmares cannot find me through the light of your soul." She caught a breath as he stood and lifted her up off the swing and into his arms. "It always unnerves me a little when you do that. And it's really kind of sexy. Maybe you don't have to behave yourself."

"There *are* people sleeping on the floor of your room, you know."

"Damn. Good point. Just sleep it is."

She not only slept more peacefully in his arms, she slept long past sun up—which was as unusual for a Protea child as it was for a Delphinium one to be up in the middle of the night. Protea represented the day; they went to sleep and got up early. Delphinium represented the night; they stayed up and slept in late. Rocky himself woke after the sun rose, but he just continued to hold Shana in his arms. The others hung around as well since they had no classes.

Shana finally awoke closer to noon, and had one hell of a sleep hangover. Her groggy state seemed most evident in that she did not make a peep of protest as Siobhan insisted on helping her shower and wash her hair, and then almost meekly ate the lunch that Juliet prepared. It stayed down, too. She curled up on the couch for another nap after finishing her food, and the others felt downright *grateful*. Trusting that she was, finally, mending, they all began to take their leave. Siobhan and Rocky left last, and they made Edgar vow he would call them if he or Shana needed *anything*.

Shana awoke an hour or two after her nap and felt both alert and refreshed again. She finally went to change out of her pajamas, and she coiled up her hair. Feeling a need to do *something*, she went into the kitchen and got started on the dishes. Normalcy. If she could control nothing else, at least she could control that.

She was elbow deep in soapsuds in the sink when Edgar walked in rubbing a towel over his hair after his own shower. He stopped short and stared at her. His eyes filled with pain as they lingered on her bound hair. Unlike Rocky, he had never been able to remove the binds she felt. He slung the towel around his shoulders and walked over to the fridge to silently get out a fermented drink. How did he apologize for being blind to what she suffered? Only at that very last moment had he understood what she had known all along, and yet hindsight made it seem as if he should have known all along.

"You're almost as Dark as I am," she told him gently as she saw his face. "We both are often blind, Edgar. And, well, I made sure you stayed that way on purpose." To lighten the mood, she teased, "Be careful opening any gifts from Virginia on your birthday this year."

It made him laugh. "I think I ought to be more wary of you," he said dryly. "This time, you might help."

She grinned over her shoulder. "What makes you think I didn't help her back then, too?" As she turned back to the dishes, she added, "Don't apologize for not knowing what I did. I took care that no one would know. It's over and in the past; don't dwell on it."

"You should have still told Robert, Sayena, and me much sooner, Shana." He frowned. "It should not have been your burden alone!"

"It would have changed *nothing*. Truly, literally, nothing. Why would I steal away what little hope remained? I can endure nightmares far better than any other. Let the burden be mine alone."

"If he managed to defeat you, what would happen?" He hated asking, but he wanted to know, needed to know, the rest of the truth. There was still so much she hadn't told him, and he never wanted her to be alone with those burdens again, no matter how she insisted otherwise. For the first time, he thought he could truly see and understand his sister's powerful strength of will. She had no equal.

She stopped scrubbing and stared silently out the window over the sink. Then, quietly, "Nightmares will no longer be confined to the night. They'll be free during the days. Fear and terror will consume the people and the worlds will slowly rot and decay away until there's nothing left."

A chill ran down his back and he put down his drink can

quickly. She just smiled and continued to finish the dishes. He stared at her for long moments before it dawned on him that she genuinely held no fear of losing. After everything she had endured, everything she had been forced to deal with, she had no option but to win. He had seen it with Siobhan as well, where the added weight of five thousand years had pushed her to be unwilling to compromise. Perhaps that, too, had added to the need to be reborn.

"You know I will fight beside you." He moved closer to hug her tight. If he had *ever* regretted being shorter than his sister, it only came in the moments where he wanted to take her away from the things that wanted to hurt her. Sadly, he could not bodily move her against her will. He had always had to depend on Alexandria and Rocky for that; good thing all three of them tended to think the same way. "This is a matter of our Royal House, not just you. All Protean Ruler Cultivators carry the same sin, Shana. We could not do what you did, either. It is on all of us to help you fix this."

She didn't say anything to that and finished up the dishes. She had just nipped his can to steal a drink when her Sight stirred. Her entire body froze briefly as she stared at nothing.

Edgar didn't bother to wait for what she had seen; he went down the hall, grabbed the necklace that had her two Masks on it, and brought it back. The moment her eyes focused on him, he fastened the necklace around her neck.

Her communication mask lit up with fiery orange. She touched it lightly. "Sherry? What did you See?"

"The protea garden," the Aster Defender responded without preamble. "It was being filled with weeds. I know evil is there. What did you See?"

"A nightmare."

Sherry didn't ask for specifics. "Then that means Nemesis or Vermillion is trying to draw you out. Do *not* go alone. All of us will meet you there."

The mask stopped glowing and Shana pulled a face. "You can't tell me what to do," she groused. "I barely let Ginny do that!"

Edgar fought to hide a smile. Some things truly just never

changed. Poor Virginia had been banging her head on a wall for two lives in her effort to keep the Apex of Dark in line. Siobhan was more willing to defer than her partner, simply because Siobhan accepted her need to have a physical partner in order to allow her to use magic.

Shana possessed exceptional physical skills even when unarmed and unarmored, and she could also use what magic she did have in particularly brutal ways. Her Nature power could crack open the land under someone's feet, and it could also hurl vines to entrap enemies; her Dark power could form a shield capable of absorbing near anything, and it could also produce projectiles of raw power. All Defenders accepted that she might not *really* need them, and in turn, she accepted that they still *needed* to protect her anyway.

As Shana pulled her Mask off her necklace, Edgar grabbed her wrist. Black and pink swirled around him and formed his Ruler suit. Identical pink eyes glared at one another for long moments and then she gave in on a sigh. "Fine. But at the risk of sounding like Virginia, stay out of the middle! Focus on partnering Siobhan. If I need someone to cover me, and the Defenders can't do it, leave it to Rocky. That's *his* job as my Caretaker." In a mutter, she added, "I will be far happier over this entire thing once we find the eight Commanders. Then the Defenders will not only have *their* Caretakers, but you and my lover will have dedicated defense!"

Edgar looked at her a bit oddly. "You mean seven. We found one. Where we should not, but we did."

"No. No, we really did not."

He opened his mouth and then closed it. "No," he agreed softly. "We really did not."

She put on her Mask and called up her armor. She clasped hands with her brother and they transported directly to the protea garden. They were the first to arrive, but the others appeared within very short order, including Clara. Her partners and queen had entered battle, and now so would she. The two Delphinium siblings came in last. Rocky and Edgar exchanged a glance and then places so that they stood by the side of the Defender they had been made the Caretaker for.

Nothing at all seemed completely out of the ordinary for the garden. It was certainly a little lusher than it had been the day before, but since it had held the ground zero of an awakening Nature element, no one really felt surprise.

Shana held out a hand and called her claymore to it. No one but Rocky had ever seen the weapon before, and more than one whistled softly. Like the magical rod held by Siobhan, to look at the weapons of the Apexes was to underscore their role. They looked nothing like the weapons held by the others, even the Defenders of the Dark planets. Alexandria possessed a harpoon, Kellie a three-headed spear only a Metal element could control, and Desiree used a throwing pinwheel. Clara used her hourglass as a weapon that focused magical spells, so in battle, she would stay with the other two solely magic users.

Evil surged across the land. Shana and Sherry alike swung around, and Virginia snapped, "Shields!"

Yvonne and Siobhan hastily threw out shields of Ice and Illusion around everyone. The oncoming surge of terrible power smacked into the icy portions and cracked them, but it dissipated when it reached the glowing mirage within. "Brace yourselves," Shana ordered. She shot a look at Virginia. "We are in battle. Do you yield to my command as strongest Defender Cultivator of our generation?"

"Yes—but only until the point where your life is in danger you cannot escape."

Shana had to smile. "Fair enough."

The power had receded back into itself and it began to rise up out of the ground with wispy, monstrous visage. The creatures had no real defined features, no real way to claim they resembled anything. They most resembled whatever the person they opposed feared most, and they rumbled with a sound nearly inaudible that still made hearts quiver with dread. Nightmayres.

Shana looked at them and saw . . . sleep. The one thing she feared was her own sleep for it was haunted by the bloody fingers of the creature she existed to destroy. A tiny smirk touched her lips. Was this the best Nemesis had to offer? He could not scare her with the thing that had become so thoroughly a part of her life.

The Nightmayres rushed in as a whole and the fight began.

Shana dove right into the heart of the battle without hesitation, and both Rocky and Alexandria stayed near to her side. Virginia intently watched Rocky for a few moments and then felt a bit of tension leave her shoulders. Her prince could at last use the full breadth of his skills, and it made him nearly as potent as his lover. She still kept an eye on him, though.

It did not take long at all for both Siobhan and Rocky to realize that the same thing happened to the Nightmayres as had once happened to the Germs. When one was destroyed, the backwash transported away lingering fragments so that Nemesis could expend less energy creating more. They kept their mouths shut for fear that Shana might do something like the two Delphinium heirs had. It was all or none this time!

Unfortunately, Shana had already noticed the happenings. While she did not know what her counterparts had done before, she possessed an intelligence that equaled Rocky's. She leapt to the same conclusion he once had, and she also suspected she could use her transporting magic to take herself to wherever those fragments went. She just chose to keep that knowledge to herself.

She waited until she could just get herself a bit away from the others. Even Alexandria let her move as she liked because of her armor and skills, as long as she stayed within the general area, of course. Shana watched, waited, and then spied the perfect opening. She lunged forward and threw out her power in the same moment. Dark power struck the backwash and opened an odd time-space portal. She dove within and swung around at the last moment. Another shot of Dark shut the portal behind her.

"Shana! Goddess *damn* it!" Rocky snarled.

A bit of frenzy on the side of the good guys obliterated the remaining Nightmayres. No more reappeared. Why would they? Nemesis had what he wanted. No one even knew *where* to look for Shana, and Edgar could not look through Protea's eyes as long as the taint lingered. "Did you know she would do that?" Kellie demanded of Edgar.

"I didn't." Black seethed across his normally pink eyes. "I had insisted on joining her, that this supposed sin was carried on the backs of all Protea's Rulers, but she never agreed nor disagreed. Did you tell her about that?" he asked Siobhan sharply.

She scowled. "Why would I when she's too damn much like you? Rocky and I planned to go with both of you! I don't want her to pay that price alone, either, Edgar!" She stamped a foot on the ground with a powerful huff of air and then swung around with arms crossed. "Damn it! Why do I have to love two such hardheaded people? Not fair, Destiny!"

"Clara?" Alexandria asked tightly. "Can you find her?"

"Yes."

When that was all she said, Rocky's hands curled into fists. "But you won't. Because you shouldn't?"

"I like Destiny no more than most of you do," the Librarian admitted a bit tiredly. "And I like her less when she makes sure I know where not to interfere—even when I could."

* * * * *

Shana dove out of the portal on the other side and rolled across the ground before nimbly gaining her feet. Her eyes swept over the scenery and realized immediately that she had landed right outside her own castle. It looked surprisingly intact for having been neglected for five thousand years, but Protea herself had tried her best to salvage what she could.

The only thing about the castle that belied what lay within was the bloody hue to the stone. Shana walked forward calmly and reached out to touch the wall. Her gloves did not actually cover her finger tips, and so her skin itself came away stained with blood in a mimicry of her newest nightmare. She did not wipe it away as she turned and walked into the castle. She knew where to go.

Halfway there, she felt a familiar presence join her. She smiled. "Why don't you just escort me to him? Am I that terrifying?"

Vermillion stepped out of the shadows near her, his face expressing a combination of fear and hate, and then he nodded shortly and fell into step beside her. He had always secretly admired her even though he had hated her. She had always commanded respect in many ways, even from those who were her enemy.

"You do realize I will destroy you as well." She watched where they were going rather than look at him. "That is, if Nemesis doesn't do it himself."

"I'm aware of that," he agreed. "I'm not concerned with it since I chose this path."

"Why did you?" She finally looked at him and stopped in the middle of the hallway. "Didn't you feel any remorse for what you did? Don't you realize the pain you caused when you simply disappeared? Robert nearly lost his mind when you could not be found!" Her eyes narrowed sharply. "What did you do to Chance and Diego when they came after you? I know they found you. I could See it."

"Rubeo never should have followed me!" he admitted bitterly. "Nemesis killed him." His face tightened. "I had to pretend it didn't matter. As to where he is *now*, I don't know that either. I don't feel my brother on the planet."

That would have to be revisited eventually; it didn't bode well that someone of power had not been reborn, and Chance had indeed possessed intriguing gifts. "And Diego? I assume you killed him."

"No. I wanted to! But that idiot . . . he tried to protect *me*. Said that as long as Robert wanted me as his Commander, that he would do anything to ensure our prince had such a thing. Called me an idiot, but he died protecting an enemy." He made a disgusted noise. "What would he have known about how I felt?! He had everything he ever wanted! Robert loved him more than me, and he would have been a Commander if he had not been too young. I was only second-best!"

"Whether Robert loved Diego more is irrelevant, Vermillion." Her cool voice contrasted the hint of black moving across her eyes. "He did love you. And you betrayed him. But why Nemesis? Why release my enemy? How did I ever offend you?" Understanding suddenly filled her as he shot her a fulminating look. "Because Robert loved me."

"He had nothing left for me or anyone else. You consumed him entirely."

She just sighed as she started walking again. "You really don't understand how love works, do you? It's not a limited force. It's not something you run out of. You can love many people in many different ways. Will Robert only ever love me as a lover? Of course; he's a Cultivator, and that's how we work. Does that mean he uses up all of his love on me and has none for anyone else? Absolutely not. It doesn't work that way, especially not for those of Delphinium! They have a well of love to give that will never run dry."

"So you say."

"So I *know*," she retorted. "Why drag Nemesis into this? You could have just gone after Diego and me directly. Or did your hate expand to include Protea as a whole because I embodied the essence of the world?"

"All I know is that I hated you, hated Protea, and hated Diego." His hands clenched into fists. "I wanted all of you gone. It was easy to hate you, and I knew that if I unsealed Nemesis before you were ready, he could take care of everything. He promised to spare Robert for me if I did his bidding."

"And you called Diego an idiot!" she exclaimed in exasperation. "Damn it, Vermillion." She stopped outside the main door of the dungeons and turned to glower at him. "Nemesis has no care to abide by that promise, and he hates Robert as furiously as you hate me! Even if somehow Nemesis kills me here, he will go after my soul mates next!"

"Then I'll be reunited with my prince in the afterlife."

She lifted a brow. "You think that you'll earn that gift? Think that Robert will *ever* forgive you for what you've done?"

"He forgives everyone." He opened the doors. "Unlike you who never forgives and never forgets."

"You have to earn my forgiveness, sorry. Hazards of being Dark." She walked into the room lit by bloody spheres and looked around with ease. She could see in absolute dark, let alone where light lingered. Honestly, she actually saw *better* in the darkness. She often suspected it was only her Nature element that allowed her to see in the light at all, just as it was only Siobhan's Illusion element that allowed her to see anything at all in darkness.

Softly, a voice that had haunted her sleep said, "So, there you are. Just like I wanted."

"There's an old adage from Gladiolus that fits here. Be careful what you wish for." She slowly swung up her sword, and sunlight radiated from the blade. The darkness of the room drew in toward her and flowed over her skin. Nemesis' familiar form revealed itself in the middle of the room, and she shook her head. "Like all nightmares, you're not so terrifying once the dawn comes."

A surge of necrotic power swept over him and he abruptly condensed into a visage not unlike his Nightmayres. He stood bigger than the Protea High Queen by a bit, and acidic blood poured down his body from open wounds. He moved closer and leaned down to be face-to-Mask, and she did not flinch. "Are you afraid yet, Your Majesty?"

She smiled. "No. But you should be." Fear her destined battle? How could she? She had every advantage, including strength, power, and training. After everything she had endured, she couldn't fail now.

She just couldn't.

Back in the protea garden, no one really knew what to do or where to go. It felt like an hour since Shana had disappeared. The only evidence they had to any of the goings-on lay in Rocky. His entire focus had turned inward as if to find the bonds connecting him to his soul mate, and he occasionally flinched as if he had been struck—or rather, Shana had.

"How is that possible?" Siobhan whispered to Clara.

"He is merely extending beyond the natural level that exists between soul mates. Only lover soul mates can do such a thing, however, because they are interlocking rather than merely overlapping. Alexandria can feel when Shana is in danger, but she cannot feel if Shana suffers physical pain, nor deepen their bond to share it."

"I can feel Shana's pain, or share it as well if I try," Edgar admitted, bringing many startled eyes. "We found out as children. It was after the accident. She had been hurt far worse than I. I wanted so badly to make her not hurt, to share her pain, and . . . somehow I did. I didn't even think anything about it until what you just said."

"I can feel Rocky's pain too," Siobhan whispered. "Either if it's so strong it echoes, or if I deliberately want to make him feel better. I never even thought of it as unusual."

Alexandria drummed her fingers on her arm. "Then that means that we were not wrong in thinking that both sets of siblings are soul mates of some sort. But how do you have aspects of a lover bond and a twin bond alike? It's odd enough for someone to have three."

"That I honestly do not know," Clara apologized.

Rocky's head suddenly snapped up. He stood from where he had been sitting on the grass and turned around. Vermillion appeared in front of him a moment later.

A low snarl of rage vibrated inside Juliet's chest. "You son-of-a-bitch!" she snapped. "How *dare* you betray our prince?!" She would have gone for his throat if Virginia had not grabbed her arm to restrain her.

Rocky fought to keep his voice even. "Mind explaining?" No memories of friendship, of how much he had loved this person, could take away his fury. His own Commander had joined with the creature trying to destroy his soul mate. He barely noticed when Siobhan stepped up beside him and slipped her hand into his.

"You saw me as second-best." Vermillion had only intended to taunt everyone with the knowledge that Shana struggled, but the bitterness had welled up the moment he saw his prince. "You spared barely any time for me compared to the others! Diego and Shanae took all of your attention!"

Rocky suddenly felt old and tired. "No, they really didn't. Diego spent more time with me, sure, because he was my companion-at-arms, but I loved him no more or less than I loved Talon and Ulyen. If anyone took the majority of my attention, it was Shanae as my lover soul mate, Sabin as my twin soul, and Sayena as my soul-sister." He held tighter when she squeezed his hand. "I loved you, Vermillion. As much as I loved the other Commanders? Well, no. But you know what? You never wanted me to."

Vermillion recoiled a bit. "No."

"Actually, yes." He sighed. "Vermillion . . . you don't understand love. And because of that, you always kept a little wall between yourself and others. Of course you were not as suited to be a Commander as Diego. Diego proved himself on the first day with his willingness to try to be a Commander even though he was too young. Would *you* have ever done that?"

Silence stretched long and painfully. "No," Vermillion finally admitted in a low voice.

"You could have had what you wanted, Vermillion," Siobhan told him quietly, "had you been willing to give what needed to be given in return for such a gift. You cannot ask someone to love you unconditionally if you are not willing to give the same. Defenders and Commanders alike must love without condition, must give all of themselves, to the High Prince or Queen that they are to defend, for you must be willing to die for us if it is needed." Her chin lifted slightly. "You do not deserve to be called a Commander, and is my right as High Queen of Delphinium, I revoke your position."

Shock and pain filled Vermillion's eyes. Millennia of beliefs and hate shook on their foundation. He found himself staring at what he had done through the eyes of another, and self-loathing rose.

Very softly, Rocky said, "If there is any real love inside your heart for me, you will cease to be my enemy. That is the one thing I never wanted."

Vermillion's eyes closed as he felt the rising waves of guilt. What had he been doing? He couldn't even comfort himself with the idea he had been controlled. He had done what he had done willingly. He had deliberately set out to destroy the one person he should have protected for she was critical to his prince's existence. Slowly, he sank down onto one knee with his head bowed. "There is much I have to ask forgiveness for, my liege."

"Stupidity tops the list."

He found his first smile in a long time. "I still can't argue you with you when you're right."

Edgar moved forward. "If you want to make amends, you will take me to wherever my sister is and allow me to help fix what you made wrong."

"Not just Edgar." Siobhan's chin lifted. "Rocky and I as well. She needs us! I won't let her face what I did! If she is to pay a price, then we will be there to help her endure!"

If Vermillion took them to the castle, then he would forfeit his life for a new betrayal. But, so be it. If he could give his life to protect the one his prince loved, then perhaps he might be able to make amends in the end. Instead of standing in Shana's way, he could clear it for her. "Alright. I will take you there."

Shana snapped up a Dark shield in order to protect herself and it absorbed the evil energy Nemesis had just hurled. Dark red blood streaked her skin where a few attacks had gotten through her armor, but the same also stained him. It had become a battle of stamina; neither of them could gain an advantage. She just needed *something.* Some little thing to take her over the edge.

Magic suddenly swirled around her body with a soft pulse of light. She swung around in surprise and discovered that Siobhan, Edgar, and Rocky had appeared behind her. Edgar moved closer and held up a hand. She laced her fingers to his, and he smiled. "I should yell at you, but I suppose I expected this."

She smiled. "I knew you would find me if I needed you." She looked at Siobhan and Rocky. "Magic only. Cover Edgar and I."

Nemesis could only stare at the scene in mounting shock. For just a moment, he could only think that Shana had sent out a call to the others, but he did not recall seeing her grab her communications mask. They had come of their own will, which meant they had come through his barriers, and there was only one way that had happened: Vermillion had brought them there.

The great evil roared in sheer fury at being betrayed by the great betrayer. "VERMILLION!" The ground rattled in the wake of his rage as he clawed at the walls. "Where are you?! I will tear you apart!" He whirled around and saw Shana and Edgar watching him, and to the side of them stood the two heirs of Delphinium. The absolute forces of Shana's power had just become more absolute by adding her brother to bolster her Nature and her lover to bolster her Dark.

Nemesis began throwing wild blasts of power that forced everyone to scatter and dodge. Neither Siobhan nor Shana could throw shields when they had to constantly move, and Nemesis kept up the barrage with such violence that there proved no time to pause. One blast landed in the middle of the room and created a shockwave that knocked everyone into the walls.

Shana and Siobhan weathered it well enough thanks to armoring, but their brothers hit a bit hard. Both slumped toward the ground and tried to catch a breath in order to get up and make less of an easy target. Nemesis saw his opening and savage satisfaction filled him. He hated the High Prince of Delphinium only slightly less than he hated the High Queen of Protea. Rocky would be the first to fall as punishment for Vermillion's actions, and destroying him would gut the Protea Defender irreparably!

The blast came on too hard and too fast for anyone to react. Rocky tried his damnedest to cast a shield spell, but it refused to form because his magic just did not work that way as a Ruler. Siobhan and Shana had thrown their skills as well, but Nemesis' power had gotten a head start and would land first. Rocky could only brace for the inevitable impact.

The blast never landed. Vermillion interceded a few feet in front of him and took the full strike in his chest. It sent him smashing into the wall beside Rocky where he then crashed to the ground with a meaty thump. Blood pooled under his body.

"Vermillion!" Rocky scrambled over to his side. He blanched as he saw the gaping wounds in Vermillion's chest; the blast had shorn clear to the bone and his uniform now bore blood for reasons other than his master's power.

"Oh gods!" Shana and Siobhan had already been running to reach Rocky, and now they skidded onto the ground beside the fallen former Commander. "You idiot!" Shana shouted. "You only had to *ask* for forgiveness!" She barely noticed when Edgar knelt beside her and held onto her in support.

"I can't heal him!" Siobhan managed to say. "Why can't I heal him?! Why did he do that?" she demanded raggedly.

Rocky took a long breath. "He knew. He knew he would die if he brought us here, Siobhan. His death was inevitable. The moment Shana destroyed Nemesis, he would have taken Vermillion with him. And . . . he won't be reborn. He abandoned that gift when he chose to betray our house."

"Your visions . . . were always vexing." A tiny smile touched Vermillion's lips. "Could never stay a step ahead of you. Only . . . Sabin could do that." His breath rattled in his chest. "I want you to find Diego," he managed to whisper. "Give him the position he always deserved. It never . . . belonged to me."

Pain blossomed inside Shana's chest as he slumped over and she could no longer sense his life. Too much death. There wasn't supposed to be anymore death in order for her to finish her destiny. Fury erupted. "That is *it*!" She lunged to her feet and whirled to rush at Nemesis. Her sword came to her hand and she hacked violently into his body before he could dodge. A pink glow began to radiate around her as hot as the sun, and she seemed to disappear as she plunged all the way into his essence.

She bore deeper and deeper through the muck of his existence and ignored the gouges cutting into her armor and skin beneath. When she could go no deeper, she stabbed her sword into the very center of his decayed soul and released the full force and might of her blended Dark and Nature power. Black-pink sunlight exploded away from her body and began to eat Nemesis alive. She listened to his screams without remorse.

On the outside, the other three only knew that Nemesis had begun to scream horrifically. Siobhan desperately clamped her hands over her ears to drown out the sound. The screams spiraled higher, and then Nemesis just . . . evaporated. He disappeared as if he had never existed, and his erasure caused a shockwave of Nature power to rip through time and space. It burned past the Cores of Hyacinth, Orchid, Daffodil, and Statice and unfroze all of them. It may be millennia as well for them to recover to support life, but at least now they *could.*

In the place where Nemesis had once been, Shana appeared instead. Power still moved over her body. She looked far more ragged than the last they had seen her, and only her sword served to brace her so she stayed on her feet.

Rocky and Edgar moved forward as one, and Rocky caught her safely when her knees buckled. She was already unconscious even before he lowered her to the ground. Edgar removed her Mask, and her armor disappeared. Siobhan moved closer and unfastened the first few buttons on Shana's shirt to yank it partway down her arms to see her Flower Marks. The sight of both stopped them all cold.

They had not changed. No sparkling edge to the crowns, no second blossom to her Defender Mark.

"Sh-she didn't evolve," Siobhan whispered. "I wondered. She didn't change like I did. She didn't awaken as an Apex!" Horror rose. "Does that mean . . . oh gods. Nemesis wasn't the price of her birth?!"

"Then what *is*?" Edgar asked a bit raggedly. "What more does Destiny want her to do? It wasn't enough to place the burden of the destroyed kingdoms on her, to make her live eternally within a nightmare she cannot escape? What could be worse than that?!"

Rocky's arms tightened around Shana. "Unfortunately," he said softly, "we're going to find out. But maybe, perhaps, she will have some measure of freedom now. The sin has been cleansed." He glanced toward Vermillion's body. "In more ways than one."

* * * * *

"It's done."

Shanta had been standing in the shade of her favorite fir tree, and at hearing her descendant's words, her eyes closed as her knees buckled. She slowly sank down to the ground and buried her face in her hands. "Finally," she whispered raggedly.

Genevieve knelt to hug her, and Shanta turned to hold on in turn. They grieved equally for what Shana had suffered; as Edgar had said, the sin had rested on the shoulders of all Protea Ruler Cultivators. "There's only one concern," Genevieve admitted in a low voice. "Shana did not awaken as an Apex."

Shanta's head jerked up. "What?" Her eyes slowly widened. "No. That's impossible. Orion said . . ." She broke off as she realized her husband had never said that Nemesis was the price of the Apex of Dark's birth. He had said that there would be an unknown price to the birth of the Apexes, and the one of Dark would destroy Nemesis. They had all just simply started assuming that Nemesis *had* to be the price. "What could possibly be worse?" she whispered.

Genevieve took a long breath. "I may . . . have a suspicion. Someone came to Protea from another world, under the cover of secrecy. I looked at his world. It is . . . ravaged."

Shanta began to frown. "So then the wars will continue."

"Removing Nemesis does not remove the weeds he already planted. We can only wait, Grandmother."

With a little nod, the High Goddess got to her feet. "Indeed. And in light of that, I need to go find my husband and demand he give me answers for what he *does* know."

Genevieve watched her stalk off, and smiled a bit ruefully to herself. "Good luck with that."

* * * * *

Life settled down and went on. Shana's crown moved to her apartment and took up residence in a trunk at the end of her bed. Alexandria and Virginia, in full Masks and armor, reported again to the world leaders on behalf of High Queen Shanae Protea to say that the queen had returned, but she would wait to retake her throne until Delphinium arose as well. There was much disappointment at that, yet it was accepted as given. It really did seem only fair for the queens to wait to rule together.

Concern lingered among all of the Cultivators over Shana's lack of awakening as an Apex but no one said anything about it. Talking about it would change nothing, and all they cared about right then was that Shana had healed. She no longer got sick, and she seemed to finally be sleeping every night through even if her lover didn't share her bed—rare as that may be.

As Siobhan and Shana shared a parfait at a shop after classes, the former noted, "You're laughing again. It's nice to hear."

"It feels nice to *want* to laugh."

"No more nightmares, then?"

Shana smiled. "I'm much better, promise. I feel more rested than I have in a *long* time." She stretched largely. "Still feeling a bit odd, I suppose, to no longer have *him* looming over me as an inescapable destiny. I hope to eventually become complacent with the events."

Siobhan highly doubted that would happen for a long time. No one could actually mention Nemesis' name without sending Shana into a heart-racing, palm-sweaty sort of brief terror. She had developed a ripe case of survivor's stress, and they lacked anyone with Spiritual Healing to help her get better. But, at least, they could diminish the effects by carefully avoiding the topic entirely. It was not difficult; no one else wanted to remember. "You and me both."

Shana glanced out the window and saw a familiar figure waiting. She smiled. "If you'll excuse me, I have a date."

Siobhan glanced, saw Rocky, and grinned cheekily. "Well if you're going to be like that, I'm kidnapping your brother."

"Ha! He's all yours." She kissed Siobhan's cheek and then headed outside. She then burst into laughter as Rocky swung her up into his arms and around in a quick circle. He did it *just* to make her laugh, and she did not mind at all.

Most everyone knew they had gotten engaged, and a flabbergasted Rocky had discovered that more than one person at university had been eyeing him personally since they expressed dismay at the change. Shana had only laughed at him; and they called those of the Dark blind! He and Siobhan alike could be adorably oblivious to those who couldn't help falling a little in love with their generous hearts.

To help make the transition easier, Shana and Rocky had obtained stone rings to wear on each thumb of their hands to mark their engagement. Rocky had gotten the stone for hers from Delphinium, and she had gotten some from near her palace there on Protea. The average person needed no such trappings, but they were both Ruler Cultivators, and they felt the need to uphold the traditions of their first lives. Siobhan and Edgar, seeing what they had done, had also obtained the same stone and updated their own engagement rings. It had never even occurred to them to do such a thing.

"Speaking of," Rocky noted as they walked down the lane toward the studio where they wanted to catch a stage theatrical, "do you still want that wedding band I promised you five thousand years ago? It's not the tradition these days, so no one will be suspicious. I can see the symmetry of rings for our pinkies, though. We'll get those, too, when we marry in this life."

She smiled. "I like that. And, yes, I do still want my band! It feels a little superfluous, sure, but I want it." Her breath caught as he swung around to face her and held out his hands. There, on his palms, were two beautifully made wristbands of shimmering opal. She lightly touched one and felt the soft and tender pulse of Delphinium. "How?" she whispered. "Delphinium barely healed!"

His eyes softened as he began to fasten the bands on her wrists. "I asked," he said simply. "I went there, and I asked my Mother for what I needed. Siobhan came with me, and we were gifted with the opals needed for your bands. And, yes, as that implies, she knows we consider ourselves married. She had been suspicious already." He brought her wrists to his lips and pressed a kiss to the tender skin near her bands. "You wear the jewels of my world, my wife. Will I wear the jewels of yours?"

"Yes," she promised. Her eyes began to sparkle. "If I can find an amber stone as sassy as you are!"

"That could take another few millennia to find," he teased. He released her wrists only to wrap an arm around her waist and begin heading once more toward the studio. "Are you sure you want to be with me that long?"

She looked up at him, and all of her love glowed out of her eyes. "I think I can handle something like that."

The Chaos War

21

Life settled into a comfortable pattern. As October rolled around, Siobhan's twenty-fourth birthday came with it. For the next month, she and her brother would be the same age, and poor Shana would feel even more like the baby of the lot until her own December birthday. Siobhan had no desire for a big party, especially because she wanted her introverted loved ones to be happy, so instead, she had one small party with Octavia, her brother, her sister, and her lover, and then she had another with all of the Dual Cultivators.

Even Clara attended, and she joined Juliet to take over all cooking duties. The party itself really felt more like a casual get-together that involved cake, and that suited everyone fine. They played some games, and watched film theatricals. Siobhan considered it a special gift to get extra cuddling from Shana. Oh, Shana could be cuddly, to be sure, but Siobhan tried really hard not to use up all of her introvert's ability to recharge others. It was only fair to share, especially with Rocky.

Huddled together in a large bean bag and swathed in blankets so only their faces could be seen, the two sisters critically studied the newest film theatrical that they had put on. It featured the new actor Byron Rancul, whose popularity seemed to just keep climbing as time passed. Not only did he possess his Virtuoso voice, but he also had genuine acting skill, and anyone who worked with him said he was likeable and easy to get along with. The fact that he had a very handsome face with almond-shaped eyes just helped the entire package. At just under twenty-five, he had a maturity not expected from someone not quite an adult. But then, rumor said he had been given independence on the young side.

"I like his coloring too," Siobhan told Shana. "Hazel eyes and hair are so fun because they all but change color from green to brown to gray depending on the light they're in. Always a shame when they stick him in a wig."

"Well, with hair to his hips, unless he wants to always be cast as the romantic male lead, he needs to change his looks now and then." Conspiratorially, Shana said, "Remember me saying I might get a new actor naked in front of the camera? This stays between us, but it might be Byron. Lux opened that new and improved theatrical studio to produce both film and stage shows, right? Well, he's considering coming to Lux to record here, and the owner of the studio came to university to find filmers and photographers, and I got tapped for the second. So . . . maybe!"

"That would be so fun if you got to work with an actor! He models, too, right?" Siobhan giggled. "We'll get Sherry to make him some clothes to show off. Oh!" She whispered into Shana's ear, "Wait until you see what she made me for a birthday gift. It's almost as much for Edgar as me."

Shana bit back a laugh. "He's doomed. And I'll probably have to expect one for my birthday soon enough."

"Oh to be sure. She said something about hand dying pink lace." She snorted softly. "Really, at this rate, the two of us should either just swap the man we live with, or maybe all four of us live together. I'd really rather the latter, actually. I miss that, from when we were little. We'll have different room sharing to be sure but I just want us all to be together in the same house again."

Shana looped her arms around her knees as she watched a dramatic battle with weapons happen on the film. Byron had real skill on top of his stage ones, so she had to admire that, too. "Maybe someday soon. There might be a place. Edgar and I know about it, but it's . . . out of our reach for the time being."

Siobhan studied her. "Does this have anything to do with your trusts, and your degrees, and your not-common surname, and the fact that I heard Mom tell Edgar that she would be giving him something she's been holding on his birthday this year—you know, when he's a legal adult—and Clara earlier said something about looking forward to, and I quote, 'getting her hands dirty again'?"

"Maybe."

Sensing she would not get anything else, Siobhan hugged Shana tight. "Okay. Fine. I won't press for anymore answers unless I feel that neither of you can do whatever it is you intend to do alone."

Rocky plopped down next to them and told his sister, "Time to share."

"No, I have dibs!" She stuck her tongue out at him briefly. "Go cuddle Edgar if you need a battery."

"I did. We just decided it was time to swap."

Shana just shook her head. She had missed this far too much while she had been in Axium. It made her question her sanity, but at least she couldn't deny she never lacked for feeling loved.

* * * * *

The Ephemeral Plane had not yet regained balance. It had suffered too greatly across the two wars against Nemesis, and Pallas had only begun to see signs of majik returning within the last thirty years. Strong majik, to be sure, but not yet nearly enough. He knew his prince and queen had regained their full skill and memory, and knew that his queen could help restore the balance as only a Ruler Cultivator of Protea could, but he had not been able to reach out to them yet. He had honestly been afraid to try for fear of making things worse. They likely didn't even know how bad things had gotten; Clara was the only one who did, but there was nothing she could do personally as her domain lay within the Hall.

Pallas felt the land move under his feet and turned his green eyes toward the distance where he could see swirls of light and dark violently crashing against each other in a way that created sparks. That did not bode well at all. His hand tightened on the long broom that served as mark of his position, and magic moved around the crystal sphere embedded at the end. He had to try to reach his Rulers.

The Plane depended on it.

* * * * *

Shana's sleep had become less fearful to her thanks to defeating Nemesis. Nightmares still came with more frequency than the average person, but not every night. Not all the time. Even without her lover to hold her, she did not have to dread closing her eyes. Perhaps unusually, if she did not have nightmares then she rarely had dreams at all. Their frequency had tapered off significantly without Pallas specifically sending them to her as his role as Archon and hers as Ruler dictated. That hadn't happened in over five thousand years.

Things changed shortly after Siobhan's birthday. Shana had been contently sleeping alone in her bed when she suddenly heard a whisper across her unconscious mind. No words could be determined, but she heard a familiar voice regardless. A flash of scenery came with it. Familiar scenery, though more ravaged than she remembered.

Help us.

Her eyes flew wide and broke the dream as she went from sleep to waking in an instant. She carefully sat up in bed and shoved at her hair as it fell in her face. When she could see, she slid out of bed and walked over to open her door fully. She stepped into the hall just as her brother's door opened across from her. He looked as groggy as she felt.

The siblings turned as one and headed for the kitchen to make some hot tea. Only after they both had cups did Edgar finally say, "That was unexpected."

"A bit." Shana stared down into her cup and watched leaves float. "But maybe not. We knew things would be bad. It was inevitable after us not being there, and everything lately with Famine and Nemesis, especially the latter."

"Mmm." Edgar slowly stirred his tea. "It's been too long since we visited, I guess."

"Well, death will do that to you."

As was their way, neither Shana nor Edgar mentioned the dream they had received or the possible meanings of it. They just did not feel as if it was worth bothering the others until Pallas actually could contact them wholly and tell them exactly what he needed from them. That did not mean it didn't bother either sibling, however, and their sudden excessive quiet and propensity to be thinking to themselves more than usual sent up red flags in both Siobhan and Rocky alike.

Rocky tried tentatively asking Shana and then Edgar but only got diverted. Siobhan tried bribery of both equally and still did not get a direct answer. A few days ticked by with no progress, and after the third night of both Chivantis unusually turning down the offer for a sleepover, Rocky and Siobhan alike had reached the edge of their patience. Their loved ones would share and tell *or else.*

Shana genuinely had no idea of the coup about to happen until she left her last class for the day and hands grabbed her unceremoniously around the waist, hoisted her, and tossed her across an all-too-familiar broad shoulder. She felt no startle or surprise at the gesture because the only one she could not sense sneaking up on her was her Light lover. Her lack of sensing him meant she didn't get surprised; even she knew that to be odd.

On a sigh, she propped an elbow on his back as he calmly strode through the university past dozens of snickering and giggling students and faculty. In a way, she had expected this a bit sooner. He and his sister had shown unexpected patience. "Am I being kidnapped?"

"Correct. But don't feel bad. Edgar is too."

She blinked. "But he's . . . Siobhan is . . ." There was no way at all Siobhan would ever be able to physically manhandle or move the Protea Prince against his will, so Shana could not help but be a bit curious as to how she would pull off a kidnapping. Still, "Damn it, Rocky. You cannot carry me all the way to your apartment!"

"Watch me."

She scowled and crossed her arms as he proceeded to indeed carry her the few blocks to the apartment he shared with Siobhan. Not for the first time in her life, she felt grateful for her lack of shyness as all too often her Light companions did so love to push their luck in provoking her Dark temperament.

He walked into the apartment, and she blinked at seeing her brother sitting on the couch. He had been trussed up with what looked like bands of Illusion magic. He looked at her in turn and said politely, "Did you know that Illusion magic under the Defender category can effectively make someone fly by imitating weightlessness?"

She felt an absurd urge to laugh rising. "I did not! Do tell more."

"Someone of particular magical skill could just, you know, truss another person up and tow them along through the air like a living balloon. It might actually be fun if the balloon in question had had *warning* their feet would leave the ground."

Shana dropped her arms and head alike as laughter welled up against her control. "Of all the things. Damn it, Rocky Toulume, put me *down*!" She found herself put lightly on her feet and walked over to plop down next to Edgar. A flick of Dark magic from her fingers absorbed the Illusion magic holding him; lucky for Siobhan, Edgar's lack of using Dark despite technically possessing it meant that for all his own unexpected magical skills, he could not absorb magic cast on him.

Siobhan had been sitting on the bean bag, and she hopped to her feet to plant her hands on her hips as she aligned herself beside Rocky. "You are almost more trouble than you're worth!" she scolded. "We're your family, and we're your soul mates! How many times have we told you to just *share* your burdens with us? Something is bugging you, and we're not budging until we find out what it is!"

"So maybe we can't help," Rocky added firmly, "but we can listen and we can let you vent and we can tag along behind you with moral support and sparklers to help make you feel better!" He huffed out a breath. "Also, we're lonely. But it's your fault that we're addicted to you, though, so no apology there."

Shana and Edgar exchanged a look and then both started laughing. "Eternal optimists," Edgar said fondly.

"Someone has to do it!" Siobhan leaned over and gave him a smacking kiss.

"Alright," Shana sighed. "We'll explain what we can but better we tell everyone at once. In a way, it affects all Cultivators and not just the Protea Royal House. I'll call my three and you call your four. Clara can skip this conversation for now since not only is she aware of why it will happen, but she may not necessarily be needed at the moment."

It did not take long to have the other seven Defenders assemble at the apartment. All had noticed something off about the two Proteans, but even Alexandria had been willing to bide her time a little bit more. As she walked into the apartment, she told Rocky, "You saved me the effort of a kidnapping personally."

Shana scowled at her. "I wouldn't let you get away with what he pulled. I love you equally, but I only tolerate certain behaviors from certain people!"

"Like letting me boss you around but no one else." Virginia tugged on her hair as she sat beside her on the couch. "Under duress, maybe, but you do allow it." She settled back and crossed her arms. A hint of a look in her gold eyes heavily implied that perhaps a third kidnapping may have been in the works. "So what's been going on?"

Shana stretched out her legs and studied her sneakers. "The Ephemeral Plane. What all do any of you know about it?"

Yvonne frowned thoughtfully. "Honestly, not much. We never used it, or accessed it, and it never really came up as a necessary sort of knowledge. I mean, we know Clara lives there in the Hall of Records, and that there's another space called the Immortal Fields—I remember Liena talking about that one—and we know that the worst of all existences become trapped in the Underbelly of the plane. That's where Famine and—and Him broke free from. I think everyone knew about the Plane back in the time of the kingdoms, but no one really knew anything about it, so to speak. It is connected to the Protea Kingdom, I think."

"All of that is correct," Edgar said. "To clarify, the Ephemeral Plane is sort of the slough of the physical realm to hold that which isn't capable of being on our plane, and it plays a critical role to existence because it is where all the memories—in the Hall of Records—and dreams—in the Immortal Fields—are housed. Clara is in charge of the Hall, of course. The Archon known as Pallas is in charge of the Fields. However . . . the Fields need more than just an Archon. They need a

Protea Ruler Cultivator."

Shana nodded. "The Plane as a whole relies on the Dark and Light of Protea and Delphinium as much as the rest of our universe, but especially the Fields are dependent on Protea in particular because we provide the power of Nature. So, back at the beginning, our ancestor Shanta become the Ruler of the Plane to help Pallas keep balance. Every Ruler Cultivator of Protea since has been equally the Ruler of the Plane."

Desiree cocked her head. Even she and the other two Defenders of the Protea House had not known these details. "So . . . how did having two Activated Rulers of Protea affect the Plane and Fields in our generation?"

"Positively!" Edgar held up a finger. "The duties split between Shanae and I. We co-rule meaning we have to make any decisions together, but the other aspect of being Ruler is split between us. I defend the Plane, which means it is my particular Nature magic that provides the intensive shields that keep just anyone from entering the Plane anywhere they like. The *only* people who can walk the Fields without expressly getting permission from me are witches of the Faith. Their majik ability to even enter is basically a tacit agreement with Destiny herself to serve as gatekeepers themselves. On the other hand, appropriately, Shana fights for the Plane, which means it is her particular Nature power that allows the Plane to continue the cycle of growth and death, and she alone can help maintain the balance of the Fields specifically."

Siobhan turned that over and then said softly, "No wonder you were fit to fight *him*."

Something pained flashed through Shana's eyes before she banished it. "Yeah. But that doesn't mean Edgar isn't fairly embroiled in the Fields personally. We could swap roles should it ever be needed. And, for the record, yeah that's why you and Rocky all too often will share our dreams when we have them. That is a byproduct of being our lover soul mates." She rubbed her hands over her arms. "Anyway, the Plane is in bad shape right now, particularly the Fields. For one thing, it hasn't had a Protea Ruler Cultivator in five thousand years.

For another, remember me mentioning those of the Faith? Turns out the Plane is almost as dependent on them as on Protea! Ever since they went into hiding and stopped practicing so openly, the Plane has suffered from that too."

"I was wondering about that," Juliet mused. "If the fact that I have literally never met anyone of the Faith in this life, and that it isn't even talked about by most people, would have some sort of impact in a way we didn't see. They have incredible gifts, needed ones for us Cultivators as Liena proved, so it just felt . . . odd they might have disappeared."

"Can you find them?" Alexandria asked curiously.

"We *could* if we looked through Protea, but there's something that needs to happen before we make an attempt to restore the Faith." Shana waved it off literally with one hand. "Right now, it's most important to get Edgar and I back to the Plane so we can restore the balance and help everything stabilize. Pallas is struggling terribly to do it by himself, but he honestly can't. His role is to watch and oversee and report to Edgar and me any changes we need to address. He's *trying* to contact us, but, again, imbalance. He's a Nature element too, so he's sort of reliant on us as well."

"Can't we just go there?" Sherry shook her head. "I would assume you two can just enter at will, and we can go with you to help if possible."

"Well, yes, under normal circumstances. We're not kidding about this imbalance thing screwing up everything." Edgar shrugged. "We could normally just open up a transport right here and through we go, but we really don't dare because there's no knowing whether or not the Plane can actually support that. Instead, we can use one of the few places on Protea where there is a physical connection point."

"So where are they?" Rocky asked.

"Good damned question," Shana muttered. "It's been five thousand years. No knowing where they moved."

Sherry slowly lifted a brow. "But I could find them via some divination related to my Sight. Is that what you were going to say next?"

"Maybe?"

Virginia barely stifled a sigh that Alexandria echoed. "So," the former said pointedly, "then you *did* know we needed to be told because you actually *do* need our help—or at least Sherry's—in order to get back to the Plane. You might have the strongest Sight here, and be the only one besides Clara with All Sight, but you can't use divination because you never learned how."

Divination could be learned by anyone with any form of Sight, but what could be learned or obtained by the deliberate application of Sight directly related to the form of Sight possessed by someone. Present Sight limited to current events, for example. Shana with All Sight could conceivably divine information from just about any time period, but she had never bothered to learn how to use the skill since she so rarely had need—and in the past she had had access to three different people possessing the skill personally: Liena, Asheria, and Jayden.

Of the three, Sherry had always had a particularly potent Sight of her own and though limited to Future, she skirted *very* close to having Present as well; her future visions could be anywhere from years to hours to even *minutes* from happening. That meant her particular gift for divination could find objects in all but current time, as long as they were stationary.

Shana merely glared at Virginia. "If Pallas can contact Edgar and me in order to tell us what exactly he needs and if the Plane can support transport, then notifying you lot would have been merely a footnote because we could go there, fix things, and come back."

"You really think it'll be that easy?" Alexandria retorted.

"Rocky wants me to be more positive, and I'm trying. I can't please you people, sheesh."

Muttered Rocky, "There's a difference!"

She ignored him a bit pointedly. "Let's find a portal we can use. It's basically a place where physicality and metaphysicality connect. Usually we find it in a piece of glass since Glass has a propensity to show reflections, and only reflections can offer a glimpse of things not really there."

"Sherry isn't enough to go along with you. I, Alexandria, and Kellie will go along as well. Siobhan, too, for extra magic."

Shana glared at Virginia for several moments and was met by an equal glare. Desiree, ever the pacifist, calmly walked over and caught Shana's face to make her look down at the shorter Defender. "Shana," she said with utter calm, "it's not worth your effort to fight this fight. If it's really no big deal like you think, then why is there an issue with others going along to observe? Think of it as an outing with everyone. You enjoy those." She poked Shana in the nose. "Maybe we did wait too long to let you wear your Mask. You've gotten too self-sufficient."

Shana sighed and relented. "Okay, fine."

"Water elements," Juliet intoned. "Capable of taming even the untamable Nature!" She grinned at Alexandria. "Makes me wonder why Air ended up being the twin soul to the Apex of Dark, she who is the best and worst of both Nature and Dark alike!"

Alexandria grinned. "Because there's literally nowhere she can hide that I can't find her—which has saved not just my sanity but also Gin's more than once!" In a mutter, she added, "I count my blessings she's Nature and Dark and not Dark and Light. *That* would be a terrifying combination." She thought about it and then decided, "But potentially entertaining, to be sure."

"Is there such a thing as a pessimistic optimist?" Siobhan wondered. "That'd be someone thinking things will always work out but probably be terrible along the way, I think." She giggled. "Okay, that does sound funny."

Sherry snorted. "I'll hope that person is a Defender, not a High Ruler, thanks!" She nodded firmly. "Alright, let's see what I can do to find one of these portals." She sat down on the floor from where she had been leaning against the kitchen counter and closed her eyes as she held out her hands, palms up, before her.

A few moments ticked by and then her eyes opened swiftly. Her yellow irises had completely consumed her pupils. "A broken bottle," she said, almost monotonous. "A piece still sits near a shop corner. When someone kicks it tomorrow, it will shatter entirely and something will come out." She took a little breath as her eyes went back to normal. A scowl darkened her face. "Yeah, you're not going alone. That was *not* a pretty 'something.'"

"That doesn't bode well," Kellie muttered. "A portal to the Ephemeral Plane is going to spit out something potentially evil?"

Edgar shrugged one shoulder. "Considering the state of the Plane and everything lately with the Redemption Wars," the moniker applied equally to both fights and avoided naming Nemesis for Shana's sake, "it doesn't seem so surprising that lingering or festering evil may exist."

Shana coughed as more than one pair of eyes glared at her and her brother. "So let's go then and get this over with."

"The boys stay here." Virginia's voice booked no argument. "No, I don't *care* if Edgar is Protean and Rocky can push the Apex of Dark. Until I know exactly what we're walking into, those without armor are not allowed."

"Sometimes I wish we weren't Ruler Cultivators," Rocky complained at Edgar.

"Well, you are," Siobhan shot at him, "and there's probably a reason for it, but until then, Ginny's word is law. I mean, you could *probably* petition to Shana and see if she can override Ginny as the stronger Defender but I see this as being something they would totally agree on. I think she and I equally won't forget seeing you two smack into a wall without armor and be completely defenseless!" She went up on her toes to kiss Edgar's cheek to take the sting out of her words and then whispered, "When we find the Commanders. It'll be okay then. Gin won't be as afraid for you. Max and the others multi-tasked really well. They can directly protect you and Rocky and also step in to act as Caretakers personally."

A little pang of pain and loneliness went through Edgar's heart that he stamped down fiercely. There would be time enough for everything. He did at least know the Commanders lived on Protea somewhere. He had not actively gone searching yet simply because the time had not felt right. He and Rocky alike had agreed to exercise patience until Shana's sense for the future said it was needed. She knew *something* would clue them in, so they waited. "Alright," he conceded. He looked at his sister. "I'll wait here for you to bring the portal back so we can go together."

She smiled. "That's fair." She snorted. "Sorry that when Ginny and I *do* agree, it happens to be about you two staying safe! Whoop!" She hastily grabbed Rocky for balance as he yanked her off her feet into his arms. Before she could blink, he had kissed her with an edge that sent her senses spinning. When he released her, she barely noticed their laughing friends. "What was *that* for? Are you trying to distract me?"

"No, I was sharing my strength with you, as I can as your Caretaker." He grinned. "Which, yeah, I could do without touching you, but this seemed far more enjoyable."

Alexandria fought back laughter as she grabbed Shana's arm. "Enough of that." She pulled Shana over to where the other four Defenders had gathered closer together. It only amused her more that Shana did not resist; if she had, Alexandria could never have held her, particularly with the Delphinium Prince's own considerable strength bolstering her own. Edgar could share his surprising magical gift with Siobhan as well; standard for most Caretakers, but particularly potent here as the two men had had to work extra hard to gain their gifts.

Because she was both Ruler and Defender, Sherry could use her transport magic to take them to where she had seen the shard. As they landed, she said musingly to Shana, "As much as it really would be easier for everyone involved if Rocky and Edgar were not Activated Ruler Cultivators, I feel as if it is as much because Destiny wants something from them personally as it is that they have to be that way to support you and Siobhan."

Shana nodded. "That's been my thought for two lives, really." Softer, she added, "And everyone else may be Dual Cultivators because of *me*. I had to be one. I *had* to, in order to do what I did—and to do whatever else it is that Destiny intends to demand of me. I have not paid my price yet, to exist, and whatever it is means I needed to be as much a Defender as a Ruler. I couldn't be that way alone, and, truly, Siobhan had to be that way, too. So . . . . to better understand us, to better support us, to better protect us . . . you all had to be that way too. Maybe we do make your lives harder, and I am sorry for it, but . . . I need to look at you and see you all *know* how it feels to love your world enough to not just support it, but to willingly die for it if needed."

Alexandria tangled her fingers gently in Shana's hair. "Does it make you feel better to know that we may be willing to die for you, but that we won't stay dead for long since we have yet to meet our soul mates and produce heirs for our worlds? It's only *after* we have kids that you should really be concerned."

It made Shana smile, as she had wanted. "Well, maybe a little? I mean, knowing you will return will in no way make me handle losing you better, but maybe I won't completely crumble and collapse in grief."

Siobhan found it extremely hard to believe Shana could *ever* crumble or collapse, but she fully understood the sentiment. She also didn't entirely like the way Shana had phrased her words, almost as if she *knew* it would happen for sure. Then again, maybe that little seed of hope of the return of their Defenders in the event they lost their lives might be the push needed to help her evolve and unleash her Whisper. A terrifying thought, to be sure, but Siobhan squared her shoulders. She would do whatever it took to save her beloved sister. Period.

Sherry lightly ran a hand down Siobhan's hair in support and understanding and then looked around. The slimy dripping sensation down her skin told her that evil indeed lingered close. The fact that Shana's foot tapped unconsciously on the ground implied she felt it too. A second quick look told her they stood alone in the area, for which she was grateful. A third look caught a glint of a sparkle, and she turned quickly to see a shard of broken green glass. "There it is. I'll grab it."

She had taken two steps toward the glass when a sudden wave of evil energy poured out of it. She dodged with fiery grace and rolled up to a crouched position in front of Siobhan. Virginia moved to join her even as Kellie and Alexandria put themselves in front of Shana. All grabbed their Masks and braced themselves.

The energy rolled back into itself and then lifted upward where it formed an oddly shaped visage, like a monstrous creature made from millions of facets. Each little flat space acted almost like a Visuality and showed battles against evil from Defenders of past times and other galaxies. The creature did not seem wholly capable of movement, however, as its lower half trailed down into a smoke that affixed to the glass shard on the ground.

"What the windy hells is that thing?" Alexandria demanded.

"A Projection," Shana told her. "A definite sign of issues on the Plane, and proof we will need Clara. Basically, the imbalance of the Plane has begun to affect the Hall as well, and the lingering evil energy still leaking out of the Underbelly from where Famine and—and *he* came from is gobbling up past records in order to strike out. Cleansing the Plane will clear the issue, to be sure, but it's going to be dangerous until we get there. Masks on, everyone."

They all donned their Masks to call up armor and weapons, and both Shana and Virginia went in directly at the same time. Kellie had defensive magical gifts, so stayed with Sherry to cover Siobhan. Alexandria played decoy and kept the Projection constantly diverted so that the other two could start smashing through the facets.

The Projection's inability to move proved advantageous, though it did have an exceptional strength and ability to predict oncoming attacks that still made the fight vicious. When Virginia's halberd hacked off an arm, the Projection screeched like nails on glass and sent out a wave of pure evil. Shana shot forward before she could be stopped and planted herself in front of Virginia. The wave smashed into the breastplate of her armor and dented it before suddenly being absorbed into her body rather than diverted. The Projection, infuriated, threw more and more power at her that she kept absorbing until her pink eyes turned black and glowed hotly.

Without warning, the Projection went immobile and turned into a solid glass statue. A well-placed blast of smoldering fire shattered it and left behind nothing except the shard on the ground. Shana staggered only slightly and shook her head hard. She felt hands on her face and opened her eyes to see Alexandria frowning at her. She smiled, and her again pink eyes looked normal. "I'm fine."

"Scared all of us when you did that," her twin muttered. She looked at Virginia. "Though I can't complain *too* much. That could have done real damage to you, Gin."

Virginia grimaced. "Considering the denting it made to Shana's armor, no kidding. Takes a lot of punch to harm our armor, especially the metal portions." She studied Shana. "Is there a cap on how much you can absorb?"

"I genuinely don't know." Shana held still as Kellie worked to the mend the breastplate. "Really, Ginny, I don't. And if it makes you feel better, I have no desire to test my limits."

"It does, thank you." Virginia walked over to pick up the shard and found it clouded and murky so that no light passed through. She tried applying her Glass magic, but the shard did not clear. In fact, it outright shattered in her grip. "This is useless because of the Projection. I guess we have to wait for Pallas to contact you or Edgar."

Kellie pulled her Mask off even as the others did, and she sighed. "Great. Another war. I shouldn't be surprised by it, and certainly we've all gotten used to it across two lives, but . . . I always long for peace."

"We all do," Siobhan told her. "But that's why we fight."

"As long as there is unbalance, evil will come," Shana admitted softly. "And as long as evil comes, there will be unbalance. Until there is a day where we can erase all evil at once from the universe, we will always have wars. I will always fight."

Like her words of before, her words then held a ring of prophetic truth that unnerved all of her friends equally. With nothing more they could do, they transported back to the Toulume apartment to update the others as to what had happened, and just how potentially complicated things might become.

Everyone stayed on edge for a day or two since they did not know whether or not more Projections would leak out into the physical world, or if Pallas would be able to push through finally to contact either Shana or Edgar. Not even Clara really knew what to expect; she had not been back to the Fields in a very long while, and as always, events that directly affected her own future would forever remain hidden from her Sight.

With everything out in the open, Rocky and Siobhan found themselves no longer effectively barred from spending the night with their lovers. Rocky got more disgruntlement out of it than his sister, however; he had to share cuddling of Shana with Bastian. Luckily enough, the ferret liked him almost as much as he did his owner. Shana found it strangely soothing and also utterly adorable to wake in Rocky's arms in the middle of the night and find Bastian curled around his head instead of hers.

On the third day out from the fight, Shana had been enjoying a dreamless sleep when she felt a familiar presence and sense of Nature power sweep over her subconscious mind. A hand held out to her that she accepted, and in the next moment, she found herself consciously within her own unconscious mind and looking at a familiar figure she had not seen in five millennia.

She had to smile. He looked the same as ever with his matching green eyes and hair and sun-kissed skin. He also still stood slightly over half a foot shorter than herself. On the surface, he did not bear much resemblance to either his full sister or even his half-brother who had helped start Shana's own Protean lineage *but* if the three had been put together one could have found similarities in their eyes and especially their smiles.

He placed his broom on the ground between them and then kneeled respectfully. "Greetings, my queen," he said formally. "It has been too long."

"Oh, enough with that." She rolled her eyes. "You *know* that we aren't big on the formality with you. You've always been more like family than not." She snorted softly. "And definitely don't try that when you inevitably meet my hu—betrothed, or my brother's betrothed. They're even more casual than we are. Friends with everyone!"

Pallas scooped up his broom and straightened on a smile. "So I had observed." The smile faded from his face. "I wish I would be meeting them under better circumstances." He gestured with his broom. "As you can imagine, things are terrible right now. I have been trying to reach you or Edgar for over a month now, ever since you destroyed Him." Pallas, too, knew of Shana's scars and would be damned if he cut them open anew. In many ways, he understood better than even her own brother just how deep they ran.

She nodded. "Yeah, that was my feeling." She took a long breath. "Alright. How terrible is it? Can we transport there? And what do we need to do?"

"To answer the last first, it will take you and *Siobhan*." He nodded when her brows shot up. "Nothing short of a pure cleansing of Dark and Light will aid the Plane in regaining its balance. Not even the harmony of the Dark and Nature inside you will work now thanks to the Chaos already formed in the imbalance wrought by evil."

She cocked her head slightly. "Chaos? Why would that be present?"

"Because the Light power exuded by Siobhan in defeating her enemy joined the Dark power exuded by you in defeating yours, and there is nothing and no one to control it." He sighed. "How very like the power of Chaos to do this. Its presence was almost . . . mandatory. Five thousand years without a Protea Ruler Cultivator for the Plane and the planet, the loss of majik from the Faith, and then the two worst of evils tearing free of the Underbelly only to be erased in the shockwave of Light or Dark." He hesitated and then added softer,

"Too, there is Chaos power boiling on another world outside Blossom Field. It is sloughing into the Fields as well, meeting that which is here, and making it worse."

Shana rubbed her hands over her arms. "What happens beyond Blossom is the work of other Defenders. I hate saying that, but it is true. If they seek aid, we will give it, but for now, my duty and the duty of my fellow Blossom Field Dual Cultivators is to protect our worlds and the Ephemeral Plane for *all* depends on it. We have to help here before we can plausibly help anywhere else. You just need Siobhan and me to cleanse the Plane, then?"

He hesitated anew. "That would be potentially detrimental to you both unless the other Cultivators can support you better. They need to enter into their final tier and fully bloom in order to have personal cores strong enough to support the two of you so you are not destroyed by the Chaos power."

She winced. "It's that bad?"

"Worse. Chaos is born where Dark and Light strike against one another. That's what happens when you and Siobhan hold hands, in fact. Those sparks are the tiny birth of Chaos. Nothing dangerous as long as you two are not actively using power. If you were, then it could be devastating to you both. Because Chaos is both Light and Dark, you are both very weak against it."

"Yet it is as critical as Dark and Light themselves," she murmured as she thought about what she had learned from her Sight across her very long life. "It completely encompasses all that involves emotion, stripping away all lies until the rawest truth is bared. It is both magic and combat, a harmony even more difficult to obtain than my own." She grimaced. "No wonder Mother and Aunt Hannah were pushed to become so close and reunite the two worlds."

"Trust me," Pallas said almost ruefully, "any of us observing from the outside had some nightmares of our own at the idea of the worlds being at war when you and Sayena were born. You two being at war would have created a Chaos power the likes of which would have destroyed all existence without a third Apex to control it—and the universe just can't handle three."

Yet. The word hovered unspoken between them, and their eyes met. "I know something of my own future," she said softly, "and I accept whatever may come. In some ways . . . it comforts me. I think you can understand why."

"Yes," he agreed even softer. "I can." He shook it off. "The solution stands. In my best knowledge as Archon of the Immortal Fields, you and Siobhan must enact a cleansing that can only be successfully achieved so long as the four Dark Defenders empower you and the four Light Defenders empower her. To empower you, they must enter into their final tier and fully bloom. It likely would not hurt Siobhan to do the same."

"And me?"

He shook his head. "I truly, honestly, do not know, my queen. I would grant you any knowledge of why you have not evolved or what the true price of your birth is if I knew. But I just do not. My best suggestion is to see if what works to evolve the others will work for you, and as to the process of that evolution as an act outside of being forced within combat . . . that is in my sister's realm of knowledge as Librarian."

She smiled. "It's okay, Pallas. I know you would help me however you could if you could. Sometimes we just have to do things on our own. And that's not just the Dark person being all self-sufficient! Sometimes there really are things only we can do." She lifted her hands in farewell. "We will return shortly. I assume, then, that we *can* transport providing we are strong enough to deal immediately with Chaos?"

"Correct."

"Then we will do our best."

As Pallas began to disappear, he murmured, "The best you can obtain is far more than what any other can. You are truly special, my friend."

Shana abruptly opened her eyes and found herself staring at Rocky's chest as he slept contentedly beside her. A ball of fur that was surely her ferret had curled up on his stomach, and his arm had somehow tightened around her unconsciously. She did not lift her head from his shoulder as she turned over everything.

Her lover suddenly murmured sleepily, "Did you know that I can sort of hear you talking in your dreams inside my own?"

She looked up at his face and smiled. "I imagine that was odd."

"Like hearing an unrelated voice over a speaker and not understanding a word." He tugged her as close as he could and gently pressed a kiss to the top of her head. "Pallas get through?"

"Mmm. To me only; possibly because I am more powerful than Edgar." She sighed. "And things are, of course, complicated and terrible and chaotic. After dawn, we'll call everyone. Go back to sleep."

He pointedly moved Bastian to the end of the bed and then shifted to lean over Shana. Even inside the dim room, the Light inside his soul swept out to caress her skin and illuminate her. "I'm starting to be fond of very early morning," he murmured as he nipped at her stubborn chin.

Her lips curved. "You've certainly made me fond of late evening, so I feel that's a fair trade."

Not long after dawn, Shana got breakfast started in the kitchen. Edgar hadn't had the same dream of course, but he had certainly felt something odd from his sister so had woken even earlier than usual. Siobhan proved the last to stumble out yawning, but became much more alert when brought up to speed.

After they had all eaten, they once more contacted the Dual Cultivators to have them meet, though this time at the Chivanti apartment. Shana called Clara as well this time, with the direct order to report in. The Statice Defender showed up last, and walked out of a transport without any shame or care for bothering with the door. "I expected the call," she admitted as she sat down on the couch beside Desiree and Yvonne. "I had a feeling I would be needed."

"Well, I always need you," Shana told her, "but this time enough to call you into action." She ran down the events and conversation with Pallas very briefly and then said, "And that's the other reason we need Clara, because she can tell us how to do what we need to do."

Clara nodded as eyes turned. "Under the most normal of circumstances, a Defender can only evolve under the pressure of battle when he or she needs to access more magic to drive back evil. I have never actually evolved personally because my partners have always forced my retreat right at the time when it seems most likely I would most need that magic. Perhaps, too, my very age lends itself to my particular potency. I am the only one of Statice after all." She crossed her arms. "There are a couple other methods of evolution that can be had, and a couple are too extreme to ever be needed. The best one for our course of action is for a Defender to astrally walk on the Plane to my Hall of Records and access the knowledge of the Cultivators before her in order to force her magic to evolve via their blessing."

"That sounds a tiny bit dangerous," Juliet muttered.

"Actually, under normal circumstances, it would have barely any repercussions." Clara winced. "But the imbalanced and chaotic Plane makes things particularly dangerous this time around because I can't say whether or not the Projections will attack an astrally walking Cultivator. They haven't yet actually gotten into the Hall—I'd have noticed—but if they even exist at all then that means the Hall is under pressure anyway."

"Alright, that sounds fair enough, but . . ." Virginia studied Clara. "As you said, you are the only one of you. How will you evolve? Do you even need to?"

"To answer the second, yes." She looked right at Shana. "For Shana, I will do anything needed to keep her safe, and I will push myself to a final tier I've never before needed if it ensures she survives." She looked back to her Lead. "To answer the first, I will not petition to my forbearers but instead to Time herself. My grandmother whose power I protect."

Glances exchanged among the others; it was not the first time they had noticed Clara's love for Shana went beyond what she had felt for Genevieve, or even Siobhan. Shana just walked over and leaned down to hug Clara fiercely for a moment. Lavender eyes widened briefly and then filled with powerful emotion as the eldest Cultivator hugged her queen back. "I would do anything for you," she murmured. "I hope you know."

"I do." Shana let her go but only to sit beside her on the couch. It could just barely hold four, and Desiree scooted over as much as possible to give her space. "What about Siobhan? She's sort of in your shoes as well, being the only Defender of Delphinium. And . . . can I do this as well?"

"Siobhan can petition directly to Delphinium herself and ask her Mother for the power she needs to enter her third and final tier. Unfortunately, the state of the Plane means you cannot petition Protea to do the same. You're going to have to go as you are, and we will all hope that we four Dark Defenders are enough to support you until whatever price you have to pay is finally revealed." She laced her fingers with Shana's. "I would tell you if I knew, Shana. I swear."

"I know."

Clara glanced back to the others. "I will do this first as I have the best understanding of how it should work, so I can tell you what oddities to expect if they occur. While I am doing so, it should be safe and simple enough for Siobhan to travel to Delphinium and petition there. She doesn't need to astrally walk for her potential evolution — but I highly suggest *someone* go along just in case."

"As if I'd let her go alone!" Sherry groused.

Siobhan grinned at her. "As if I'd go without you! At least I know I'm squishy and need extra protection, unlike someone *else* we all know and love."

Shana ignored her pointedly. "Then that's the plan. Clara and Siobhan start things off and then everyone else will follow suit. Once everyone who can fully bloom has done so, we'll brace ourselves and drop into the Immortal Fields to cleanse it."

Clara took that as her cue and got to her feet. She opened a transport to return back to her comfortable home within the Hall of Records and then moved far deeper beyond. The location would intrigue her friends when they visited. She knew it to be an unusual and fascinating place; as her title of Librarian implied, it resembled an endless library. Infinite rows of billions of books that stretched endlessly into the distance and loomed miles into the air. Seemingly no ceiling other than a soft wisp of foggy air, and the ground reflected back echoes of important historical events.

She moved ever deeper to where a nearly hidden space at an odd dead end held nothing but a candle that cast flickering lights and shadow. She reached out to touch the candle and felt the distant presence of the omniscient force who watched over almost as much of her life as Destiny herself did. "Time," she said softly, "I beseech you."

A soft swirl of color lifted from the flame, and a feminine voice answered. "I am here, my child. What do you need to ask of me, Claret?"

Clara shook her head a bit. "I need to evolve. I need to reach full bloom in order to support my queen. There has never before been a need for such a thing from me, but there is now."

"Why is that?"

"Shana is . . . special to me, Grandmother. More than any other Protean Ruler." Her voice softened unknowingly. "From the moment she was first born, I knew I would love her more than any other. I don't know why."

"It is a sign of change," Time answered. "Great changes soon enough. You will know them as they happen. In the meanwhile, I grant your request for it is more needed than you may yet understand."

Warm power swirled down around Clara in a swirl of statice blossoms. Her two Marks burned briefly and she looked down to see the one on her arm changing. Not only did it gain a second blossom, but both they and the one of her Ruler Mark opened into full bloom. The sparkling edge to both Marks, present since she had been claimed by her Mother, seemed to sparkle only brighter. A new, stronger, magic moved inside her body that she could nearly taste.

A feeling of evil swept over her body. She swung around sharply and found cracks forming in the reflective floor. A Projection rose from one and clawed at her with razor tipped fingers. She hastily dodged out of the way and grabbed her Mask from her bracelet. A second dodge had her moving deeper into the Hall, and the Projection followed her by moving from crack to spreading crack. She pulled on her Mask as she swung around, and her armor formed.

Magic welled up around her hands and created a shield around her just as the Projection got close, and it smashed into the barrier hard. It immediately shattered into a half dozen pieces that reformed and came after her again. Before she could prepare to call for backup—she had neither offensive magic nor real weapon—a different power entirely surged into the Hall. The feel of majik swept down her arms so hotly that she felt goose bumps rise. The silvery majik shot toward the Projections in a tangle of Ice and Illusion and Nature, and the evil entities shattered to bits. Clara bypassed her magic entirely for her gifts as a Librarian to erase all remaining fragments from her Hall, and they luckily disappeared.

The majik also ebbed as swiftly as it had arrived, and she slowly looked around the now empty and silent Hall. Only the briefest surprise inside her turned quickly to more thoughtful speculation. "I didn't know you were out there," she murmured. "But then, perhaps I just did not think to go looking. Thank you."

Knowing better than to not warn her partners, she grabbed her communications mask. "Open all," she ordered. A pause, and then a swirl of gradient color began to move over the mask. "Successful evolution, however, I indeed encountered resistance from a Projection. Don't be alarmed if it happens, though. It would seem we have some . . . unexpected alliance from someone. Someone majikal."

"Shana?" Virginia's voice asked.

Silence from the obviously open Protea line.

"Fine," Virginia sighed, "we get it, it's not important right now other than just being grateful it's here."

Clara fought to hide a smile though no one could see her. "Indeed. Siobhan, for certain have Sherry go with you to Delphinium. When you're done there, Sherry can then undertake her own Walk and evolution. Each one of us who completes this task needs to notify the others because it would be a bad idea for us to all go at one time."

"What would it do if we did?" Kellie asked curiously.

"You *really* don't want to know. Get moving, everyone. We're on a borrowed clock right now."

Without time to spare—and Clara would be the expert on that—Siobhan gulped down her nerves and accepted Sherry's hand for support. Sometimes she thought she only managed to be brave because of those so willing to hold her hand. Her twin, her lover, her brother, and even her sister. It was as if they somehow just gave her a bit of their own bravery just by holding her hand. And if Shana couldn't do this yet, then Siobhan damned well would work all the harder for her!

Delphinium looked almost no better than the last time either Cultivator had visited. Barren, empty, and struggling to heal. In a few places, life had begun to push through, and little sproutings pockmarked the ashy ground with bits of green. Siobhan's hand trembled briefly in Sherry's grip, and the Aster Cultivator tightened her hold. "Hey," she said softly. "I'm here. I won't let anything hurt you."

Siobhan moved closer as they walked toward the empty castle. "I know. I also know that because you love me is why you always push me to do better. You nag and nag and nag until I get things right. I'm so terrible with numbers but you just kept feeding them to me until I yelled at you about it and then I ended up passing my class with high marks."

"I just know you and your brother have a propensity to run from the things you feel hold you up, so I made sure you could not run far. I yell at Rocky too, you know."

Siobhan had to giggle. "But not as much as at me."

"Well, to be fair, that's not necessarily my being nice to him. If he actually gets to that place where he needs a push, then *Shana* is the one to do it, and she's much scarier than I am because she doesn't even have to raise her voice." She grinned. "And Gin will kick *me* for admitting it, but I do sort of take a perverse humor in watching her try to give Shana orders."

"We all do," Siobhan confessed in a mock whisper, "but that's okay because Ginny knows we do and doesn't really mind. She's really aware of her own personality and shortcomings and strengths, so she knows when she's getting her just desserts."

"I look forward to seeing who she ends up with as a soul mate."

Siobhan bit her lip briefly as she thought about Maxim

Montague, the second-in-charge of all Commanders, the head of Evan's contingent as well as his twin soul, and the *only* person who had *ever* made the Carnation Defender give as much ground as she demanded from others and made her stand on the side safely. Mentioning him would open a can of snakes she had no desire to stir yet, so instead she focused on something else that had bounced in her mind since getting her memories. "I think she met him already."

Sherry glanced at her, more with speculation than surprise. "When Juliet and I convinced her to do that summer-long study abroad in Valerian Heights across the sea from Axium. She came home very . . . subdued for a while after. I admit, I wondered as well if maybe her heart had been broken—which, really, could only mean she met her soul mate—but she never spoke about it. You think so too, then?"

"I really do." She giggled. "When we have a free moment, Shana and I will get her drunk and make her spill the truth. Then we can fix it!"

"Okay, you and Shana in cahoots is almost as scary as you and your brother. You lot really, really like to have your way." She let go of Siobhan's hand as they entered the castle. "Okay, kneel down." She knelt as well and automatically supported her twin when she inevitably slipped on the still ashy marble ground. "Close your eyes and imagine yourself getting very light, so very light you're flying," her Shaman voice took on a beautiful cadence that could not be ignored, "and think only of Delphinium."

Siobhan could do nothing except obey as she never had a desire to ignore her twin's gift; it only got used for good. She could feel her head going light, her entire body feeling as if it had been made of cotton, and she thought of delphinium blossoms floating on the wind. A little chill touched her skin and she opened her eyes on a gasp to discover she no longer knelt in her castle entry.

Nothing but pure white filled the space around her, though golden sparkles floated through the air now and then. At the feeling of a presence near her, she swung around and tripped over her own feet only to land on nothing. She floated for a moment on a scowl. Only she could manage to trip over her feet in a place where she did not actually have feet!

What she had sensed, she saw then, was an immensely large and beautiful bush of flowering delphiniums. Her eyes lowered, and she caught a little breath as she saw it growing out of a giant opal.

What need have you of me, my Daughter?

The soft voice seemed to whisper from all around, sounding tired and old and yet so very full of love that Siobhan's eyes filled with tears. "I'm so sorry," she said urgently. "I know you're still so hurt and that you need to heal more, but I need you to help me so I can help everyone else! I *have* to fully bloom. There's something really bad happening, maybe more than even Famine, and I have to be ready to deal with it." Even quieter, she added, "And I need to be ready to help Shana. Do—do you know how terrible it will be?"

Yes.

When that was all that was offered, Siobhan could only sigh. "Okay. I get it. I'm just scared! I'm so scared for her!"

Be there, Siobhan. Be there for her. Give her the Light she needs when she is lost inside her own Dark. You are as critical as your brother in her continued sanity. A brief pause, and then, *I grant your request, my Daughter. Let yourself rise as the first fully bloomed Defender Cultivator of Delphinium.*

Siobhan's heart skipped a beat. To say she was the first seemed to imply there would be at least another. Her future daughter with Edgar? The idea scared her more than a little, and suddenly she had a whole new respect for Hannah and Genevieve alike in knowing that terrible things may befall their children. "Thank you," she said only.

Warm power swirled around her, and her two Marks burned briefly. When she looked down at her arm, she could see that a new blossom had added, and all three had opened into full bloom. She had to smile for it almost looked as if her crowns had become planters of sorts that held their flowers. One to her chest, and three to her arm, all in bloom. Freshly charged magic moved under her skin with a tingling force that she recognized yet knew had gained strength. "Thank you," she told the sheltering bush from which her Seed had been birthed. "I am honored to be your first Defender."

Siobhan?

The voice belonged to Sherry and she blinked. In the space of the blink, she abruptly found herself back in her body, in her castle, staring at her concerned twin soul. She looked down hastily and saw her Mark over the top of her v-cut shirt. It had fully blossomed, just as she had seen it do in her visit to her planet's Core. "That . . . that was strange and sort of wonderful and I have no words so don't ask me to describe it!" she said in a rush.

Sherry smiled. "I don't need to ask." She got to her feet and drew Siobhan up as well. "We will return to Protea for safety. If a Projection is to attack me while I Walk, I would rather it on Protea where the world is more stable."

Siobhan nodded and accepted her offered hand to reach for transport. She paused, thought of the ramifications of what she had learned, and then put it aside. It would be important soon enough, and she more than anyone knew that no one could change destiny. Well, *almost* no one, but the one person who had ever managed it had long since passed. They would have to muddle through Destiny's plans on their own.

Over the course of the next day, all Defenders except for Shana sent themselves into a meditative state that allowed them to astrally walk to the Hall of Records, enter, beseech their predecessors, and emerge fully bloomed. In every instance, the Defender found herself under attack from one or more Projections, and without fail, all found that mysterious majikal force moving in to give aid. It had more than Clara suspicious, to be sure.

Evolution brought tangible changes to Defenders. In those with defensively oriented magical skills, the strength and potency of their shields and blocks and reflects reached new limits. In those with offensively oriented magical skills, the speed and range and strength with which they could strike the enemy also reached new limits. Virginia, as Lead Defender, had access to both the defensive and offensive magic of her world's Glass Flower Element, and she discovered both equally pushing to a new cap.

More than one person felt uneasy about Shana. Observing as she and Siobhan had a spirited discussion over just what the cleansing may entail, Virginia muttered at the others, "I really, really, *really* am not liking this."

Alexandria shook her head a bit. "In some ways, we can't say we're surprised. Remember, the nature of Dark is to absorb where Light repels. We saw it recently with Shana absorbing that powerful evil energy without even batting a lash. I think because she absorbs so readily and easily that it will take *far* more pressure for her to evolve. It's going to take one hell of a lot to hit her with something she can't absorb and therefore has to evolve to deal with. Honestly . . . I'm scared of what it will be."

They made plans to transport to the Fields on the following day, but that very night they discovered they had run out of time faster than anticipated. Nightmares flooded the city in an uncontrolled force, and anyone with any measure of majikal or Sensing ability found themselves suffering in all manner of creative ways. Shana made the order to assemble, and this time, Edgar and Rocky demanded to go along.

"I may be needed," Edgar insisted fiercely to his sister. "I am as much responsible for the Ephemeral Plane as you are! Besides, if all Defenders go, then who will be here to watch over Rocky and I in the event the Projections spill out again?"

"Hitting below the belt, Edgar!" Virginia snapped at him before Shana could. "If we're doing our job right, then the Projections won't get to either of you!"

"Argh!" Rocky raked his hands through his hair and made it stand only more on end. He felt sleep deprived and already cranky without this on top of it. "You *do* remember that at least me but also Edgar *are* as skilled and powerful, or more, than a lot of you, right?"

"You don't wear armor!" more than one voice retorted.

In a dangerously quiet voice that somehow still carried, Shana said, "I am the strongest Cultivator of our generation, and I am the High Queen of Protea—only Siobhan does not bow to my order. You and my betrothed will stay, Evan. *Period.*"

"*Dammit.*" In a rare display of temper, Edgar stalked away from the confrontation and stood for a moment, visibly seething internally. Arms slid around his chest, and his sister rested her chin on his shoulder. Temper drained. "Let me support you," he said in a low voice. "Too much is asked of you already. You can't hold up existence alone."

"I'm not alone. I'm never alone." She hugged him tighter and then let go. She turned to the others and nodded. "Let's move. Masks on before we land. It'll be safer." She walked over to the other Dual Cultivators and all put on their Masks at the same time to call their armor. Once they had, Shana reached out with her power. "Brace yourselves."

Having never visited the Fields, no one other than Clara or Shana had any idea of what to expect from the largest section of the

Ephemeral Plane. Their vision cleared as they landed, and more than one person caught their breath. The Immortal Fields had been well-named. Endless, and endless, and *endless* rolling fields of every flower known in existence. An eternally sunset sky swept by over their heads, symbolic of the time when light and dark met. It could have been the most perfectly beautiful place ever made . . . if not for the evil that had consumed it.

Projections ran rampant across the flowers, devouring every little wisp of energy they saw. The natural little crystal spheres that dripped from flowers like dew shattered when grabbed, and each little fracture seemed to make a distant voice cry out in pain across the Fields as if the owner had felt their own dreams break. Some crystals turned an ugly blood red and released demonic wisps into the air. Nightmares.

Pallas stood in the middle of the mess with broom in hands and fought to sweep back the violent black and white lightning bolts of Chaos that kept creeping in closer. The uncontrolled Chaos power seemed intent on gobbling everything it could.

Shana took in the entire scene briefly and then ran forward two steps from her friends. "To me!" she ordered. Her lashes flinched as the nightmarish wisps immediately surged to her to be absorbed, but she merely squared her shoulders and accepted them. She lifted her hands, and clean, comfortable, dream wisps rose from her gloved palms.

Horror churned inside Siobhan as she moved closer. "Is . . . what are you doing?" she whispered. "Are . . . are you actually absorbing the nightmares?"

"It's my job." If she felt discomfort from the absorption, it did not show on what could be seen of her face behind her Mask. Her two Marks could not be seen under her armor, but they did glow briefly, hotly, with pink-black color that was quite visible. Nothing came of it, and more than one Defender cursed softly under her breath. What would it take?

The Projections noticed the newcomers and changed course to immediately come surging at the ten Defenders. Siobhan very nearly took a step backward, but Shana's hand curled around her wrist and just that little touch gave her a boost of her sister's courage. Still a few hundred yards from the team, the Projections began to pull together into a single, giant, monstrous creation. Moving in behind it came the force of Chaos, dark and light and mingled gray with wild bolts of emotion.

Pallas ran over to join the Defenders and he brushed off Kellie when she moved closer. "I can be healed later," he told her. "It is nothing terrible right now." The tattered state of his robes and the blood staining them seemed to deny his words, but no one pressed. "I will aid you as well," he told the two Apexes. "My role as Archon as well as my own Nature power and Light core can be of use to you." He took a breath. "This is going to sound utterly crazy to you, but, you have to create Chaos."

"We have to make Chaos to fight Chaos?" Siobhan echoed.

"Unfortunately, it is a power that is only weak against itself, which is why it is so utterly devastating. If you two release Chaos power, and that force is coming in the other direction, the resulting shockwave will form the cleansing we need and erase all of the Projections."

Shana and Siobhan turned to face each other and linked their hands. The four Dark Defenders lined up behind Shana, and the four Light behind Siobhan, and the ten together formed an almost mirror of the way their planets hovered in space. The two Apexes began to draw in their power, and as they pulled from their cores, they could feel as they pulled equally from the ones who supported them. Light and Dark met at their clasped hands and began to produce violent sparks. Black and white became gray as the sparks kept growing into black and white lightning bolts. Matching looks of pain swept across Shana and Siobhan's faces behind their Masks but they did not let go of one another. Pallas fearlessly stuck his hand into the middle of the Chaos and let his own power well.

A wild shockwave released from the power and smashed through the approaching Projection as if it had been made of paper. It collided with the oncoming Chaos force of the other direction and the entire Plane shook as the two forces merged and then exploded outward. As it swept across the land and began mending what had been unbalanced, the Defenders braced themselves for the wave to hit them all.

Silvery majik swirled around the Defenders from out of nowhere and erected an impossibly powerful barrier. The Chaos touched it, recoiled, and diverted. If it could have made it through would forever be a question for it seemed obvious that the Chaos did not even want to *try.* It went around the shield and continued on as if it had never paused. Gray color welled and blinded everyone, even Shana and Siobhan, and then faded. Into the silence that followed, almost no Chaos remained. Just a few wisps here and there as evidence that unbalance still existed *somewhere.*

Shana and Siobhan slowly let go of each other's hands, looked at one another for a blurry moment, and then collapsed. Alexandria and Sherry hastily caught them before they hit the ground and held on tight. Desiree and Juliet removed the two Apexes' Masks, and everyone let out a little breath of relief since they looked only tired and not truly injured. Still, unease churned. Without her armor, Shana's two Marks could be seen again, and they had not bloomed. The skin around them looked red and irritated, but nothing had really changed.

"That majik definitely felt familiar," Yvonne finally said. "Even more than when it helped me on my Walk. I mean, I'm not saying I know the witch owning it personally, but maybe I knew someone like them."

A little tiredly, Shana said against Alexandria's shoulder, "You're not wrong. We'll meet them soon enough, okay?"

"Okay." Virginia brushed at her hair and then at Siobhan's. "Both of you just rest." She looked to where Kellie had finished up healing Pallas' wounds. "How are you, Pallas?" she asked. "You took almost as big a risk as our queens did, by sticking your hand in that."

"It just burned me something terrible, though nothing Kellie could not fix." He picked up his broom where it had been dropped. "I could not enter into the circuit you ten had made, so I had to be more direct. Clara and I may be siblings, but our powers are vastly different in all ways."

Desiree grinned. "I honestly keep forgetting that you two are directly related. Not distantly and almost not at all like the relation of Destiny or Love to the two High lineages, but actually literally sharing the same parents."

It made Clara smile. "Most everyone had forgotten within the first few hundred years, let alone after several million. Just as most everyone entirely forgets that Pallas' and my own half-brother is Orion—that figure through whom Protea claims its connection to Destiny."

"Is that why you love Shana most?" Juliet asked solemnly. "Because she's most like Orion?"

Clara thought about it. "Actually, she's not that much like him. She's *very* like Shanta, though!" She grinned a bit. "Which may be why I am so fond of Rocky, in fact, because *he* and Orion do share many personality quirks! Perhaps because of their so alike soul mates. At the least, it may also account for why Shana and Edgar alike have always been particularly fond of Pallas, and feel he is more like family than not."

"Out of pure curiosity," Virginia asked, "who is eldest?"

"Orion, myself, and then Pallas," Clara offered.

Pallas snorted very softly. "I wholly sympathize with my queen in being the baby." He turned to Virginia and smiled. "If I may ask, will you please create a few glass orbs? One for all Defenders, other than Shana and Clara who have no need."

She lifted a brow but obligingly lifted her hands where red and gold magic became swirls of liquid glass. The swirls broke into eight pieces and then hardened into colored orbs. Showing off only a little, each orb held the colors of its Defender and a petal from their flower hovered in the center. She collected the orbs and offered them to Pallas. "Why?"

The orbs lifted to hover in the air around him, and he lifted his broom before his face. Each orb glowed briefly and then he gently swatted each to its proper owner. "These are personal portals so you may all come to the Fields at your will. I would not turn away *any*

Cultivator, let alone ones so beloved to my sister."

"Thank you so much!" Yvonne told him for everyone. "If we're done, may we take Shana and Siobhan home now? They need to rest."

"Of course!" Pallas swung his broom up and created a transport for them all to walk through. He watched as Alexandria and Sherry picked up and carried their twin personally, and then all disappeared through the transport. He closed it behind them and murmured, "All of our lives are inextricably entwined in some way or another. My own future connects to yours. How curious."

Shana and Siobhan had recovered within a few days and returned to normal. As per usual, Virginia reported on their behalf to the world leaders to inform them of why the brief nightmare wave had happened. Cultivators had honestly never tried to live their lives in such secret that no one knew what they did; Defenders in particular felt it was their duty to keep the worlds they protected abreast of the evil that tried to harm them.

As they walked together in the park, Siobhan held to Shana's hand and murmured, "So those sparks when we initially clasp hands are Chaos."

"Seems so. Long as we're not actively using our power, it's brief and harmless."

Siobhan grinned a bit. "I guess we're lucky our lovers are only *rivals* for our Light and Dark cores. If they were perfect matches, then we would be making *literal* sparks in bed!"

Shana started laughing. "You're so terrible!" She bumped her arm against Siobhan's companionably. "But I guess I and Edgar both need that in you and Rocky alike, that ability to always make us smile when we're so sure we can't smile anymore. Has Mom started in on the 'when do I get grandkids' thing with you as well?"

"She started years ago," Siobhan complained with good-nature. "I sort of danced around it with a 'well we don't know when it will happen because you know medical science' which was the only way to say we literally don't know when the kingdoms will be resurrected and realistically we can't expect to have kids until then anyway, and *especially* not until the other Cultivators meet their soul mates because the generations are always the same age—and Mom doesn't even know we are Cultivators!" She scowled. "Why didn't you ever tell us you were a nightmare filter?"

The two Toulumes' ability to move from one subject to another without literally a pause had long stopped confusing Shana. After almost two decades, she had following their minds down to an art. "Well, it seemed irrelevant, I guess. It's honestly no big deal. It means I have more nightmares than the average person, to be sure, but Pallas honestly does make up for it by sending extra good dreams as well. It's the nature of my particular role as a Ruler over the Plane. That thing about my particular power helping with the balance. Too much of either sort of dream has to be filtered off, so, through me it goes!" Much softer, she added, "And as much as it explains why I could fight *him*, it also helps explain his obsession with me. We knew each other down to a molecular level."

Siobhan held her hand tighter. "Well, I know that neither Rocky nor I can help with any of that, but, at least we can help make you feel better. He can snuggle you more, or if I'm the only one there, I will completely get up to make you some tea." She nodded firmly. "Even at midnight. Any time."

"That's how I know I'm loved: Delphinium children willing to wake in the middle of the night!" She abruptly stopped dead in her tracks, and her eyes stared blindly at the distance. A feeling of dread swept through her as she watched Chaos consuming alive everything it touched. It devoured her Defenders in an unending surge and then ate her brother and lover alike. Even her sister. Pain gouged deeper and deeper into her soul as she watched the Chaos bearing down on her personally.

"Shana!!"

She blinked and found herself sitting on a bench with Siobhan holding her face in her hands. She could feel the tears in her own eyes, and the look on Siobhan's face was a combination of terror and dread. "Siobhan?"

"Oh gods." Siobhan grabbed her around the neck in a fierce hug. "You scared me! I mean, your Sight often does scare me because you never get the happy fluffy good things but you *cried*!" Her breath hitched. "I always wish you would cry more because it's so bad for you to dam it up, but it's so much scarier when your Sight drives you to tears! What did you see? Tell me! Let me share it!"

"I can't," she whispered. She closed her eyes and turned her face into Siobhan's shoulder for a moment. "Did anyone call us?"

"No."

"Then I am the only one who saw it. It will remain my own until it is time to share it, if I have to."

Siobhan intensely hated the unspoken rule that Destiny only shared visions of the future with those who could handle it, particularly when it meant truly terrible things if she only shared with her Apex of Dark, she who could handle *anything*. She eased back and once more framed Shana's face in her hands. "I will help light your soul when there is too much for Rocky to handle alone," she vowed. "You never let us get lost into our Light. I will never let you get lost into your Dark. I was born to balance you, Shana."

Shana smiled a little. "We are equals, Siobhan."

"No one is your equal, Shana."

She sighed and closed her eyes. "Yeah. I know."

Another month went by, and in November the next year at university began. For the older nine Cultivators in school, that meant they began their final year of classes and study and all would graduate in June of the following year. Siobhan still had two years of classes, minimum, and then would move to a specialized medical school to continue toward being a doctor like Octavia. Shana had an even odder schedule thanks to her advanced placement. She technically had the same two years as Siobhan left, but the skewed schedule meant she was still in the middle of her current year while the others changed over. She would switch to her final year in April, months ahead of her sister.

The shuffled schedule meant she never shared any classes with her friends, but she did at least share similar times on campus. She suspected more than one person had deliberately sought to make their times align to hers, but she did not mind. Even introverts liked having lunch with their friends, and hers were always nice enough to find a quiet spot for her and Edgar alike to enjoy themselves.

The siblings would have liked to have shared some classes, particularly since they aimed for a matching degree, but they settled for taking similar ones at roughly similar times so they could share notes and study together. They also could walk together to some classes, and Rocky and Siobhan tagged along since they had decided to take a theatrical illusions class together that ran at the same time—Shana considered it semi-unfair of the two Illusion Flower Elements, but she also thought she would get to take advantage for her photography, so did not complain that much.

The four had gotten halfway toward the building they shared classes in when a fellow student came hurrying up. "Okay," she told

Edgar and Shana alike, "I drew the short stick to ask you two: you have the same last name as the university. Are you related to the Chivanti Corporation?"

"Yes," Shana said.

A moment ticked by where that was all she said, and Edgar looked no less forthcoming, so the student sighed. "Okay, fine. I get it. It's none of our business. But you can't blame us for being curious! You don't have a common name and some journalism students were looking at old reports and found stuff that just felt coincidental."

"Whether we are or aren't related to the company is irrelevant right now," Edgar said easily. "We're too busy being students to bother with much else."

The other woman took that as given and walked away with a wave, but Rocky and Siobhan exchanged a brief look. Edgar would graduate the next year, and Shana shortly behind him, and even before her graduation, Shana would have reached full adulthood. The timing felt suspect, to say the least.

Being November, something else of importance other than final years of school came around: Rocky also turned twenty-five, making him the first of the High heirs to do so. He also opted for a low-key birthday party out of deference for his fiancée and brother-in-law. One with their mother and a few other family members, and then just one with other Cultivators (including Clara). As they were enjoying a picnic, he teased to Shana, "At least we don't need big galas in this life."

She snorted at him. "Mine back then would have been much more enjoyable if *someone* hadn't decided to wait for me to figure things out. You really should have just been much blunter after I turned twenty-one and started noticing you were attractive."

He snorted back. "Pardon me, but you hid that well enough that I didn't see it until it couldn't be hidden at all." He caught her shirt front and tugged her closer so that he could kiss her contently. "I like us being closer to the same age," he whispered teasingly. "I don't have to wait so long for our marriage. It's just a formality, really, but I like some formalities. Like seeing you in wedding attire."

"And just imagine." Her voice sounded no less teasing. "With

Sherry around, I'll get to have something . . . special to wear under it. Just for you."

"Does she take requests? I have ideas."

"Break it up you two!" Desiree bopped them both lightly on the head as she stopped behind them. When they looked up, she held out the plate heaped with tasty treats that she held in her other hand. "Food! Juliet went overboard, as usual."

"When feeding this lot, there's no such thing," Juliet countered dryly. "I never have leftovers!"

An hour later, full and feeling lazy, the Cultivators stretched out on the giant blanket to rest. Half of them were asleep, and the other half just rested with their eyes closed. Shana, in the process of playing with her camera, stopped and looked at the image they made. The light through the trees overhead was almost ethereal with little beams of light drifting to the thick cloudy blue blanket. The force of pure Flower Element magic seemed to echo out of everyone in a very subtle color aura. All were so different, yet so alike. She looked down at her camera and then flicked off the flash and adjusted settings to compensate. She wanted to maintain that dreamy effect.

Because the camera was silent, no one batted a lash when she snapped a few quick shots; in fact, most of them weren't even aware of the photos being taken. Rocky was, however, and he opened his eyes to grin at her. All of them had gotten used to Shana taking their photo, sometimes without them knowing, and her collection of figure studies also continued to grow. Alexandria had started off the set, and Rocky had matched the challenge by going second. She really only had Yvonne, Virginia, and her own brother left to blackmail. Actually, no blackmail for Virginia, really; they had saved her toward the end because Shana wanted a challenge, and the talented model would be too easy to photograph without planning something special.

She suddenly went very still even as Sherry jerked into an upright position from sleep to awareness in a second. "Get down!" the Aster Defender shouted at Shana.

Virginia, barely awake only by the sound of the shout, grabbed Shana's ankle and yanked. Shana landed unceremoniously on the blanket just as a blast of unusually colored magic whizzed past where she had been standing. It woke everyone up, and all scrambled to a kneeling position. All except Rocky and Edgar, that is. Alexandria and Sherry shoved them flat again. "Stay down!" they both snapped.

"Masks!" Shana ordered. As they donned them and called armor, her eyes narrowed visibly. "That magic felt wrong." Not necessarily evil, but not *right* either. Evil magic existed as a wholly different level from the normal Flower Element magic of Cultivators of both types. "Siobhan?"

Siobhan slowly shook her head. "I agree with the assessment but I don't know how either. It felt maybe like Glass, but it also felt like something else." She sensed more magic approaching and told Yvonne and Clara, "Help me!" Her rod appeared in her hand, and she fired off a powerful Illusion shield around everyone that Yvonne and Clara reinforced with their Ice and Memory magic.

The oncoming magic struck the shield, smashed through as if it did not exist, and landed in the center of the Cultivators with such force it sent everyone flying. Perhaps ironically considering their lack of armor, both male Rulers got the least amount of damage thanks to those who *did* have armor being directly in front of them. They in no way landed safely, however, and everyone felt bruises blooming.

Dark red blood slid down Shana's face under her cracked Mask as she pushed herself to her feet. Darker red than her friends remembered seeing it last, and it belied her lack of awakening as an Apex. Those of the purest Light and Dark always had blood that echoed to that power. Edgar's blood looked a very dark red that nearly passed for black in the right light; Rocky's looked a very pale pink that nearly passed for white. Siobhan's blood had gone utterly white in her awakening, and every passing fight seemed to be visibly pushing Shana ever closer to fully black blood of her own.

"What was that?" Virginia demanded as she forced herself to her feet as well. Her halberd appeared in her grip as she did. "It hurt all of us equally!"

"Chaos," Siobhan said a bit grimly. "It has to be if it could not be repelled by me or absorbed by Shana." Her stomach churned with sudden nerves that she fought down. Again, her Sight stirred with the future rather than present, almost as if Destiny knew she *needed* to know. Her hands tightened on her rod as she moved closer to Shana's side. "We can't block it, so we won't try."

"Agreed." Shana's head jerked up as she felt the magic approaching again. "Move!"

Rocky and Edgar dove under the closest picnic table to safety, and their Ruler suits appeared as they did so in order to give them some measure of protection. The Defenders managed to avoid the worst of the blast but all still took damage, and more than one now had either a cracked Mask or dented and torn armor.

"You can't hide!" an unfamiliar female voice raged at them.

They turned as one and found a figure had appeared in the air behind them, held aloft by what looked like Chaos power. She did not look at all familiar in any way, even from the past. Her possibly naturally fair skin had been stained and corrupted by gray, and her eyes and hair alike had gone from some sort of brownish hue to an alarming clash of black and white. Lightning bolts crackled over her entire body, and not the fizzy sort belonging to Thunder elements. These were a terrifyingly familiar chaotic black and white. Her clothing, however, provided the most horrifying evidence of her identity: a tattered and torn gown that loosely resembled some sort of flower, now perverted from whatever its true color should be to mottled black and white and gray.

"Holy shit," Alexandria breathed. "She's a Ruler Cultivator!"

"I am Mania." The nearly empty glaze to her eyes underscored the statement. "I will take the Seeds of Protea and Delphinium to empower my Chaos and become its master!" She started to lunge toward Shana and Siobhan alike but hastily diverted when a pinwheel almost struck. The weapon whipped back around to Desiree, and the Orchid Defender brandished it warningly. Mania merely snarled. "You will never stop me! Chaotic!" She hurled Chaos magic at the ground where it exploded upward into a jittery, terrifying, almost draconic creature. "Tear them apart!" she raged. "And bring me the Seeds!"

She disappeared as abruptly from the scene as she had arrived, and the Chaotic rushed at the two High Queens. Shana shoved Siobhan safely to the side and then shot forward with her sword at ready. She flinched, visibly, as sparks hit skin not covered by armor, but she persisted. "I have it distracted!" she snapped at her friends. "Use an opposing combination to try to destroy it, especially anything with a one-hit kill possibility!"

Of all elements, Ice and Glass had the possibility to one-hit kill enemies thanks to encasing them wholly in the owner's magic. It fell under attacking type magic, though, and therefore Yvonne could not use her Ice in such a way—no Defender of Iris ever had. Virginia, on the other hand, fully could make her Glass liquid enough to encase an enemy and then harden it to a point that it shattered from internal pressure. The most opposite power to Glass lay in Metal, so Kellie linked one hand with Virginia as they mutually called on their magic. Kellie had defensive magic, but did not need offensive skills to enhance the ones Virginia had. The fusion of liquid elements shot through the air and engulfed the Chaotic opposing Shana. It clawed wildly to be free and stretched its fingers toward the Protea Defender's face. It froze only centimeters before touching her Mask.

As the liquid kept hardening, cracks formed across the surface. Siobhan smashed her rod into it with all her strength, and it shattered into billions of pieces that began to dissolve. Nothing remained of the Chaotic in the aftermath. Nothing else came in to attack them, and neither Shana nor Sherry sensed any further evil. The latter slowly lowered her sword and then turned to look under the table she and Alexandria had been protecting. "How are you two in there?"

"Stuck," Rocky muttered.

"No wonder." Alexandria sent her harpoon away and turned to help get him and Edgar alike out from under their cramped and impromptu shelter. "At least you were semi safe in there, especially with us on the outside." Her eyes narrowed as she looked at Shana and Siobhan. "I don't like this. More than any other war, I *really* don't like this."

"Join the club!" Shana shot at her. She looked at Clara. "You will remain for this war. We need all of us. We can't predict what will happen; Chaos is never predictable to begin with without adding in a corrupted Ruler Cultivator! She has access to not just whatever she has as a Glass-based Ruler, but whatever that Chaos is giving her on top of it." Her eyes narrowed slightly as she thought of what Pallas had said about Chaos boiling on another world. She could not determine which world thanks to Mania's complete corruption, and there would be no time to go looking, but that answer may come as the fight progressed.

Clara had thought much the same, though she already had suspicions. "I will stay with the other Dark Defenders for convenience. And, Shana? Siobhan?" She shook her head. "Absolutely do *not* combine power. If you must hold hands, pull back your magic. This is not the time for you two to produce even accidental Chaos. Yes, we normally fight Chaos with Chaos but Mania is not in control of that power, and attacking her with more may just make things worse."

"For now," Virginia added as she pulled off her Mask, "we will not strictly confine either of you or demand a constant guard, but expect that to change at a moment's notice depending on what happens over the next few days. Mania may be chaotically crazed, but she's clearly not without intelligence. She knew exactly what she was doing by attacking us when we were most unprepared." Under her breath, she added, "And I am now oddly more grateful than ever that we have *two* Defenders who can sense evil moving."

"You're welcome," Shana countered dryly. She grimaced as she also removed her Mask. "About as much as I'm grateful my boyfriend got himself a healing skill because we're all a mess and it'll take more than just Kellie and Siobhan to put us all back together!"

Even after they all split up to go home, everyone remained more than a bit on edge. They hid it as best as they could, with those of the Dark cores hiding it best, but it still lurked under the surface as they all headed to class the following day. It was a rare day where all those in school happened to be on campus at the same time, and a rarer one still where Shana had more lecture time than she did lab.

She had just started to flip through her language book when she felt an unfamiliar Glass Flower Element magic brush her skin. In light of the recent events, it should have alarmed her, but it came with such a pure force that she knew it could only be good. She turned toward the door just as it opened, and she slowly lifted a brow as she found an unexpectedly familiar figure in the entrance.

Long hazel hair tied at his neck, matching hazel eyes in a beautiful almond shape, and strikingly handsome good looks that added sultry appeal. The man of the hour, most popular new actor, and generally adored celebrity Byron Rancul. He had a relatively normal height only a few inches shorter than Shana, but he had a frame that looked more muscular than she had expected or seen on screen. Not on par with a Protean, to be sure, but he clearly worked very hard in some fashion or another.

She happened to be the only person in the room at that moment, so he looked at her fairly quickly after glancing around the space. He then walked over and smiled. "I'm torn with how to greet you," he told her, and a slight hint of an accent colored his words that felt familiar. "After all, it's not every day one meets a High Queen."

She grinned as she got to her feet. "Well, thank you for confirming I was right and you're a Cultivator. I felt your Flower Element before you came in, and I can feel your Seed up this close. And as far as greeting me goes, I'm only a High Queen on the random Tuesdays. Just Shana works for me. Shana Chivanti to get the whole thing." She offered her hand palm up.

Rather than place his hand on hers, he instead performed the more formal honor of bringing her hand to his upper left arm where his Mark would appear. It acted as a sign of respect from a Defender Cultivator for a Ruler Cultivator, and it also implied his willingness to fight for her should it ever be needed. He released her hand, and his hazel eyes looked more green than brown with his humor. "Byron Rancul, of course. It's nice to meet you, Shana. And your name is familiar. Are you the photographer that the studio owner has been insisting I need to strip for?"

It made her laugh. "For your sake, I hope so. I'm good at what I do, and I promise no one is ever uncomfortable with me behind the camera!" She sat down and then pulled him onto the seat beside her. Strangely, he did not feel unfamiliar to her, so she didn't feel at all uncomfortable. "I thought you were just coming to Lux to maybe film some things. I wasn't expecting you to be in classes."

"Only one class. To be frank, I've always had a trouble with your language," he admitted, "coming from fairly far away, so it seemed best to brush up on that skill. Why are you in here?"

"Freebie grade toward my degree." She ruffled his hair as if he were her brother. "I'll be your study partner if you like, alright?"

He glanced at her with a bit of surprise, and the smile on her face made his heart clench a bit. She had looked a little aloof when he had first spotted her, but she actually seemed to simply pour out love and acceptance into the air around her. He felt safe and secure. Part of her Dark element? "Thank you," he said softly.

"You do know," she added calmly, "that you came to Lux at a terrible time. And that your timing is in fact a bit suspicious, shall we say?"

"I would never," he started fiercely only to stop when she held up a hand.

"That said," she continued as if he hadn't spoken, "know that I trust you. It is so exceptionally rare for Cultivators to ever do evil deeds that, literally, Mania is the only one I can think of ever hearing about. By nature of our blessing as either Rulers or Defenders, or both, by our Mother planets, we just can't do evil. A Cultivator's Seed has to be wholly corrupted by an external force for that to happen, and achieving that is *damn* hard."

He stared at her for a moment. "That . . . that easily?"

She propped her cheek on her hand. "Well, to be fair, it is almost out of character for me to trust people that fast, *but*, that applies to people who aren't Cultivators. It's hard to distrust someone who you know is very like you. Are you Ruler or Defender or Dual?"

He hesitated a bit and then said, "Defender."

"Planet?"

"Ranunculus."

"Oh!" She grinned anew. "Okay, that explains why your accent seems familiar to me. Good goddess, I think Blossom Field and Ranunculus have been trying to form an alliance since long before my first life!" She pursed her lips. "Lady Yura. I remember her from Evan and Sayena's engagement. Five thousand years ago, so I doubt you know her name."

"Actually I do!" He grinned as well. "Would you believe she is actually one of my ancestors? The universe keeps getting smaller every generation!" He dug in his bag for his book for class. "Maybe when the dust settles, we can finally get that alliance going. I have some weight with Ranunculus."

"As a Defender Cultivator, I imagine so! Even if my Defenders were not also Rulers, I would entirely listen to their opinions on such things." She reached over and flipped pages for him. "We're here, still at the beginning since we're not far into the year. Don't worry." She smiled. "I'm a great tutor."

That little odd clench came again but he found a normal smile. "I believe it!"

Lunch came around after class, and Shana made Byron go with her to meet the other Blossom Field Cultivators other than Clara who was not on campus. No one actually felt surprised to see Shana walking with Byron since they all immediately recognized him, but as they got closer and everyone else could feel his magic, smiles turned into frowns. Eyes narrowed. Only Siobhan, Rocky, and Edgar did not actually feel alarmed, though.

"Oh!" Siobhan brightened and ran over to take Byron's hands. "I'm so excited to meet you! And you're a Cultivator, too! That's so wonderful. I'm Siobhan Toulume! I'm also High Queen Sayena Delphinium, but that's not important right now, okay? We're equals as Defenders!"

Byron blinked at her and then looked at Shana in bemusement. She smiled wryly. "You'll get used to her and her brother. Speaking of!" She gave names and flowers briskly as she went around and she ended with, "Gin is the Lead Defender for Blossom Field. She shares your Flower Element, too."

Virginia reached out, caught Shana's arm, and forcefully pulled her away from Byron. "Look," she said curtly, "I think you will fully understand why none of us are entirely pleased by your presence or the timing of it. Okay, yeah, you've been here on Protea since long before Mania arrived, but you *happen* to reach Lux the day after she does?"

Byron crossed his arms, and he suddenly looked as much a Defender as the ones around him. No acting; in fact, it felt a little as if he had *stopped* acting. "I understand your feeling," he responded calmly, "and I appreciate where it comes from. I respect it for I myself protect a Ruler Cultivator of my Ranunculus. However, I am far from a threat to you. I am here to stop Mania. She nearly destroyed my world and killed my elder sister in her mad pursuit of Chaos power. I will not rest until she is no longer a threat. Things she said when she attacked us made me realize she would come here. I determined to get here first."

"And you didn't warn us?" Sherry asked as she shifted slightly to be more in front of Siobhan and Rocky equally.

"Do tell me how I was to find you."

"Alright," Virginia said. "We concede that point. However . . ."

"Ginny." Rocky sighed deeply. "Would you guys please calm down? He's not an enemy! Can't you at least give him a chance to prove it?" He grinned. "Besides, he won over *Shana* on first meeting. That has to account for something."

Edgar held up a hand. "I like him."

"Delphinians waking at midnight, and now Proteans trusting someone on sight," Alexandria muttered at Yvonne. "The universe is going mad after all."

All four gave her a dirty look, and Byron fought to hide a smile. He opened his mouth to offer more reassurance when he saw matching looks cross Shana and Sherry's faces. He instinctively tensed even as the others did, and he reached up to grab the small Mask he wore on a chain under his shirt. A familiar chill swept down his skin in turn. "Chaotics are coming," he warned. "I can feel them."

The frenzied beasts appeared only moments later, and they landed in the center of the Defenders. Everyone dove for different directions though some landed with less grace than others. "Masks!" Shana ordered. She looked at Byron. "That includes you. We will not turn down any help. Will we?" she shot at Virginia.

The Carnation Defender kept her mouth shut and merely put on her Mask. The others followed in turn, and armor appeared. More than one person studied Byron curiously for his armor looked like nothing the rest of them wore. It resembled a ranunculus, to be certain, yet it had a different overall feel to it by having more cloth than metal. It, strangely, somehow looked oddly familiar, too, especially to Sherry who knew clothing best.

As Defenders scattered into teams to start tearing into the Chaotics, Byron moved to where the two princes had tried to duck back to be out of range. They had on their Ruler suits to help their defenses, and they intently watched their lovers, but they would try their best to stay out of this fight. Byron moved to stand in front of them, and a javelin appeared in his hand. "Allow me to protect you," he told them. "I have built up something of an odd immunity to Chaos power thanks to Mania attacking my world." He glanced at the two queens and then back. "If you have a need to act as a Caretaker, I will follow you to protect you."

"I really like him," Rocky muttered at Edgar. "He *gets* it."

By the time the dust settled and the Chaotics had been erased, once more the Defenders looked more bloody than not. Byron had taken a fair number of wounds himself, and the sight of them made the seven Dual Cultivators look among themselves. He had visibly risked himself to protect the two High Princes, and they could not help but both respect and appreciate him for it. His efforts had freed them to think only of the enemy and their queens.

Everyone removed their Masks, and Virginia told Byron, "Thank you."

He nodded. "You're welcome, though I don't think I need thanks for doing what I was born to do."

"You're good with that javelin," Alexandria offered by way of compromise.

"And you have good magic skill," Yvonne added.

He smiled as he realized they were attempting to warm to him. "Thank you both as well. I promise that my intent is to help you however I can in defeating Mania. I truly am a valuable ally in this. Chaotics do less damage to me."

"Sure," Shana said, "because you've been fingerprinted. I can see it on your soul as a sort of gray smudge on your naturally Light core. You must have been at the scene of the first direct attack and taken the full hit. Amazing you survived."

"It was not . . . comfortable survival."

Virginia winced. "No details. We've been there, I guarantee it." She looked at Shana and then back on a sigh. "Alright, Byron. We'll try to be more accepting. We'll be watching you, to be sure, but we won't necessarily question your every motive. Do you have a communications mask?" At the nod, she nodded back. "Then you can contact us in case of emergency, and we can contact you."

"Done." He grinned. "And to make things friendlier, I'll take the heat for the fact that you're *all* going to be late to your next classes."

"Okay," Juliet told the four heirs. "I'm starting to like him too."

Siobhan grinned cheerfully at Byron. "Welcome to Blossom Field!"

25

Byron may have intended to keep his presence low-key on campus, but word traveled fast. In addition to his already intended filming at the Lux theatrical studio, he found himself being in high demand for fashion shoots for local companies and illustrated periodicals. He had the time for them as he only had one class, but the excessive demands made his head spin with decisions. His manager always let him pick his own photographers for shoots, but that meant he received a stack of several dozen to review. He almost didn't bother until the one on top caught his eye. Well, *that* made the decision easier.

Shana had just finished hanging a background for a shoot when the studio door opened and Byron bolted inside. He shut the door hastily behind himself. Before she could ask, she heard the stampede of feet going past. "You are popular!" she told him dryly. "And either you knew I was in here, or you have better luck than I expected."

"I knew, thankfully. I was looking for you when the horde spotted me." He winced wryly. "Hopefully it will taper off soon." He walked over and peered curiously into the bucket of props she had plopped on a table. A strange array of hats met him. "What are you up to in here?"

"Experimenting with montage." She adjusted a light. "I'm going to bribe someone to wear lots of hats and act differently depending on the hat. It should be a fun little set of images. The assignment is to capture as many differences as I can with minimal change."

"Me!" He held up a hand on a grin. "I could be bribed. Actually . . ." he side-eyed her, "on a related topic, it seems I'm in high demand in Lux, and some nearby other cities. I need to find a photographer with a certain . . . skill set. Not just talent behind the camera, but maybe the ability to juggle multiple projects? Someone who enjoys theatrical and fashion work. Conveniently enough, I think I know that person,

pg. 380

and her resume sat on the top of the stack my manager handed me, so I'd guess she might be interested."

"Is she going to be paid?" she teased.

"I can offer both money *and* my housekeeper's ridiculously delicious flat sweetbread as payment."

"I'll take both!" She turned to smile at him. "Honestly, I had applied as soon as I heard you were coming to Lux because you've always intrigued me, and the owner of the studio somehow got me in his line of view, so I would have been interested anyway. But . . . I like you, Byron. As a person now as much as an actor or model. I don't really make friends easily, except for Cultivators." She shrugged one shoulder almost wryly. "It's hard for me and Edgar to let people in, you know? But there's something about you that just makes me comfortable. I don't think we're wholly kindred spirits because we're not *exactly* alike, but . . . close. Pretty close."

He reached out to take her hand. "That is a big compliment, and I feel the same. I would be here to ask you to do my shoots even if I hadn't seen your portfolio because I really do feel comfortable with you too. I actually can make friends easily, but you're special somehow." He nodded firmly. "Let's start here! Tell me what to do, boss."

She grinned. "Put on a hat, sit on the chair, and act in a way that somehow befits said hat. And don't be offended if I issue orders arbitrarily."

He grinned back. "From a queen, I would expect nothing less!"

One shoot turned quickly into several others as they both mutually got sucked into the whirlwind of jobs. They had so much fun working together that they both forgot it counted as *work*. In the space of a week, they took almost a thousand photos together that Shana had to knuckle down to process quick enough to meet short turnaround. Thank *goddess* she had switched to the digital system. Things went so very much faster. She could also utilize the studio's printing facility to make the review proofs for Byron to go over, which saved on time and cost alike.

As they sat together at a table in the studio, he felt a little speechless as he shuffled through the images. "You take better photos of me than anyone else," he finally murmured. "I'm a little surprised. I just don't look like I'm acting in any of these."

"You're not." She smiled when he looked at her quickly. "Byron, you show me an unguarded you when we're together. That's something I treasure. You don't feel like you have to build up walls because there are things I can't know. I think, also, that you have gotten so used to being what people expect you to be that you maybe forgot how to be *you*. I don't expect anything of you, so you relaxed with me."

"Maybe I did." He took out an image that came from the hat shoot, and he had pulled a suitably ridiculous expression to match the jester hat on his head. "You know, I can't remember the last time I goofed off like this. I haven't done a comedy before, either. I guess it's another form of letting go."

"You should do one before you go home." She put one of the approved photos to the side. "I assume you will when the dust settles."

"Mmm. I only intended to be here to stop Mania. Still not wholly sure how I ended up in this position. Okay, that's a lie. I was singing for my supper not long after I arrived, and my now manager happened to be present. He grabbed me up."

"Well, you *are* Virtuoso. Sherry's a Shaman, by the way. She likes your voice and was hoping to maybe work with you when you arrived."

"She doesn't like me much now," he groused.

"Nah, they do. They're just overprotective. By the time the dust settles, as you said, Sherry will be making you new clothes and singing with you, Juliet will be compelled to feed you, and Desiree will be demanding to style your hair."

"I'm not objectionable to any of those, really."

They sorted through the rest of the photos until they had narrowed it down to his particular favorites with a few secondary options. He would pass them to his manager to be handed off to the appropriate parties for final review before being printed in publications. Shana had already been paid for her share of the work, and more than she had been expecting. Her protests had fallen on deaf ears, too; Byron had insisted she be paid like a professional, so that was what she got.

As they walked away from the studio, she offered, "Want to join us for dinner? It's a night out for me and Edgar and Rocky and Siobhan. We alternate nights at our places or with our mother and once a week we go out." She grinned when he eyed her. "The use of 'our' is applicable. Edgar and I were orphaned shortly after I turned five. Octavia Toulume, Rocky and Siobhan's birth mother, became our caregiver in the hospital and then adopted us and brought us home. So she's really as much our mother as a future mother-in-law."

"Well, if they don't mind, I'd love to go along."

The other three had no objections at all, and Byron felt bemused at how both Siobhan and Rocky guiltlessly held his hands to make sure he felt included. For the similarities between the two sets of siblings, there clearly appeared significant differences. He half wanted to meet their shared mother and commend her for surviving to raise four such fascinating individuals. He could imagine it had not been easy with two of them wanting to save every stray and the other two refusing to share their burdens.

They grabbed dinner at a restaurant owned by the Chivanti Corporation, which Byron did not comment on, but both Siobhan and Rocky suspected showed ulterior motives. The fact that the management there seemed to know Shana and Edgar personally also just made the mystery more so. Just what did they intend to do when Shana became legal?

After dinner and dessert, they opted for a walk through the sunset park. Shana said nothing about the steadily growing sense of dread inside her chest but her companions noticed something wrong anyway because she had grown agitated in a very un-Shana way. She barely held still, and her foot tapped on the ground almost unconsciously if they stopped walking. She seemed to all but disappear on them, drawing deeper into herself so the conversation flowed around her.

"Shana!" Rocky stopped and swung around to grab her

shoulders. "What is wrong? What do you See that I don't?"

Her eyes stared through him for a moment. "Death."

Chaotics burst out of nowhere and landed on the ground in a closed circle around the five Cultivators. The three Defenders hastily donned Masks and armor, and the two Rulers activated their suits. Both also grabbed their weapons; too many enemies and too few Defenders meant *everyone* needed to fight until either Alexandria or Sherry felt the danger to their twin and rallied the rest.

A moment ticked past before Shana's communication Mask lit up with blue color. "Lex?" she asked. She hacked a Chaotic in two parts with the sword in her other hand. "Are you on your way?"

"We're trying! We got halfway toward you when we got attacked as well." Something shattered in the background. "Mania is trying to keep you undefended! Here's your chance to remind us why you don't need us, Shana, and for Byron to prove himself. *Stay alive.*"

The connection abruptly cut out, and Shana dropped the mask back where it belonged. She fought off another Chaotic and took in the scene. Siobhan had managed to avoid most damage by staying behind Rocky who physically muscled away anything that came toward them; he looked a little bloody for the effort but nothing critical yet given his sister healed him as fast as she was able. Byron and Edgar alike tore apart anything that was weak enough for an easy kill, leaving the heavier hitters for Shana herself to handle.

It took only a few minutes to begin to see the intent. The Chaotics had a clear goal: Siobhan and Shana. They all but ignored the men entirely unless the men happened to be in the way. As several Chaotics merged to form bigger and more powerful beasts, Edgar grabbed Byron's arm. "Byron," the prince said low, "whatever else happens, you can*not* let the two Apexes lose their Seeds. They are more critical than anything in existence, and Mania possessing their power would literally destroy the entire universe. Don't focus on me or Rocky; we're not as important, and as their Caretakers, their safety is our first concern as well."

Byron very did not like it, but he nodded in understanding. "You have my vow."

The newly merged Chaotics released blasts of Chaos power that sent everyone painfully reeling. Siobhan could not manage to get her feet under her and her head throbbed painfully from the blast more than the landing. A sound jerked her head around, and she bit back a yelp as she saw a Chaotic lunging for her with odd magic on its clawed hands. She threw out a shield almost desperately only to see the Chaotic punch through as if it did not exist. On a cry, she threw her arms over her head.

Edgar moved with almost unnatural speed and threw himself over Siobhan protectively. The Chaotic's claws plunged into his unprotected back, and dark blood flew. He slumped against Siobhan, nearly knocking her over, and she watched in horror as the Chaotic pulled its claws away with a glowing object caught in its grasp.

A Cultivator Seed.

Agonizing pain tore through Shana and Siobhan equally as they felt Edgar ripped out of their souls by the root. Shana dropped her sword as she scrambled to reach her brother's side, and tears ran unnoticed down her face. Byron and Rocky moved just as fast, and Byron fiercely blasted other Chaotics when they tried to lunge at Shana's now unprotected back.

A high-pitched cackle of crazed joy had everyone's heads jerking around just as Mania appeared. A glazed look filled her eyes as she took the Seed her Chaotic offered. "Finally!" she crowed. "An Immortal Seed!" She broke off and looked closer at the Seed, and she frowned. It looked . . . odd. Almost as if it had been broken away from something. Still, it glowed with all the Dark radiance she would expect from the brother of the Apex of Dark. She sent a sneer toward the others. "I'll be back for yours next!"

She disappeared just as the eight ragged and worn Dual Cultivators finally made it to the scene. They stopped in sheer horror at what they found, and then they nearly tripped over each other as they tried to get to where Edgar had fallen. Virginia reached out toward him, but not fast enough. His body dissolved into shimmers of color that flowed away just before her fingers touched his cheek.

Siobhan found her arms holding nothing, and her soul gutted.

A soft sound of anguish slipped free and then she doubled over in gut-wrenching sobs. Her Mask fell onto the ground with a thump and her armor faded. Shana stared blindly at where her brother had been, and tears slid down her face behind her Mask as pain writhed inside her soul. Rocky yanked her Mask off, and she stared at him for a long moment before her entire control crumbled and she nearly fell to her knees.

Byron scooped up Siobhan into his arms, and his lashes flinched as she only cried harder against his shoulder. "Where do we take them?" he asked Virginia in a low voice.

"The Chivanti apartment." Virginia picked up Siobhan's fallen Mask and handed it to Sherry. She kept her voice even with sheer effort, and only her trembling fingers gave away the potent blend of grief and fury churning inside. "Rocky, carry Shana." Once he had lifted his lover, Virginia opened the transport for everyone. They all passed through, and she pulled off her Mask. "Take them to Shana's room. All we can do is let them cry it out and maybe sleep."

Clara nodded slightly. "I can aid a bit with that if they cannot reach rest by themselves." She slowly sank down to sit on the couch, and her mouth tasted bitter. No, it was never easy to fail to protect a Ruler Cultivator she had vowed to protect, and it had happened more than once in the past. The whim of Destiny.

Rocky and Byron put the two sisters onto Shana's bed where they curled together instinctively. Even Rocky suspected they did not really notice their presence around the newly torn hole inside their souls. He tenderly brushed at their hair equally and then sighed heavily as he followed Byron into the hall. His own grief and pain would stay tamped down as far as it could be. He would cry when he could do it where it wouldn't hurt Shana or Siobhan more.

As they reached the main room, he told Clara tiredly, "Just go ahead and help them sleep. Siobhan might be able to cry herself there, but Shana won't. We know she won't. She'll buckle down and make herself stronger and just bleed where we can't see."

Clara lifted a hand, and pink and lavender magic moved over her fingers before flying down the hall. Of all Cultivators, only she and

Siobhan could use sleep-based spells on allies and enemies alike. "Now what?" she asked in a low voice. "And, no, before you ask, I did not know of this. I know nothing important of the coming days. My future entwined inexorably with it the moment Shana demanded I remain for the entire fight."

Juliet's hands slowly curled into fists at her sides and then she abruptly whirled on Byron. "How dare you?" she snarled. "You let Mania take our prince's Seed! What were you doing that was so important that you did not defend a High Queen's soul mate?"

With unexpected fury, he snarled back, "I was doing exactly what the High Prince ordered me to do and protecting his sister and lover!" Temper and frustration turned his hazel eyes nearly brown in the dim lamplight. "Edgar outright ordered me not to concern myself with him or Rocky, that as Caretakers, they were not as important as Shana or Siobhan! Do you think I liked watching that Chaotic steal his Seed, or that I at all enjoyed watching Shana fall apart?! I would sooner have given my own Seed than see what we just witnessed! I will protect the two queens with my life as I vowed, whether you Blossom Field Defenders like it or not!"

Virginia looked at him a little sharply, and then glanced at Rocky. He looked unsurprised by the outburst. In a way, she suspected Byron himself did not fully understand it personally. And hearing it, and feeling the truth of it in her Empathy, she felt her trust finally cement. "Alright," she said quietly. "That's enough out of both of you." She rubbed her hands over her arms as eyes turned. "Byron, I trust you. The way you spoke now as much as the words themselves tell me all I need to know. However, if you truly intend to remain, then you will defer to me as Lead Defender for I am stronger than you."

He slowly nodded. "I will accept that, Virginia." A hint of a smile came back to his face. "But I think you'll understand if I say that I will defer first to Shana, and then Siobhan, before I defer to you."

She managed to match his smile. "Spoken like a true Defender. I accept that condition as well." She slowly sat down on the couch beside Clara. As Shana had so presciently noted, the belief that Edgar could as yet return in the aftermath of the war because he and Siobhan had not borne a child in no way changed the fact that his death deeply gouged them all. The little voice whispering *what if* could not be hushed. "Here's what we will do. We have it now confirmed Mania cares most for getting to Shana and Siobhan. A Defender will be with them, and Rocky, at all times if they leave their home. With Byron, we can assign three Defenders per each High heir as needed. Would that we could just keep them locked in the apartment, but we really can't. We have to let life carry on, but as safely as we can manage."

Edgar's absence got passed off as an unexpected illness keeping him at home; they would play that lie as far as it could be taken. If anyone noticed how haunted both Shana and Siobhan looked, and Rocky as well to a slightly lesser extent, no one commented. A day ticked by with everyone on edge. Shana herself did not help the tensions any. She had become even more agitated, and she almost stopped speaking entirely to people.

That first evening, when Alexandria and Yvonne joined Byron to keep Shana company in her now empty apartment, all three Defenders spotted something happening to the queen's Marks. Both had turned a dark, almost bloody, red color. Yvonne examined them yet found nothing wrong, per se. As she watched Shana pace between windows, she whispered, "What is going *on*?"

Alexandria's fingers tightened on her arms where she had them crossed. "She's on the cusp of *something*. My gut tells me what it is but it terrifies me." Softer, she said, "A price worse than death."

The second day went the same as the first, but that evening, Shana insisted on being alone. No one liked it, but not even Alexandria could batter through her persistence. Rocky did not bother to try. He merely showed up on the doorstep and let himself in with the key he and his sister shared. He found Shana standing at the window across the room, and the setting sun made the darkness inside her almost *burn* around her body. No light could touch her skin. He could barely even see her. A sense of panic made him move fast, and the moment he caught her arm, his own Light brought her back to visibility. "Shana!" he said raggedly. "You're breaking my heart! I can't fix this. I want to, but I can't." He gave her a little shake. "Let me in! Let me help you! You know what is coming, don't you?"

"You know I have All Sight." The words came out with bitterness. "The most powerful Sight of anyone alive, more than even you. I'm bound to Destiny by her blood and her choice. I have premonitions and visions even when I don't want them. I hate it. I hate it so much sometimes." Her eyes closed as a chill moved through her that the sun could not stop. "The death won't stop. It will keep coming. I can't stop it." She opened her eyes and watched pale blood pour down his chest from wounds that did not, yet, exist. Another nightmare. "Just hold me. I will pay the price to exist soon enough."

Her voice broke on the words, and he jerked her into his arms. His own Sight had told him far too much of coming events, too. Events he now suspected she knew of personally. As her Caretaker, his duty lay in saving her soul, in holding her together when the weight of her duty tried to break her apart. Yet now he saw a terrible truth. Nothing could shatter Shana except her own hands. He would only be able to sweep up the pieces in the aftermath and try to put her back together with his love.

Another day, and tensions ran higher than ever as even Sherry began to become antsy with the sense of evil moving. Byron had been scheduled for a photo shoot that he tried to cancel, but short of an apocalypse, he had no out. A bit of bitterness made him want to yell at his manager that, in fact, an apocalypse did lay on the horizon but somehow he refrained. His unease for the situation became no better when Shana showed up to the evening shoot with only Rocky in tow. "Where are the Defenders?" Byron demanded sharply.

"Whether they like it or not," Shana countered, "I am as capable, if not more capable, of defending myself than they are, and even without armor, Rocky outclasses the others as well. Nature of our own existence and my role within it. You are magically oriented, though physically skilled, so between us, we can handle something if it happens."

"Byron," Rocky said quietly, "I think it fair to tell you as well that I actually trust you more than I trust any other Cultivator besides Alexandria to help protect Shana. You would *never* let her be hurt."

"I don't think the others would agree with that," he muttered.

A little smile touched Rocky's lips. "Virginia does. And her opinion matters most as Lead."

They headed into the studio, and proof to professionalism and inner strength, both Byron and Shana worked almost completely naturally together. Rocky could almost believe there was no danger or weight of an axe hovering over the back of Shana's neck. Events set in stone. He glanced out the window at the setting sun. Sometimes he hated his Sight, too.

The shoot done, they all three headed back outside only to find a familiar carriage parked outside. Alexandria and Desiree stood beside it, and both had scowls on their faces. "You let her do this?" Alexandria demanded of Rocky and Byron alike.

"I don't like it either!" the Defender retorted.

"Too bad!" Rocky snapped at them equally. "I trust Shana's Sight as wholly as I trust my own, and we both felt this had to be done. Some things cannot be stopped, Lexie, and you know it as much as you hate it!"

No one got the chance to respond. With no warning, as if she had somehow cloaked her presence, Mania appeared in the air. Magic fired from her hands before anyone could blink, and the unnaturally chaotic liquid Glass fired directly at Shana. The attack would surely hit her—she had nowhere to dodge, and no Defender stood close enough to protect her—but Rocky had literally Seen the events coming. Without guilt or hesitation, he shifted his weight to place himself in front of his Cultivator as any true Caretaker would.

The Glass struck his chest, punched through, and emerged on the other side with a glowing Seed in its grasp. It continued its path with enough force to gouge across Shana's shoulder before angling up into the air and bending around to return to Mania. A shout rose as all three Defender Cultivators lunged toward Shana and Rocky. Alexandria and Desiree managed to catch Rocky as he fell, and Byron grabbed Shana's shoulders to keep her standing. She did not even seem to see him. Her darkened pink eyes stared only at the Seed clutched in Mania's grasp. Like Edgar's, it looked oddly shaped, but it glowed hot with Light instead.

Fresh pain boiled through her already gouged soul. New holes ripped open as she felt her soul mate torn away from where he had been interlocked to her. She almost stopped breathing as the agony came from a place she had never imagined could hurt. Her gaze lowered to her lover's form, and she watched as his body dissolved into shimmers of color.

Tears streamed without control as her eyes turned wholly black. Her hands curled into fists at her sides. Byron gave her a little shake but she did not see nor feel him. She barely felt Alexandria inside her soul around the pain, and she certainly did not feel when her twin grabbed her arm to help restrain her.

Mania looked down at her, and her lip curled into a sneer. "Is that all you are, great Apex?"

Dark power erupted around Shana with such force that it knocked Byron and Alexandria back a step. She shot into the air on the force of her power alone, and her sword appeared in her hand. Her first attack cut open Mania's cheek with such precision that everyone *knew* she could have killed the evil Cultivator on her first strike. Her next attack cut through the cloth over Mania's chest and stopped *just* short of piercing flesh. Shana looked at the warped Ruler Mark that then revealed itself to her, and then looked into the Heart of Chaos through Mania's eyes. "I wondered about you," she said softly.

Mania felt terror well inside her shredded soul as she could not break away from the Apex's burning black gaze. A little desperately, she reached for her magic and blasted Shana pointblank in the chest with Chaos power. It sent the other Cultivator reeling painfully, and Mania took what little window she had to escape.

"Shana!" Alexandria scrambled forward and managed to catch her queen as she fell. Only Desiree and Byron hastily bracing her kept her from landing on the ground personally. She could physically lift and carry her twin, but having her full weight hit her from several feet in the air could not be overcome. She reoriented herself and briefly nodded at the other two in thanks. "Shana?" she asked softly.

No response came, and it seemed no surprise. The Chaos had

done as much damage physically as losing Rocky had done internally. Blood, darker than ever, seeped from dozens of burns and cuts. Her sword fell from her lax fingers and disappeared before it hit the ground. Tears continued to fall even deeply unconscious. Her two Marks that had been so bloody red now slowly turned black.

Desiree's communication mask lit up with bright red. "I'm here, Virginia," she said tiredly. "And it's worse than you may think."

Just as tiredly, the Lead Defender responded, "Based on Siobhan's reaction, I don't think it is. Clara has knocked her out. We're at Siobhan's apartment. Bring Shana." The mask stopped glowing as the connection ended.

Byron reached out with trembling fingers to touch Shana's cheek. "I should have done that, not him."

Alexandria looked at him for a moment. "You're in love with her."

He froze briefly and then pulled his hand back. "I . . . yeah."

"You didn't notice until now?" Desiree murmured. She found a smile. "Byron, don't be upset by it. Everyone is in love with Shana to some level or another. Siobhan, too. There are so many ways to feel love. So many different types. Enjoy loving Shana. She gives as much as she gets. More, really. And someday, when you find your soul mate Caretaker, I guarantee you'll be all the more dazzled by it because you will appreciate it more." Softer, she added, "And I suspect Virginia and Rocky alike knew already. That's why they trusted you. Knowing it now myself, I also trust you."

"As do I," Alexandria agreed. She looked him in the eye. "If something happens to me . . ."

He nodded in acceptance for the duty he knew she offered. "With honor."

They used a transport to get back to the apartment, and Alexandria tucked Shana into bed with Siobhan, whose face looked paler than usual and showed even more ravages from tears. Even in sleep, the two sisters' fingers laced together as if to hold one another when their souls wanted to shred.

Everyone spent the night for fear of leaving either Apex alone.

Clara periodically throughout the night would reinforce the sleeping magic to ensure both slept as deeply as possible. A brief contact to her brother had him helping ensure they remained dreamless as well.

Shana awoke after dawn to an emotional hangover the size of her palace, and a sort of numbness spreading in place of the pain. Siobhan stirred beside her, and then opened her eyes and looked up. Shana tightened her grip on her sister's hand. "We'll make it," she said softly. "We'll survive and they'll come back."

"I believe anything you tell me." Siobhan burrowed closer for a moment and then forced herself to let go. "Let's talk to everyone." She studied her sister's face. "You know something we didn't before."

"Yeah. Best to share it at once."

Kellie had gotten to Shana long before dawn, so no wounds remained externally. Just the blood from her lover as well as her own. Everyone kept clothes at each other's place, so she changed into something clean in Rocky's room. Just feeling his presence permeating everything around her cut into her anew.

She reached the living room behind Siobhan and found all other Cultivators awake and alert. Juliet and Clara worked on making breakfast. Shana looked around at everyone for a moment and then at Byron. She walked over to where he stood and reached out to touch the Flower Mark on his arm. It had a sparkling edge, of course, because he was the only Defender of Ranunculus. "When were you going to tell us?" she asked him calmly.

He winced a bit as eyes turned, but at least they looked more curious than hostile. "I really did intend to tell everyone, but it . . . is painful to discuss." He hesitated and then sighed. He tugged down his shirt collar, and there, on his chest over his heart, lay the empty outline of the same Mark as on his arm. The evidence of a Deactivated Ruler Cultivator. "When I said Mania attacked my world and killed my sister, I was not lying. A year ago, my sister, Tara, who was Ruler Cultivator of Ranunculus, started getting curious and experimenting with Chaos power."

Virginia began to get a sinking feeling. "It didn't go well."

"To say the least. No single Light or Dark core could ever handle

Chaos. The power went out of control and began to destroy our people and our world. She chose to save our world by sacrificing herself. She absorbed all the Chaos into her own core and only managed to kill herself in the process." His eyes closed. "She became Mania, and obsessed with taking the Seeds of the two Apexes. She disappeared from Ranunculus, leaving it in near ruins. As both Defender and potential Ruler, I *had* to come here first, to be ready to stop her."

"So that's why," Sherry said. "We all felt it, I think, but especially me, that something about your armor felt oddly familiar. It's because we were noticing its resemblance to Mania's ruined Ruler Cultivator gown." She looked at Shana. "How did you know?"

"I had a gut feeling right from the beginning when I met Byron," she admitted. "But I knew for certain when I attacked Mania last night. I needed to see her Mark, so I went after it. It is horrifically warped, to be sure, but there could be no mistaking for anything less than the same Ranunculus as on Byron's arm. Also, up close, I could see her natural coloring better and it reminded me of Byron's hazel coloring." She turned to Byron. "She can be saved."

He froze. "What?"

"She can be saved. If she was truly dead, if her Seed had been ruined beyond redemption, you would have become Activated as Ranunculus sought to protect its future. Somewhere, deep inside the shell of Mania, Tara is there." Her eyes hardened. "I will plunge into the Heart of Chaos, and I will save her."

A chill swept through everyone equally at the idea. To plunge into the Heart of Chaos would be to open herself wholly to Chaos power and risk destroying herself in the process. And yet . . .

Siobhan moved forward and slipped her hand into Shana's. "I believe in you," she said softly. "And . . . I think that you are the only person who can do this." She looked at Byron. "Can you track your sister?" At his nod, she looked at the others. "Then we'll go. Today. We can't let this drag on." She glanced at Shana's Marks and their dark, angry, color. "We're running out of time."

Byron's ability to track Mania—his sister—made far more sense now that they knew not only of his connection to her, but also Shana's insistence that Tara still lived and could be saved. No one expected that salvation to be easy, though. In fact, they anticipated a bloody battle that would very probably demand something *someone* should not have to pay.

Following the invisible lines of magic between Activated and Deactivated Ruler Cultivators, Byron pinpointed Mania's hidden location as being somewhere on one of the tiny islands that surrounded the landmass where Lux sat. The little fragments of land had been shorn off over five thousand years before in another war no one liked to remember. Only abandoned buildings remained as a memory of the past.

They used a transport to reach it, but they had no option for catching their breath. The moment they landed, Chaotics erupted into the air around them. Hundreds. Thousands. The Defenders waded right into the horde with weapons and magic alike, and Byron as much as Alexandria stayed near to Shana to help cover her back as she efficiently tore through enemies. Sherry and Virginia mutually stayed near Siobhan for the same reason.

Unknown to either Apex, a plan had been made by the nine Defender Cultivators. Yvonne used a perfectly timed blast of Ice magic to create a thick fog obscuring sight, and Virginia snapped, "Move deeper!"

Everyone dove through the open door of the sole building in the area, and Alexandria threw the door shut. Ice sealed it to keep out the Chaotics, but a low crackle and growl from beneath their feet implied more waited down deeper into the basement levels. Siobhan turned to ask Yvonne if she could maintain the seal at range, and horror rose to choke her as she did not see her Iris Defender. She did not see the Daffodil Defender either.

She jerked toward the door and belatedly noticed the ice on the *outside* of the door. "Yvonne!" she shouted. She leapt toward the door only to be intercepted by Sherry who held her despite her struggles. "Kellie! What are you doing?" she cried. Her head jerked toward Shana who had neither moved nor spoken. "*Stop them!*" she shouted. "They're going to die!"

"Siobhan." Shana kept her voice quiet. "They're doing the only thing they can to help us. I . . . I had wondered if they might do this." She looked at Virginia. "It's something I might have determined to do, had I been Lead." Her eyes moved back to her horrified partner. "What are we supposed to do? Keep fighting endlessly in one place and either never advance or become so worn that we don't survive to reach Mania? She can create as many Chaotics as she wants. She can just wait for us to be so tired we can't fight anymore. You and I . . . we have the best shot at saving Tara. We *have* to make it there to save her, because if we save her, we can save everyone else. If we don't make it then . . . then all of the death is worthless. Without Seeds, no one can ascend to the Realm. It will end. Permanently. And in all too short a time, all of our worlds will end, too. Blossom Field will cease to exist—which will eventually take the rest of the universe with it."

Siobhan stopped struggling, and Sherry let her go. She walked over to the door and pressed her hands against it for a moment. Nothing hurt more than to let the Defenders make this sort of sacrifice. Her eyes flew wide as that terribly familiar glow flared bright enough outside to leak around the door, and she did not resist as Sherry pulled her away. Even in death, strong enough magic from a Cultivator could not be erased. Nothing would get through that door. "Maybe," she said softly, "that's another reason for us to all be Duals. It . . . it gives us such a more powerful need to survive, and the greater and necessary type of magic *to* survive."

They moved down deeper into the basement levels and found another floor drowning in Chaotics. Shana said not a word as she forged a path toward the next trapdoor and stairs, and only five of the seven remaining Dual Cultivators as well as Byron followed her. She slammed the door closed behind her, and her lashes flinched behind her Mask as Water and Thunder sealed it from the other side. Cracks just seemed to keep spreading within her soul.

Siobhan spared a moment to heal the worst of whatever she could see on those who remained. Tears ran unchecked down her face that she ignored fiercely. As she healed a nasty gouge on Sherry, her twin covered her hand briefly. "I know," Siobhan whispered. "I will make my decision as well. I think . . . I already know. If my Sight told me accurately what is happening now, then . . . I know."

Another floor, and a larger horde. As Virginia and Clara stepped forward, Shana finally spoke up. "Claret." Her Defender turned, and she lifted her chin. "You cannot sacrifice yourself for me. You tried that once before, and Pallas retreated you. You are attempting to do it again here, and there are no words for how terribly humbled I am that you not only want to do this, but that Virginia will even *let* you. However . . . *I* will not allow it. You have another duty more important than I."

Clara tenderly cupped Shana's chin. "There is nothing more important than you in my world."

"In that we disagree, no matter how much I love you for saying it." She closed her eyes and reached out with her gift of transporting magic. Clara disappeared abruptly from the scene, and Shana opened her eyes slightly. "I'm sorry," she whispered.

Byron stared at her for a moment and then looked at a silent Virginia. "I thought . . . I believed that only a Lead had the power to force the retreat of an ally Defender Cultivator."

Virginia did not look away from the Chaotics tauntingly creeping in closer. "The curious thing about our generation is that Shana *should* be Lead. But there will come a day when she hangs up her Mask to rule a High Kingdom. That time will happen long before the time when the rest of us may need to hang up our Masks, therefore Destiny made me Lead—but she gave Shana many of the same gifts." She did look back then, and she smiled at Shana. "Maybe the reason we butt heads so terribly is because we are the same sort of Lead." She turned back to the Chaotics and held out her halberd. "We're not there yet. I believe in you, Shana."

Shana's expression did not change as she swung her sword up into an offensive position and then lunged forward. She cut viciously through the monstrous creatures until she reached the next trapdoor. She held it until Siobhan, Byron, and the two twin souls dropped down inside, and then she dropped down as well. She slammed it shut behind her, and only a little sound of pain escaped her control as Glass sealed it closed. Her darkened eyes stared a little blindly at the chunks of unbreakable glass as the future closed in on her.

The deeper they dove down into the building toward Mania, the more powerful the Chaotics became. Each Seed she claimed only empowered her more, and having the Seeds belonging to Rocky and Edgar had already made her terrible enough. Siobhan *knew* what would come next, and tears already filled her eyes for the oncoming agony. She knew Virginia had chosen to make her final stand sooner rather than later just to buy Siobhan and Shana those precious few moments, and that hurt just as much. Love. So small a word for such a powerful force a Defender could feel.

Shana jumped down the final trapdoor and looked up to see Siobhan hovering at the edge. On a little gulp, Siobhan jumped down followed by Alexandria and Byron. The door slammed shut, and Fire engulfed it before hardening to unbreakable obsidian. Pain punched through Siobhan's already damaged soul with all the force and fury of losing her lover and her brother. She would have fallen to her knees if Shana had not caught her. She clung on for long moments, fighting through the tears to breathe. "It's okay," Shana said softly. "I can be your strength."

Siobhan shook her head fiercely and pushed herself to her feet. "No!" she vowed. "For once I will be *your* strength!" She turned to look at the empty space, which felt eerily so after everything else they had gone through. None of the four who remained were wholly intact. Masks had been cracked, and armor showed rips, and dents, and tears. Blood stained everyone. "What now?" she whispered.

A door sat at the end of the room. Shana lifted her chin and calmly walked forward. She opened the door only to wince painfully as a flood of Chaos washed out and bit into her body and soul alike. Somewhere inside the middle of the force, a tiny sound that seemed so very out of place made her head come up. Chaos was . . . *crying*.

The force ebbed enough they could all walk into the final room. Nausea turned Byron's stomach as he beheld his sister's manic form. She had been corrupted only more, nearly no vestiges of her former self to be seen. Her gown had not been mended, so the rip Shana had made still showed her Mark. It had been warped to almost non-recognition. A hot throb from his Deactivated Mark told him they stood on the verge of being too late.

Siobhan took one look at Mania, at the Chaos power wildly whipping around her, and knew one thing with absolutely clarity: her Sight had been right. She turned to face Shana and caught her hands. "Shana," she said intensely, "I am a liability here. Mania will target me first for I am truly the easier target. I can't run and cast at the same time." She drew her sister's hand up to rest over her breastplate and beneath which lay her Ruler Mark. "If she takes my Seed, you will be in terrible danger, because the Light inside Chaos will be so much more than the Dark inside you that you might be destroyed in a single hit."

Shana said nothing, and neither did Byron or Alexandria.

Siobhan shook her head a bit. "Only you can do this, Shana. In fact, only you *should* do this because this is surely the price of your birth. I don't know what you have to do in order to awaken, or to find the Hope that I *know* burns inside you, but I do know that I will become the Light that makes you more Dark." She smiled tremulously as she drew out her Seed and pressed it into Shana's hand. "I believe in you. You can do anything."

Shana's fingers trembled as she closed her hand around the Seed and watched Siobhan dissolve into shimmers of color. It burned to hold the Seed, even through her glove, and sparks flew at the connection before ebbing. "I will cover you," she told Alexandria in a low voice. "I will use Siobhan's magic as well as my own minimal skills to cover you. It is less risky for you because Mania wants *me*."

Alexandria nodded and then looked at Byron. He obeyed the unspoken command and moved to stand closer beside Shana. The Hyacinth Cultivator hefted her harpoon and braced her shoulders for what she knew surely lay ahead. On a shout, she lunged at Mania as concentrated blasts of Light and Dark streaked past her shoulders in a potent double attack.

Mania had been so utterly shocked by Siobhan's action that she did not get a shield up in time to stop Alexandria. The Defender punched past her guard, and her weapon blade slashed across Mania's chest. The pain, as much as the pain of the day before, shocked Mania only more. She had not felt pain in ages. Fury welled up and she fired Chaos power right into Alexandria's chest to send her tumbling backwards. With all the frenzy of the condemned, she began lobbing blast after blast of Chaos power, but not at Alexandria. She aimed right for Shana. If she could take down the Protea Defender, she would claim both her Seed and Siobhan's alike! "You can't stop me!" she raged.

Byron knocked Shana flat and planted himself in the way. What little immunity he had gained served him well as the Chaos power did far less damage to him than it should have, and certainly less than it may have done to Shana. His Mask cracked, and his armor flickered, but it continued to hold. Glass magic welled around him, and he hurled the immolating blast back toward Mania. It punched her right in the chest and sent her crashing into the wall behind her. She landed on the ground with a little thump, her skin burning as molten glass dripped from it.

Her head jerked up and she screamed as she released a return wave of Glass magic. It looked exactly like the blast that had taken Rocky. Alexandria shot to her feet and leapt between the blast and Byron. It shot through her chest as if her armor did not exist and emerged on the other side with a blue Seed in its grasp.

She did not fall as the Glass recoiled to Mania. Somehow she stayed standing. She glanced back only once, and saw tears streaming from Shana's now black eyes. Had she done what Destiny needed her to do? She looked instead at Byron, and he closed his eyes in acceptance. With a little breath, she let go, and she dissolved into shimmers of color.

Even expecting the pain had not prepared Shana for the ambush. She hunched into herself with Siobhan's Seed clutched in her grasp and fought to simply *endure*. The gaping holes inside her soul wanted to destroy her. She stared a bit blindly at the Seed in her grip and then, without warning, pure fury began to boil her blood. With it came a moment of pure clarity as her sister's Light brightened her Dark.

She slowly rose to her feet and her Mask disappeared as her armor began to dissolve. Without fear, without hesitation, she reached for her own soul and shattered it to pieces. Pain engulfed her as she forced it to reforge, and Dark power surged wildly up her body until it and black-pink protea blossoms were all she wore. Her darkened Marks abruptly cleared and began to glow with more and more force until the one on her arm took on a second blossom and all bloomed wholly. Her crowns began to sparkle. Wings of glowing black burst from her back with such force they cracked the floor, and the crown on her Marks appeared on her left cheek.

The Apex of Dark took one step forward and then lunged for Mania. "Call Tara!" she shouted at Byron, and then she somehow disappeared as she plunged right into Mania's body and the Heart of Chaos. In shattering her own soul and reforging it personally, she had given herself *just* enough immunity against Chaos to survive.

She dove down deeper and deeper through the muck and mess of Tara's ravaged soul, and she could hear Byron's beautiful Virtuoso voice singing a tender ballad to his sister. She ignored the pain of her dive, focused on finding the Seed so nearly lost. When she finally could go no deeper, she closed her eyes as she felt the Chaos power trying to eat her alive. It couldn't do it, for inside her, Hope had been born. She slowly lifted her free hand and then curled it into a fist. "Let the Dark ring out with Hope," she whispered.

A soft voice welled on the air around her as if to repeat the Whisper, and it merged to the voice still singing in the distance. Hot Glass magic began to well as the Chaos retreated from the Whisper. A hand reached out, and Shana reached out in turn. Their fingers met and meshed, and a shockwave ripped from Shana's body.

On the outside, Byron kept singing, his heart pounding dully with terror. He didn't know what was happening. Mania only screamed over and over again, ripping at her own hair and body as the Chaos power fought against the Dark power spilling from cracks across her skin. The two forces met, and the shockwave erupted free. Byron had to stop singing as he threw his arms in front of his face protectively. Somewhere, inside the rush of hot power over his skin, he almost thought he heard a whisper.

It ebbed and he lowered his arms. Tears briefly choked him. "Tara?" he managed.

Mania had disappeared. In her place stood the familiar figure of his sister, her Ruler gown intact and her coloring returned to normal. Her Mark glowed through the cloth over her chest, and it had no longer warped. The Chaos power in the place evaporated in the air as it dispersed back into the universe, and only the lingering presence of Dark remained.

Byron was running forward before being aware of it. Not just to Tara, but to the one his sister supported. Shana looked . . . horrific. Black blood poured from wounds that should have killed anyone else. She had shifted back from her Apex form, but her clothes looked no better. She did not even have the strength to stand on her own. He caught her arms gingerly around the wounds, and shock filled him when he saw her eyes still open. How was she *conscious?!*

Tara let him take more of Shana's weight—the delicate Ruler stood quite a bit smaller than her savior—and then tenderly lifted Shana's hand to pry her fingers open and free the Seed she clutched still. Tara lifted it, and the others she had gathered floated into the air before scattering across the floor of the room. Each Seed glowed, and then the lost Cultivator it belonged to reappeared. UnMasked and without armor, and certainly more ragged than normal, but alive and healthy and restored.

Rocky was the first to shove himself up to his feet, and he looked around sharply as he felt writhing pain inside his body that surely came from his lover. He turned, and bile rose when he saw her being held up by Byron and Tara. He took a step forward and then started running, nearly tripping over his own feet in the process.

Shana pulled free of Byron and tried to move forward but her legs gave out. She landed safely in Rocky's arms, and she curled her fingers into his shirt as she felt her reforged soul at last healing as the three she loved most returned to her. Alexandria and Edgar reached her only a moment later, and Siobhan tripped over them both in haste to help with healing magic. Tears ran down her face. "You did it," she whispered. "I knew you could. Sleep, okay? Sleep now. We're safe. You saved us." She pushed the magic a little harder, and Shana's entire body went lax in Rocky's grip. "Oh god, oh god," she managed to say around a little hiccup.

"What happened?" Virginia asked Byron and Tara alike as she and the others walked closer. "We were in the space between the Plane and the Realm, so we saw nothing." Her head turned as Clara walked out of a transport. "Clara?"

Clara slowly shook her head. "I did not see it either, though I . . . have suspicions. The power of Chaos blocked the Plane and Realm alike from viewing anything, so even if you had ascended, you'd have been left blind to the events." She cupped Shana's cheek for a moment. "Pallas will work to keep her dreamless as long as he dares with her need to be filter. It is all we can do."

"And neither of us will talk of the events unless she does first," Byron vowed.

Tara nodded. "It is her choice to share her horror."

Edgar brushed at Shana's tangled and sweaty black hair. "She will never tell," he admitted in a low voice. "She never shares her nightmares, even when sharing them might well save her from more."

"In a way," Byron said softly, "I can't blame her at all. I'll have some nightmares of my own after this." He held onto Tara tightly as she moved to hug him, and he buried his face in her hair briefly. The burn from his Deactivated Mark had faded entirely, and their world would be able to recover. Everyone would.

Everyone except, perhaps, the one who had ensured it happen.

In the days that followed, life returned to normal. Shana recovered with great speed physically thanks to a combination of magic from Siobhan and Kellie and incessant nagging from her loved ones to take it easy for once. They played off that she and her brother had caught the same illness, and their teachers did not mark down their grades in response. The nice thing about being reliable academic stars was that they got more leeway than the average student.

However, saying that Shana had recovered only referred entirely to her physical health. Her lingering survivors' stress from fighting Nemesis had become exacerbated from her evolutionary battle, and rather than risk sending her into a panicked terror, her friends did everything they could to effectively not speak of the events at all. It would have to be addressed someday, but, again, without a spiritual healer, they could only take what little actions were actually available.

Watching as she and Tara chatted casually with Siobhan about alliance, Yvonne murmured to the others, "I didn't even think it possible someone *could* shatter their own soul. We break in order to heal—not evolve. And doing that . . . reforging herself like that . . . she just made it harder for herself to break or heal at all." Softer, she added, "I don't think I'm wrong in saying she may well be the greatest of all Cultivators that Destiny has ever made."

Desiree nodded. "If ever anyone is more deliberately created by Destiny, I think the entire universe will change." She rubbed her hands over her arms. "At least she's smiling again." She found a smile of her own as Siobhan waved them all closer. "Have we figured things out?"

Siobhan nodded firmly. "I don't know why this was so difficult in the past, really. We're blaming Destiny for it. We've got the details all done up, and we'll have Virginia take them to the world leaders for

pg. 404

us when she reports on the recent war." She nodded again. "Also, there's something else to report."

Shana braced her hands beside her hips where she sat on top of a picnic bench. "We felt it this morning, that there's been a *really* big shift. As in there was an actual shift in the fabric of Time. Clara confirmed it for us. With all of our generation, including her for once, being fully bloomed as Cultivators, we have unintentionally ended an era. The Royal Era will end next month in December of Year 5104, and the following month will be January of Year 1 of the Rebirth Era."

"Rebirth, huh? Well, that sounds fitting," Virginia decided. "I wonder how long that era will run until. It usually changes over with a generation." She grinned. "We'll have to watch for it once we start having kids eventually."

"We need soul mates for that first!" Kellie told her dryly. "Maybe we should be watching for those instead?"

Siobhan bit her lip to hide a smile, and Shana briefly glanced at Rocky and Edgar who mutually looked amused. None of them said a word. "Anyway," Shana continued smoothly, "I guess it's just about time to say goodbye to Tara and Byron."

Byron nodded and then smiled. "It was a little easier than I expected to get everything in order to go home. I told my manager outright about being from Ranunculus and sort of stretched the truth by saying I came to form alliance, and with that done, I am returning home. I'm apparently going to break hearts all over Protea, and there will never be anyone to take my place," he clasped his hand to his heart dramatically, "and if ever I return again, the masses will weep for joy."

It sent several of the others into a fit of giggles, including his sister—a sound he did not think he would ever tire of hearing. "It was only a *little* stretch," Virginia assured him. She walked closer and held out her hand palm up. When he placed his hand on hers, she held on tight. "Byron, by my right as Lead Defender for Blossom Field, I would like to offer you honorary standing as one of us. If we need help, we will call you, and we hope you will call us."

"In an instant!" he vowed. "And I am both honored and humbled you would give me such a position."

"Well," her eyes flicked to Shana and then back, "you more than proved yourself to all of us." She gave him a hug and then moved back so everyone else could do the same. She then changed her mind and hugged Tara equally. "I'm glad we saved you," she told the Ruler. "Byron would hate being a king."

"Yes he would," Byron grumbled.

Tara laughed. "Oh, you. It's not that terrible." She hugged Siobhan, and then Shana, and held on a little tighter to the latter. "You are my savior," she whispered into Shana's ear. "And no matter what, no matter how small, if ever you need me for *anything*, I will be there."

Shana hugged her back. "Thank you." She felt Siobhan and Rocky each take her hands, and they watched with the others of their galaxy as the two Ranunculus siblings walked away. It felt a little less like a farewell than it did a promise to meet again, so no one felt any real sadness. Neither time nor space could separate friends, and even those with Dark cores knew it.

Everyone scattered to various events, and Shana and Rocky headed off in their own direction. It felt nice to not be worrying anymore, and to be allowed out without bodyguards. He tugged her under his arm and teased, "It's so hard to find privacy with so many overprotective people dogging your every step." He nibbled teasingly at her ear. "Sure you want to just go get lunch? We could pick something up and take it home. My home, that is. Bet we can convince Siobhan without any difficulty to take Edgar back to your place instead."

She smiled up at him, and with more ease than she had in a long while. "You do tempt a woman." She laughed and caught his shoulders for balance as he swung her around into his arms properly. She eased up the bit needed and nibbled at his lip the way he had teased her ear. "Maybe we can just call for delivery," she whispered. "Juliet would be willing to run us over something."

"Well, you've convinced me." He swept her up against his chest just to make her laugh again. "Delivery it is." He contently began walking down the lane, and he ignored the giggles and laughter from observers who saw them. "The Rebirth Era, huh? My Sight seems curiously quiet about anything it will hold. What have you got?"

"A few things here and there. Nothing set in stone, and nothing that bothers me." She rested her head on his shoulder with a contented sigh. Maybe, just maybe, she did sort of like it when he moved her places against her will; possibly because it never actually went against her will. Just her stubbornness. That seemed fair. "I think we'll handle them as they come, you know? And for now, just having everyone by my side is enough for me."

He could not argue with that. They knew inevitably more wars would loom on the horizon for, as she had said before, they would always come so long as unbalance and evil fed onto each other. Loose threads left from the start of the Royal Era five thousand years before would soon have to be woven into the new fabric of the Rebirth Era, and unaccounted for friends would have to be found. A distant future with resurrected kingdoms also loomed, as did the end of the freedom they all coveted so greatly—especially Shana. Yet, for right then, everything could be perfect.

The price had been paid. They had all fully bloomed. Their galactic garden could be a beautiful one once more.

GLOSSARY

Because the universe of the Kingdoms' series is complex and detailed, here's a quick reference for some of the terms used frequently within the story.

Activated – A term referencing a Cultivator who is in full possession of their magic and skills.

Arcanery – The proper term for the infinite power inside the Apexes of Light and Dark because they have far more than just magic inside them. Technically both do possess infinite magic but Shanae's actual magic use/capacity is very limited to little more than what a normal Dual Cultivator would have (other than Shanae having both offense/defense as a Lead). Sayena, conversely, can use her magic in ways that no other being alive can do. Therefore, when Shanae is using arcanery as an Apex, it is easier to see than if Sayena is doing it (because there is the expectation that Sayena's magic can do anything). There IS a significant difference between magic and arcanery, particularly since arcanery—as the name implies—draws on the literal Light and Dark and Hope forces of the universe to make things happen.

Caretaker – The term used for the soul mate of a Cultivator. Caretakers are specially chosen to have unique traits and qualities that enhance their Cultivator, and they are usually given one magical gift from either the Ruler or the Defender category depending on the need of their mate. Caretakers to Defenders are particularly special since they inevitably have the ability to enter battle at their Defender's side, and have the strength of will to hold their heart and souls together.

Core (capitalized) – The soul and life of a planet that gives it will and holds its Flower Element power. Like living beings, a planet's Core is either Light or Dark. Light Core planets rely on Delphinium to keep them alive while Dark Core planets rely on Protea. This is true for the entire universe, and not just Blossom Field.

Core (lower case) – The most basic component of all living beings that helps determine much of their personality. They are also Light or Dark. Some cores in people can have speckles or aspects of the other, but never in a perfect blend.

Cultivator – People with a Seed inside who possess Flower Element magic based on their world's flower/Core. Cultivators are divided into Rulers (who literally rule their worlds), and Defenders (who literally defend their worlds). Both Rulers and Defenders possess very different sorts of magic even when sharing an element/world. Dual Cultivators—as the name implies—fill both roles and therefore possess both types of magic.

Deactivated – A term referencing a Cultivator who does not have access to magic or skills though the potential for such exists inside them. A Deactivated Cultivator is all but completely powerless, including lacking immortality, unless they happen to be a Caretaker for another Cultivator.

Era – The term for a section of time marked by the flow of power within it. Eras change when power levels reach an absolute peak for that era. Typically, power will climb across Eras, plateau, drop, and then climb again higher. The shift of an Era can be tangibly felt by those with magic, especially High Rulers and very specifically those with the Memory Flower Element. Eras can vary in length from a few decades to thousands of years. For the sake of continuity, Era shifts are not 'officially' begun until January of the following year. Typically, the birth of a generation of Cultivators will cause the change of an Era, or at the least, will mark the 'real' start of it. Other times, it will be marked by the first marriage of a Ruler Cultivator of the first generation.

Flower Element – The literal elemental forces that shape all of existence. The Flower Elements determine what sort of climate/landscape a world will have as well as the individual magic or majik inside Cultivators and witches. Nine Flower Elements are considered common as they can land in just about any hands: Nature, Illusion, Ice, Fire, Thunder, Air, Water, Metal, and Glass. The Memory Flower Element is restricted solely to those who are involved with or critical to the Hall of Records. Even more limited are the Dark and Light

Flower Elements as they cannot be controlled by anyone except an Apex with arcanery—because both Light and Dark are technically arcane forces that support the universe. Rarer *still* is the Chaos Flower Element, which is actually as critical an arcane force as Light and Dark to all existence but it does not have an Apex to control it. There exist two 'sub-elements' of Time and Shadow, which derive from Memory and Chaos respectfully. The subs have some similar properties but work in vastly different ways, making them less dangerous to be owned—though no less rare in their own way.

Flower Mark – The mark on a Cultivator that denotes which world birthed their Seed. A Ruler has their Mark on their chest over their heart; a Defender on their upper left arm (Duals of course have both). A Deactivated Cultivator only has an empty outline of their Mark, where an Activated one has full color. A starting Mark will have a single blossom of their world's flower. Rulers cannot evolve, but Defenders can, and each evolution known as a 'tier' adds another blossom. When the Defender reaches their peak, their blossoms open into full bloom. Evolution is a necessity for most Defenders to increase the strength of their magic while fighting against evil. Additionally, if a Cultivator is the only one of their world, their Mark will have sparkling edges. Only the Apexes have a crown wrapped around their Marks, and the crowns sparkle upon their full evolution to Apex, which is separate of their being fully bloomed (though Shana reaches both at the same time).

Flower Mark (additional): Touching a Flower Mark belonging to a Cultivator is a very personal thing under any circumstance, but has specific meanings depending on who/how is doing it. A Defender who places a Ruler's hand on their Mark is outright offering respect and protection for that person. A Defender placing their Caretaker's hand on their Mark is *asking* for love and support from their lover. Likewise, a Caretaker touching their Defender's Mark is showing respect and love and of course support for the role they fill; this is also applicable to Rulers, but more poignant with a Defender given the danger they face. Between non-mated Cultivators, touching Flower Marks is all but casual, and is seen not unlike holding hands or hugging. Suffice to say, a non-Cultivator/Caretaker who *dares* touch a Flower Mark without permission has effectively violated the Cultivator in question, and has earned a powerful slap in the face—or worse.

Magic – The force of Flower Element power inside all Cultivators (and most Caretakers). Each Flower Element works in very different ways, though there is some overlap, and it can have as much effect on someone's personality as their core. The color of someone's magic directly relates to their world's personal flower rather than any assigned color to the element itself. This is why perverted/evil magic always looks off or putrid in color. A Caretaker's magic—if they do not have their *own* Seed—will have the color of their Cultivator's flower. All magic, if it is strong enough—usually once reaching full fruition as a skill inside at least a Caretaker—can be used to hold select items like weapons. Nearly all Caretakers and Defenders alike carry their weapons inside their magic. It is far more convenient and secure than any other option.

Majik – The force of Flower Element power inside all witches. It is alike to magic but very different and so called slightly different. It can also have as strong an impact on someone's personality as their core. The color of someone's majik directly relates to whether or not the witch is closer to the Goddess or the God, and this applies even to those not actually in the Faith or following the Path. Closer to the Goddess will make the majik silver in color, and closer to the God will make the majik gold. A subtle under color of either white or black will follow the gold or silver depending on the witch's core, but it is rarely ever noticed by the average person unless something is wrong with it. Majik works exactly like magic in only one way: the ability to carry select objects. In the case of witches, they usually carry their wands or other majikal objects for convenience.

Mask – The item used by a Defender to summon their armor. A Mask is a condensation and manifestation of the Flower Element magic of each world, and donning it will both shield a Defender's identity as well as give them magical armor for protection. A Defender does not need to wear their Mask in order to access their magic or weapon, but it is usually safer to put on a Mask before pissing off evil things. All Defenders of a world have the same Mask, and armor is identical on males as well as identical on females (which is determined by the Defender's identity).

Power – A catch-all term that can apply to magic/majik/et al as well as the various smaller levels of gifts and skills inside people. Power can either be manifested wholly as a properly named item, or simply exist to make people feel/act/respond differently to stimuli. Typically used to describe someone who either does not yet know what sort of gift(s) they have, or someone who doesn't have gifts strong enough to be named at all. This term is especially used where the planets, gods, goddesses, and demi-god(dess)s are concerned since they don't really fit into any of the categories and not unlike the Apexes use gifts/skills outside normal defined scope. If someone references Shanae's 'Dark power', for example, they are implying a combination of all she possesses, otherwise they would name them specifically. Power is also the term used to apply to musical gifts since those particular gifts are not Flower Element-based. *(Note: Holy power specifically refers to god/goddesses/demis, divine power specifically refers to Destiny, and arcane power is Light/Dark/Hope forces wielded by the Apexes.)*

Seed – The item inside a Cultivator's soul that *makes* them a Cultivator. Their entire soul comes from their Seed, which is why ripping out a Cultivator's Seed will kill them. A Cultivator can choose to willingly sacrifice or burn out their Seed to release greater and stronger magic/power, but it will kill them. This applies even to the Apexes.

Author Notes

Twenty years ago, at the age of 15, I was inexplicably bitten by the bug to start writing. The first thing I ever wrote, the first story I ever conceived of, was the, well, *seed* that led to the story you just read. That's right. The Kingdoms Series is the final incarnation of the first thing I ever wrote. It started life as a fanfiction, but then began to deviate so far from the source that it was nearly ninety percent original. Every rewrite over two decades as I honed my skills moved it further and further from where it had begun. Finally I realized that maybe it had never been meant to be attached to another story at all. So, after hours and hours of research, and revisiting all of my old favorite shoujo anime/manga, I came up with the final version of this book and the ones that will follow. The Kingdoms Series is my love song to that which shaped my imagination as a teenager, and what propelled me to start writing in the first place. Stay tuned for book two THE UNSEEN KINGDOMS in 2019!

If you loved this story, or any of my stories, please leave me a review on Amazon! Reviews are the bread and butter of an author's life, and even a simple "More, please!" will keep us going.

You can keep up with me on www.facebook.com/stacyjgarrett or www.stacyjgarrett.com or follow my blog at stacyjgarrett.wordpress.com. I sometimes lurk on Twitter (@stacyjgarrett), and Tumblr as well (stacyjgarrett.tumblr.com).

Additionally, if the cover art makes you swoon as much as it does me, please go follow Allexis on nearly all social medias as "whispwill". Check out her comic on Tapas while you're at it!

I can't wait to share more stories with you. Until we meet again in another world, or perhaps another galaxy, keep dreaming of those happy endings.

Stacy J Garrett

Stacy J. Garrett was made in England but born in Sacramento, California, and like the redwoods of the state, her roots have dug deep. Her destiny as a bard was somewhat inevitable. Little else can explain how she constantly told her mother tall tales so outlandish that she couldn't even get grounded for them. Her mother and grandmother had her reading by age three, and that love of a good story propelled her through so many books that Scholastic Books gave her a medal. A love of worlds created by others eventually brought out the desire to create her own, and she has never looked back.

Stacy has seen both good and evil in her life, and her stories, like life, have no half measures. Even in a fantasy world of dragons and faeries, even in a modern city where magic abounds, she knows that the constants of real emotion never change. Dreams come true, love can be found at first sight, princesses can rescue their princes, and maybe there really can be happily ever after. Her happy endings never come without cost, though, for she truly believes we can't appreciate the good and the joy without the bad and the pain along the way.

Her current haunt is a comfy house in her beloved Sacramento where she wrangles three feline fur-kids and consumes peppermints like mana in order to balance a calendar filled with more creative venues than a sane person should realistically undertake. If she's not chained to her desk, she's stomping through the scenery in search of equally fantastical photographs.